GHOSTS OF BLACK BEAR MOUNTAIN

MARC MONORE

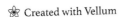

For everyone who has ever been too fearful to take the first step
into their dream. Believe.

Liam – I love your blog and
I really appreciate you taking
the time to read it. I hope you
enjoy it. Best wishes –
Marc Monroe

S aturday, October 31st, 1964
Sunrise 6:56 AM Sunset 5:37 PM

T he gates of hell were at the gas station at the end of
the street in my small suburb north of Atlanta.

Today was the day of my grand escape. I'd even changed
my diet of laced pills and arrived sober. My brain itched and
kicked at my skull every time the facade of one of my many
bad dreams fell and shattered, revealing that each dream
was, in fact, reality. I was never surprised at how unforgiving
the "real" was.

My car, a 1960 Ford Falcon, had been running on fumes
for days. Someone had finally agreed to meet with me about
a job, but getting past the gatekeeper wouldn't be easy. The
station's owner hated me, and rightly so.

I parked at the small, simple gas station and sank down
in the seat twisting my beard. For a clear Saturday, the
station was lifeless. It could have been due to the cusp of

winter-cold, or . . . I stopped myself. I didn't dare jinx it. There was no such thing as luck. People who lived lives as tragic as mine couldn't believe some random metaphorical wheel of fortune could be so cruel. We have God to blame for that.

I shuddered.

I needed to get Mr. Marbert alone. Maybe then he would listen to my weakly formulated plea, rather than taking another swing at me. But he wouldn't agree to anything if anyone else witnessed it. Except the truth was terrible and unforgivable. It was his youngest daughter, eleven-year-old Darlene, I assaulted.

It happened during one of my blackouts after I'd taken more pills than usual. I needed them. I was told I snapped in my classroom and attacked her in a drug-induced rage. I couldn't believe I did that. I usually gave myself plenty of time to enjoy my LSD trips, but that morning I'd taken more than just acid and lost track of time. It was a miserable excuse.

I sighed again and slid my glasses back up the bridge of my nose. I deserved to get fired. I deserved the punch. Either way, I'm glad I didn't remember the incident.

The service attendant tapped on my window, and I jumped. The attendant was a former student. Four years ago, Zack was the smart, twelve-year-old redhead with freckles from my first class. He used to think I was a riot, but Zack's sorrowful eyes reflected my shame.

I cranked down the window.

His face was cautious and full of regret. "Mr. Christian, Mr. Marbert told me to tell you I can't pump your gas."

"Good grief," I muttered.

"He told me to tell you some other stuff too, but, oh boy, I won't repeat it." Zack glanced back at the station. "You should probably leave before he comes out."

"Thanks, Zack," I said with a flat grin. I could understand his situation.

He paused. "Sorry about everything. Hope it works out."

He was a good kid, and his kind words were the first I'd heard in over two weeks. I tried to smile, but couldn't. "Hey, how's Darlene?" It was an honest question. No one would talk to me, so I hadn't been able to check up on her.

Zack lowered his head and glanced quickly at Marbert, Darlene's two-hundred-and-fifty-pound father. "Oh man, Mr. Christian, I don't wanna get in trouble."

I nodded and peered into the station. Marbert glowered at me through the window, his arms tightly crossed over his round belly.

"Damn it," I hissed.

Even if Marbert was fuming, I couldn't detour from my plan. I'd lost my remaining pride months ago. I had no problem saying I wanted to run, but for me to split I needed Marbert to do one thing: forgive me long enough to spot me a tank of gas.

I ran my fingers over the little, laced aspirin in my shirt pocket, but I left it there.

Drumming up my courage, I forced myself out of my car. With what little wisdom my twenty-four years had given me, I took off my suit coat and laid it on my seat. Lowering my eyes to the pavement, I moved toward the station door like a man walking to the gallows. My heart was in my throat. I tried to swallow, but my mouth was too dry.

The door flew open, and the little bronze bell clanged to the concrete.

"Do you want me to cream you again?" Marbert shouted.

I avoided his eyes. "If you have to. You're the only one who can—"

The pitch of his voice rose to near laughter. "What? Help you?"

"I'm desperate."

He shoved his finger in my chest. "I'll beat you to death if you don't leave right now."

"I don't want money. I need a tank of gas. Just one tank—"

He grabbed my shirt and twisted it in his hand, causing the collar to tighten around my neck. He pulled back his massive arm, and his fist shook in anger.

I squeezed my eyes. "I didn't mean to do it! You know that!" I blurted out the words as I braced myself for the punch.

"You hit my little girl, you piece of shit," he barked, shoving me against the brick wall of the station.

"You know I lost everything!"

Marbert jerked me but held his punch.

Words raced out of my mouth. "You went to the funeral. Darlene offered to sing, remember? She said every funeral should have 'Amazing Grace,' remember?" My eyes stung with tears. "Pound me, do it. Do it, please, but then let me get out of here. Just one tank," I pleaded.

Marbert stood frozen in a tense ferocity. I searched his face hoping for some glint of mercy, but then his expression narrowed, and his right fist plowed into my stomach, causing me to fold around his punch like tissue paper. He let go and I hit the ground, struggling for air. Zack rushed toward me.

"No, leave that trash on the ground," Marbert warned.

I gasped.

The adrenaline coursing through me wasn't enough to

mask the dull, warm pain in my gut. I rolled onto my hip and hauled myself up, holding onto the wall.

Marbert stood over me. "Get out of here before I call the police!"

"One tank and I'll leave town," I pressed, emphasizing each word.

"I'll kill you," he spat.

"Please!" I coughed. "I'll never come back ... Just one tank."

Marbert didn't say anything, instead he left me there and stomped back into the station. Part of me was grateful; my stomach burned. Another punch would have put me in the hospital, then I'd miss the interview for sure. He would call the police, and that would hold me up as well. Either way, it was time for me to leave. I'd failed.

I pushed off the curb thinking it would help me stand. It didn't. I crumpled and staggered back to my car.

Leaning on the hood for support, I circled to the driver's door.

My thoughts raced. I had to find a way to get some money. Some of the ideas were new lows even for me, but it didn't matter. There were always people who could find a use for someone down on their luck, but there was no use in doing any of those things clearheaded.

I reached into my pocket and put the LSD-laced aspirin under my tongue.

Ding.

The gas pump rang behind me.

My soul froze.

I trembled as I turned toward the station, but I stopped short. *Who cares who turned on the pump,* I thought.

Shoving the nozzle into my car, I kept my head low and counted the seconds with extreme fear as the pump flowed.

I waited for it to shut off. The sweet fumes wafted up into my face until gas spewed out onto the ground in front of me. I inhaled it, the smell of freedom.

Holding my aching stomach, I slid back into the Falcon. I cranked the car and watched as the gas needle moved to Full. Giddy with excitement, I pulled out of the gas station and left my past behind.

2

M y last teaching job hadn't ended well, but there I was in my Falcon swerving to yet another damn teaching job. It might not be a different career, but at least it was a chance at a fresh start in a new state.

I'd been calling around for work for weeks, but no one would talk to me after the school informed them about my predicament. I received rejection after rejection. Until last week. After calling eight times about a position in north Georgia, the school secretary must have felt sorry for me. She gave me the scoop on an older, unlisted post in eastern Kentucky. She was a friend of a relative of someone in the town. Until she mentioned it, I'd never heard of Middwood, but then again, I'd never been north of Nashville.

All I knew of Kentucky was from a spread in *Life Magazine* titled "The Valley of Poverty," which may have influenced President Lyndon B. Johnson's War on Poverty. When I thought of Kentucky, what came to mind was the popular Sunday funny, *Barney Google and Snuffy Smith*. The strip told the tale of an old hillbilly, Snuffy, and his hefty wife, Ma. My grandmother—who I called Rose-Mary Grand—stated on numerous occasions, while she sipped her coffee and flipped through the paper, that if she were the size of Ma she wouldn't have married such a tiny man. But then there's someone for everyone, she'd say.

The secretary warned me it wouldn't pay much, but perhaps their dire need would overlook my situation.

So, I searched all through my car, and even walked the roads searching for change on the streets, but fifteen cents was all I could find. That's how I ended up on the receiving end of Marbert's merciful fist.

In Middwood, no one would know me at all, and my past would stay buried. Maybe in the new town, people would think I was just quiet or shy. Perhaps if I got the job, I could move out of my car and afford to rent a room. I missed having running water and sleeping on a bed. My face stretched with the foreign sensation of a smile. My grip loosened on the steering wheel and my knuckles returned to their natural, pale color. Heck, maybe get a place with a little porch.

The euphoria of my escape carried me two hours from Atlanta and into Tennessee. Even in the middle of the fall, the Tennessee grass was still green. I loved the large, plush fields on the tranquil, sloping hillsides. The sky was open with picturesque blueish-gray mountains in the distance. It was lovely. The roads swelled, and, because I was tripping or because I'd lost my mind, I imagined the hills were the laughs to come. Maybe that was silly, or hopeful, or it might have just been sad. Over the last few years, any happiness I was allowed was short-lived.

Four hours in, gray clouds gathered on the horizon, and a storm loomed. The storm clouds hung frightfully low. It took me several minutes before I realized they weren't clouds, they were mountains, ugly and oppressive. Without looking at the map beside me or even seeing a sign, I knew it was Kentucky.

~

There was a sense of flying, soaring in the air as though the Falcon had become her namesake, like a bird rising beyond the canopy. I could see all of Appalachia. The various sized pointy, gray and black mountains were covered in naked trees and cloaked in mist.

I didn't realize how high I was until my stomach quivered, somewhere between floating and crashing. I looked down at my speedometer, which read fifty-five miles per hour even though there was no road beneath me. Several feet below, the road pitched heavily downward, like a death-drop on a roller coaster.

I screamed, "Holy—!"

My car slammed into the pavement, throwing me forward onto the steering wheel. My hand knocked the gear shift into neutral. And I must have hit the radio as well because it sprang to life, preaching at me with imperative anger: *"Though I walk through the shadow of the valley of death..."* The prophetic words blared as my eyes bulged at the steep slanting road ahead. I cranked the gear shift back into drive, making it kick back with a nasty growl.

"...I will fear no evil."

Gravity pulled me down and my speed increased to over sixty. I pressed the brake, but the car barely slowed. "For Christ's sake!"

My vision blurred as I frantically gripped the wheel and quickly put on my seatbelt. For the first time, I was glad my

Rose-Mary Grand had insisted on the seat belt option when she bought the car.

"A thousand shall fall at thy side, and ten thousand at your right hand..."

I gasped, peering at the sharp elbow-curve below. "Come the fuck on!" Panic seized me. I wasn't going to be able to stop.

I stood on the brake pedal. My car groaned as it fought to resist the building momentum. The Falcon slowed a bit, but it didn't matter, at my current speed, I'd lose control on the curve before tumbling off the mountain.

"Shit!" I shouted, clenching my teeth and butt cheeks.

"...but it shall not come nigh thee."

I glanced over my shoulder, out the window at the trees whipping by like a switch being beaten down on a child by an angry father.

"...with thine eyes shalt thou behold and see the reward of the wicked."

I returned my gaze to the road ahead while I continued to bear down on the brake pedal with both feet. The car barreled toward the turn in the road. "Come on, Matt! Think!"

I spotted an extra-broad shoulder along the curve below that looked wide enough for two cars. It could have been a sight-seeing spot, a turnout—or a place designed for idiots like me, who had never driven in the mountains, to stop. Whatever it was, that extra chunk of the shoulder was my only chance at saving myself.

I released the brake pedal, then slammed down on it again, trying to stay on my bitter course.

I ran off the road and hit a dip between the pavement and the dirt. There was a loud *pop*. The car's momentum shifted forward. My car spun around, dirt and rocks pelting the undercarriage.

My heart pounded as the vehicle slid with a fluttering resistance, grinding toward the cliff. My eyes widened as the expanse of dirt and gravel that made up the shoulder quickly diminished, and the vast view of sky and treetops opened. I threw up my arms.

BOOM!

T he car crashed with the driver's side taking the brunt of the impact. Glass sprayed across me, biting and slicing into my exposed neck, hands, and head. The Falcon finally rocked to a halt, slamming my body against the crushed driver's side door.

Everything was silent. Everything was numb. If my heart was beating, I couldn't feel it.

There was a sense of judgment buzzing in the air, a debate. I was on the scales of fate. There were distant hisses... chants calling for my death, my poor soul that dared to change it's destiny by crossing over the mountain.

3

Am I dead? My mind demanded to know.

I gasped and opened my eyes as cold autumn air, and gnawing pain rushed over me.

"The altar is open, brothers and sisters. Tomorrow is not guaranteed to anyone and—"

My chest heaved as I gaped out the windshield at the now-calm mountain road. The radio preacher droned on. I tried to reach out to shut him up, but my arms wouldn't obey. I wanted to throw up. I didn't do either.

"It's okay. I'm okay," I told myself, then took a breath. I pushed out my hand, the broken glass on my coat glittering in the sunlight. I didn't remember putting my jacket back on. My fingers trembled as I managed to turn off the radio. I flipped the rearview mirror toward me and lightly touched the sides of my head, checking myself for injuries. I winced as I ran my fingers over tiny pieces of glass sticking out of my scalp. When I looked down at my fingers, there was blood, but the pain wasn't bad. Luckily, I had thick hair. It was the one trait I didn't mind sharing with my father.

I gazed out across the hood again to the narrow, curved

strip of the shoulder. Somehow the Falcon had fit. I slowly turned my head to the steep road I'd barreled down. My car had spun around and was now aimed up the hill. I shivered.

I gently craned my neck to the left; more glass cut into me. Muted sunlight shone through the top of the window, but a brown boulder blocked more than half of my crumpled door. I wanted to reach out and touch its rough surface, but recoiled my hand, fearing the slightest contact might cause the boulder, my car, and me to plummet over the cliff.

I took one of the duffle bags from the back seat and shook off the shards of glass. I used it to wipe the seat clear, then tossed it back over the seat. As I climbed across to the passenger's side, the crystalline bits ate into my shaky legs every time they touched the seat. The pain was subtle and welcome. I needed the anchor to tell me I was alive.

I finally managed to pull myself out of the car. I carefully took off my suit coat as I stood shaking. I bent over and rested my palms on my knees, trying to stop the ringing in my ears. Mixed with a constant high-pitched noise were the amplified sounds of nature: limbs creaking and cracking in the wind, squawks of unfriendly birds, and the roar of the harsh, cold wind. It was like hearing for the first time, and it was deafening.

I swallowed, and my ears popped. Everything returned to a gentle silence. My hands hovered next to my ears. After all the chaos, the peace was just as foreign and, for a moment, just as frightening.

The mountain air pierced my clothing and hit my face and cuts. The chilled breeze consumed the heat radiating from me. I pulled the frosted air into my lungs. I coughed hard but took another deep breath.

Dropping one hand, I used the car for support as I circled to the hood. The right front tire was blown out and the bumper was beaten up. I looked over at the serrated break between the pavement and the shoulder; it was more than a foot deep. The rain must have carved the empty channel. I ran my fingers down my face. The blown tire saved my life.

Still using it for support, I followed the body of the car around to the side closest to the ledge. *What saved me?* I wondered. It wasn't good clean living. I could have said it was Fate or God, but, instead, I thanked the lone boulder nestled in the curve. I was shaken but alive, saved by a rock resting less than a foot away from—

I gulped. Another foot and I would have soared over the cliff and arrived at my appointment on time. Dead, but on time.

My eyes moved sluggishly over the grayness of mountains, mountains, and more mountains. They were devoid of color, like a black-and-white photograph. It all looked so sad, as if my trip had been a reverse version of *The Wizard of Oz*. I continued to stare and slowly discovered a few drops of orange, yellow, and red leaching from the vast image before me. There was still hope.

I couldn't see the bottom of the ravine, so I inched closer to the edge, grasping the hood of the Falcon with only my fingertips. My glasses slid down my nose, but I couldn't risk letting go of the car to adjust them. And I *wanted* to see.

Jagged rocks blocked my view, so I side-stepped, causing my fingers to slip from the Falcon. One... two baby steps closer to the edge... and there it was, the gaping mouth of the valley with no bottom or end in sight.

My head swam at the depth. My stomach churned, but I managed to keep everything down. I hadn't eaten in two days so I wasn't sure what would come up. The dry, bare branches of the oaks and birches looked like a graveyard of brittle witch fingers. I tried to break from my brush with death, but instead imagined my car burning below with my impaled body roasting in a tree above it.

Finally, I was able to make out the little town, through the branches, down in the valley with its smoking chimneys. It looked like a village nestled in the fog from a painting I'd seen a long time ago.

I found I was unable to take my eyes off the bottomless image. The view below me was foreign, like when you look in a book and see a picture of a Chinese palace, tribes in South America, or imagined the surface of Mars; the valley looked just as unreal to me.

I shook my head. I couldn't help but think it seemed magical, as if the little town had been formed by an ancient god and then set there, cupped in his caring hands. Except the mountains had fallen, trapping the god's arms and wrists. He could free himself, but then the town would be crushed by the massive mountain rocks surrounding it, so the god held his hands still. The town appeared protected, though long forgotten. Maybe my God's hands had also been tied, and that was why he allowed so much death and sorrow to run rampant in the world. I tried to shake off the negative emotions, but there was an intense sadness that shrouded me.

A sputtering vehicle climbed the hill. I stood watching the empty diagonal road until an old, orange truck drove past me. The middle-aged driver wore a blue trucker's hat and shot me a questioning look as he slowed. I held up my hand in a tentative wave, but the old man sped up the winding hill until he was out of sight.

I sighed, and then focused on my task of changing the flat tire. I still had an appointment to keep.

4

After I changed the tire, the remaining trip down the mountain was cold and tense. I couldn't help but think about having another blowout and tumbling to my death. The road continued to wind and dive. My right foot was numb from riding the brake all the way down, so I had to alternate using my left foot.

As I drove farther into the valley, the higher and heavier my dark, rocky surroundings grew. I was a worker ant on a termite mound. I sighed with relief when I reached the base. It had been a hell of a ride, but luckily it was a one-way trip.

A train whistle blared. The taunt was so powerful and close that my gut clenched. Who the hell would put train tracks at the bottom of a death trap like this? "Come on!"

The Falcon screeched and came to an abrupt halt, causing all the various pill bottles in the duffle bag behind me to rattle. It sounded like I was smuggling baby toys.

Seconds later the train blew past, blurring in front of me. I whipped my head in the train's direction, attempting to match its speed and catch a glimpse of its cargo of black rock, coal.

Once the train passed, I turned right onto Highway 421, which ran parallel to the tracks. The landscape still swelled and curved, but nothing like what I'd just experienced. From the appearance, the railroad tracks and highway had once been part of the mountains, cut out of the thirty-foot slanting rock that remained and unnervingly loomed. I couldn't imagine the dynamite and machine-power it must have taken to level the terrain. The rock face looked like petrified charred meat ripped by the teeth of some enormous prehistoric beast.

A chill came over me; I didn't belong here. I didn't think *anyone* belonged here.

The highway also ran parallel with a small river, which, according to a sign, was named Looney Creek. Even though it was the widest creek I'd ever seen, I acknowledged the name with a cocked eyebrow and grin.

Beyond the creek, the bare-bones woods were broken up by the occasional lone shanty. Some of the shacks were far off the road, while others were stacked on the mountain, and some even appeared to be in holes. It was at this point I noticed the crosses. Small, white crosses were nailed or painted on just about everything: trees, rocks, mailboxes, and phone poles. A pattern developed as I drove: shack, burned shack, cross painted on a rock; shanty, caved-in shack, shack, cross painted on a pole.

After I passed the third partially demolished home, I couldn't help but think of my own recent near-death driving experience. Images of out-of-control cars diving off the mountain filled my head. I cringed, turning my eyes away from the homes, not out of judgment, but out of empathy. My father and I had lived in plenty of roach-infested rooms and apartments, and for the last two weeks I'd slept in my car. I wasn't better than anyone else.

A green sign with a black bear on it greeted me:
Welcome to Middwood, Population 3,013. The low number
was a culture shock. It was more than twenty-thousand
people less than the Atlanta suburb I'd left behind.
Good grief.

About three miles later, a small collection of buildings
appeared on my left beyond the creek. It was too small to be
a town, but the buildings weren't uniform like a college or
an industrial park. There were houses farther up the hill. I
slowed down and glanced at my directions, then peered out
the window in disbelief. This was it, I knew it.

I shook my head in disbelief, but there were no streets or
apparent way to drive into the town.

"How the hell do I get into this place? What am I
supposed to do? Jump the river?"

A quarter-mile down the road, I came to a worn, narrow
wooden bridge. I stopped my car on the road and studied
the overpass. It was wide enough for a vehicle but appeared
decrepit, and I wasn't even sure it would hold my body
weight much less my car.

"You can't be serious."

My watch read 3:45 PM. I was already an hour late.
Seeing no other way into the town, I made do with what
presented itself. I'd already survived the mountain, so it was
only poetic I would face the river, but I was determined to
be smarter about it. I turned the wheel, pulled onto the
shoulder, then parked. I grabbed the directions and slid out
through the passenger side.

There were no other cars on the highway, and except for
the rippling gushes of the creek and the breeze, it was quiet.
It was possibly the most silent place I'd ever been.

I bit my lip and looked down at my directions. Was I in
the right place? I frowned. "Middwood, in the middle of

nowhere." I scratched the back of my head and hit a stray piece of glass. I examined my index finger and squeezed it. A little bubble of blood formed, and it was enough to dislodge the shard. I shook my head and thought about getting back in the Falcon and seeing how far Marbert's gas would take me.

There was nothing behind me but the railroad tracks and the remains of a mountain with more peaks in the distance. The directions read, *Once you cross the bridge, turn left onto Main Street.* My eyes widened at the short row of buildings. "That's Main Street? Oh, brother."

I ran my eyes along a few rows of houses up to, of course, another mountain. The town looked out of place, like a Western but with an overabundance of looming mountain peaks.

I took off my glasses, closed my eyes, and listened. A woman laughed, a screen door snapped, a dog yipped, and somewhere a man sang in a distinctive country twang. My frown faded, and I took a deep breath. There were at least two living people and a dog in Middwood. That was good enough for me.

Even on foot, I paused and warily eyed the bridge. I managed to grunt out a laugh when I imagined the bridge was the remains of some ancient drawbridge and I was walking across a moat.

To the right was a small gas station with two pumps, though one of them was wrapped in a rusted chain. A reedy young man about my age in a blue and white flannel shirt studied me. I assumed he was the station attendant and from his dark tan it was apparent he worked outside. He was wearing a blue baseball cap, but his dark hair peeked out in messy, unkempt tuffs. His sparse beard matched his hair. At first, I wondered if he was the man in the truck that passed

me, but he was too young. He sat in front of the station
eating a box of Cracker Jack. The longer I stood building up
my courage, the more his curious gaze shifted into a wary
stare. I wasn't sure if he was nosy, friendly, or shocked that I
was stupid enough to attempt to cross the fragile wood
bridge. So, I decided to do what we always do in the South
when we are in doubt—wave, the universal greeting for "hey
y'all." It didn't seem to ease the attendant's suspicion.

I surrendered and took a step onto the bridge. The
planks creaked, and I froze. "Hey!" I called to the attendant.
"Is it safe?"

He stuck out this chin, making his long nose appear
longer. "What do ya mean is it safe?" He said in a thick
southern drawl.

It wasn't a sarcastic question, but he acted like he
needed more explanation, which was silly since the bridge
looked like nothing more than termites holding hands.

"The bridge—is it safe to cross?"

The guy tensed and leaped behind one of the gas
pumps. He had been sitting down, but when he moved I saw
his legs were so very long, he reminded me of a frog. He
grabbed something resting out of my sight, something long.
A smooth metal rod?

He threw up the end of the barrel and demanded, "Who
are you?"

Oh crap, it's a shotgun.

hy is he pointing a gun at me? I thought.

I definitely didn't belong here. I could still leave; get back in my car and keep driving. Chicago couldn't have been more than seven or eight hours away.

I held up my hands, eyes wide. "What did I do? I'm just here about a job."

"There ain't no jobs in Middwood."

"I'm obviously in the wrong place. I'll just be on my way."

The hammer clicked back. "No, sir, you are on the bridge now. You gotta cross."

"Look, I'm just going to get back in my car and leave."

"I hate shootin' a man in the back, but then again, the ones I shoot ain't real men. I'll leave that up to you."

"Fuck," I whispered in shock. "Wait...I have an appointment about a job—"

"Which mine is hiring?"

"Um, no. At the school."

"We ain't had no school for years." He tightened his

muscles and pressed, "Why'd you park your car over there? Why didn't you just drive on over?"

"I already crashed my car coming down the mountain, and the bridge looks old as hell."

He shot a glance to the Falcon and then back at me. He shifted uncertainly.

"Look, I'm already late, can I just pass?"

He stiffened then cocked his head. "I don't know. Can you?"

What kind of game was this? "I don't know. Are you going to shoot me?"

"If I have to."

What did that mean? And what was it with me and gas stations? He hadn't pulled the trigger yet, but he was still pointing the gun at me. "Okay... um... what do I have to do so that you don't shoot me?"

"You can try and walk across the bridge," he instructed in a tone of profound sensibility.

"What do you mean 'try and cross the bridge'?" I asked, trying to remain calm.

"Them's the rules. If you can make it across, then I won't shoot you."

Bewildered, I paused. "That doesn't make any sense."

"Makes plenty o' sense," he said through his teeth.

"What if I turn around?" I asked.

"Then I'll shoot you! Stop stallin'."

Where the hell am I? I thought.

He took a step closer. "Hurry up, stranger. I thought you said you was already late?"

"I am."

"Then start walkin'."

"I don't understand this!"

He ran his tongue along his lower lip. "You've already

stepped foot on the bridge and there ain't no steppin' off 'til you get to the other side here. And here I was thinkin' I wouldn't get to shoot anything this week."

I started to speak, but I realized that words were pointless. I shook my head.

"Shake your head all you want, but if you don't start walkin' in three seconds, I'm gonna pull the trigger."

It was one of those moments where you would pinch yourself to make sure you were awake, only, for whatever reason, you couldn't move your arms to check.

It was the first time someone had pointed a gun at me. It was also my first time in Kentucky, so maybe this was a common thing. But I did what the guy with the gun told me to—I walked.

I kept my eyes fixed on the end of his gun. I wanted to see what came out of it before I died. The breeze picked up, and the piece of paper with the interview address blew out of my grasp. In a panic, I stumbled over my feet trying to catch it.

CLICK! I froze with a hard jerk and waited for the spray of metal pellets to pierce my chest and head, but they didn't come.

"What the hell? I just tripped!" I protested.

Still holding the gun on me, he let out an excited laugh, "It's a double barrel shotgun, stranger. Keep walking!"

I swallowed. *He's playing a trick on me. It has to be some crazy, country-ass, bullshit trick.*

My eyes darted from the twin shotgun barrels down to my shaky legs. My feet slid and shuffled across the boards like sandpaper until the scuffs were replaced with the gentle crunch of dirt and gravel.

With my hands still in the air, I stopped in front of the gunman. "What do I do now?"

He huffed, then lowered the shotgun. "You thank the Lord God in Heaven that yer still alive. I guess it wasn't yer time."

He dropped the outlaw act and greeted me with a smile. "I'm Eddie. Sorry I had to do that to you, but it's part of my job."

I let out an exasperated breath, ignoring his greeting. "What kind of job is that?"

"Security," he said with a proud grin.

I glanced at the gas station.

Eddie noticed my confusion. "Yeah, I pump gas, too. Like I said, I'm Eddie," he repeated, stretching out his hand farther. "I'm pretty important here."

Was he being serious? I paused, but reached out to take his hand. "Matt."

"Nice to meet ya, Matt," he said as I shook his dry, calloused hand.

"You, too," I wearily said, releasing my hand and pointing to his gun. "Eddie, is that thing loaded?"

"Oh, it's loaded," he said nodding. "Strange though, it's never misfired before. Like I said, thank God you're alive."

I cocked my head. "You pulled the trigger?"

"Yep. Crazy, huh? Lord must be watchin' after ya."

"About time."

Eddie rotated on his boot heels and walked away. He opened the shotgun barrel and popped out one of the shells, placed it in his pocket, and replaced it with another. He put the gun beside the old pump and sat down. I watched him as he took off his hat, gave his dark hair a shake, and went back to scanning the rock wall beyond the train tracks.

He did all this like nothing had happened, like it was just another ordinary day. What the hell?

I started to leave but stopped. I'd lost the address on the bridge. "Eddie?"

He whipped his head around and lifted his chin with a questioning face.

"Don't shoot me for asking but...can you tell me where Thornbrook Lane is?"

"Oh? You really do have a meetin'?" He raised his chin higher. "Who's it with?"

"Um, Franklin Mullis? Fourteen Thornbrook—"

"*Sixteen* Thornbrook Lane," he corrected. "Frank told you to meet him up there? Wow. That's wild. Okay, well, Thornbrook's the last street up the hill." He pointed toward the dirt road lined with shops. "That's Main Street. Just go to the end of that, then turn right on Windy Hill Lane, 'cause that's the only way you can turn, then follow Windy Hill up, and there's Thornbrook."

"Last street up the hill. Thanks."

"Sure thing. Givin' directions is one of my jobs, too." He smiled, then turned back to the wall.

I stared at him for a moment, wondering what he was watching for.

The whole valley was like a medieval castle with the stream running along one side of the town like a moat, the railroad tracks circling half and the mountain behind it like a castle wall, and Eddie, the Knight, guarding the bridge. All Middwood needed was a dragon and it would be set. All hail, Macbeth.

I wanted to ask him if I could walk back across the bridge to get my car, but since he had a gun and was possibly unstable, I decided to walk away. At least the trek would help me get acquainted with the town.

I continued onto the dirt road that was Main Street. *Lots of dirt here,* I thought.

I didn't know when Middwood was founded, but it looked temporary, like an afterthought.

Directly across from the bridge and over the stretch of road sat a humble Catholic church. I'd never attended a Catholic church, but after my recent near-death experiences, lighting a candle for myself seemed like a good idea, even though I wasn't sure what the candles represented.

The first storefront on the right was a small diner called the Bucket, which was good since I didn't cook. Next to the Bucket was the First Bank of Middwood. It was the first display of money I'd seen since I crossed into Kentucky. The outside walls were covered in sheets of polished stone. A young man about my age stood on the other side of the glass, staring at me with enough of a sneer on his face for me to return the look. He turned his head and called back to someone farther inside. I glanced back at the gas station. From the door of the bank, anyone could have seen my exchange with Eddie. Less than five minutes in town and I was already getting looks like that.

On the left side of the street, across from the bank, was a small pharmacy, Bill's Pills. Other than one or two other businesses, Main Street was a row of blackened windows. At first, I thought it was dead because it was cold out, but then I noticed several yellowing "For Sale" and "Going Out of Business" signs.

The last storefront at the end of the street on the right was Magnolia's, a small grocery store. A woman in a simple dress carrying a quart of milk and a can of something had just stepped out. She wasn't wearing makeup, but she had a semblance of a bouffant hairdo like Jackie Kennedy's. The style was a few years behind, but it was still a classic look. Maybe the town was too far behind after all.

After less than seventy-five yards I came to the end of Main Street. The road was so short they didn't even have a stop light. I glanced back down the street and blinked. At least there was a street lamp, located next to the bank. I didn't have time to dawdle any longer.

I turned back to the end of Main Street and was greeted by Jesus and the First Methodist Church. I turned right, and as I continued, I peered up Windy Hill Lane to see if yet another church anchored it. Instead, the First Baptist Church of Middwood sat up the steep hill on the left, beyond a large four-story building.

The church was shaped like a traditional country church: the double-door entrance, stained glass windows, and a tall, stretching steeple. But it was its burnt orange color that set it apart. It was made from large, rough, orange clay bricks.

Three large churches, all in the smallest town I'd ever seen.

Not many places for a sinner like me to hide, I thought.

I took a deep breath and looked at my watch. I hurried my stride and began the climb.

6

I tried to focus as I rushed up the incline. There were too many questions I needed to avoid, or at least give answers that were heavily sugar-coated. I was in the middle of a question-and-answer scenario when I noticed the houses up on the right. Across from the Baptist church and the large building, were two-story homes that were much better maintained than what I'd passed driving in. The houses were simple, clean, and had a certain charm. I let out a breath that I hadn't known I was holding for most of the climb.

Past the Baptist church, I turned right onto the last street off Windy Hill, Thornbrook Lane. I passed two more houses on my left. Then I stood on the dirt road in front of a picturesque two-story, pale-blue house with teal shutters. Sixteen Thornbrook Lane sat on a slight hill with a porch that ran the length of the front of the house. At the base of the road was a weeping tree of sorts; it looked like someone had planted the bones of a large mangled umbrella.

Regardless, it was a beautiful older home. All the setting

needed was someone to erase the ugly mountain behind it, put an old rocking chair on the porch, and it would be perfect. However, instead of a rocker, there stood a scowling, older man with a curved back waiting for me.

The white-haired man on the porch was easily in his early to mid-sixties, dressed in wrinkles and all shades of brown from his beige slacks to his tan cardigan to his light tan, button-up shirt. I couldn't help but think he resembled an old English bulldog guarding his food bowl.

I stepped onto the brown grass of the yard that curved up to the house. As I approached the porch, I hoped I wouldn't have to face another shotgun.

"You must be Mr. Christian?" he asked.

"Yes, I am." I grinned. It was time to try and turn on the charm. I had to make a good first impression.

"You're late," he said with a scowl.

That didn't take long, I thought.

"I had a blowout. I apologize for—"

"I heard. Glad to see you Atlanta boys at least know how to change a tire."

A sense of confused embarrassment came over me. My tire blew less than an hour ago. How did he find out so fast? Was it the shit-head that drove by?

"I heard a blue Ford Falcon with Georgia license plates crashed coming down Black Bear Mountain. I figured it was you. Speaking of that, why did you park outside the town?"

"I couldn't find the way in, so I parked on the highway." I cocked my head, "Who told you about that?"

He ignored my question. "You couldn't find the way in?"

I held my composure. "I only saw that little old bridge, and after what happened to my car I didn't want to take any more chances."

"Mr. Christian, that bridge is the only way into the town proper."

"I didn't know that. But anyway, that's also why I look like such a beat-up mess—the wreck." I swallowed, and I could still feel Marbert's fist in my gut. It was an extreme coverup, but my ordeal on the mountain masked everything.

He took his time staring into each of my eyes. I felt like a math problem he was trying to solve.

"What is it, Mr. Mullis?"

He held up his hand. "We will deal with your car later. Let's just get on with the interview."

I couldn't believe it. The old man ignored me again. Everything inside me said I should leave, but I didn't have anywhere else to go, not yet anyway. My shoulders bowed in defeat. I reminded myself I could always get in my car and leave at any time. Then again, I only had fifteen cents to my name. I took a breath. If nothing else, I could use my first paycheck to get out of here. Until then, surely, I could play along. I was always good at that.

Franklin pulled a set of jangling keys from his pocket. "Your car issues have put us behind schedule, and one thing you will find is people here are very particular about time, especially when the moon is rising. The blowout was understandable since you don't know how to hold a hill, but I'm sure you won't make a habit of needing excuses for punctuality."

"No, sir."

"Good," he said, flipping through the keys. He growled as he pushed on the door. My guess of his age kept getting higher.

"Do you need some help, Mr. Mullis?"

"No," he grunted. "You'll see the doors here are heavier

than they look." He gave another shove, and the door opened.

We stepped inside, and inches away from the reach of the door was a set of stairs that led to the second floor. The main level opened into a small, cream colored plastered entryway. The foyer ran along the ten feet of the wall that masked the stairs and ended at the open kitchen door. The opposite side of the foyer's width was marked by the arrangement of furniture. To the right, the living room was separated by a small, thin table that sat behind a purple sofa. My eyes continued to the right to a chunky, dark, purplish-blue armchair with ruffles that looked more than a decade behind the times.

Groovy digs.

A faded rug on the hardwood floors centered the space. It was cozy, like going to your grandparents', except my grandmother wouldn't have gone without a TV. In the living room, facing the front yard, was a large, floor-length window with impressive, ivory-colored plantation shutters. They were nice, but they didn't match the rest of the house. Through the open door on the far side of the living room, I saw the dining room at the back of the house, and it also had two of the same impressive windows and shutters.

I crossed to the living room window and opened the shutters. "I love the windows. I bet the view of the mountains is great." The view was the homes across the road, Main Street, the town, and the seemingly endless sea of mountains.

The four two-story houses were all different colors: yellow on my far right, the two in the middle were light coral and pink, and the one on the far left was a bright hue of green. The colors were whimsical, and that was the trend with the shanties across Looney Creek as well. On the highway the houses were basically shacks, but off Windy Hill Lane the homes would be considered beautiful even if they had been located in Atlanta. They were nice, but they didn't compare to Mr. Mullis's home. Not only did he have prime real estate and a view of the entire valley, but he also had an armed guard watching over them at the only bridge into town.

I turned my eyes back to the massive mountain. My smile diminished. "There's a lot of rock here."

"In front of you is the highest point in the great state of Kentucky. Middwood was built in its hollow."

"What's a hollow?"

Mr. Mullis rounded the sofa. "Lowland between two mountains."

"I see," I said dryly.

The old man grunted out a laugh. "Black Bear Mountain is over four thousand feet tall."

"Four thousand? Jeez. No wonder I felt so small. Back home, Stone Mountain is only about a quarter of that."

Mr. Mullis joined me at the window. "And we aren't even on the valley floor."

"Where is the bottom?"

"Not far from here. Over the creek and the railroad tracks. See that cut there?" He pointed straight out over the houses and beyond the town.

"Cut?"

"Well, there used to be even more mountain here. We had to blast our way in to lay the tracks for the train." He peered at me over his glasses, looking for a sign that I was following him. He must have been convinced because he continued, "Well, beyond that cut, the valley drops a good three hundred feet."

"Jeez. That's huge."

His hand floated to the right. "About five miles that way is the new mine." He faltered, "Well, we call it that, but it's almost thirteen years old now. You'll hear the whistle every morning and every afternoon. It's better than a rooster or an alarm clock."

"It's a charming town." It wasn't a complete lie. From this angle and height overlooking the town, it was "quaint," as my Rose-Mary Grand would say.

Franklin grunted. "Well, folks didn't come here for the view."

"For the coal, I assume?"

"For the money, Matt," he corrected.

"It's a completely different world here."

"Lots and lots of money."

I tried to smile. "Well, I'm a teacher, not an adventurer."

"We'll make an Appalachian out of you yet." He patted me on the back and crossed from the living room window into the dining room. "Besides, the town isn't what it used to be."

"You mean the coal mine?"

"Coal mines. The town opened up a new small operation about ten years ago." His mouth twisted, and his chin bounced with slight nods. "It was lucrative once, but...Well, the Lord giveth and the Lord—or someone—taketh away."

This conversation about the past made me nervous. I was worried he was using the story of the town as a segue. I didn't want to jeopardize the only job offer I'd received in six months. Following behind him, I changed the subject. "The house is beautiful."

While I focused on the bald spot on the back of his head, his chin nodded in appreciation. "The house is a historic site in Middwood. It was one of the first houses in town to have running water. She's much older of course, but still a looker. It was modern for its time, and some parts of it still are. As you see you can enter the kitchen from the living room or the dining room, two doors. I always thought that was nice."

"You could run laps through the place," I grinned.

M r. Mullis furrowed his brow, and my grin subsided. He let out a little huff in a curious sort of laugh. "Plenty of other places to run around in circles. Do you cook much?"

"I know a few basic things, but I guess I'll be eating out mostly for a bit."

Franklin turned his head giving me a curious stare. "And where will you be goin' to eat?"

"I think I saw a diner on Main Street? Is it any good?"

"The Bucket. Decent place." He nodded. "Mediocre food, but they serve up some pretty good corn fritters. And you can't really screw up coffee, can you?"

I gave a gentle laugh. "No, you can't. Any other good places around?"

"Nope. Mr. Christian, you'll be needin' to learn to cook," the stoic instructed. He nodded and completed the circle back to the living room.

He returned to the large window and looked down over the town with his hands behind his back. "Now, let's get the biggest question out of the way."

My eyes widened and my body tensed. Mr. Mullis was going in straight for the kill. He was about to ask me about Darlene, the drugs. Even though I planned out responses to those questions, my mind went into a non-verbal stutter. "Well, I. . .really need to go to the bathroom." I nodded. "It was a long trip."

"Yes, of course, just up at the top of the stairs."

"Thank you. Excuse me."

It wasn't a complete lie, I hadn't gone to the bathroom for over five hours. I lowered my eyes to my zipper as I spun to face the toilet.

I met a demon's blazing eyes.

7

I jerked back, ramming my shoulders into the wall.

The gruesome, snarling face of a devil hung over the toilet. It was painted in thick strokes of various reds and black. "Good grief."

Pushing my glasses up my nose, I leaned in to examine it better. Sticking out of the paint were bits of dried straw, and the color was mixed with dirt and chips of rock.

Franklin called from downstairs, "Everything okay up there? Did you drop your pecker?"

"Yes. I mean, no... Just the ... painting gave me a fright," my voice bounced around the tiled room as I replied.

"Well, clean up any of the fright that may have gotten on the floor," he said.

I zipped up, quickly rinsed off my hands, and checked my shirt pocket. I dug out the small, white pill and I kept a watchful eye on the painting as I dropped my face under the faucet and took a slurp.

I stood, making a sour face. The water's taste was almost as bad as its thick mineral odor. I dry heaved and spit out the contents of my mouth. The pill bounced off the top of the basin onto the floor. I bent down to pick it up. It was wet and covered in dust, but there was no way I'd let it go to waste. I wiped it off the best I could, snarled my lip at the thought of it being on the floor, but popped it in the back of my throat and swallowed it dry. I thought about wiping out my mouth with toilet paper, but I was just stuck with the lingering taste of tainted water and chalky dust.

As I stepped out of the bathroom, Franklin stood at the base of the stairs. "I suppose you are wondering about that painting?"

"Yes. I've--"

·He filled in the words for me. "Never seen a painting of the devil above a toilet?"

"No." I was starting to get a headache. "It's a different kind of choice than I would have made."

He leaned back and stretched. "Actually, everyone in Middwood has a similar painting."

"Why?"

"Mr. Christian, it's just a painting. Something that caught on with the locals, mainly to support a dear, local Shawnee lady."

"I see."

"Are you superstitious, Mr. Christian?"

"No."

"Good. Are you Baptist or part of the frozen chosen?"

I stopped. "The what?"

"Methodist. Are you Baptist or Methodist?"

My brain still fumbled, "I have to choose?"

"Or are you one of those Mormons?"

"No." I let out a relaxed, nervous laugh. "Honestly, I haven't been to church in a while."

He furrowed his eyebrows so much that his eyes were almost closed. "Do you feel guilty about it?"

"Um... Yes?" I answered, confused.

"Then you must be Catholic? Plenty of Catholics, first church you see when you drive over Keeper's Bridge."

I raised my eyebrows at the name of the scary little wooden structure, but the name was fitting. "I'm not Catholic. I guess I'm Baptist."

He pointed his index finger to his nose. "That's the right answer. I do know a few Methodists, but I'm always slightly suspicious of them. They drink, you know?"

With feigned concern. "I didn't know that."

"Do you drink?" Franklin asked.

"Sometimes I wish I could, but no. It doesn't agree with me," I said.

"The Baptists hate drinking. Most of them still do it, but come Sunday they hate it. So mind your business."

He pointed out the window down Windy Hill Lane to the right. "The Baptist church is the first building. You can easily see it from here." He turned back to me. "Well, it's getting late."

"Are we going to the school now?" I asked.

"No. It's getting late, and since neither of us have a car handy, we'll have to walk."

"I don't mind. It's only five."

He gave a single nod as he crossed to the window and closed the shutters. "I'm sure you don't, but when the sun goes down, the town closes up. Here in Middwood, we go by the light, not by the clock. Besides, you've had a long drive. Why don't we call it a night?" He moved to the front door. "We'll meet up first thing tomorrow morning."

"Okay," I said following behind him scratching my neck. "um, Is there a local motel you can point me to?"

Mr. Mullis craned his face toward me, his eyes narrowed and confused. "What do you mean?"

"I didn't arrange for a place to stay. Hopefully, there are some places on the less expensive side."

"There aren't any motels in Middwood."

I sighed. I'd be sleeping in my car again. I had enough gas to drive a few miles out of town. Then I thought about the gossips who told Franklin about my blowout. I'd have to drive farther, but it was doable. I covered, "I'm sure I can find a motel farther up the—"

Franklin held up his hand again. "Matt, you'll be staying here until we figure out other arrangements."

My jaw dropped and my mind went silent.

Mr. Mullis raised his brow and leaned in. "Is that okay with you?"

"I-I get to sleep here? In a house?"

The man's eyes searched to his left then right. "Yes."

Again I was silent, but I wanted to shout! A bed, a real bed!

"Are you okay, Mr. Christian?"

"I'm just—"

"Thankful, I know."

My mind started to work again. "I *am* thankful. How many other tenants are there?"

"None. It's just you. If you'd rather stay with a local family—"

"No! This is— It's great." After sleeping in my car for the last few weeks, a free place to stay was a Godsend.

"It's only temporary. I'll be honest, you were going to stay somewhere else, but there was an accident."

"What type of accident?"

"A fire," he said with no hint of emotion.

"Oh, is that common? I saw some burned homes on the

way in." I realized I put my foot in my mouth by asking the question.

"Many local houses weren't built for the long-term. They were built for the miners, but there's lots of moisture in the air here and when people don't upkeep them ..." He shook his head. "Well, seasoned wood burns quickly. You won't have that problem inside this area."

"So I got the job and the house?"

"Why the hell else would I have stood here and talked to you for so long?" He extended his hand. "One of the bedrooms is locked--old papers, storage, and such, but the rest of the house is yours."

I gave his hand a firm shake. "Thank you, Mr. Mullis."

He didn't seem to care much for emotion, and he waved it off. He reached into his pocket and handed me the house key. "If you want your car you should go and get it now."

"Yes, sir. I might look around the house first. It's just—"

Franklin held up his hand. "Go and get your car right now. I'll walk you down to the street to make sure you go."

I shrugged. "Yes, sir," I said beaming and babbling after him, "You won't regret this, Mr. Mullis.

We reached the street, and he stopped. "I'm going to stop in on one of your neighbors, Thad Tippet. He runs the smallest mine. You run on down and get your car."

"I know I've already said this," I said as the sting of tears threatened to fall. "But this job means the world to me. Just tell me what I need to do and I'll do it."

"Let's just start off with you making it through the night," he said with a concerned face.

"Yes, sir," I laughed.

"Go get your car then get back into the house." He raised his hand, and I immediately responded with my full attention. His tone was steady and serious. "Once you get back here, close the shutters, and lock the doors." Concern must have faded my smile. "Nothing to worry yourself with, animals, some break-ins. Just do as I say, close the shutters and don't open this door until after sunrise. Do you understand?"

"Yes, sir, I might have lived in a big city, but it's still the South, so I understand," I lied with surprising ease. I needed to keep this man's trust, and more importantly, I needed to keep the house.

"Just remember, it's an old house, but it's a new place to you, so you might hear a bunch of noises. Just ignore them. I'll meet you at the Baptist church when it gets light out, and then we'll go see the school."

"I have to go to church?" I asked, trying to hide my worry.

"Yes. You'll be introduced to the town tomorrow morning, and the parents will be told to send their children to school come Monday. Besides, folks seeing you there will help ease their minds about what kind of a person you are. In Middwood, it's real simple, if you want to fit in, then you have to be seen. And, Mr. Christian?"

"Yes, sir?"

"Make sure to take a bath."

His comment caused a wave of self-awareness to wash over me. "I stink?"

"One step away from catfish bait."

F ranklin and I separated. He crossed the street, and I continued to the right toward Windy Hill Lane.

I couldn't help but count the steps to the Baptist Church —166 steps. It was the closest I'd ever lived to a church. I wasn't sure why that amazed me so much, but it did.

Walking to my car meant I'd have to cross Keeper's

Bridge. Eddie was still at his post. His attention went from a stick he was whittling with a knife to the view across the highway, down the railroad tracks, and back. I glanced to the top of the cut, as Franklin called it, but didn't see anything except oppressive mountains and the sky of a setting sun. I doubted if he ever saw anything. When I turned back, Eddie was staring at me.

I swallowed. "Hey," my voice cracked. "I'm getting my car. Is that okay?"

He shrugged. "Sure. Why wouldn't it be?"

"Because of earlier?"

His attention went back to his knife. "Like I said, once you get over the bridge you're gold. How'd the meetin' go?"

I was shocked at the difference in his manner since our previous encounter. "It went well. I got the job."

He shot me an honest smile and toasted me with his stick. "Well, that's just great. Congratulations. I know the town will be hootin' and hollerin' about it."

I paused. "Just so I'm clear... I can walk across the bridge and you won't shoot me?"

He let out a grunt. "You'll be fine. And buddy, trust the bridge. She's stronger than she looks, made with the leftover ties from when they laid the railroad track."

"Thanks." I found comfort in his words but still walked with care.

I glanced over my shoulder to make sure Eddie wasn't going to shoot me in the back, but he wasn't watching me. Still, I held my breath and walked over the bridge. The river flowed beneath me with continuous gushes and gurgles. Earlier, my heart must have been pounding so loud in fear I didn't notice the sounds of my surroundings.

I crunched over the dirt and slid into my car. "Hey, baby.

Guess what? I got the job. I know you're excited." I cele-
brated, scooting over to the driver's side and put the key in
the ignition. "Wait until you see the house." I turned the key.
"It has—"

The engine sputtered but didn't crank.

8

"Oh come on." I pumped the gas a few times and turned the key again. The engine groaned like an alcoholic demanding another drink, then passed out.

I got out and inspected my car like I knew what I was looking for. I had almost completed my circle when I noticed the puddle in the back. I knelt, and the mind-numbing scent of gasoline fill my nostrils.

I got back in, and sure enough, the gas gauge read empty. "Dammit, wasted money on the ground." I tried not to get upset. My car had done the best it could, and the final leg of the Middwood trip hadn't exactly been smooth. I grabbed my keys and got out.

A whistle blew over the mountain.

Circling to the trunk, I grabbed two gym bags and threw one over each shoulder. I stacked the smaller box with personal items on top of a larger box filled with books. Finally, I carefully placed my Heinz 57 green milk-glass soup bowl—my holy grail—snuggly into the top box. It was heavy, but it was the only way I could think of to get every-thing back to the house in one trip.

"Something wrong with your car?" Eddied asked as I walked by.

I paused holding my haul. "She won't crank."

"What do you think it is?"

The box started to slip, so I pushed on the bottom with my knee and readjusted my grip. "Other than gas leaking out, I have no idea. Hey, I need to get my stuff up to the house. I'll talk to you later."

"Yeah, get on up to the house before it gets dark. I'll be packin' up soon, too." Eddie waved his knife and went back to cutting on his stick.

I struggled, balancing the top box on my books, but since people were walking about, I didn't stop to take a break. The burn in my arms was manageable, but I knew it would intensify. I had to think like a shark, if I stopped moving, I would die.

A man's voice called out, "You need some help there?" I shifted my eyes to the left, but my green bowl blocked his face.

Oh, Eddie, shoot me, please. I kept walking.

"Can I give you a hand?" the man asked.

Two bullets in the back of the head.

"Hello?" he asked again.

I slowed but didn't stop. "Oh, sorry. I couldn't hear you over the top of my box." I turned to make eye contact with him, but he moved, so again his face was hidden.

The man laughed. "Son, do you need some help?"

My arms shook as I lifted the boxes two inches higher. "No, sir. Thank you, though."

He continued, "I run the pharm—"

I shifted the boxes again, and a book fell.

"Oh, let me get that for you." I still couldn't see his face, but his body was long and slim. Gritty scratching dug at my ears as he dusted off the cover. "*The Diary of Anne Frank*. That's the Jew girl right?"

I clenched my teeth and rolled my eyes as the box cut into my fingers. At least he didn't call her a kike. "Yes, a story from the Holocaust."

"I haven't read that one yet since they never proved it happened."

I hid my struggle. "I'll have to let you borrow it. I'm the new teacher, Matt."

He gave a surprised gasp. "Is that so? Well, I'll be."

I groaned. "Yes. If you will forgive me. I need to get home. Darkness falling and all."

"Oh, you betcha." He put the book back in the box. "Nice to meet you."

I tried being polite. "Sorry about rushing off," I said while hurrying away.

With the additional weight of my belongings, the incline up to the house made my upper legs and calves burn.

By the time I got to the yard, I had no feeling from my shoulders to the tips of my fingers. I couldn't wait any longer. I dropped to my knees until the boxes rested on the brown grass. I couldn't just let them fall since the green bowl had been given to me by my grandmother. It was the only thing I had left of hers.

I held out my curled, white, stone-like fingers until I was able to extend them again. I peered around, sneaking glances to make sure no one was rushing over from across the street to help me. Luckily, the road and yards were empty. I picked my boxes up and sped to my front door.

Looking over my shoulder, I turned the doorknob.

"New guy, huh?"

"Jesus shittin' socks!" I jumped away from the door, gripping the boxes tighter.

A short, slim man stood next to the door. He was dressed like an undertaker.

I regained my composure and gave a nervous laugh. "Sorry, you scared the sh-—I didn't see you there."

He lifted his chin, stretching his neck. "Did you get everything you needed from your car?" The slime of this guy oozed off of him. It started at his hair and dripped off him to the floor.

"Yeah, I got everything."

He scratched his ear. "Are you okay, Matt?"

It sounded like he was using my name against me. "I'm fine. How do you know my name?"

"Sorry, I didn't mean to scare you."

"Don't worry about it. It was the surprise of it, not actually you." The guy was creepy, but hardly someone to be afraid of. Marbert was a big man, this guy was five-nine and maybe one hundred forty pounds. "What do you want?"

"I'm a teacher, too. I'll be working with you at the school."

My heart sank.

He cackled. "I'm only kidding. I'm not a teacher. I can't stand kids."

"What do you want?"

"I beg your pardon. We don't often get new people around here. I don't think I've had to formally introduce myself since... Well, since I got hired at my job three years ago." His thin lips all but disappeared into a line that curved into points on each end.

The box pulled into my chest. I wasn't sure if it was the

strain from holding it or my body reacting to him, but my chest ached. One thing was for sure. I didn't want to touch him.

He held out his hand. "I'm Clint. I work at the dentist's office."

I stepped back.

His eyes narrowed and he twisted his lower jaw.

I swallowed. "Sorry. Mine are full. I'll catch that hand-shake next time."

"Of course." He retracted his hand. "I guess I need to just come out with it." He rubbed the end of his nose nervously. "Matt, I just want to make sure Frank was completely honest with you."

"About what?"

"About the town. How strange it is."

"He warned me."

"That's the problem, Matt." He paused. "He needed to scare you, not warn you."

"What's it to ya?" I asked, my tone short.

He cocked his chin, not like a confused puppy, but more like a snake drawing back before a strike.

"I'm trying to help you, pal."

"Then help me a bit quicker. I want to get settled in."

He grinned. "Frank didn't tell you the rules, did he?"

"What rules?"

Clint shifted his eyes to the mountain. "There are always threats, Matt."

"I see—"

"Well, actually, you won't see. That's the whole point." He placed his hands behind his back and circled me. "Mid-dwood has a few quirks, if you will. Did Frank mention the windows, Matt."

Every time he said my name my skin crawled.

"'Close them and lock the door,' he told me."

"No, Matt. There's more than that. There are rules and I can't with a clear conscience let the sun fall without telling you."

9

Clint was turning out to be just another weirdo. I fought the urge to roll my eyes.

"You don't believe me."

I shook my head.

"I saw Eddie hold his gun on you."

"You were—"

"Yes, I was watching, Matt. This is a small town. It's boring. I watch and listen, just like everyone else. The bridge is nothing compared to the rest of the shit in this town."

I scowled at him and fought against my growing aggravation, I put the boxes down on the porch. "Okay. Tell me."

He extended his hand.

I ignored it. "Tell me."

He focused his eyes on me and slowed his words like I would do with a student when I needed to make sure they were listening. "You said you would shake my hand the next—"

"Skip it," I snapped.

If my car would fucking crank and if Eddie didn't have a shotgun, I'd get the hell out of this place.

He grinned sourly and made his way down the steps.

"What about your clear conscience?" I insisted.

Clint turned and hurried back up the steps. "Matt, you were rude to me. You dismissed me. I do what I do for the good of this town. You might not be the one for the job, and the town might be too much for you to handle. If that's the case, then so be it. But while you settle in tonight, stay inside."

I couldn't help but wonder what his game was.

I bit through my childishness. "Clint, forgive my disrespect."

He nodded. "I appreciate that."

We both cooled off.

Clint walked back down the stairs. "It's getting dark. Good luck." He waved over his shoulder and continued down the yard.

I watched him, making sure he didn't stop and hide in the bushes.

The farther away he walked the more relaxed I felt. If I hadn't loved the house so much, I might have asked Franklin to put me into witness protection.

"No one will ruin this moment for me; not Marbert and not Clint. I'm going to sleep in a bed. *My* bed!"

Grinning, I stepped into the house and shut the door.

Once I was inside and alone, I stopped. I took in the quiet and the stillness. There were no motors growling, no horns honking, and no police tapping on my window telling me to move along.

I opened my eyes, and it was all true. The house was real. "Thank God."

I dropped my box on the thin table behind the sofa and let out a deep breath. Circling the living room, I ran my fingers along the arm of the big purple sofa, pushing my fingers into its deep, cushiony arms. I spun around on the hardwood floor and sat in the armchair next to the fireplace. I rested my feet on the ottoman, careful not to touch it with the bottoms of my shoes. Then I smiled and pushed off my shoes, letting them *thud* to the floor; I could do that now. I took a huge breath, and I snuggled into the chair. I closed my aching eyes again.

My mind was plagued with doubt. None of it was real. It was just another dream; an escape from the horror that was my life. When I opened my eyes I would be in the cramped back seat of the Falcon, on some stranger's sofa, some stranger's bed, or at the end of someone's fist. I was on another trip, dropping out of reality into... I stopped myself.

I opened my eyes and frantically studied my surroundings. I was in the house. I really was in a house with a roof, windows, and doors that I could lock or open legally.

I laughed through unshed tears.

Even my mind would have never created a paradise in Eastern rural Kentucky. "That would take a hell of a lot more than a bottle of laced aspirin," I muttered.

I kicked up my legs and scooted my socked feet to the staircase. The butterflies flew away when I noticed how dark it was on the second floor.

At the top of the stairs was the bathroom tiled in teal and painted in a pale yellow. *At least it's not pink,* I thought. The thick, ivory ruffled curtains were pulled shut. The only natural light was the ambient glow from downstairs. I peeked in, there was your basic tub, sink, and toilet.

In the hall to my left was a stark transition from dim to complete darkness. The light from downstairs barely reached more than an inch or two into the pitch-black abyss before me. I could make out a small linen closet on my right, but whatever lay beyond was hidden. I hesitated, then moved forward.

Why don't you turn on the light switch? I thought.

"Good grief, the light switch." I shook my head at my silliness.

The hall light illuminated two bedroom doors at the end of the short stucco hallway. Franklin mentioned one of the rooms was locked. I went to the door on the left first. I tried the handle and the knob resisted my strength. It was indeed locked, which made it intriguing.

Directly behind me—on the right side of the hall—was what I assumed would be my room. I turned the knob and pushed, but nothing happened. I grimaced. I tried again, but it still wouldn't open.

I knew how to open a door. It just wasn't working. Again, I pushed, leaning in with my weight, and it started to give. I finally pushed with both my upper and lower body and the slab gave way. Except the door didn't open immediately into the room. It had a depth to it. I held my hand up against the threshold; it was at least seven inches thick. Then I took in the closed-in musk.

Panic stabbed at me. Images of something locked in the darkness made me withdraw. Thoughts of running fired off in my head, but I held my place.

I stared into the dark room. Even with the hallway light on there were deep pockets of shadows.

I listened.

10

"Jesus, it's just a bedroom," I barked at myself. I couldn't believe I was jumping at phantoms after I was given what I most wanted, not just a job but a tremendous place to stay as well.

The room had to have a light. I simply had to flip the switch. I moved into the deep threshold and reached in. I ran my hand along the wall but found nothing. Rolling my eyes, I withdrew my arm, then inched closer.

I stretched out my arm again, huffing uneasily. Finally, my hand stumbled on the switch. I flipped the lever, and the room lit with a crackle. "That doesn't sound safe."

The overhead light washed over the space, but the ivory-painted room was muted and stuffy, though it was a nice size. There was a double bed centered along the wall opposite the door and covered in what looked like a homemade, Southern quilt with floral blocks. However, even with the bed's softness, the dungeon door made it feel unnatural. My eyes burned. I wanted to rub them, but I resisted fearing my hands were covered in dust, and then they'd really start itching.

Exhausted, I plopped the bags down and collapsed onto the bed. A plume of dust shot up and settled on and around me. I sat up and brushed myself off and sneezed. "Oh, brother," I said, then I sprayed another sneeze across the room.

I looked at the windows. There were two windows on each side of the bed. Opening them would make a huge difference in alleviating the underground feel of the room, but each was covered with heavy, ruffled, chartreuse curtains.

The frown grew on my face as I crossed to them. Chartreuse was my Rose-Mary Grand's favorite word but her least favorite color. We always made sure to point it out whenever we saw it, and she would feign an over-dramatic reaction, "It's not the fifties anymore," then we'd both laugh.

I held my breath as I pushed back the curtains. Through the dust cloud, instead of a warm setting sunlight and a view of the street, I found a solid, ivory-colored wall.

"What the hell?"

I hurried to the other window. It, too, was blocked. I stepped back, lifting the curtain. There was no enclosure, no seal where the window had been.

I moved closer and examined the wall. The wall had a faint bumpy pattern that didn't match the rest of the house's plaster covering. I ran my fingers along the walls and they came away covered in dust. I wiped them on the sides of my slacks in disgust. Looking at the clean spot from the swipe of my hand, I reached out again.

"Concrete?" I asked in a confused whisper. The beautiful house I would be staying in had a bedroom lined with cinder blocks.

I shivered. "It's a tomb."

My lungs tightened in a wheeze. I didn't know if it was the dust or panic of the enclosed space.

Questions about the oddities of the house were flying around inside my mind. My next meeting with Franklin was going to be interesting, and I was afraid to hear what the reason might be.

When I started scratching, I knew it was time for a shower. I searched through my bags and found my soap. When I left my apartment in Georgia it had been half a bar, but that was two weeks ago. I found a loose white sock in the bottom of the first bag, my classy soap holder. I dug in and pulled out two poor slivers of soap.

I took off my shirt and made my way down the hall. I lifted my arm and sniffed my pits. It must have been a while if I couldn't even tell I stank. I was embarrassed that Franklin had to point out my musk. Two years ago, before she died, that would never have happened.

I let the tap run for a bit, which was a good choice as the water came out brown. I twisted my face in disgust. Either the house had plumbing issues, or it had just been sitting unused for too long.

I bit my fingers. It was a lose-lose for me: sleep in the tomb or shower with Satan.

An itch climbed up my back. My skin's reaction to the dust and glass didn't believe in the devil, but my mind took it a step further imagining nails inching up my skin.

"Stop. Stop," I told myself rolling my shoulders back.

I took a deep breath and huffed it out. I stretched my neck to the left and right, then finished undressing.

The hot water on my skin was the first warm embrace I'd had in a long time. However, I couldn't relax. The water had a sharp smell that made me nauseous. Plus, I kept peering over the shower curtain to look at the painting. I'd never had so much face-time with the devil. It was like a new, bizarre take on Psycho. Granted, I wasn't in a motel or a movie, but, again, I didn't really know Franklin or anyone in this strange little town.

I thought about Franklin. I'm sure he had another key to the house, and the scenario played out in my mind: the shower curtain pulled back, a knife raised, and Franklin, or worse yet, Clint, dressed as an older woman would stab me to death. Eek, Eek, Eek.

The sense of being watched continued as I dried off. I kept hearing things I was eighty percent sure were ghosts in my mind, but still, to be safe, I cracked the bathroom door and peered out. The yellow lit corridor was clear, and I hurried down the hall back to my room.

My stomach growled as I put on my pajama bottoms. There was at least a small chance that there was food downstairs in the kitchen. That slim chance was enough for me.

At the end of the hall, I stopped at the linen closet for a clean set of sheets, but the sets I found were for a single bed. On top of that, they were as rough as sandpaper. No big deal, I would pick up bigger sheets later.

I chucked a couple flat sheets down the hall and they landed at the doorway to the bedroom where I could pick them up later.

I walked softly through the kitchen, opening all the cabinet doors. There was nothing. The sour smell of the refrigerator pushed me back. It was empty and only beginning to cool. Franklin must have plugged it in right before I arrived.

I consoled my stomach as I moved to the living room. I stared at the large shutters, Clint and Franklin's stern warning echoed in my mind. Even though they were closed, part of me expected the boogie man to come crashing through them.

"Stop being stupid. It's just a damn house." However, I continued to stand there, looking at them.

"Fuck it." I flung the large, white wooden shutter open. No boogie man in sight.

I stared out at the unfamiliar setting of pastel houses with warm yellow light glowing from inside the living rooms. I looked again. Searching all the homes, none of them had visible light coming from any other place in the house.

I wrapped my arms around my shoulders, reminding myself that regardless of all the crazy, I'd done it. I'd accomplished multiple goals in less than twelve hours. I'd gotten a job and a place to stay. Despite the dust, it was a beautiful place, and it only cost me a punch to the gut. I was starving, yes, but I'd been starving for days. I would think about food tomorrow. All in all, it was the best day I'd had in years. That's right, I thought, be grateful.

Stepping closer to the window, I frowned, thinking about the Falcon alone out on the highway. I said a little prayer for her to be safe. After all, I'd called that small, light blue Ford home for the last two weeks.

Again I gazed out into the nightfall. As silly as it was, I wanted to make a wish. A wish for a hopeful future in my new place, but the lights around me suddenly darkened. House by house the curtains and shutters were drawn shut. Most of the remaining light was only specks shining through gaps of cloth or lines shining through shutter slats. Nimble hands must have been at work because even those little slivers of light were quickly folded and closed away.

The hollow was totally dark. The town had spoken, it was time for bed.

Unnerved by the sudden darkness, I forgot my wish.

11

F ollowing Franklin's instructions, I closed the shutters. I checked the dining room shutters behind me, but luckily, they were already secure.

I hurried up the stairs, went to my room, and shut the door. The sleeping arrangements weren't ideal. The bed sheets were like burlap and, even though it was November, the room was warmer than I liked. I felt claustrophobic in my decorated, block-box room.

I gave my ill-fitting sheet a tug and moved to the light switch. I mapped out the steps I would need to take, turned out the light, and got in bed. I rested there for a few minutes, blinking at the darkness that surrounded me. There was no peace in the room. The blackness moved around me, settled on me, harmless at first, but the weight of the room grew heavier, pushing on my body.

Back at my old apartment, I always slept with my door closed and locked. I liked the sense of security it gave me, but I needed to be able to breathe. It was stupid that all the bedrooms in the world had windows except in Middwood. My backseat bed in the Falcon had windows. Even jails cells had windows, or at least I remembered that mine did. I got up, went to the door, and pulled on the knob with both hands, pushing off with my left foot against the frame until the door opened. I cursed under my breath, then laid back down. I glanced at the open door, made peace with it, and closed my eyes.

It was better. Air moved around the room and the tightness in my chest released. I took a deep, satisfying breath. It was cozy.

I lay there for a few moments, trying to find peace, but it wasn't working. I wasn't relaxing.

I opened my eyes and stared into the hallway. *"An open door is an open invitation."* That's what my Rose-Mary Grand would say. I imagined some dark figure walking by or waking up to some townsperson standing over me saying they hadn't known anyone was home. What if a coyote or a bear got in?

I rolled over, so my back was to the door. That way if anyone came in I wouldn't see them. My anxiety grew. I was haunted with images of hairy, brittle fingers dancing inches away from my spine.

I swatted at the phantoms and calmed my goose-bumped skin by running my hands down my sweaty lower back.

It was ridiculous. Not that I was freaking out, it was ridiculous the town didn't have windows in their bedrooms.

I flung myself out of bed, turned on the light, and knelt on the floor next to one of my bags. When I picked it up, the bottles inside clattered. I searched until I found the one I wanted.

I hurried into the bathroom, unscrewed the cap, and tossed a pill on my tongue. I kept a watchful eye on the painting as I dropped my face under the faucet and took a slurp.

I shook off the taste, and the devil caught my eye. "Enjoying the show?"

Back in my room, I laid back down on my bed with the door open. It would take some time, but the medicine would knock me out soon enough. I waited. I went through my exercise of trying not to think of anything. Sometimes I would imagine a cloud, nice and soft, forming around me. It was a good, relaxing image, but the devil wasn't having it.

Every time I tried to relax I imagined not just someone walking in my room, but the demon from the painting stalking in to drag me to hell because I pissed him off with my parting comment.

I pounded my fists down onto the bed and exclaimed, "My God!"

I got up, stomped to the bathroom, and jerked down the painting. I caught his gaze as I was carrying it.

"Don't look at me." I threw it in the hall closet, the face against the wall. "Now stay."

Victory.

I walked back to my bedroom then froze.
Skrrtch.

I inched back to the hall closet. Images of the devil peeling and fighting its way off the canvas filled my mind. He was probably already free of his prison and standing behind the door. Another scratch.

Some sounds arouse curiosity, but I'm not sure I wanted to know what was creating it. Another scrape, but it sounded farther away. I carefully and quietly crept along until I was a foot from the imprisoned demon.

I stopped and listened.

Bump.

I released a relieved sigh when I realized the scratching was coming from below. I moved to the stairs and peered down. It was coming from outside.

I remembered what Franklin said and repeated it, "It's a new place for you, so you might hear a bunch of noises." I shook my head. "It's just a cat. Bunches and bunches of noises. Good God, it's time to go back to bed."

Skrrtch.

I got to my bedroom and looked with worried eyes down the dark hall that led to the stairs. I listened for the scratching. I thought I could still hear it. I could have stood there for hours, waiting for the noises. However, luckily, a haziness covered my fears as the pill kicked in.

Tomb, vault, noises or not, I locked the door. It wouldn't matter. The drug would do its job. It might make me a helpless victim, but at least I wouldn't know about it until I woke up dead.

12

A photo at the end of the hall was tilted off center. I always wondered how that was possible, how a family photo could shift. It's not like a herd of elephants trampled through the house.

I walked around the corner into the dark living room. I flipped the switch, but there was no light. I hated that my father used the string from the overhead light instead of the wall mounted switch.

I didn't need to count my steps, my body, my brain just knew. I reached up, found the string, and pulled. The light popped to life.

"Why did I come in here?"

I turned around, scanning the room. Looking over the items on the floral sofa, the brown arm chair, and the coffee table. They were all bare. "What did I come in here for?"

"Matt," a voice called from the back of the house.

"Rose-Mary?"

I spun to the darkened hall.

"Matt," her voice tightened.

I hurried into the shadows but came out onto a misty foot trail.

The ground was squishy beneath my feet.

A distant voice called, "Matt?"

I searched, but my sense of alarm faded as someone walked toward me.

She was a beautiful woman. She wore a simple white cotton dress and a smile. We were in the forest, and she was walking toward me. The forest was alive. It was a different season. I knew because the landscape had life. The birch and oak trees and grass were green. Instead of dull gray clouds the sun was out, shining onto the canopy of the trees. It was warm. We were on the top of Black Bear Mountain. The sky was full and open around us. I could breathe, and I made sure to take advantage of that.

The trees clicked, flickered. There was a distorted twitch. A black curtain spread across the mossy forest floor like the shadow of an approaching giant. Black blades grew, jutting out from the ground in different directions. They crystalized and turned to shards. The trees disintegrated, and a purple mountain erupted out of the brittle ground. The woman continued to walk. Her strides remained smooth even as the black rocks cut into the bottoms of her feet and blood began to flow.

I tried to tell her to stop, to tell her I would help her, but I couldn't move. My feet wouldn't or couldn't listen to me. I shouted, but only the faintest of muffled sound came out, a distant echo even in my own head.

The woman rose off the ground. I wasn't sure if she levitated or was lifted by some unseen force. She peered down to her left and right, but she didn't seem concerned.

The shards vibrated, then doubled in size. The matte black rocks reflected what little sun there was as the light hit the smooth sides. One of the crystals pierced the bottom of her foot and broke through the top.

The black earth moved. The very ground turned and rotated. As the earth wheeled with increasing speed, she was lowered into the rocks. The shards hit her feet, digging into her skin and bone. Her eyes became aware of the pain her body was experiencing, but she remained quiet and still.

The sharp teeth made easy work of her lower legs. The rocks gnawed at her knees, but she didn't cry out. The gentle smile turned to an emotionless stare as the splinters scraped at her supple skin, cutting and tearing the flesh into scarlet ribbons.

She lowered her eyes to mine and our gazes locked. I tried to look away, but she had some sort of control over me. She started to move her mouth, tried to speak to me, but the beating of the rocks stopped her.

I wasn't affected by the shards. Somehow, I was immune. What was she going to say?

Her lower abdominal muscles were already gone. The ground picked up momentum like black forks as it ripped and pulled at her. Her bits and pieces spattered my legs and chest.

Finally, one of her eyes glistened and a tear dropped. What was left of her dress was torn off from the remains of her body. Her face strained as her eyes turned red. She looked like she was about to scream, an eruption was only moments away.

I could feel that scream building in us both. It was more than I could handle. *Stop it! Stop it!* I tried to scream.

Banners of her flesh sprayed my body. I couldn't turn. I couldn't get away.

Knock. Knock.

Soon she would be gone, eaten away.

Knock. Knock. Knock.

I twitched.

Knocking. Someone was knocking.

Wake up, Matt. Wake up.

She opened her mouth.

"Say it!" I screamed. "What? What is it?"

My mind called, trying to wake me.

We stood staring at each other, but I was being pulled away. I could see her, and I could see us both looking at each other. The distance continued to grow.

The knocks turned to banging. The further I was taken from her, the more relief I felt. My sorrow lessened. I would forget her when I woke.

"Faster. Wake up, Matt. Wake up."

The banging grew more determined.

The world she and I inhabited dripped away.

She reached out to me with her only arm, but it was too late. She was only a shade.

Like a cannon, she shot across whatever plain we were on. She moved so fast the remaining flesh blew from her bones. In an instant she was skull to nose with me.

She gripped my face with her blood-stained fingers and hissed, "We want you to see us."

13

Sunday, November 1, 1964
Sunrise 6:57 AM. Sunset 5:36 PM.

I shot up in bed, flinging my arms out in terror against the darkness, pushing away the bits of flesh that clung to me.

I had no light to guide me, no air; it was stifling. Moisture covered my skin. In a panic, I swiped at my arms and legs. It could have been water, sweat, urine, her blood, my blood, bits of her body. I tumbled and fell, landing on a hard, firm surface.

My hands spread out on the ground and searched for answers to where I was.

The ground was hardwood floor.

I panicked as I got to my knees and clawed at the darkness until I found a wall. I stood, sliding my arms against the surface. "Where is the fucking—"

Click.

The light came on.

I gasped, taking in the room.

I was in a strange place, but at least I was alone.

Middwood. Franklin. A house. No windows, my mind flipped through the images of the last day.

It was just a dream. I exhaled and collapsed against the wall, with my chest heaving. As rough as last night had been, I'd woken up in stranger places in the last month.

My hair was soaked. I leaned over and pushed, cracking open the bedroom door. The change in air temperature was drastic.

"We want you to see us."

The words from the nightmare that woke me were still digging through my head, spoken to me by a mutilated woman who was ground down like a piece of wood.

What and how much had I taken the night before? I couldn't remember.

I grabbed the doorknob and climbed to my feet.

The amplified bangs continued below.

I wanted to scream out and let my visitor know they should get the fuck off my porch, but even the thought of yelling made me wince.

"Mr. Christian? Are you there?" Franklin's muffled voice came from downstairs.

Fitting for a Sunday, I found myself praying for a better day. I mumbled to myself, feigning sincerity and rubbing morning crust from my eyelashes. "Is that you, Franklin? I'm sorry. I thought you were a mountain goat."

"Mr. Christian?" he yelled and continued knocking.

I stumbled down the stairs. "Norman Bates, I thought you were going to kill me while I was in the shower," I whispered with a snicker.

"Matt, are you okay?" he shouted in a concerned tone.

I opened the door. "Mr. Mullis, you could wake the dead."

He exhaled. "Oh, thank Jesus."

"Speaking of Jesus, my room is a tomb. I thought I was going to suffocate."

He lowered his head. "I was afraid you didn't make it through the night." He looked like a sweet, worried grandpa.

I relaxed against the door frame. "Mr. Mullis, I'm fine. I just didn't hear you knock at first. Concrete doors and all."

"That's why I banged so hard, and they aren't made of concrete. They're wood."

I rapped my knuckles on it. "That's the heaviest wood I've ever...pushed."

"It's called bloodwood."

"Bloodwood?"

Examining the door, I realized the color resembled streaks of thick, dried blood.

"The windows—"

Franklin frowned at my hair. "Matt, you look like hell. Why are you all wet? Have you showered?"

"As a matter of fact, yes, the devil painting and I both showered last night."

He waved me off. "Get dressed. We can talk about it later."

"Why? What time is it? I thought we were meeting after church." Not able to hide my sarcasm, "Oh, no, did I sleep through it?"

"No such luck. That's why I'm here, to make sure you get to the church on time. I have to admit, I'm a little surprised. I thought a city boy like yourself woke up with your hair combed."

I returned a slight laugh. So much for the sweet-ole-grandpa act.

He pulled his chin back. "Haven't brushed your teeth either. Well, get ready. I'm taking you somewhere."

My eyes widened. "Where am I going?"

"To the Bucket for breakfast."

"Breakfast?" The word was so beautiful it hurt to even say it. Except I didn't have any money. "Breakfast and church sound like a full morning."

"Yes, that's the spirit," he said. "Let's go. I'm starving, so hurry."

"Would you like to come in?"

"No, it's a beautiful day out."

"Okay. I'll be out shortly."

He stood in front of the door, still looking at me as I shut it. I was amused by how extremely odd he was.

Back upstairs, I tried to be quick. To keep all the questions about the house and the dread of being forced to go to church at bay, I let the need for food be my motivation. I only had fifteen cents, but I was going to find a way to eat. My stomach growled in agreement.

Besides my stomach, I kept hearing Franklin in my head, and found myself saying his words out loud, "If you want to fit in, then you have to be seen."

I accepted my fate. Since I was going to be seen, I decided to put on my finest. I rummaged through my bags for my only clean outfit—the suit I wore to my father's funeral. I picked up the tie and stared at it. It used to be my favorite tie, but now it was a reminder of ...

"Stop thinking so much."

I snapped out of the past and I dug out a collared shirt. I gave it a shake. It wouldn't be ironed, but I hoped it would be good enough for the Baptists.

I ran into the hall.

Franklin stood there with his back to me.

"Mr. Mullis—"

He shut the door to the second bedroom. I shifted my eyes into the room, but he closed the door before I could make out anything.

"I'm sorry, I thought you were waiting downstairs?"

He put his keys back in his pocket. "I just remembered something I was going to give to Mr. Bankward." Mr. Mullis waved off his words. "He runs the bank."

I gestured to his hands. "I guess you didn't find it?"

"Excuse me?"

I gestured to his hands. "You aren't holding anything."

"Oh. No, I couldn't find it. No matter."

"After breakfast, I could help—"

"No, thank you, but after breakfast, you're going to church."

My stomach growled.

"I agree with your stomach. Let's go eat."

~

Other people were out and about as we walked down Windy Hill Lane past the Baptist church. It wasn't a bustling neighborhood, but we saw about a dozen or so people. Franklin must have been well-known because the few people we passed all said hello to him. He was short with small talk, explaining that we were running late, but told them all to "be ready for a surprise in church." That comment made me more nervous every time he said it, but I kept my focus on the most important thing, bacon.

"Mr. Christian, slow down. You are moving like a dog ready to hunt."

I stopped and let Mr. Mullis catch up. "I'm sorry, Mr. Mullis."

"I understand, you're a young man. Simple thoughts."

I laughed.

He chuckled, "I didn't mean to offend, but I see you didn't take it that way. I just mean that young men think about certain things."

"A man has to eat."

"Food, water, shelter—"

"The water here is terrible."

"Yes, it is. You have to boil it. You didn't drink much, did you?"

"I had some for dinner last night."

"For dinner?"

"Sorry, I always think I'm funny when I'm hungry."

"Matt, when is the last time you ate?"

I didn't know if I should tell him how broke I was, but I'd have to tell him something so he'd pay for my meal.

"Young men, simple thoughts. Don't worry, I'll pick up the tab for breakfast."

Oh boy, I had finally made my way up to purgatory. My southern upbringing tugged at my soul to decline, but my simple thoughts rose above the noise of etiquette. "Mr. Mullis, I promise, I'll pay you back."

"Well, you are a bit puny."

I shot him a glance.

"Well, tall, but puny."

"Hey, you can call me whatever you want if you're buying."

Franklin didn't laugh.

14

Franklin explained that the Bucket got its name from the buckets the miners used to carry their lunch in to work. But upon entering the storefront, I wondered if it was named after its size and smell. It was a cramped space that didn't appear to be clean enough to eat in. There was no bar-top seating, and the kitchen was hidden in another room behind a standard, half-shut door without a knob on it. The Bucket was a hole-in-the-wall muddled with black coffee, the sour-sweet scent of old grease, and man-sweat.

Franklin wove his way through the ten to twelve square, mismatched tables, toward the only empty table in front of the street-side window. It was prime real estate in the restaurant and, luckily, because of the window, there was a draft.

A tall, thin, middle-aged redhead brought us two cups and a pot of steaming hot coffee. After she poured us both a cup, I held it under my nose for relief against the putrid smell.

"Are you cold or is it the smell?" Franklin asked.

I was completely put on the spot in front of the waitress. "Um, I just like coffee."

"Then you two will get along great. Frank drinks a few pots every day."

"Well, it keeps me chipper. But, Matt, as far as the smell goes, this used to be the boot shop."

"Boot shop? I had no idea."

The waitress twisted her tongue around in her mouth before she broke into a clumsy grunted laugh. "He's an awful liar. Better keep an eye on this one, Frank."

"Will do, Petunia. Let's get some food."

Without a menu, Franklin ordered scrambled eggs with grits and corn fritters, both with extra butter.

The waitress rocked her weight back on her hip and pointed her front foot out slightly. "Frank, don't you want your salt pork?"

"That's the reason I come here, Petunia. You take such good care of me." Franklin was a flirt. I couldn't blame him, though. Having something pretty to check out from time to time makes even old frowns show their false teeth.

"And what about you, handsome?" Petunia smiled as she looked down at her notepad.

"Um," I was distracted by the comment, but flattered. "I'll have—" My mind froze up.

"Honey, I promise the food ain't that bad."

"Oh no, I've already eaten." *What the hell was I saying?*

Franklin narrowed his eyes. "Really? What did you have?"

My eyebrows went up. "Well, I ..."

Petunia snickered. "Bad, bad liar. I hope you're going to church after this."

Franklin grunted, then pointed to Petunia's notepad. "Bring him some eggs, grits, and fried pork, too."

"Will do, Frank." She cocked an eyebrow at me. "Biscuits or corn fritters?"

"Biscuits. Can I get my eggs scrambled too?"

"That's the only way they come here, honey."

"And um, what is fried pork?"

"It's just sausage without the casing."

"Oh. Sounds perfect."

Petunia laughed. "Oh boy, Frank, where did you find this one? Food will be out in two shakes of a lamb's tail."

"Thank you, sweetheart," Franklin said, eyeing her as she walked away.

"So, is Petunia your favorite waitress?"

"Well, look around, young man. The other ones are much too old to look at. Petunia is what the young folks would call a 'fox.'" He sipped his coffee.

I scanned the room. There were only two other waitresses in the diner, but if he meant the youngest of the waitresses, then I guessed he was correct.

"Are you ready for church?" he asked.

"I'll just say, I'd rather be standing in front of a classroom instead of standing in front of a church."

"It won't be that bad. It's just town politics. Come noon everyone in the town will know who you are."

"That sounds intimidating."

"Ha! Matt, you're in a small town. If you walk outside your house, you will find yourself surrounded by your students. And if not them, their parents."

I pushed my glasses back on my nose. "Have you worked with the other teachers in town?"

He went blank. I was about to apologize for whatever I said or did, but our food arrived.

I picked up my fork.

"Lord, honey, let me put the plate down first."

I put the fork down and took the plate from her. "How did it come out so fast?"

"'Cause we only serve scrambled eggs. They should still be warm."

I picked up the biscuit. Smiling, I looked up at Franklin, but he wasn't amused. "What?" I asked.

"We haven't said grace."

"Oh," I said, then with great pain I put the warm, buttery biscuit down.

While Franklin prayed silently, I stared in gluttonous lust at the plate before me, praying I wouldn't lick the butter off my fingertips.

"Amen."

"Amen, yes."

As I stuffed my face with a biscuit as slowly as I could, I noticed Franklin's salted pork slice was bigger than his plate. The ham was seared, but the fat touched the table. I tried not to stare, but every time Franklin moved his ham it would leave a little grease trail like a slug. I checked my plate. I was glad he'd ordered me "fried pork."

I picked up my fork again and went to town on my breakfast. It wasn't that bad at all. I stared back at Franklin's ham slug, but I made sure to look out the window before he caught me.

An attractive, darker-complexioned woman in her late twenties with long, straight, black hair was standing across the street. "Is there a substantial Indian population here?"

Franklin turned to the window to take a look. "Ah, her name is Litonya."

"Litonya?" I repeated.

"It's an Indian name—Shawnee. Used to be lots of them in these parts."

"She's waving at you," I said.

"What?" Franklin asked.

I pointed with my spoon. "Litonya is waving at you."

Franklin gave a smile and a little wave. A teenage boy was standing with her. She tapped the boy on the arm, who wasn't paying attention. She pointed to us while she talked to him and waved. The boy looked directly at us and turned his head away in disinterest.

Franklin furrowed his brow back to its usual state. "She is an interesting woman, but her son, Peter, well, he's a... bit of a troublemaker."

Litonya continued to wave.

"You're being rude. Wave back to her," Franklin said, talking with his mouth full.

I realized I was staring. "Oh. Yes." I waved to her, and she nudged her son on the arm, prompting him to wave, again, with no result.

"If you haven't noticed," Franklin leaned in, "she's the tastiest thing on the menu."

I turned back to look at her. Mainly to give me the chance to look away from Franklin's horny, wrinkly, food-smacking face, but he was right, she was attractive.

"But, Mr. Christian, 'steer clear of the Sirens, and their enchanting song.'"

I turned and looked at him.

"It's from *The Odyssey*," he said.

"I know. It's just—"

He smacked his lips. "Caught you by surprise. And just think, you haven't even been here a full day, but I'm being serious with you. There's a reason she's single, Litonya's a wild one," he warned.

I cocked my head, "Well, what if I like wild women?"

Franklin burst into laughter. Many people turned their heads. But not out of shock or disgust, they seemed amused by Franklin. His laugh was so hearty I laughed myself. It was the first time I'd laughed in weeks. Once he started coughing, I realized it was something he rarely did. However, I'm not sure what it said about me since I delivered the punchline.

"Oh, Matt, you're a funny one," he said as he gained his composure.

I looked out the window again but Litonya and her son were gone.

～

F ranklin patted his belly in delight, but my stomach was like a balloon being played with by a mischievous child.

Franklin waved to Petunia. "Sweetheart, put his on my tab."

She winked and called from behind the counter, "Sure thing, Frank. You two have a good day. Nice to meet you, Matt."

I smiled at her as Franklin and I exited. I stretched my back as I held my stomach. "I'm ready for a nap."

"No, young man, you are ready for your big reveal. You didn't get anything on your clothes, did you?"

Looking over my shirt and tie I stated, "No, I don't think so."

"All right, I'll let you go. Good luck. Church starts at eleven sharp. Afterward, I'll meet you outside the main doors."

I tilted my head. "Aren't you going to church?"

He frowned. "Matt, the Almighty and me don't get along so well."

"Should I ask why? Or is that being too bold?"

He frowned and gave a slight nod. "A bit too bold."

Even though I felt like I just had my hand slapped, I admired his honesty. "Ya sure you don't wanna come?"

"Nah, I'm going to have another cup of coffee."

Petunia came outside. "Frank, we're going to close up and head to church. You comin' back inside?"

"Yes, thank you." He turned to me and said, "Good luck," and returned to the diner.

Petunia held the door for him, then walked out onto the street. She shot me a smirk. "Is he throwing you to the wolves?"

"Oh brother, I hope not."

She laughed. "Which church are you going to, Matt?"

"Baptist."

She frowned. "Baptist? Ekk."

"You're making me nervous." I shook it off with a smile. "What about you?"

"I'm a good Catholic girl. Best of luck. But you better hurry, it's ten fifty-five. Middwood is all about being on time."

J esus only knows why a town so small needed three
churches. I thought all their prayers were supposed
to be going to the same place? Though I knew reli-
gion wasn't simple enough to sum up into one
building, it was something I thought about when I was high.

It was only three blocks back up the hill, but I was
wearing down fast from the incline, or perhaps it was the
weight of dread. I wanted to go home. I'd already eaten with
Franklin, and he had exhausted me with all the town's crazy
nonsense.

If I were lucky, I'd be able to slip in unnoticed and find a
seat in the back row.

I hurried and merged into a short line of people filing
into the church. I made my way up the steps. A tall, hefty,
black-haired man exited the gray double doors and greeted
the line.

I sighed, so much for an undetected entry.

The man bellowed, "Good morning, brother. How
are you?"

My shoulders hunched from the weight of his presence. "I'm doing well. Thanks."

He threw out his arm and took my hand. "Are ya strong in the Lord?" he asked with his full, deep voice.

His question caught me off guard, but then he clamped down into our handshake. "Um, yes, sir," I winced. "I'm trying to be."

"Are you new to the area, son?"

"Yes, sir. I'm the new schoolteacher."

"Boy, I know who you are," he laughed. "I was just playin' with you. I'm Pastor Jimmy Gresham. Franklin filled me in on the game plan for today. Well, praise the Lord," he shouted. "What a blessing to have you."

He was the widest preacher I'd ever seen, and I imagined him playing the defensive line on the team of Jesus. "I'm Matt Christian."

"Amen! You were born with a holy name. Welcome, and I have to say I love the tie." He finally released his grasp.

"Thank you," I said as I cradled my hand.

The sanctuary was directly across from the outside doors separated by a simple, narrow foyer. The hardwood floors vibrated with excitement. With the inner doors open, conversation and laughter blared out.

It was too loud.

I turned around, but the preacher was blocking the door, so I couldn't sneak out. I looked to the right and read a sign labeled Balcony. The upper level would be the perfect hiding place, but a group of teenagers had entered behind me and headed up the stairs amidst hushed giggles. An older couple in their mid-fifties also climbed the stairs. The man carried a sobbing little blonde girl around three years old. Her snotty nose dripped onto his worn overalls. It was enough for me to search for courage to face the full brunt of the church. I just needed to find a seat and get this over with.

Franklin was right, everyone went to church on Sunday. The service hadn't started, so people were squeezing past one another to hug or shake hands. An aisle ran down the center of the church dividing the space into right and left seating with about eight pews on each side. Thinner folks were able to maneuver along the side walls where the stained glass windows met the end of the benches.

My head swam. It was so cramped. I pulled at my tie.

A man marched up to me. I swallowed my anxiety, took a breath, and braced myself for the encounter. I was always terrible at this sort of thing.

He was a tall and slender built older man, maybe in his late forties. The oddest thing about him was the size of his mouth, it made him look like a fish. He moved closer and smiled, and I tried not to stare at his jaw full of frightful teeth. He shot out his hand. "Praise the Lord. Are you blessed?" he asked, slurring his words enough to catch my attention. Surely, Skinny Mouth Man wouldn't break my fingers, he wasn't anywhere near as big as Pastor Gresham.

"Yes, sir, I am." I smiled, growing less intimidated.

"Nice to meet you again."

He clamped down his grip, but I held my smile. Whoever he was, he was strong. My hand had only been shaken twice, but it was already throbbing. Coal mining men had firm hands, but Big Teeth must have been on something because we had never met before.

He continued, "How's the new schoolteacher doing?"

He must have seen the question on my face because he turned his head and narrowed his eyes at me. "Can you hear me? I know it's hard to hear with all the squawking going on."

I spoke up, "Yes, I can hear you."

He pointed to himself, "Do you remember me? I helped you with your boxes yesterday. *Anne Frank*?"

"Oh, that was you? Thank you, I appreciated that. I couldn't see your face."

"No problem. Now that you've seen it, you will never forget it." I nodded dumbly in agreement. The man had some teeth. "We are so happy to have you in the house of God with us. I'm Bill Self; I run the new pharmacy."

My ears perked. A lustful grin grew on my face and the angels sang hallelujah. I wanted him to be my new best friend. "Thank you. I'm happy to be here. A new pharmacy, isn't that exciting?"

"Well, it's more than ten years old, but it's still new to everyone here. Had to open one when the one in the big store closed. If you need anything at all, you just come on by."

"Actually, I do need something." I stopped myself. I couldn't start the conversation in church, so I changed my question. "Where's a good place to sit?"

"You can sit anywhere you like, Matt. Anywhere at all. I like that tie. It's sharp." He walked away moving on to the next person.

He was the second person to point out my tie. Other than the men walking around shaking everyone's hand, I was easily overdressed. Since when did the Baptists not require a shirt and tie to get into Heaven?

I settled on a thin, pea-green-cushioned pew hoping no one would sit near me.

An older couple stood over me, hovering.

"Good morning," I said craning away from them.

"Yer in our seat," barked the older man.

"I beg your pardon?"

"He said, you're in our seat," growled the older woman.

I got up. "Oh, I'm sorry. I'm new here."

I was halfway up when they hurried to claim their seats, shoving me out of the way. As rude as they were, they might be kin to Franklin. Come to think of it, Franklin never mentioned his family. But then again, I hadn't asked.

I slid past a man to an open pew three rows along. I was almost in the middle of the church. I made sure to ask the young couple behind me if it was anyone's usual seat. They were in their early twenties. The girl's small mouth closed up as her eyes hardened into a frightful stare. "What's it to ya?"

"Because... I need a place to sit," I said.

The guy put his hand on her arm. "No, no one sits there anymore. Welcome to our church. I'm Coy Scotts, and this is my fiancé, Judith."

I nodded and gave a grateful grin. "Thank you. It's nice to meet you. And, congratulations."

He beamed. "Thanks. We announced it to the church last week."

I sat down on the springy pew.

Judith pressed, "Honey, he really shouldn't sit there."

I half rose, paused, then stood. "I'll just find somewhere else."

I thought about waiting in the back until the sermon started to see what seats were still open.

Coy reached out to me. "No. It's fine. It's just... Someone used to sit there, but they passed away."

"I'm so sorry to hear that. I'll sit somewhere else out of respect."

"It was thirteen years ago. Those respects have been paid." Coy said and gave the same awkward smile I make when I don't know what else to say.

"Oh. Thirteen years? I guess I understand. I was told not many new people move into town." I sat down for good. I hoped.

"Are you new to town? We live way out, so we don't get out much to hear all of the gossip," Coy said.

"Yes, I'm the new school teacher."

"Lord have mercy." Judith turned white.

She seemed to look into my soul. "What is it?" I asked, a wave of guilt and shame coursing through me. Was it possible the Marbert's had family here?

Coy again put his hand on Judith's arm. "It was the old school teacher who used to sit there."

16

I sank into the pew. "Shit." I tried waving off my curse. "Oh, I'm sorry for the..." I grabbed my beard. "Are you serious? What are the chances?"

Judith murmured, "I was just about to say the same thing."

"And you said she passed?" I asked.

"Yes," Coy said, "very tragic."

"Tragic? Was she older?"

"Lord no, she was just a bit older than you."

"I haven't been told anything about the previous teacher."

Judith sat back in her seat. "Well, it's a sin to gossip. Lord forgive us."

They looked at each other. "Do us a favor," said Coy. "Don't tell anyone we told you. It's not something the town, and especially Franklin, likes to talk about."

"Oh, gosh no. Of course not."

"Please," Coy insisted.

The organ began to play, and everyone stood.

"I give you my word." I turned around in my seat.

The man who greeted me at the door called out, "Sing the first two verses of 'Blessed Redeemer.'" I thought he was the preacher, but there was a red-haired man sitting in a chair on the pulpit. Perhaps, Gresham was the music director, I thought.

The church began to sing. There was no page number given, but I quickly found it in the songbook by looking it up in the table of contents.

I'd heard the song before many times as a child, but I hadn't sung in a long time, so I hummed quietly. By the end of the second verse, I was catching on.

Gresham called out, "While Wallace plays the third verse, take time to shake hands with your neighbor."

The organ played as the congregants started turning to each other and shaking hands. The old couple who'd kicked me out of my original seat shook others' hands with smiles on their faces. If people never moved seats, they must have shook the same hands every Sunday. It seemed pointless.

I sat still. I looked around, wondering if anyone would greet me. Even in a room full of people, I was all alone. There was a tap on my shoulder. I jumped.

"Oh, I'm sorry."

I pivoted in my seat.

Coy grinned and held out his hand. "I didn't mean to scare you. I don't want you to feel left out."

I smiled. "I appreciate that." Surprisingly he didn't crush my hand. "I only jumped because I thought you were God sneaking up on me."

He chuckled.

"Hey, Coy, do you mind if I ask you a question?"

"Sure. Shoot."

"I was going to ask you about the previous—"

Coy cut me off. "Matt. He's pointing to you."

"Who?"

"Pastor Gresham, up on the stage."

I turned and made eye contact with the husky man. "God snuck up on me," I whispered.

"There. Now we have his attention," boomed Gresham. "He was wrapped up talking to new friends. What a blessing. Everyone, welcome Matt Christian, he is our new schoolteacher. He has moved all the way from Atlanta."

Every eye in the church was on me. I could feel my face turning red. I didn't know what else to do so I did what Rose-Mary always did. I stood and gave two waves. "Good morning. Good morning." Then I sat.

"Come on up, Mr. Christian. Tell us a little about yourself."

My eyes about popped out of my head. *Oh, God no. I repent. I repent.*

He smiled and waved me up on stage. "I do believe he is a bit nervous. Let's give him a round of applause."

The church clapped. Luckily it gave me the confidence I needed to walk up onto the stage.

I stood there and finally stuttered, "H-hello, everyone, I'm happy to be here at the First Baptist Church of Middwood. Oh, and my name is Matt Christian."

People in the congregation shouted, "Amen!"

"No, I mean that's my name, last name, my last name is Christian. Not to say I'm not a Christian, because I am—"

Gresham put his arm around me and I froze as the man pulled me into him with a side hug. "Okay, Matt, what a blessing it is to have you here. Will you be transferring your letter?"

"What letter is that?"

Gresham and the red-haired man chuckled, and so did

many of the other members. "I do believe we have stumped the teacher."

The congregation laughed.

Gresham held up his hand. "Isn't it nice to have laughter in the house of God? Remember we will start back to school tomorrow and Franklin wanted me to impress on each of you to send your children. Let's keep the spirit flowing with our next hymnal, 417, 'I Gave My Life for Thee.' I gave the hymn number for Matt since he seems a bit lost this morning. Please take time after the service to welcome him to our town and keep him in your ongoing prayers. God bless you, brother."

I stood there for a second, smiling, then walked back to my seat. I wished I could bury myself behind my hymn book. I'm sure my face matched the maroon cover.

Coy leaned forward and patted me on the shoulder. "You're pretty funny. I think you'll get along great here."

I didn't turn around, but I nodded. I realized once the sermon was over, other people were going to come talk to me. All I could do was wonder how the hell was I going to survive. Gresham preached on obedience. The red-haired man stayed seated in his chair. Maybe they were both preachers?

The sermon was over precisely at 11:55 AM, which gave five minutes for the benediction—"Because He Lives"—and the altar call. It was strange because, after the song, I noticed a few of the members glanced over at me. I guess my sin was written on my face. Sorry, folks, no altar call for me.

Church was over precisely at noon, as perfect as God's Holy Plan. That is one thing I can say about the Baptists, they know when it is time to leave.

I tried to avoid people by staying in my seat. That may sound like a bad idea, but because the rude old couple made me move I was in the middle of the church and both exits were being flooded. I imagined every family was either racing to the Bucket to beat the line or hurrying home to save their pot roast from the slow-cooker. My Rose-Mary Grand always used the food cooking on the counter as an excuse to avoid people she didn't care for after church. I missed her pot roast.

The older couple who kicked me out of my first seat came up and the man asked, "You're the new teacher, huh?"

"Yes, sir, I am."

The elderly man extended his Godly duty. "We haven't met."

The old woman smacked the man's arm. "We met him earlier, honey. He's the young man who stole our seats."

"He is?" asked the older man in disgust.

"Yes," answered the wife.

"Oh, I thought he looked familiar," he said, then they shambled away.

I couldn't help but grin and shake my head. *Amen.*

I spotted Coy talking to another man. I searched for his fiancé, but she was across the church with a group of ladies. I inched toward him, and once he was finished talking, I stepped into his path.

He smiled. "Matt, I'm glad you came. It's been a long time since we've seen a new face that wasn't a newborn."

"Yes. It was"—I forced it out—"a blessing."

"What do you think about the town so far?" Coy asked.

"I like it. It's exactly what I needed." I smiled.

"And what was that?"

"Just some good ol' peace and quiet."

"Absolutely," he said, "we have lots of that around here."

"Mind if I finish that question I was going to ask?"

"Go ahead," Coy said.

"About the previous teacher."

He tensed and looked around. "I'm sorry, but I think Judith is ready to go."

I turned, but she was still talking to the women with her back to us. I turned back. "I'm sorry, but I'm just curious. How did she die?"

"I'm afraid I can't answer that question."

"Listen, I won't tell anyone—"

"No, you listen." He spoke with a quiet intensity. "It was a mistake for me to say anything in the first place. Do us both a favor and forget I told you *anything*."

"What's the big deal?"

He swallowed, his face red. "The fact you're asking that is enough. Look, Matt, you seem like a nice guy, but this town isn't like where you come from. Sorry, I just want to keep my job."

As a teacher, I knew when someone was feeding me a line. I frowned. "I see."

"It was nice to meet you. Hope to see you next week," he said, then called out to his wife. "Honey? Are you ready to go?"

I watched him as they walked away. He whispered into Judith's ear. She whipped her head around and gave me a stern look.

Great. Now I look like a troublemaker. Maybe I should have gone to the Methodist church...

17

I hurried outside, and Franklin was waiting on the church's grass with a mammoth-sized man. I moved toward them, but a woman stepped unapologetically in front of me.

Her face was like stone, long and thick. Her eyes were on my face, but it was like she was focusing on my nose instead of my eyes. "These are my children." Her voice droned. "They'll be at school tomorrow."

I looked at her daughters. They were twin girls of about eight or nine years old with matching yellow dresses. I grinned. "Hello. Your dresses are pretty. I'm Mr. Christian."

The mother drew my attention back to her. "Their names are Kate and Meg. They don't talk much, or at all. However, they are listening. They'll hear ya."

What a freak, I thought. The twins narrowed their eyes. *Oh, brother, they're freaks, too,* I thought. *How did I end up in this town?*

I inhaled. "It was nice to meet you, and you two as well."

I received blank stares from the three of them, then they left.

Franklin waved to me. "Matt, come meet one of Middwood's finest."

My shoulder muscles tensed, not just because he was a cop, but because the man was massive. He wasn't fat by any means, but he was huge, even bigger than the preacher. A real tough guy. I was glad he smiled at me because in any other situation he was a man I would avoid out of pure fear. His smile gave him an approachable and handsome quality that reminded me of a mix of Marlon Brando and Li'l Abner. He was in his early to mid-thirties, clean-shaven, and wore a conservative, slicked-down, side-part hairdo.

"Matt Christian, Sheriff Philip Rollin."

I looked up at the man. I'm six feet tall, but standing next to the sheriff I felt small. He was not only around a foot taller than me, but he was at least a foot wider.

He did what I feared, he reached out his hand. I did my best to hide my reluctance, but I accepted Rollin's greeting. I had average appendages, but my hands were like a child's in comparison. To add further insult to my manhood, Rollin gave an intense squeeze. I tried not to wince.

So, Eddie was the guard on the castle wall and Rollin was the dragon. Just seeing the sheriff was enough to keep outsiders in check. It was like he was saying, *"Welcome to our town, but know I'm bigger, stronger, and I could easily destroy you."*

The sheriff unclenched my hand and I hid it behind my back.

An older lady walked up to the sheriff and wrapped her pudgy arms around his midsection. "Hello, sweetheart."

"Hey, Mama," he smiled and gave her a side squeeze.

She wasn't a giant like her son, but she was still tall for a woman, standing eye to eye with me.

"Welcome to town, Matt," the jolly, older woman said. "I'm Phyllis Rollin—"

"My sweet mama," grinned Philip as he squeezed her again.

"But you can call me Grandma Rollin." She gave me a warm grin and shook my hand. "How's your wife adjusting to the big city of Middwood?"

"She hates it." I grinned. "I'm kidding, I'm not married."

"Oh, my word, then that must be why you are so skinny. I don't understand all these handsome men holdin' out and being bachelors when we have so many single girls around."

"Ma," warned Philip.

Grandma Rollin pointed to Philip and mouthed the words, "He's single, too."

Sheriff Rollin changed the subject. "If there is ever any problem, Matt, you just let me know."

"Of course, Sheriff."

He continued, "We want to keep you around as long as we can." He slapped me on the back with his heavy hand. I almost fell over. "Uh oh, watch it there, buddy. Have you been drinking?" he and Phyllis laughed.

I attempted to join their humor.

Franklin stepped forward. "You two have a great Sunday. Matt and I have a trip ahead of us."

We exchanged "it was nice to have met you's" and they went on their way.

I pointed to my right at the four-story building beside First Baptist. "Mr. Mullis, before I forget, what is that building?"

His voice filled with past pride. "Mr. Christian, that is the big store, or what used to be the big store." I wrinkled my forehead and he explained, "Like I told you, the town is small because it was built for one reason, coal. It's like all the other little mining towns up and down the mountain ranges. Companies bought the land where coal was, and to have a workforce, the company erected the houses and everything else you see. The big store—the building here—used to provide just about everything the miners and their families needed: doctors, dentists, drug store, bank, clothes, everything."

"The mines are still running though, right?" I asked.

Franklin shook his head. "More or less, but, Matt, it's nothing like it used to be. The company that owned this mine left, and they took all their money with them. So the people they left behind took over the town and the old mine."

"Sounds rough." I knew Middwood was in bad shape, and now I knew why.

"We manage, and we'll get Middwood back to its former glory," he said with confidence, a dreamy rasp in his voice.

I didn't say anything, but even with my decent imagination, Franklin's vision seemed utterly unrealistic.

"And guess what, Mr. Christian?"

I raised my eyebrows.

"It all starts with you, the new teacher." He shifted to me. "Are you ready to go up?"

"All right, I'm ready."

"It's not that far, and I'm sure you are in better shape than me. Do you smoke?"

"No."

"Good, then yes, you are in better shape than me."

According to Franklin, getting to the school was simple, you take a left after you cross Keeper's Bridge, walk for ten minutes, make a right up the dirt path, then hike up the slope for ten minutes.

Less than halfway up the steep incline, I started feeling the burn in my upper legs. Franklin was also having a bit of trouble, wheezing in between his huffs. I guess he wasn't joking about the smoking.

"Are you okay, Mr. Mullis?"

"Of course, I do it a couple of times a week, and for the last time, call me Franklin. Mr. Mullis is good and dead, and I'm not ready to see my father again anytime soon."

"Force of habit. Sorry."

He huffed. "And stop apologizing all the time."

Franklin was an old crab, but I couldn't help but grin. I liked the guy.

I was nervous, though there was a sense of adventure to all of it. I knew it would be a small school, but I was looking forward to meeting the other teachers. With the town being so small, there might only be three of us total. I would need to dodge questions about why I left my previous school. Secretly I believed Franklin already knew about Darlene.

An old school bell tower appeared and grew as we crossed into the sunshine away from the mountain's shaded path. "Oh wow, a school bell. Do I get to ring an actual school bell?"

Franklin stayed silent.

As we reached the top of the ridge, I stumbled. I looked down and saw my shoes were covered with dust. Loafers weren't the best option for hiking.

I looked up and the path led to a flat, leveled open space.

I wasn't from the mountains, so I didn't know what it was called. "It's almost like a floating island—"

I stopped. There was no school in sight.

About ten yards away, off center from the dirt yard, was a single dead tree with a stump hiding under it. A few yards behind that sat an old, off-white shack of a building.

I wrinkled my forehead.

Simply stacked, cinderblock stairs led up to a set of faded black double doors. Hanging beside the entrance were two sheets of weathered plywood covering what I assumed was a window. Under the plywood to the left of the doors was a worn bench.

Granted, I had never been to the mountains before, but everything around me from the ugly mountains, the rotten tree, and the miserable, pitiful shack... it was truly a different world than Atlanta. With all the backward shit that had happened to me, I didn't know if I was still on a job interview or had become a soon-to-be sacrifice for a town cult.

18

I stood there, frozen. I never wanted to be wasted out of my mind as bad as I did at that moment. I knew what I was looking at, and I was terrified. "Mr. Mullis, where are we?"

Franklin dismissed my question. "Hop up on that bench and take a look through the window. There's a gap there you can peek through."

"Do you have a key?"

"Of course, Mr. Christian, but it's been closed for thirteen years. We best look through the window to check it out before we open the door."

"You mean this is the—"

Franklin continued: "A black bear could have made the place into its den. There are lots of them around here, though there's still a few weeks before denning time."

I started at Franklin blankly.

"Wake up, Mr. Christian. It means hibernating."

"I see. Black bears?" My mind became more numb by the moment. "Um, shouldn't we have a gun or something?"

Franklin urged me on. I nodded and attempted to hide my concern about the shack.

I faced the building and closed my eyes. I gave the bench a shake with my foot. It didn't collapse and seemed sturdy enough, so I stepped up, pulled back the corner of the plywood, and peered in, keeping my face as far from the opening as possible. The windows were dirty, so my view wasn't clear. I inched closer. The room was dim, but I was able to make out the wooden back support of a chair.

Fuck, I thought, *it's a desk.* It was the school. My heart melted in the fire of the hell I found myself in. I wished a bear *would* kill me.

Rawr!

Hands slapped at the glass, and young faces materialized.

I rocketed into the air and fell off the bench, landing on my ass.

"You scared the—"

"Bejesus out of you from the looks of it." Franklin laughed and slapped his side. "You city boys are too much."

One of the kids inside laughed with a shout, "Did you see that? He jumped like a cat."

"Yeah, but cats land on their feet," said another kid as they opened the door and piled outside. There were four in all.

The Shawnee woman I had seen outside the diner stepped out of the school as well. She pushed one of the boys. "Peter help him up."

I was instantly embarrassed she had seen me fall.

"Our joke got a little more out of you than we expected," she apologized.

An older blonde girl stood inside the school's doorway with a broom. "See, Peter, I told you it was a bad idea."

A joke. Prank the new teacher. *Hilarious,* I thought.

The boy who was with Litonya earlier dragged his feet down the stairs. "You don't have to be sour about it," he griped.

"I wouldn't say I'm sour about it, but I do wish I had a bit more padding on my backside."

He reached out his hand. I wasn't sure if I should trust him, so I stood up myself.

"See. He's an okay guy," the chubby kid said.

Just then, a young girl of around twelve hovered in front of me. "Hello, Mr. Christian, I'm Carla. I just wanted to introduce myself and tell you I'm pleased to hear we're finally startin' school again in Middwood."

I cleaned my hands off on my slacks. "It's nice to meet you, Carla."

The boy with the attitude still hadn't introduced himself. "And who are you? The bear hiding in the outbuilding?"

The chubby boy pointed to me. "See, Peter, he's not a square."

The teenager, Peter, grunted. "Weezer, he wasn't making a joke. He doesn't know this is the school. He probably thought it was just an outhouse."

Everyone turned and looked at me.

I didn't know what to say. The window had been a trick. Was this just another hoax?

Peter burst into laughter. "Oh boy! He doesn't know!"

"Peter, that's enough," Litonya warned.

"Come on, mom. It's funny."

I held it all in until the pain was so great that it burst out of my mouth as a laugh. I stroked my beard as I feverishly nodded until the laughter stopped. "This is the school?"

No one laughed.

I pushed a grin on to my face. "It's quaint."

Weezer looked to the other children. "What's quaint?"

"It means, charming, Weezer. Like Prince Charming," said the blonde girl.

Peter leaned against the school laughing. "Amy, it means he hates it."

I gave a plastic smile. "No. It just means... it's not what I expected."

"He doesn't hate it. Do you?" Amy, the blonde, asked.

Carla stepped forward. "Mr. Christian, you hate it? You won't leave, will you?"

Peter pointed to me with both palms. "Didn't you hear me? He—"

"Peter! Hush!" his mother snapped.

Everyones gaze was on me.

Franklin was wearing his bulldog face, and my laughter didn't amuse him.

I cleared my throat. "But ..." I bit through my insanity. "I'm so grateful for the opportunity. Someone show me the school."

Carla hopped to attention. "Yes, sir, Mr. Christian! Right, this way."

Franklin spoke up. "Okay, kids, let's clean this place up for tomorrow."

"Just a second, Carla. Mr. Mullis, I can help."

"Oh, no." The blonde moved back to the school. "We don't mind, Mr. Christian. And I'm Amy."

"Nice to meet you."

She smiled as she pushed on Weezer's shoulder. "Besides, we're good at cleaning. Aren't we, Weezer?"

The chubby boy ignored her.

"Weezer, come help me."

"I want to sit outside and watch the new teacher."

Franklin spoke up. "Weezer, he's not doing anything."

"Then just let me rest a minute," he whined.

Franklin threatened, "Get up, fatty."

Carla pulled my arm. "Come on, Mr. Christian."

The Shawnee woman approached. She and Peter both had dark, straight hair, but her complexion was slightly darker. I had seen Litonya this morning at a distance and thought she was attractive, but up close she was beautiful.

"Carla, you're doing such a good job at helping Mr. Christian. Can I talk to him for a moment?"

"Of course, Ms. Tonya."

Carla took a few steps away and waited. Litonya regarded her with a warm smile.

I tried to speak, but nothing came out of my mouth.

She grinned as she took in my awkwardness.

"I-I'm sorry, I'm Matt Christian."

She smiled. "I know who you are, Matt. I'm Litonya Janowski, Peter's mother. But please call me Tonya." She held out her hand.

"Nice to meet you."

Her hands were small, but her grip was firm, and her hands were rougher than I expected. Without thinking, I examined our handshake.

She pulled back. "Did I get something on you?"

"Oh, no," I answered. "Or I don't think so..." I looked down at my open hand, trying to concoct a reason to cover my surprise.

"I was working earlier; I paint. I'm probably still covered in it," she apologized, searching her simple dress.

"No, you look just fine. I'm just weird." I let out a nervous laugh. "But you paint. That's amazing. I should really try and get one of those, a hobby, I mean." I grinned hoping my joke wasn't too lame.

"Well, I refuse to learn to type."

"I support feminism."

"Feminism?" She laughed. "Do you read a lot?"

I widened my eyes. "I do. Can you read minds?" I grinned and gave a boyish laugh.

Good grief, I hated myself.

She laughed politely. "You are going to be the talk of the county, you know? Oh! And my son, Peter, will be coming tomorrow."

"No, I'm not!" the boy called from some hidden place.

Trying to ignore my hesitations about her son, I replied, "I'm lucky to have found such a charming town."

She leaned in, grinning. "Mr. Christian, there is no need for lies with me. The valley is incredibly boring."

Her frankness was the relief I needed. "Well, it's different, but that is part of its appeal."

"Carla," Franklin called from the school's doorway. "I know you are waiting but let me show him the inside of the school."

She pursed her lips. "I'll just wait for you right here."

"Thanks, Carla."

Tonya touched my shoulder. "I need to get home. Good luck tomorrow, Matt."

I smiled. "Thank you. I'll need it."

As I moved toward the school, I bit the dead skin off my lip, hoping the inside was better than the outside.

Franklin stepped into the dim schoolhouse ahead of me. "We got new desks about fifteen years back. They're still nice."

I climbed the unsteady blocks and entered the shed, the stale air inside held notes of dirt and mold. Franklin walked through the room and dust danced up from the floor and the tops of the desks.

"Don't worry, we'll get it cleaned up by tomorrow," he said, moving to pick up an overturned stool next to the window. "I guess it's gotten a little dusty since it's been closed." He sat the stool down next to an old stove. "And look, I put the stove in myself. It's coal burning, of course. Nifty isn't it? If you've never lit one before I can show you." He smiled with pride. I didn't speak but stared at the floor for many moments. Finally, he pushed, "What do you think, Mr. Christian?"

"Um, yes, these desks will be fine. The two-seaters will help us if we have a limited number of books."

"That was the idea."

I couldn't hold it in any longer. "Oh, God." I blurted the words out in painful despair. I pushed my hands through my hair and sat down on one of the dusty desktops.

I'd left Atlanta. I had no money, and the gas that was supposed to be in my car had dripped out onto the dirt road in front of the most fucked up town with the most back-woods people I'd ever come across. My savings were the two coins in my pocket, and they wouldn't last long. I didn't even have enough to get a hotel. I'd have to sleep in my car again, if I could get the Falcon's engine cranked, then I could... I didn't even have enough gas to get to the next town.

"Mr. Christian?" Franklin prompted.

I nodded. "Like I said, it's just not what I expected."

He shook his head. "What were you expecting?"

I released a nervous, panicked grunt. "A school."

"It is a school—"

The words flowed out of my mouth. "A school has teachers, office clerks, and a coffee pot. This is a one-room schoolhouse. When you offered me the job, you said—"

He cut me off. "I hired you to be a teacher—"

"Not just *a* teacher, Franklin, *the* teacher."

We stood there with our gazes locked. He was like a stone, but I was finished with the game. I turned and shook my head. "I'm sorry."

"This is the backwoods, Matt—"

I stood. "I'm sorry."

A truck pulled up. The man called out as the kids walked over to him. "We got all kind of things, brooms, shovels, rags."

"Let me go help unload the truck. I'll be right back."

19

I stepped outside and, luckily, Carla, along with everyone else was preoccupied. Unless, they had a few gallons of gasoline in the back of the truck, all the brooms in the world wouldn't help that shack.

I made a beeline for the trees behind the school. Despite being on top of a mountain, I needed air. I wanted to run screaming down the hill, but that wasn't an option unless I stole a car.

Maybe I could hitchhike back to Atlanta and face my past. I scoffed; no one there would have me, all those who would were dead.

Body heat warmed by back. I turned around, but there was no one there. I searched the trees between the school and me, but, again, there was no one there. Just my crazy imagination, I guessed, maybe my make-believe super-human telepathy was weakening. But I was usually correct when I felt I was being watched.

I was making my way through the trees toward the schoolyard when I heard muffled voices. It was a sound I knew well, the chatting back and forth of little girls.

I straightened and looked around. "Hello?"

My question was answered by giggles, but they were behind me. I turned and looked, but there was nothing there except the empty, slanting, cliff. I spun in a circle. No one there.

My chest tightened.

The laughter rang out from behind me again as branches moved. I hurried and broke through the limbs to the open schoolyard.

Amy jumped and turned as someone darted back into the trees. "Oh!" She laughed nervously, "Mr. Christian. I'm so sorry I didn't know you were there. I was just...um..." She wiped her mouth. "I'm sorry did you need something?"

"Who was here?"

She broke into high laughter and waved her hand. "Just one of the kids—"

"Mr. Christian!"

Amy and I both jumped.

Carla stood with her hands on her hips. "Can I show you the schoolyard now."

"Yes, Carla. I found him for you. Enjoy, Mr. Christian, I'll see you tomorrow. 'Bye." Amy turned and walked away quickly.

Carla pursed her lips and stared after Amy. "I pray she doesn't become a Jezebel." She peered up at me. "Shall we begin?"

After we walked the perimeter of the mountain island and Carla gave me a tour of the schoolyard, including the tree, the stump, and the bench, it was time for me to go back and face Franklin. I wasn't sure how long I could make this work, but my options were severely limited.

I readied myself as I climbed the cinderblocks again. I paused outside the door, then stepped through. Franklin was cleaning out the coal stove.

I cleared my throat. "Carla is a thorough child."

He stood. "Yes, she's very bright. I'm hoping she won't be let down."

I relaxed my shoulders and blew out a breath. "I'm sorry I reacted like that."

Franklin frowned me.

"I have never been in a situation like this before."

Franklin put his hands behind his back. "Meaning your personal situation?"

I folded my arms. My suspicions about him knowing about Darlene deepened. I couldn't let that throw me. I needed the house, I needed the job, and I needed for everything to work, if only temporarily; I needed the little bulldog man to like me. I would do whatever it took, including eating crow.

I lowered my arms. "I was referring to the situation of being the only teacher at a school. I mean, teaching that many different grade levels—" I halted my tangent and took a breath. "Please forgive my earlier outburst. It's hard finding a job mid-year."

"I reckon it's hard to lose a job mid-year as well."

That was a jab.

I sat on a desktop. "Yes, well, not as hard as you may think. You see..."

He held up a hand and waved me off. "Matt, one thing you will find out about the town is that no one will know your business unless you share it."

I exhaled. "Thank you, Mr. Mullis. I'd like to take the job."

Franklin cocked his head. "Are you sure?"

It was time to lay it on thick. "My passion is teaching. I'm hoping I can teach the kids, and that they can teach me about...Appalachian life as well."

Franklin gave a victorious nod and grinned. "Okay then, you'll be the teacher."

"How many students will I be teaching?"

"Well, we only have eighteen seats, so I reckon eighteen."

"I can handle that."

He moved to the double doors, but then stopped himself. "To be honest, I have no idea how many kids you'll have. They'll be behind in their studies." He shrugged. "Most of the older boys probably won't even come."

"Why is that?" I asked.

"Well, Middwood is a coal town. Mind you, not the hopping business it used to be, but still. If one of those young boys is lucky enough to get a job at the mines, they won't leave it."

"What about their futures—"

"Matt, we ain't in Atlanta. A man feeds his family with his hands and sweat. If a man can't do that here, then he isn't much of a man."

"I can respect that." The words came out. I meant them, mostly, but I held education at a higher level than most people.

"But the little ones will be here," he gave me an excited smile.

"I have my lesson books with me. I'll have to change them a bit for different ages, but with a few pots of coffee I'll figure it out," I grinned through my terrified lie as I scanned the room for a place to put the coffee pot. "There isn't electricity is there?"

"No."

"No problem."

"Good. I'm sure you need to prepare, so we should start heading back to town."

~

We walked down the hill in silence, which was nice. I needed the quiet. Mostly because I didn't know what to say, but I could tell Franklin was pleased.

Once we got down the hill and crossed Keeper's Bridge, I couldn't help but look at my car, wishing it would crank. If it would, everything would be different, but it shouldn't take too long to get it fixed. "Franklin, about my car—"

"Yes, yes, I'll see what I can do about helping you find someone to work on your car."

As we approached Main Street, Franklin proposed, "Do you need to stop in Magnolia's, the grocery store?"

"I was planning on unpacking, then going out later."

"Mr. Christian, it's already four o'clock. The sun will be going down soon."

I gave him a flat grin.

"You see, the whole town shuts down a good hour and a half before the sun sets."

"What time does the sunset?"

Right off the top of his head, "Tonight the sun goes down at five thirty-seven."

"Are you being serious?" I asked.

"Mr. Christian, be glad it's open on Sunday at all."

I raised my hands. "Okay, I surrender."

"Good. The store—"

I held up my hands again and he stopped. I tried to think of a better way to voice my dilemma, but instead I scratched my head lamely. "Um, I'll hold off on the store until I get paid."

His forehead returned to its original old man frown, and he raised his chin in a dismissive little shake. "Mr. Christian, we can't have our new teacher starving to death. Don't worry about the money, I'll loan it to you. I hope you are a good teacher; you're turning out to be an expensive hire."

As touched as I was, I shook my head in disapproval. "That is more than generous, but I can't accept—"

"Matt, kids without food in their tummies are like books without words. I'm sure that goes for teachers, too."

I chuckled. "Sounds like something a teacher would say."

"Yes, it does." Franklin cleared his throat. "I can take the groceries out of your first pay."

I downplayed my desperation, "If it wouldn't be too much trouble."

"Good. It's settled."

My mouth opened, but no words came out. After everything that had happened I knew I didn't deserve this kindness, but damn I was grateful and starving. I nodded and bowed my head. "Thank you, Mr. Mullis. I can get another job and pay you back—"

"There are no other jobs in Middwood. You got the last one."

We made our way down the street and into Magnolia's Grocery. The store was small, with six aisles, all with low shelves. There were only two other people in the store, and one of those was a kid sweeping in the back corner.

"Cutting it close, Mr. Frank," the young man sweeping said, looking at the clock.

"I know, Bobby. We're just making a quick stop. We won't keep you long at all. Five minutes, tops." Franklin nodded to me. "Make it quick."

It was like an egg timer had been wound in my chest, but with a store this size, it wouldn't take long.

The floors were filthy, but with the dirt roads in town, keeping them clean would be impossible. The selections were small, but it had all the basics. I just had to figure out what I needed and not get overzealous with my buying.

Franklin hovered the next row over. He approved when I stopped and picked up shaving cream. "Yes, a clean-shaven man always looks more professional."

"I will only be shaving my neck. The beard stays."

He frowned. "I'm going to go wait by the door while you finish up."

"Yes, sir." I returned to my shopping. By the time I made my way to the checkout counter, I had a loaf of SunBeam bread, two packs of American cheese, butter-like stuff, three boxes of Corn Flakes, milk, Lifebuoy Soap, a can of coffee, and the tube of Barbasol shaving lotion.

"Who is he?" a husky female voice behind me asked.

20

I turned, and there was a middle-aged woman with wiry, chestnut hair playfully stalking toward me in a near sideways dance. Her curvy, slinking hips said everything, and their language made me uncomfortable.

Franklin must have played football back in the day because he intercepted her, stepping between us. "Magnolia, this is Matt Christian. He is the new teacher."

She opened her mouth and inhaled the world with her overdramatic admiration. "The new teacher? I didn't know we had a new teacher," she said in a raspy, smoker's voice.

"It was announced at church," Franklin grumbled.

"Franklin, you know I don't go to church anymore." Magnolia grinned, her voice dripping with sarcasm.

She pushed past Franklin and put her arms around me, giving me a tight hug. "Oh, what a surprise. The kids are going to be so happy. And, Franklin, you old devil, you know how to pick 'em." She pulled away and looked me up and down. "He is just as tall and handsome as he can be. Damn!"

"Magnolia..." Franklin murmured.

She swatted at Franklin and extended her hand. "Yes, I

am Magnolia. You can get anything you need here. Do you hear me, Matt?"

"Magnolia..." Franklin warned.

She glared at him. "Oh, I heard you the first time. I'm just being friendly." She started taking the items from my arms and set them on the counter. "Bobby? Bobby, come check out Middwood's only clean drink of water." The teenager walked up and listed the groceries in a small journal. The store didn't have a cash register.

"Speaking of that. Matt, you will need to boil your water before you drink it."

"You're welcome, Frank."

"Thank you, Magnolia," he huffed.

"I noticed it had a zing to it."

"A zing?" Magnolia laughed louder than my ears liked. "You've got a zing, too, but listen to Franklin. Mining is good for the pockets of bigwigs but bad for the water. Broken souls and drinking water don't mix."

"Broken souls?"

Magnolia gestured toward Bobby. "Check him out. He works at the mine. Doesn't he look like a broken soul?"

I smiled at him. "What do you do at the mine?"

The boy eyed Franklin. "I pick out the slate from the coal." He looked at Magnolia with earnest eyes. "It's getting really late."

"You do a fine job, Bobby. And you're right, we need to hurry," encouraged Franklin.

"Will you be coming to school tomorrow?" I asked.

The boy kept his head low writing up my items.

Magnolia slid up next to me, pushing her shoulder into mine and whispered, "No he will be too busy dying at the mine in the morning." She raised her chin to look up at the boy. "What is it, Bobby, six cents an hour?" She whispered to me, "He works a fine job, but the boy has no soul. Just like a ghost child; the town's full of them."

"Ghost children?" I asked.

"Yeah, them dead kids floating around, scaring up the damn place. Even my cats—"

"Put the stuff on my tab," Franklin instructed Bobby.

"Mr. Mullis—" I protested.

He corrected, "Franklin. And you heard me, Bobby."

"Franklin, are you sure you don't mind? Should I put some of the things back."

"It's time for final selections," Bobby insisted.

"Can I put somethin' on your tab, too?" Magnolia asked with a straight face, then started laughing, practically falling over the counter.

Franklin ignored her.

She moved to him and put her hand on Frank's arm. "I was just kidding, Frank."

Franklin pulled his arm away.

"Sourpuss." She turned to me. "I'm still kidding. Ain't he a sweetheart, Matt? The town is full of helpful people. Just be careful when they start being *too* helpful."

I grinned to be polite, but Franklin groaned. I was missing something. The history between them was confusing.

"It is," she feigned as she moved behind the counter to start bagging my groceries. "Middwood is so helpful. When my husband was killed—"

"Died," corrected Franklin.

"Oh, that's right, Franklin. When my husband died—"

He tried to cut her off. "Bobby, let's hurry it up."

"He writes slow, Frank! Like I was saying, when he died, the town was nice enough to take my store and my house from me—"

"Magnolia, are you drinking again?" Franklin asked.

She fake-smiled at him. "As a matter of fact, I never quit."
With a smoker's cough, she turned back to me and continued, "The bank said we owed more money than we did."

"But," Franklin jumped in, indicating the store, "we let
you keep your job."

She joined Franklin's words like a rehearsed performance. "They let me keep my job." She shook her head and
smiled at him. "And I am very grateful."

"I'm sorry to hear about your husband."

Her cloudy eyes hinted at a sparkle, and a big, proud
grin grew on her face. She squealed as she ran around the
counter and hugged me from the side. "I'm going to keep an
eye on you, handsome."

"You're embarrassing me, Ms. Magnolia."

"That's right, Matt. And I'm a miss."

I gave her a purposeful grin, stepped up to the counter,
and took my bag along with a gallon jug of water.

"Oh, sweetheart. You have some lint on the back of your
shirt," she whined as she moved close behind me.

"Oh?" I craned my neck to look at my back.

"Don't worry, honey. Mama will get it for you." She
steadied herself by grabbing and squeezing my right shoulder, then slowly brushed off my upper and lower back area.
"There we go."

"Thank you, ma'am."

"No problem, honey. Anytime—" Her words were cut
short as she lost her balance and caught herself by throwing
one arm around my waist and the other arm, or hand rather,
clenched my right butt cheek. "Oh hell!"

I jumped and dropped everything. I turned to catch her.
She stood slowly, facing me. She gently brushed her hair out
of her face, then gliding her fingers over her lips, she said,

"I'm real sorry about that, hon. I lost my balance. I could have rocked you over."

"It's time to go," Franklin barked.

Magnolia uncoiled herself from me. "You heard the man, Bobby."

"Ms. Magnolia, there isn't enough time to clean this up."

I bent down and re-bagged my groceries that were laying in a puddle of water."

"What a mess," Bobby whined. "My mom is going to kill me if I'm home after sundown."

"Stop cryin'." She groaned. "We'll leave it there till tomorrow."

"I can help you clean it up," I offered.

"Nope, it's time to go. Welcome to Middwood, handsome."

I stepped out onto the street and motioned to the store with my wet bag, "She's an interesting woman."

"Matt, she's done this before."

"I'm sure she just—"

"Nope. She's a whore. If you ever have the need, she has the itch. Just watch to make sure you don't leave with that itch breaking out all over you. Let's go before she walks out and asks you to walk her home." He gave a grunting laugh. "And here I was beginning to think you might not like women. Well, that's good. There are a few single girls your age, but they are few and far between. Lots of older women, though."

"Why lots?"

Franklin frowned. "Sometimes the mountains can be unforgiving. It's something that the town doesn't like to—"

He broke off. He didn't want to talk about it, and I didn't want to hear it.

A howl exploded in the distance.

Fear grabbed me so hard I cowered. "What was that?"

"That's a coyote. Lord, son, haven't you ever heard one before?" He chuckled. "You about made my teeth fall out."

I held my chest. "A coyote?" I turned to the darkening mountain, trying not to let him see me rubbing away the goosebumps that had popped up on my arms. "God, it sounded like a... woman wailing."

"Nope, thems coyotes," he continued, having fun. "City boy, you are so out of your element here, I tell you what." His grin subsided, and he smacked his dry lips. "I don't need to remind you that you are in a new place, you might hear a bunch of other noises you aren't used to. Don't be alarmed. It's just mountain life. And when you get home, remember to lock your door—"

"You have to lock your doors here?"

"We have bedrooms with bricked up windows, so you best believe we lock our doors."

He stopped, and concern washed over his face to the point of shame.

"What is it, Mr. Mullis?"

"Matt, I haven't been honest with you."

I stayed silent, but my anxiety rose.

"Go on."

He paused. "But there is a sort of folklore that you need to know."

I raised an eyebrow. "Folklore?"

"Yes, Matt." He frowned. "The town has rules. There are three. The first is, never turn your back on an open window."

"Thank goodness it's winter," I joked.

"No, Matt, this is serious."

I waited for him to laugh or at least grin. He didn't. I readjusted my grocery bag.

"All right." I waited, then scratched my head.

"The second rule is—"

"Wait. You mean, odd duck Clint was telling me the truth."

"I can't speak for Clint, but I decided to wait and tell you after you'd taken the job."

"Good grief. You are being serious. Is this why there aren't any windows in the bedrooms?"

"You can't turn your back on an open window if there isn't a window, now can you?"

"Mr. Mullis—" I protested.

"Matt, the windows were for security."

"Security against what?"

"It all started with Kennedy's advice on building fallout shelters, but we took it a step farther."

Good grief, Middwood was full of quacks. "It all seems a bit extreme. The Cuban missile crisis was years ago." I pressed. "I turned my back on a window since I've been here."

"Open, meaning you can see out of it."

"I could see out of the window earlier when I was inside. I turned my back then—"

"The rules only apply after dark."

"Only after dark? Okay ..." I exhaled. "That's good, I guess."

"The second rule," Franklin cleared his throat. "Never go out after the sun goes down or before the sun comes up."

My jaw gaped. "Are you fucking serious?"

"I know they might sound odd, but that is just how Middwood works."

I put the bag down. I didn't know why, but I did. I didn't want to ruin the one thing I might be walking out of the town with.

"Man," I huffed.

If my car would fucking crank and if Eddie didn't have a shotgun, I'd get the hell out of this place. I folded my arms. "And the third rule?"

"Since you are having difficulty with the first two, I'll save that one for later. If you follow the first two, you won't need rule three."

"And are there reasons for these rules?"

He avoided the question. "They are just for your own protection."

"I—" I held my breath but found it too difficult to look at him. Town rules and folklore were a new kind of batshit.

"Matt, we're a mining town, built on coal; all the towns around here were built on coal, and coal is money. Big money. There was a time when neighboring mining companies would try and run us out of town, scare our workers away, grow their domain. But, Matt, that was long ago."

I searched for the words, but logical thinking and this town didn't match up.

"Is it safe?"

He reassured me with a smile. "Nothing in life is certain, but, yes, it's safe. We just keep the doors and windows covered up to remember, and, of course, against the slim chance anything like that does happen." He watched me for my response.

I was aware he was waiting for me to speak. I bobbed my head to buy myself some more time to think. "That is some story."

"Coal in these parts has a sordid past. Make no mistake

about it, Mr. Christian, we have our ghosts, but we go on living."

When he explained it that way it seemed less dangerous. Crazy, sure, but there was a part of it that was exciting. I felt silly for making such a big deal out of everything.

He stared at me for a moment. "Do you still want the job?"

Oh brother, I had been around some crazy shit, but this was by far the most insane. I exhaled again. One thing I knew all too well was insanity. "I might just be crazy enough to stick around."

Franklin sighed in relief himself. "Good."

"Sorry for asking, but I just—"

"No, no. I would have been more concerned if you didn't ask any questions. We don't want just anyone to take the job. Regardless of social status or windows, a man's children are his treasure."

I laughed nervously and changed the subject. "It's a unique town."

"Yes, it is," he chuckled.

"Is the whole town superstitious?"

"Welcome to Middwood," Franklin said.

"I will do my best to play along."

"You do that," he said nodding. "You do that."

"It's late, so I need to get home," Franklin said. "Good night. I'll see you tomorrow. Remember don't turn your back—"

"—on an open window. Right." I faked-grinned.

"Correct."

"Now that I know what a coyote sounds like, and when the house creaks and such."

"Just roll over, wrap up in your beard, and go back to sleep."

"Yes, sir. And the beard stays." I grimaced.

"Good. I will meet you at the school an hour after sunrise."

"When is sunrise?"

"7:59 AM, but the mountain blocks the sun for a good thirty minutes after sunrise, so wait until then."

"What kind of time is that?"

"Valley time."

"So 9:30?"

"Children have to do their chores."

"How does that sit with the school board?"

Franklin shook his head. "We don't have a school board. This is the backwoods, Matt. We govern ourselves. Here is the key to the school." He handed it to me.

"Thank you," I said, studying the key. I couldn't help but notice it was heavier than it looked.

It was official. I was a teacher again. Correction, I was *the* teacher. I was employed, and I had an entire house to myself. Even though the town was strange, it reminded me how fast life could turn around.

21

B̲ack at the house, after I had boiled some water, I settled onto the sofa and decided that reading was the best decision. Until I started having problems a few years back, reading usually did the trick to relax me. Reading was like a friend to me. It was actually the only friend I had left. I flipped open my book, *The Diary of Anne Frank*. Nothing like some light reading on a late Sunday afternoon.

I read until the letters started to move. I blinked a few times and continued reading until I just stared at the page.

I guess sleep won because the next thing I remembered was the sensation of falling. I jerked my head up and threw both arms out to catch myself. My left arm crashed into the armrest, and my right hand gripped one of the sagging, purple, back pillows.

I was no longer lying down. I didn't remember sitting up. It was unnerving, but maybe it was a good thing. I was in a quiet little town. I was twenty-four, nearing thirty, and that was what thirty-year-olds did, they fell asleep on the sofa on Sunday afternoons reading about the Holocaust.

I tried to remember what I dreamed, but I couldn't recall exactly. Something about me being interrogated by Darlene, who was really Hitler's young bride. But then there was something about a blonde woman telling me, *"We want you to see us!"* while she was lowered into a meat grinder equipped with shards of coal instead of metal blades.

I shook off the visceral images.

I had a real, honest-to-God nap. Twisted and terrible, but a nap all the same. I was so shocked by the state of relaxation it jolted me awake to make sure I was still alive. Maybe I should give the whole "relaxing thing" a try more often. Well, minus the killing.

My eyes were still sleepy, so I took off my glasses and rubbed my face.

I made sure not to allow myself to think of anything. My conscious was standing guard like a little samurai warrior, kicking and cutting away any thought trying to gain the hot seat in my head. Money-chopped! Worry-stabbed! Work— just a firm pointing of the middle finger. Sex... well... Sleep was the only thing that mattered. I had to make sure I slept.

I went to the bathroom and reached for the bottle that read Sleep. The guy I bought it from had scratched off the label and roughly scribbled the word in black ink. I opened it up and swallowed one of the yellow pills. I had to play along with the pill, yawning and even thinking over and over, *I'm so sleepy*.

I made it to the bedroom and laid down.

I couldn't breathe.

I tried closing my eyes, but it didn't matter. The box surrounded me like a coffin. I couldn't do it another night. I pondered taking another pill, but I didn't want to be crabby the first day of school. I opened my eyes.

I got up and walked to the second bedroom, but I'd

forgotten it was locked. I wondered what Franklin really had locked in there?

I jiggled the handle. There was a burst of images, so fast and abstract I couldn't decipher them, like shouts reverberating off the darkness. Memories, my Rose-Mary Grand moving my hand from the boiling pot on the stove, backing me out of a room where my parents were arguing, shouting.

I walked down to the living room. I could just sleep on the sofa. But I hated sleeping on sofas, I was always too tall. Then I turned to the dining room. The dining room had a set of windows. Real, open windows. It was perfect because the room had two doors. Moving the bed wasn't one of the three silly rules, so it was okay. Right? I guess you have to know the rules before you can break them. Regardless, I had to give it a try.

I pushed the dining room table against the wall to get it out of the way. I dragged the mattress and box springs out of the bedroom, into the hall, and slid them down, one by one, to the main floor, then into the dining room. The tricky part was getting the mattress over the banister. I could have maneuvered around the banister by opening the front door, pulling the mattress out, then back in again. That would have been simple. But I couldn't chance one of my neighbors seeing what I was doing. Like Franklin said, "nobody knows your business unless you tell them." So instead, I lifted it and pushed it over the rail.

"Never turn your back on an open window," I scoffed. "You have to know the rules in order to break them."

If they were going to make people sleep in rooms with no windows, then "they" should add another rule which stated, "don't sleep in a room with windows." It didn't make any sense.

All of the superstition lore was rubbish.

The evening had been filled with banging and grunting. If I had lived in an apartment or a boarding house, I'm sure I would have had a scandalous reputation by morning. I couldn't help but laugh and give my best Eliza Doolittle impression. "I'm a good girl, I am!"

I set up my box spring and mattress on the floor. I put the non-fitting fitted sheet back on then threw on the flat sheet, a fuzzy, tan polyester blanket, and my two pillows.

Once I was finally done, I raised my hands. "And God said it was good."

Then it hit me. I could have just put the mattress on top of the dining room table. It would have been a high bed, but then I could feast on sleep. *That's right. You can all just eat me!* I laughed at my crudeness.

I was sweating, and I didn't want to get any on the sheets. I needed to cool down. I hated going to bed dirty. Moreover, I hated doing laundry, so I always tried to take a shower before bed.

I waited until I was in the kitchen to take my shirt off. The neighbors may not have been able to hear the noise I was making, but I did not want to give anyone reason to start talking about me. Definitely not talk of me being a nudist. I had no problem with my body, but I didn't necessarily want to show it off to any nosy neighbors, either.

Since the town was paying the bills for the first month and the devil painting was locked away, I was going to live dangerously and take a long, hot shower.

I waited until the water was steaming. It was so hot it burned my skin pink, and I had a new, whole bar of soap. It was perfect.

I went to my tomb to get my pajama bottoms, then I stretched as I walked down the stairs to the dining room. I flipped off the light in the kitchen, then crawled into bed. I grabbed the cover sheet with two hands and gave it a whip. It flew out above me as I lay down. It almost fell perfectly, but I had to readjust a bit for my left foot to be covered. I hated for my bare feet to be outside of the blanket.

Air moved around the space. Whether it was air leaks in the windows or the air in my head, my chest was light. I took a huge breath and nuzzled into the mattress.

It was quiet. I was relaxed. I fell asleep with ease.

A *bang* woke me from a deep sleep. I was disoriented. I had to remember where I was.

Knock. Knock.

I wasn't sure if I really heard it or if I was dreaming. I tried to rationalize the source of the bang. It wasn't someone knocking on the door. And even if it was, they would knock again. I decided not to worry about it and I quickly slipped back into sleep.

Skrrtch. Skrrtch.

22

I mages of a rabid coyote prowling the porch filled my mind.

More scratching, then a weighted shuffle.

"Dammit."

The first good sleep I'd had in months and some critter was trying to ruin it.

I didn't know how to interact with wildlife. I wondered if just turning on the porch light would scare it away.

I got out of bed, opened the dining room door, and inched to the far side of the living room. A *thud* sounded just beyond the front threshold.

I flipped on the porch light and peered out the living room window, but there was no change. I flipped the switch again, nothing. It was dead.

I leaned back to get a better view through the shutters. There was nothing but darkness. I clenched my jaw in dismay. I couldn't help but wonder if it wasn't a coyote. What if it was a bear or a wolf? What if it was Magnolia?

I flattened myself against the wall and slid in front of the living room window.

I could instantly feel eyes on me, like someone was in the room. I pushed my back into the shutters, causing the slats to clatter against the window frame. I held out my arms in defense, but there was nothing there. Nothing except the opened dining room window behind me. *"Never turn your back on an opened window."*

"Ridiculous." I went to the kitchen and dug through the drawers, but all I could find was a screwdriver. "It'll work."

Whatever it was made no attempt to be quiet.

With screwdriver in hand, I moved from the kitchen to the living room. It slipped from my hand. I tried to catch it, but it slipped through my fingers. The screwdriver crashed to the hardwood.

Everything went quiet.

It stopped. Whatever it was stopped. It knew I was there.

I ran my hand over my damp hair and took a deep breath. I slid my hand along the floor until I found the screwdriver.

I jerked open the front door. I leapt out onto the porch, wielding the screwdriver like a knife. There was nothing there.

A shuffling came from my left, and I turned.

There *it* was. The monster of my nightmares. A little, gray, fluffy, baby possum was crawling on my porch.

I let out a sigh of relief and leaned down.

Sure, I had seen a fully-grown possum, I was from the South, but I'd never seen a joey possum before.

I stuck out my bottom lip because even though it had a cone-shaped nose and little, black eyes, it was kinda cute. He stared up at me. He wasn't afraid. He gave me another look, then the fat little baby turned and waddled away.

Once, I was riding with my father in his truck when he ran over a possum. I remember after he hit it, he backed up and ran over the creature again. For some reason, we hate possums in the South. I'm not sure if it was a common practice or not. Regardless, that particular possum, even after getting run over twice, hadn't died.

There was a loud hiss.

I turned to my right, and at my feet was the most massive possum I had ever seen. It spat. Its feet shuffled, its claws sounded like metal pins hitting the porch.

She was a female with five more little babies on her back, but she didn't let that slow her down. I was between her and her baby.

She charged me, and I jumped, trying to avoid landing on her little stray.

I stubbed my pinkie toe on a protruding nail head. I stumbled forward onto the porch railing. She charged at me again, and I backed away as far as I could into a corner, removing myself as a threat.

She finally rushed me, showing me all her sharp, shiny teeth in a long hiss. I hopped up so my rear was on the rail and pulled my legs up so she wouldn't bite my exposed, bleeding toe.

"Shoo. Shoo!"

She glared at me with her coal-black eyes.

I was not afraid of her teeth, but I feared she had rabies.

I held myself tighter. "Go away."

I almost lost my balance, but I caught myself. I didn't want to fall on her and her babies.

She must have been walking on the banister when she or the little guy had fallen off. Her falling was the bang, and the scratching was from her trying to get back up to her newborn. She must have made a nest, or whatever possums have, somewhere around my house. Her joey finally crawled on her back. Then she swung around and scampered off like a full school bus.

I sat there on the banister until she was on the other side of the porch. I didn't want to upset her again. I watched as she clawed her way up one of the posts. I imagined those claws going into me, and I was glad I'd avoided that.

Once she was up the post and entirely distracted, I got down and ran to the door. When I put weight on my foot, a stinging pain shot up through my toe. I may or may not have screamed a bit making the possum hiss. Other sounds came from the yard as I hobbled on my heel and one good foot to get to the door. I got inside and slammed the slab of blood-wood behind me.

I spun around, and I hit my injured toe. I slipped on the smooth hardwood floors and fell right on my ass—the finale of my crazy night.

I sat there for a second staring at the door. I wondered if the possum stood, foaming at the mouth, right on the other side. To show my victory, I reached out and kicked the wooden slab with my good foot.

I pulled my injured toe close to my face. The toenail was broken, and it was bleeding. After seeing how long my toenails were, I realized why it hurt so bad. My Rose-Mary Grand would have been so disappointed in my grooming habits. I rolled my eyes. I grinned as I played out the scenario of bleeding out on the spot, although the wound wasn't that gruesome. These last few months had been crazy, and foot care hadn't been on my list of priorities. I'm sure I had a pair of clippers packed away somewhere.

I hopped on one foot to the bathroom upstairs. I put my bloody foot in the sink and turned on the water. The water hit my toe like a cold, sharp blade. I winced and put my foot down.

The acidic smell of the water reached my nose. It could either be a miracle cure or give me gangrene.

While I waited for the water to warm, I looked at myself in the mirror and marveled that I had been attacked by a mama possum. It could only happen to me. I couldn't make this crap up, even if I tried.

Something played over and over in my head. It was as I ran into the house just moments ago. I ran, looking like a fool, and even screamed once or twice. But it's what made me scream that bothered me. Yes, the possum hissed, but there had been more. There was something in the yard, something watching me. I know I heard something else, but it didn't make any sense...

I heard children laughing.

23

Monday, November 2, 1964
  Sunrise 6:58 AM. Sunset 5:35 PM.

I woke in an unfamiliar, sunny room. I turned my face away from the glowing light, but the sun battered my eyes from two adjacent windows. I rubbed my face, which was warm to the touch. It took me a few moments to realize where I was. It was my first time waking up in a dining room.

I sat there smacking my lips, like Franklin. It was a sound I hated.

The sun was up.

I twisted around until I found my watch.

"Shit!" I was late. At least I thought I was late. I couldn't remember what time Franklin said sunrise was, valley time. The watch read 9:21 and my heart sank. I was supposed to be at the school at 9:30. "And the first day!"

I sprinted upstairs, dragging toilet paper behind me as I

put the weight of my right foot on my heel. I grabbed a shirt and my teacher's bag, which held my notebook, pencils, a handkerchief, and a book, just in case I had time to read. I ran to the bathroom, wet my hands, then finger combed my hair and beard. I threw my toothbrush and paste in my bag. I would have to brush my teeth at school during lunch.

Running down the stairs, my injured toe made itself known like a pouting child as I put on my shirt and buttoned it up. With bag in tow, I hurried out the front door, stuffing my shirt into my pants.

I winced at the sight of the mountains surrounding me. It would take a few more days to get used to their crushing weight.

The town was already awake as I hurried down Main Street.

At the station, Eddie was at his post and even wished me luck on my first day. I hurried over the old bridge and was happy to see my car still had all four tires.

I turned left off of the bridge and headed up the highway, and in about eight minutes I got to the path that led up to the school. I climbed the hill to the flat schoolyard, panting like the Falcon when it was about to overheat. I couldn't help but think that once I was able to drive to work, the brakes might fail and my car would go soaring off the mountain into some poor family's trailer. I was sure that was the reason there were so many caved-in homes, cars with lousy brakes soaring off the mountain.

As I crossed the schoolyard, I noticed the plywood had been removed from the windows. On the other side of the glass, Franklin stood as I approached, and young inquisitive faces turned to peer out at me.

∾

I entered the double doors. The room was surprisingly cozy.

Franklin was standing in the center of the room to the left of the lit coal stove. "No need to go to recess just yet, children, Mr. Christian finally made it." He gave a teasing smile. "Class, say hello to your late, new teacher, Mr. Christian."

The excited class repeated, "Hello, Mr. Christian."

Franklin continued, "Class, when telling time, if the big arm is on the ten, and the little arm is on the nine. What time is it?"

"Late," the class answered in unison, then their little faces bloomed into smiles and giggles.

"AM," shouted a little girl with a big smile and frizzy, brown hair.

I was slightly embarrassed, but happy to see the children had a sense of humor. The problem was, it went against how I was taught to teach. I was always told to be overly strict in the first few weeks.

Franklin walked over to me and shook my hand. "Are you ready?"

I gave an overconfident nod. "Of course. Is there a class roster?"

"A what?" Franklin asked.

"A list of children?" I caught myself, remembering I was the only person running the show. "I'll make a list of the children's names at the end of the day."

I cleared my throat and stepped to the front of the class. A small garden of expression stared back at me: excited, afraid, cautious, and sleepy. The kids in front were all freckles, missing baby teeth, and hair bows, and in the back were near-adults; all of them in one room. There were definitely more than eighteen students.

Franklin must have seen me counting. "I had a hunch we wouldn't have enough seats, so I got some from the big store. I hope you don't mind."

"Of course not, it's nice." I heard the words come out of my mouth, but inside I was screaming. How in the hell was I supposed to teach so many different grade levels with so many kids? My stomach turned in a threatening manner.

A little girl caught my eye, and I did a double take. There were two of them—the twins. At first, I thought I was tripping, but then I remembered meeting them yesterday at church. Their mother had dressed them in the same outfits, though they were wearing their hair bows on opposite sides.

"Good morning, girls," I paused. "What are your names again?"

"Kate and Meg," they said in unison.

That confused me since I didn't know which name went with which girl, but my mind turned back to the number of students.

So many kids ...*Numbers, math,* I thought. *Math is easy.*

I grabbed a piece of chalk off the blackboard, and I divided it into four sections. The board was located across the room from the window, so the morning sun lit it nicely. "We will start with arithmetic. Please take out a piece of paper, and if you don't have any, I will pass some out. If you are between the ages of six and nine, you will do the addition problems. If you are between ten and twelve, you will do the subtractions, thirteen to fourteen—

"Sorry, I guess I'm letting my nerves get the best of me." I paused and I straightened my tie. "Hello, class...school. I'm Mr. Christian."

Amy was on the right side of the class, sitting next to a striking blonde girl of about sixteen.

The new blonde girl spoke up. "Mr. Christian, I heard you were from Atlanta."

The class became excited and chattered amongst themselves.

"What's your name?" I asked the girl.

"I'm Allison," she answered with a coy smile.

I tried to keep myself from blushing and went on, "Yes, Allison and class, I am from Atlanta."

The little girl who shouted "AM" stood and put her hands on her hips. "Well, I have a few questions."

"Ah! Scarlet, sit down and raise your hand before you speak. Mr. Christian is not accustomed to such outbursts where he comes from," Franklin said with disapproval.

Scarlet protested, "Well, Allison didn't raise her stupid paw."

The class giggled, but instantly stopped when Franklin gave them a scowl.

She plopped down into her seat with a huff and raised her hand. I gestured to her. "I'm sorry, Mr. Christian. I didn't mean to speak out of turn. But I am at school, and I'm ready to learn and make new friends and—"

Franklin held up his hands. "Scarlet, I know you are excited, but you are going to have to let Mr. Christian talk."

"Sure thing. Sorry," she said putting her hands between her knees.

Scarlet sat in front and shared a desk with Carla. The two girls were the same, and, yet, completely different.

I smiled. "It's all right. It's my first day here too and asking questions is a good thing to do, but like Mr. Mullis said, raise your paw first."

She grinned at me and shot Franklin a triumphant, over-dramatic smile.

So much for my strict-start teacher routine.

Weezer and a little, freckled boy of about ten sat in the first desk next to the door. The boy with freckles raised his hand. "Are you a farmer?"

I chuckled. "No, I'm a teacher."

He raised his hand again. "Did you have a farm back in Atlanta?"

I shook my head. "No."

The little boy was thoroughly confused.

Franklin chimed in, "Jason, Atlanta is a city, and it's hard to farm."

"How come?" Jason asked.

Franklin looked back to me.

"Because," I said, "in a city there is little farmland. Buildings occupy the majority of the land."

"If there are so many buildings, where are the coal mines?" Jason asked.

"There is very little mining for coal in Georgia since the Civil War, especially not in Atlanta," I stated.

"Then how do you make money?" Jason asked with a rising pitch.

The question set the students to chattering. It was at that moment I realized there were more differences between Middwood and Atlanta besides the mountains, windowless rooms, and devil paintings.

I raised my hands to quiet the children. "It isn't like Middwood where everyone does the same kind of work. There are lots of different types of industries with lots of opportunities."

Jason began to speak again, but Franklin shot him a look. Jason raised his hand again. "My dad said he never saw a man teacher before."

It was nothing I hadn't heard before. I wanted to correct his grammar and tell him most schools started switching to female teachers because they could control them and pay them less, but I was sure the nice little boy's father wouldn't understand.

Instead I said, "That's a common misconception, young man. In many cities, there are plenty of men who teach."

The kids whispered as I turned back to the board.

"What is a common mistconcession?" Weezer asked.

"I don't know," replied Jason.

I took a breath, turned back to the class, and asked, "Now, before we get to our math lesson, are there any other questions?"

The entire class raised their hands.

Franklin came off his perch like an old owl. "Children, there will be plenty of time for you to ask questions later."

I moved closer to the class. "Okay, I don't mind answering your questions about myself and Atlanta, but we must have our lessons as well, so I'll tell you what. Each day I will answer one question..."

I looked over at Franklin and he held up two fingers.

"One question, but only if everyone does their work and behaves. Do we have a deal?"

By all the smiles, with and without all their teeth, I could tell they were pleased. I couldn't help but smile back. "Good," I said.

Scarlet raised her hand.

"Yes?" I asked.

"Mr. Christian, you have nice, white teeth," she said boldly.

I blushed. "Thank you. That's very kind." I turned to the board. "Now, let's see where we are with arithmetic."

I wrote five basic questions in each of the assigned age-level sections and turned around. The wide eyes and smiles diminished like little, flickering Christmas lights going out.

It wasn't just the little kids either, it was the whole school-house. Franklin looked at me with concern.

I walked away from the blackboard and along the rows. I looked down at each student's paper as I passed. Some of them had managed to write their first problem down, but none of the children had written answers.

I returned to the board. "It looks like we need to take another approach. Okay, my oldest students, fifteen and up, since the division is beyond us at the moment, how many of you know how to do multiplication."

Amy, the blonde from yesterday, raised her hand. "I do, but I only know the ones and the twos."

"But Amy, you know them, so that's good," I said.

"What about the subtraction, do any of my oldest know how to work subtraction?"

Luckily, they all raised their hands. However, Allison kept looking around. Even though she had her hand up, the teacher in me knew she was afraid of looking dumb. I let it slide.

"Okay, listen, I want all of you to do the problems on the board that you do know. Even if they are just the addition problems. Everyone with me? While you do that, I will work with the youngest. Agreed?"

The children's faces lit back up again. I made sure to keep the smile on my face as I looked at Franklin. I could tell he was happy with the way I'd handled the setback.

If I was going to keep the house and the job, I had to make sure the kids learned.

24

I was finally brushing my teeth when Carla, the little girl I met on Sunday, was the first in from recess.

"Don't mind me. I wanted to make sure no one got my seat," she said as she sat in the first desk on the third row.

Her hair was neatly tied with a yellow ribbon. She was not the prettiest or even the neatest, but I could tell she'd taken the time to make sure her hair was done. I wouldn't be surprised if she insisted on doing it all by herself, without the help of her mother.

"Hey," a voice snapped from the door.

I glanced over, but I couldn't see their face. The sun back-lit the person in silhouette.

"Yes?" I asked.

"Is this just a getting-to-know-you first day, and if it is, can I ditch?"

It was, Peter, the troublemaker. His teenage attitude reminded me why I chose to work with middle-grade students.

"It's a real day. We've been working on math."

"My mom made me come. Is it only little kids in here?"

"No, there are a few older kids too."

"I'm not a kid. I'm seventeen."

"Great. Well, come on in."

"Where's Frank?" he asked as he moved to the seat next to Carla. She regarded him with a half-smile, then turned her attention back to me.

"Hey, beat it! I already called dibs on that seat," whined Scarlet in a high-pitched voice, stomping from the door.

I mused in agreement, "Oh, I'm sorry...?" I asked leaving a pause like I didn't know his name.

The boy looked from Scarlet to me. "Peter Janowski."

I gave an apologetic face. "I'm sorry that is Scarlet's seat." I paused. "She has trouble seeing the board."

Scarlet shot me a confused glance.

"Scarlet, remember? The note you gave me...from your mom?" I said slowly with a deep nod.

Scarlet caught on to my game and whipped back to him and said shrilly, "My mom said for me to sit close. Get your own seat."

He stood and threw up his hands. "I don't care if you're blind or not, dork."

"Hey! Don't call me a dork, chicken head!" Scarlet shouted.

Peter gave in and moved away. He took a seat in the back of the third row.

"Scarlet, please don't scream so loud," Franklin instructed walking into the schoolhouse.

"Hi, Frank. Can I go home?" the boy asked.

"Peter," Franklin stated firmly, "you will refer to me as Mr. Mullis, and you aren't leaving here until the end of the day. Is that clear?"

The boy didn't answer. Instead, he turned and stared out the window.

Franklin huffed, "Young man, I'm going to have a talk with your mother."

"Yes, sir, Mr. Mullis."

∼

By the end of the day the youngest were counting, and some of them were even able to add on their fingers. I encouraged the older students to help the next age group down with their work, and I promised to work with them later. All of the older girls helped, but Peter worked by himself. It was a matter of small steps. I was pleased but exhausted.

Franklin walked over to me. "Good work today, Mr. Christian. It looks like it's a good fit."

"Thank you, Franklin. They are behind, but they were all eager to learn, and that always helps."

"Well, get some rest, and I will see you again tomorrow, but be on time," he smiled, then walked out.

"Mr. Mullis," I called.

He re-entered and corrected me. "Franklin."

"Franklin, sorry. Will you be coming to school every day?"

"Until I see fit not to. Is that a problem?"

"No, but if you do stay, I will expect you to do your homework."

He looked at me blankly. It was a bad joke, but I was attempting to build some kind of boundary. I guess I would have to deal with him looking over my shoulder. Perhaps it would be a blessing in disguise.

Franklin put a hand on my shoulder. "Get some rest, Matt, you look beat."

~

By the time I cleaned up the school and packed up my bag, it was a little after four and I was mentally drained. Working was one thing but teaching a large group of kids... forget about it. My well was dry for the day.

I hiked down the hill in the brisk November air. The main thing on my mind was my car. My worries about it not working made the trip to the bridge seem longer.

As I walked past Keepers Bridge, I nodded to Eddie.

"How did the first day go?" he yelled.

"Better than I thought it would," I replied.

"Any luck with the car?"

I shrugged. "About to find out."

He toasted me with the box of Cracker Jack he was munching on. "Good luck!"

"Thanks!"

I got to my car, opened the door, and threw my bag in the front seat.

"Okay, baby, I know you've been through a lot, but I need a miracle."

I turned the key, but other than a short click there was nothing.

I re-sparked my optimism that life was worth living and decided to speak louder to her, "Come on, baby!"

The click was again followed by silence. I again closed my eyes and sighed.

~

Franklin's predictions of people coming by were true. There were two casserole dishes sitting in front of my door. I was alone, but I could feel the eyes of my neighbors, waiting for my response to the gifts. I shot a glance over my shoulder to see someone watching from the house across the street. She jumped, but then waved. I waved then gave a smile. I realized I had done the two things out of order, but there was nothing I could do about that now.

It was a nice gesture. I picked up the notes attached to each. One was in a white envelope from the Methodist church, and the other in a re-used manila one from the Catholic church. "When did the Baptists stop making casseroles?" I wondered.

The deep vibrato of an approaching vehicle made me turn. It was the sheriff. He got out.

Oh God, they found out! I panicked.

25

S ince my arrest, police made me nervous. The sheriff's passenger door opened and Philip's mother, Grandma Rollin, rounded the truck carrying a large, covered dish and a large paper bag. Philip reached into the cab and grabbed an open cardboard box that showed the shine of aluminum foil.

"Oh, my gosh, what is all that?" I asked.

The sheriff smiled. "It's your lucky day."

"Afternoon, Matt." Grandma Rollin noticed the other dishes. "Look, Philip, the other churches brought food, too. Well good." She watched her swollen feet as she climbed up the slant of the yard hill. "I was just worried sick you wouldn't have anything to eat tonight," she said with legitimate concern.

"Thank you, that's very kind," I said with surprised gratefulness.

She grunted as she climbed the hill, pushing against her weight, but she moved well for an older woman of her size. "Well, I know how it is. My Philip isn't married either."

"Ma," Philip warned closing his eyes.

I found it amusing.

"Well, it's true. I gotta make sure you boys eat. I can't stand a skinny man."

Philip shrugged. "I'm not skinny, Mama."

She finally made it to the porch. "No, you're not. You and Montana eat like horses." She redirected her attention to me. "Montana is my grandson. He'll be at school tomorrow. But, Matt, you need to eat. Do you want me to set up for you inside?"

I reached out my hands to help her. "Oh, no, I don't want to trouble you."

She handed me the paper bag and took one of the casseroles from my hands and pushed passed me. "No trouble at all. I know the way."

I stood there and imagined myself as some cartoon character who had been run over and flattened by a train. She was a stubborn old woman with food like a perfect grandmother. And even though I was surprised by their visit, it was nice.

"What's in the bag?" I asked her.

"Biscuits," Philip said walking up the steps. "My mama makes the best damn biscuits in the world."

"Philip, watch your mouth," she yelled from inside.

"He's a teacher, Mama, not a preacher."

Philip walked past me and looked down at the remaining casserole dish. "No offense to them, but you might as well leave them out for the critters. My mom is the best cook in Middwood."

She called from inside, "Mary, she's the lady that cooks casseroles at the Catholic church, she always overcooks the rice. Nobody wants that gummy mess. Bless her heart. I'm going to set it up for you on the dining room—"

Oh shit, my bed.

"Ms. Rollin, wait, I did some redecorating."

There was a shriek from inside the house, then a massive crash.

"Mama?" The sheriff rushed in ahead of me.

I put my head down and stepped into the house.

"Shut that door," Grandma Rollin instructed in a huff as she continued closing the shutters in the dining room.

After I shut the door Ms. Rollin met me in the living room. "What in Jesus's eye?" She stood firm and was intimidating. I looked behind her at the chicken and rice laying on the floor.

My head jerked around like a flapping fish. "I... couldn't sleep upstairs, so I m-moved my bed," I stuttered.

"Matt?" she asked me again.

"Mama," Philip warned in a soothing voice.

"Philip, hush. Matt, what is going on here?"

My eyes narrowed at her unreasonable reaction. "Why are you so worried about where the bed is? I mean, I know it's a little odd, but hardly anything to be so worried about."

She turned to her son. "We have to tell Franklin."

"Mama, let me handle it." Philip turned to me. "Matt, this is very serious. I need you to answer us. Why did you move your bed?"

I regarded them both with confused humor. "I couldn't breathe in a room with no windows. I nearly had a panic attack. I mean, I didn't break any of the rules."

"Never turn your back on an open window, Matt," the older woman replied.

"I closed the shutters, so the windows weren't open."

She pointed. "*They* were open when I walked in. Did you tell anyone?"

"I don't know anyone other than Franklin."

Philip tightly closed his eyes. "Franklin." He chewed on

his lower lip for a second. "Did Franklin tell you the town rules?"

I looked at both of them. "Yes. Yes, he did."

"Did he tell you all three?" Ms. Rollin asked.

I shrugged. "Sure." He had actually only told me the first two, but if the third was as stupid as the first two, I didn't want to know it.

Grandma Rollin's face appeared troubled. "What do we do, Philip?"

I clenched my teeth and narrowed my eyes. "What is the big damn deal?"

Philip regarded me like a naive child, then turned to his mom. "See, Ma. He doesn't understand."

"Son, that doesn't matter. We, of all people, can't hold this information."

"I'll just move it back," I snapped.

"When did you move it?" Philip asked.

"Last night."

Philip looked at his mom. She shook her head but relented. "It's your call, Philip."

With that, Philip walked to the mattress and lifted it with ease. I had had trouble maneuvering its bulk, but Philip handled it as easily as a grocery bag filled with biscuits.

"I'll get the dining room cleaned up," Grandma Rollin said. "Matt, grab the box spring."

"Yes, ma'am." I didn't protest, I wanted to, but Philip was the sheriff, so I went along with the unfolding absurdity. I grabbed the box spring but was disappointed when I still had to counterbalance the weight of it by leaning back. I thought maybe the same adrenaline coursing through the sheriff would be coursing through me, too, but that wasn't the case. I was ready for visiting hours to be over.

I got to the base of the stairs, and Philip was already on

the way down. "I'll help you," he said.

"No, I can get it."

He ignored me and helped me carry it up the stairs anyway.

We carried the box spring down the hall and into the bedroom.

"I can help you set it up."

"Don't worry about it." I tried snatching it from him, but I was a Ford Falcon and he was a Sherman tank.

He put the box spring on top of the wooden frame. "Come on, let's just finish it. You don't need to be sour."

A low growl gurgled in my throat.

"Matt, I didn't mean it like that."

I let out a huff and grabbed at the mattress. I strained, shifting its weight around, and we managed to get it into place.

"See? Now you are almost ready for tonight."

I went to step out into the hall, but the boulder of a man blocked the door.

I closed my eyes and sighed. What now?

"Listen, Matt." His voice was low and calm. "I'm saying this 'cause I hope we can be friends."

I stared at him with narrowed eyes, wondering what his game was.

He gave me an easy grin. "We need a teacher. Hell, we need some new blood. Don't let this bother you, but, please, take the town rules seriously."

I nodded.

"Good, now are you ready to eat?"

"Sure," I replied. "What did you bring?"

"Atta boy."

∾

I n the kitchen, Philip told his mother that we had come to an understanding and that everything would be fine. That seemed to be enough for her.

Grandma Rollin had already unpacked the food and set the table. "Cubed steak, mashed potatoes and gravy, black-eyed peas, and collard greens—both with smoked ham hocks. I put the surviving casserole in the refrigerator." She then pointed to me. "Matt, grab yourself a seat, but if you don't mind, I'll take this one." She put a plate on the side of the table that would have faced the backyard if the windows were open. "This is where I always used to sit when I came here."

I sat and spooned some potatoes onto my plate. "How often were you here?"

"Gosh, Franklin and Ellen used to have us over all the time."

I stopped. "This used to be Franklin's house?"

"Why, yes. Franklin didn't tell you?"

I took a breath of surprise. "No." I dug into the black-eyed peas. "Franklin hasn't told me lots of things."

Philip tapped me on the arm. "Do you like blackberry cobbler? If not, I'll take it off your hands." He said with a wink.

They were too funny.

"Wow," I beamed as much as I could. "There is so much food. I haven't had a home-cooked meal since—I don't really deserve it." My cheeks started to burn. "Excuse me. I need to go to the bathroom. I had a lot of coffee at school."

"Sure, sure," Mrs. Rollin said. I knew she saw my face turn red, but she played along with me. I couldn't help myself. I really hadn't had someone be kind to me in so long. It was...a blessing.

26

After the sheriff and Grandma Rollin left, I mapped out the living room for the ideal place a TV would go if I were lucky enough to afford one. With everything going on, and me living in my car for two weeks, I was behind on my favorite show, *The Fugitive*.

I sat on the purple heap of a sofa and held my stomach. I hadn't been so full since my Rose-Mary Grand cooked her last meal. My mind swam with bittersweet memories of her.

To distract myself from the past, I picked up a book.

I'm glad I like to read, I thought as I sat in the quiet home.

The house felt big all of a sudden, and the room warm. My neck tightened as a slight ringing began in my ears.

"No, no, no," I said, standing. "None of that." I craned my neck as I walked a lap from the living room to the dining room to the kitchen and back to the living room. The intensity built and I pushed my hands against my head as I walked in a circle.

"Stop!" I demanded.

Take a pill, take a pill, take a pill.

"Fine!" I shouted, and stomped up the stairs to the

bedroom for my tote bag. I jerked it off the floor, dropped it onto the bed, and grabbed one of the bottles with the scratched-out labels. I didn't know what they were called, but they helped with my sudden panic attacks or whatever they were. Regardless, I had paid a whopping ten dollars for them.

I laughed bitterly as I walked to the bathroom. I couldn't recall who I got them from, but I remembered the price. Typical.

I didn't want to go all the way downstairs for my boiled water. I took off my glasses and braced myself before I cupped my hands under the faucet and swallowed everything down.

"Everything is fine. Just relax. Think of the water as the missing... something you need." I took a deep breath and patted the top of my head.

I caught myself in the mirror. "I'm a teacher, and I have anxiety issues."

Being a teacher and having anxiety was bad enough on their own but put them together and I became exasperated. Exasperated is an excellent vocabulary word, but I have always preferred the word pissy. Yes, I got pissy easily.

I bounded back down the hall. The one thing that helped ease my pissiness was sleep. In college, if I had thirty minutes in between classes and I could get back to my dorm, I could sleep for fifteen minutes. Some people have trouble getting to sleep because they start thinking about money, their jobs, whatever. That had never been a problem for me. Even better, the busier I was the faster I'd pass out... But all that changed after my Rose-Mary Grand got sick and my dad started drinking.

I fluffed my pillow, but it didn't help as I was using one of my undershirts as a pillowcase.

I was tired, and my poor brain sagged like the over-cooked Catholic chicken and rice casserole. I wanted to sleep, but I had sleeper's block. The bed was fine, the pillows were okay, but the sheets were shit.

I wondered if this was what it was going to be like when I died, put in a tight, little box with no windows. There was no way I'd be able to rest in peace. God that would be Hell. Oh no. Don't start thinking about Hell.

I was sure just then the devil painting came to life and the eyes started moving.

Good grief.

I didn't look at my watch, but the burn in my eyes told me it was bedtime. It was like I was in a room with smoke. Oh, no, don't think of smoke, that'll make breathing in the Tomb harder.

The bathroom is right down the hallway, I reminded myself. I'd already taken a pill, but I had all kinds of medicine, and there were little yellow ones that always made me pass out. I had no idea what they were, but they always played with my mind. Sometimes they made me see things. Sleep would cut all the crazy out. I banged my head on the pillow. The tomb was oppressive and stale.

Just opening the door to the hall was a relief. The air was fresher and lighter.

In the bathroom, I felt the same relief when I opened the medicine cabinet. I grabbed my primary source of ease, my bottle of white, laced aspirin friends.

I sat on the tile floor and poured out the bottle. Some people count their money. I count my pills. I needed to know the number I had left. Plus, I wanted to make sure old man Franklin hadn't been stealing from me. One, two, five, eight, ten, sixteen, twenty ... "Twenty-one." I ended the count. They were all there, I assured myself.

I grimaced, then put the pills back into the bottle. I listened to each one clatter around, and I liked how the sound changed as I dropped more and more in.

I sighed and laid down on the tile. If I only used them when I needed them, then I could save them up. I could even break them in half, maybe even quarters if I got desperate. I could be like a crazed, pill-popping squirrel, I thought. A pill-popping squirrel fighting to survive a blue winter on Black Bear Mountain.

I sat up.

There was no way I could go to a doctor here and ask for any drugs. I wasn't even sure there was a doctor in Middwood, but there was the pharmacist, Bill Self. I needed to get to know him a bit and see if I could trust him. If I played it wrong, everyone would find out I was a psycho, or at least, that's what they would think.

"I'm not a psycho. I'm a pill-popping squirrel."

I stared at the bottle, pursing my lips. I had over twelve hours before I had to be up. There was no TV and nothing else to do. I can spare one, I rationalized. I'll break them in half when the time comes.

Without another thought, the aspirin was under my tongue.

I let out a crazy laugh and hopped to my feet.

My feet stopped. I'd already taken a sleeping pill, so I decided to play it safe. I swallowed the aspirin and went back to my room.

Laying down, I continued the game. The bedroom wasn't a tomb, no, and I was a furry little rodent safely sleeping up in a hole in a tree. "Squirrels don't need windows."

As I tried to find a comfortable spot, my eyes opened. All

fantasy and games fell aside. "Fuuuck," I let out in a long, low moan. I realized I forgot to brush my teeth.

I had a lot of hang-ups, but I never went to bed without brushing my teeth first. Not brushing your teeth was not only punishable by belt when I was younger, but my teeth were something I took pride in.

I got up and went back to the bathroom, but I couldn't find my toothbrush or paste. *Calm down it's probably just in the bedroom,* I told myself.

On my way down the hall, I stopped when I remembered I took them with me to school that morning. I slapped myself in defeat as my anxiety level grew. I couldn't go to bed without brushing my teeth.

Maybe I have baking soda in the refrigerator, and I can make my own. I quickly moved downstairs to the kitchen only to find I had none.

Wait a second. I clapped my hands. "I left my school bag in my car!"

27

"Thank you, God!"

Tired or not, I rushed to get my shoes and keys, and I hurried out the front door.

The light from my living room gave half of my yard a gentle glow as I hurried down the walking path. It was a peaceful, chilly night, but the cold air was welcome against my flushed face. The sky was beautiful. Even though I was in a bowl of a valley, I was in awe of the clarity of the stars and moon that seemed to light a path just for me. The ethereal glow above made up for the lack of street lights.

There were no honking horns or sounds of music blaring from passing cars. I took in another deep breath and blew out all the cares of the day. As I turned onto Windy Hill Lane, I marveled at how peaceful it was.

As I walked, something moved along the road to my right. I looked down and paused, but the pills dampened any real response I might have had.

It was a raccoon. I blinked a few times, but the black-masked little guy stayed put. The yellow Sleep pill made me see things sometimes, but if the images weren't real, they usually disappeared after a blink or two.

I cocked my head and looked at him. He stood on his hind legs and cocked his head at me. He was imitating me, but I found it amusing. If it wasn't for the drugs, I probably would have screamed and ran. I had never been so close to a non-stuffed raccoon, but there he was.

"Come on," I instructed, and I started walking. He followed along, waddling beside me, between me and the grass. "Welcome to Middwood, where you can walk with the raccoons."

I snickered. I shook my head because I knew I was high. I continued to shake my head because something was gnawing at me, but I couldn't make out exactly what it was. It was a puzzle that needed to be solved only I didn't have all the pieces. I was bothered. What was it?

"Thanks, pills."

Finally, my neck loosened. Again, I experienced peace. I took in the tranquility when, from my right, there was a gentle warmth, a welcome sensation like I was walking with a friend. A grin stretched across my face as I turned to my friend, but I was alone. The raccoon scampered away across the dirt road into the darkness.

"Where are you going?" I was staring off to my right after him when a breath tickled my neck.

"We want you to see us." The hoarsely whispered words spattered my ear.

I rolled my neck and ducked out of reach, swatting my hands to push back the unseen face that had to be only inches from mine. There was no one there. Where was he? Was it a man's voice?

My mind clicked, puzzle solved. I was outside. I was outside after dark, and I was standing in the road.

"Oh shit," I spat as searched around me for the stalker. I spun, but there was no one there. I stared into the shadows.

I was almost to Main Street, between the big store and the Methodist church. I turned around and gave the lonely street a three hundred and sixty-degree scan. Not a soul was to be found.

When I had imagined what Franklin meant about not going outside at night, I imagined the distant howling coyotes, an owl, or some wild beast charging at me from the darkness, but not a person.

That's because no one is there, I thought.

I convinced myself it was the drugs. My father used to take similar pills, and sometimes he would have crazed fits, seeing snakes come out of the doors. I had never encountered anything like that.

I tried to shake it off. I was in some drug-induced manifestation caused by the superstitious nonsense of the town.

I took in a fresh, deep breath and let it out with a sigh, but then I saw something out of the corner of my eye to the left. My lungs clenched, coughing out the cold night air as I jerked my head.

Nothing.

I swallowed hard as my heartbeat in my ears. My mind told me to back up slowly and get back inside. But I silenced that thought as I stared at the empty dirt road in front of me. It was cold, it was dark, and I was high.

It's the drugs man. Relax. Just go get your toothbrush. But a rush of vertigo flooded my head, causing me to drop to my hands and knees in the dirt. I held myself up, feeling the sandy grit beneath my fingers as the wave washed over me. I kept my head down as my stomach churned. I took deep breaths to calm my head and stomach.

The chilly air blew over me, and my head finally started to clear. I imagined myself as a stone sitting on the road, thrown there by some bored child. I could see myself, clear as a bell, the moon causing a shadow to draw behind me, pointing up the hill. Warmth spread over the crown of my head, which made the picture in my mind change.

I imagined four figures standing before me in a straight line, still and sullen.

I opened my eyes. The shadows were there.

I jumped back with a shout and fell on my ass with my arms holding me up and my hands pressing onto the sandy, graveled road.

The street was empty.

I got to my feet. My eyes darted around. My skin crawled. I wanted to run. Toothbrush or not, I started back toward the house.

I chuckled to myself. "There is nothing there. Don't let the town get to you, Matt." I tried to hold my grin as I continued back up Windy Hill Lane.

Within a few steps, a warmth on my right shoulder blade spread across my back, a sharp contrast to my cooled skin. The heat pulsed in a wave, but then broke into a sudden, cold shiver. I spun, grabbing at my back.

It's a muscle spasm, I thought, but my skin was like ice to the touch.

I searched around me in panic. There was nothing there. Yet something had brushed against me. My breath came in shallow pants, and my heart beat picked up. My head told me to run, but I could only maintain a steady walk.

I turned onto Thornbrook, and I tried to take control of my breathing, but my mouth was dry. I licked my lips. Then, ahead, coming out from behind one of the houses on the right, stood a figure cloaked in shadow. I could see no hint or detail other than it was big and broad.

It crouched. I mimicked it without thinking. We were both frozen, waiting. I swallowed and slowly held up my hand to wave. The figure took off running in the opposite direction like I'd threatened him with a gun.

I wanted to follow, to see where he went, but, again, I felt the warmth on my shoulder. There was pressure with the touch. A hand was on me.

I whirled as the creepy, light touch crawled over my skin. I ran toward the house, but the presence followed, a tension just beyond my skin like someone was about to whisper in my ear. I could almost feel their lips against my neck as bounded up the stairs, opened and shut the door, and locked it.

I wiped at my neck as I turned and stepped away from the door, waiting for a knock. "Get it together, Matt," I panted. "There isn't anyone there. It's just the possum. Get it together."

I ran my hands through my hair, trying to shake the phantom hand away. I sat on the stairs, and I squeezed the back of my neck, massaging the strange sensation. It wasn't a headache. It was something else, something new, crawling right down my spine. I craned my neck, but quickly stood straight when I heard it: footsteps on the porch.

There it was again, the scratching outside the door.

I stood.

The ringing in my ears got louder as the steps got closer.

I heard myself say, "Move. Move. Go upstairs."

The spark finally connected, my head started to nod, my feet pushed backward, and I scrambled upstairs. Whatever it was didn't get in last night, and I was sure it wouldn't get in tonight.

I stopped by the bathroom and grabbed my bottle of anxiety pills. I threw one back into my throat as I hurried down the hall, then locked myself in the Tomb.

28

Tuesday, November 3, 1964
Sunrise 6:59 AM. Sunset 5:34 PM.

As the crouching figure slashed its claws into me, I jerked to a sitting position, holding my side where I'd been attacked.

The figure in my dream stalked me throughout the night, while hands and claws grabbed at me from every direction. I wondered if I was awake, but the reeking odor billowing out of my mouth confirmed the fact that I had indeed not brushed my teeth.

Regardless of my mental state, I was prepared for navigating the dark void of the Tomb. I wasn't going to wander in the darkness this time. I stood, feeling toward the end of my bed, and inched forward until my hand found the wall. I still had to search for the switch, but it wasn't difficult.

I looked at my hand. There wasn't any blood, and no marks on my side. But it had been so real. I exhaled.

I heaved the bloodwood door open and stepped into the hallway. The morning glow from the bathroom window welcomed me out of my Tomb and back into the land of the living. Very poetic.

Poetry had always intrigued me, but after last night that particular thought didn't set well. I couldn't help but think about what had happened. I scoffed, hell, maybe I never left the house, it could have been a dream or a pill-induced hallucination. There was no other explanation. Middwood, as backward as it was, wasn't the gate to Hell or the afterlife. If anything, Middwood was so well hidden, God himself gave up looking for it. I chuckled.

Once downstairs, I stepped out onto the front porch. The foggy morning glow hugged the yards, the dry, barren trees, and the rooftops of my new neighbors. Then I looked above and beyond my street. I blinked at the mountains like someone with a hangover would blink at the sun.

While I was admiring the view, I noticed a figure peeking at me from a window of the yellow house across the street. I could only see their silhouette, but I assumed it was a woman. I realized I wasn't wearing a shirt. Then another woman peered out from the coral house. Small-town antics, I thought. Nosey people that gossiped the detailed account of blown out tires and questioned why the new teacher was staying in the most beautiful house in Middwood.

I waved with friendly acknowledgment to both of them, and with that, they sank from view.

After getting dressed and having a healthy breakfast of one of Grandma Rollin's biscuits, I left for the school. I looked down at my watch. I would actually be early, I marveled.

Even though I convinced myself that the previous night wasn't real, I decided to take a different route to work.

Instead of walking down Windy Hill Lane, I'd walk down
Thornbrook and turn right on the street that led behind the
Catholic church. Besides, I wanted to investigate the second
part of my hallucination. I intentionally walked past the
greenhouse, which was where I'd seen the dark figure
standing.

"Good morning!" shrilled a chipper voice.

I jumped, throwing up my fists.

A middle-aged woman stepped out from the side of her
house and hurried toward me.

With a short laugh, still holding up my hands. "Sorry,
you caught me by surprise. Good morning."

"Mr. Christian, you're up early, almost too early," she
leaned back with a prim laugh. "That's a town joke...being
out almost too early," she nodded. "You know the second
rule, right? Oh God, Franklin did tell you the rules
didn't he?"

"Oh, he did." I got the joke but wasn't sure how far I
should take my laugh, so I just smiled.

She laughed. "I got nervous there for a second. I'm Mrs.
Rebecca. My daughter, Amy, goes to your school. She's the
one with the long blonde hair." The way she pronounced
the word hair, she made it into two syllables. The Southern
dialect was considerably thicker here and had more of a
drawl than I was used to. Her face went blank and then
became concerned. "She's not the really pretty blonde, that's
Allison. Amy is the other blonde. I mean she's pretty and all,
but you know what I mean," she explained nodding.

I held my grin.

"Are you on your way to school? I know your car is
parked out there on the highway. Any idea on when you're
going to get to work on it?"

"I'm not sure."

"Eddie told my husband he was checking it out and noticed the gas on the ground. He thinks you got a crack in your fuel tank."

"Oh, did he? Well, I'm hoping to get it repaired soon." I peered past her to the side of the house where she'd approached from, which was also where the bent man had appeared.

She followed my gaze to the side of her house. "Oh, I was lookin' at my bushes on the side there. The dogs have been in them again."

"Dogs?" I guessed it could have been a dog I saw last night, if a dog stood on its hind legs.

"Well, it could have been a small bear."

"What makes you say it's a dog?"

She pointed. "Well, there's a spot hollered out against the house."

"You think so? I've never seen anything like that. Do you mind if I take a look?"

"Well, sure, if you want to."

We walked toward the spot, and she continued talking about how they'd been so busy, which was why the bushes were so high.

"No need to tell me, I'm terrible at yard work."

"Well, there it is."

It was hard to see, but between the two bushes, there was a definite freshly scratched up stretch of dirt. It could have been anything. I took a step back toward the street and turned again into the bushes. The scrape continued. I estimated it to be at least six feet long. "Good grief."

"I know, the old critter must not have been able to get settled. I hope it ain't a bitch trying to nest to have puppies. Thad will have to get the baseball bat."

I stared at her in horror. "I hope not."

She waved the thought off. "I'll let you go. Amy really loved her first day, and, by the way, all the parents think you're great."

"I'm happy to hear that. Everyone has been very welcoming."

"Amy'll be up shortly. Have a good day."

"Thank you. You, too."

She gave me a warm smile and returned to her bushes.

It definitely hadn't been her or Amy I'd seen the night before. Could it have been a bear?

I lifted my chin with a grin. It could have been a bunny rabbit, or a unicorn, as high as I was.

29

I had already written all my math review questions on the board and I still had some free time before the first student arrived. I decided if I could find enough books, I could pick various selections for all the reading levels, but I wasn't sure where they were.

"Where are the reading books?" I murmured.

A plume of dust swirled from a table in a back corner. I stared at the table, then looked at the door. I'd left it open to try to air out the wet, moldy smell that lingered after the cleaning. Still, it was odd that only the dust in that particular corner was stirred. I walked to the table and there, neatly arranged, were various young reading books covered with dust, except for one. I picked up the clean copy, *The Joys of Reading*.

"Perfect. This is a turn of luck." I smiled and gathered up as many of them as I could.

I carried them out to the old tree stump in the center of the schoolyard. Using the blackboard eraser, I wiped them off, but I hadn't tested the breeze first, and ended up inhaling the cloud dust. I sneezed loudly. "Great."

As I sniffled, I heard laughter.

I froze, then scanned the schoolyard. There was no one there. I listened again. I wasn't sure if I heard anything or if it was just in my head.

The silence returned. I wiped my nose and repositioned myself so the caked on dust would blow away from me, and continued cleaning the books.

Thoughts and questions about the previous teacher came to mind. I wanted to know more about her. Had she stood in this very spot and dusted off books? And though it was morbid, I wanted to know how she died.

The breeze picked up as little girl voices came up the hill, tinkling like bells.

There was a tug on my pants leg.

"It's not polite to sneak up behind someone." I looked over my shoulder, but the field was empty. Close to my leg, I noticed a piece of bark protruding from the stump. It must have snagged my pants.

There were no voices, no giggles, but still, I walked toward the path that led down to the highway.

"Don't be silly, Matt," I told myself.

A commotion behind me caused me to turn.

All the books were laying on the ground. My jaw dropped. "Sneaky little devils." The giggling resumed, this time coming from within the school. They must have snuck around me.

I took the clean books and bounded up the school stairs. "Would you mind helping me with the rest of these—"

The room was empty. There was no other way in or out. A chill crept over me. My heart rate picked up. "It's the same as last night," I whispered.

I heard the laughter outside again. I sighed in relief and hurried down the stairs. The girls must be hiding behind the building. My humor was fading and I was becoming irritated.

I rounded the side of the school and—nothing.

Around the back, I told myself. I walked faster as their chattering grew more excited.

"Ha! I have you now!"

There was no one there.

Anger built inside my chest. "Stop running away from me!" I rushed around to the front—and the twins blocked my path. I dodged to the left to avoid knocking them over but lost my balance and fell.

"Why have you been hiding from me?"

The two girls stared at me like stoics, no evidence of joy or laughter. "Were you two ... laughing?" The word laughing sounded strange when used in association with the twins. "Well, were you?"

They shook their heads causing their little red braids to swing against their lower cheeks.

"Did you see anyone else?" I snapped.

The twins said nothing.

"The girls I was chasing?" Aggravated at their blank stares, I pointed. "I was at the stump dusting off—" I lowered my arm slowly.

The girls stared up at me. Shame stung in my chest, I hoped I hadn't scared them with my rantings. I stood, brushing the dirt from my pants. I took a deep breath. "I'm sorry, girls. Good morning."

"Good morning, Mr. Christian," they said in unison with their unchanging, upward, wide-eyed stare.

I knelt to get at eye-level with them. "Did anyone run up the hill ahead of you just now?"

"Yes, sir," they answered together.

"Ha! Good. Who were they?"

The girls said nothing.

"You don't want to tell on them?"

They were so still and quiet. I wondered if I was still scaring them.

"Were they at school yesterday?"

The girls shook their heads no.

"Well, those girls' parents are going to get a visit from their teacher if they don't straighten up."

"Mr. Christian—"

I sighed. "You're right. It was just a harmless trick. I don't know what got into me."

"If it was just a trick, then you're lucky," one of the twins said. It was the first time they hadn't spoken together. We stared at each other for a moment.

"Would you two mind helping me pick up the books and carry them inside, please?"

They looked at each other for a moment. It was like they were communicating telepathically, which was amusing for a second, but then creepy. "Yes, we'll help."

Thank you, Satan.

They glared at me with furrowed brows, which caused me to do a double-take at their knowing expressions.

"Did you just... hear that...? Sorry, it's been a strange morning." I picked up eight of the books and gave each girl four. "Thank you, girls." I smiled.

You both freak me out, but I think I like you.

More children started coming in. It was peculiar and exciting that Franklin hadn't yet appeared. I always worked better without unnecessary added pressure, and as charming as I'm sure he could be, I didn't want him there.

"It's time to begin. Take your seats," I said with a full, loud tone. Some of the students jumped at the sound of my voice, which was the point.

I gestured to the board. "We will begin with a review from yesterday. And for my older students, I didn't forget my promise to work with you. So, let's all break into three groups. Let's get the littles over here to the right, the next group up who did addition down here to the left. I'll meet my oldest in the back."

The children filed to their assigned areas.

"Okay. Each group will work on the questions on the board. Are there any..." my words trailed off.

One of the tallest and widest boys I had ever seen loomed in the school's door. He was easily six foot six. I'm sure I looked foolish gaping at him, but from the lack of sound in the room, I wasn't the only one.

He stopped and glanced around, clearly confused by the groups sitting on the floor. Oddly, he was shy, but I also got a sense that he was used to the reaction.

"Hey, Montana," greeted many of the younger kids.

"Hey, Tiny," grinned Peter, but Peter's grin melted when the tall boy shot him a scowl.

He hesitated, but then he took two choppy steps toward me like he wasn't sure how far his feet would go. "Mr. Christian. I'm Montana. I apologize for not coming in yesterday. I was doing some repairs at my house."

I swallowed the lump of intimidation in my throat as he towered over me, "I understand. I hope you got everything finished. Your group is sitting in the back corner."

What the hell is in the water here, I thought.

30

Montana nervously glanced around the room. All the students were staring, but only when he wasn't making direct eye contact with them.

"Children, don't stare," I instructed.

Scarlet shook her shoulders in a nervous tick. "But, mister, he's so tall," she squealed. "I'm scared he's going to step on my head."

Montana frowned.

"Scarlet, stop moving so much. You're fine."

Montana made his way across the floor, but then he stumbled over a desk leg. The little children in his shadow gasped. He caught himself and continued back toward his group.

The clumsy boy is going to fall like a tree and squash my poor class, I thought.

The twins giggled. I looked at them, and they smiled. The smile melted off my face. I was starting to believe they could hear my thoughts. I was crazy for thinking that, but to be a teacher, you have to be a little crazy. *This is the backwoods, mister.*

Once Montana was seated, the whole room relaxed.

"As I was saying, we will begin with a review. Please answer the questions on the board."

Carla raised a finger. "Do we need to write out the problem?"

"Yes," I answered, "after seeing your scribbles yesterday, you all need the extra practice."

The children began their work with no groans or moans. It was remarkable.

"Montana, I'll be over to help you in a moment."

"No need, Mr. Christian. I already finished the first few questions," he said pulling his lips inward, which I took for a smile.

"That's great. Let's see." I walked over and looked at his paper. "Very nice."

"My grandmother, she taught me."

"Your grandmother? Grandma Rollin?"

"Yes, sir, that's what everyone calls her. She held 'school' at the church on Mondays. She taught the little ones the ABCs, how to count, easy math."

"I met her yesterday. Nice lady and an amazing cook. Now I see why you are so tall." I patted him on the shoulder. "Since you are ahead in math, I'll ask you to help me by assisting your group." I saw that his age group, except for Peter, happened to be all girls. "Girls, what do you think about Montana working with you?"

They all grinned, but I noticed a fleeting eye contact between him and Amy. I couldn't help but smile, too. I patted him on the shoulder again. "It's great to have you here."

I circled to the different groups, giving feedback and assistance as needed. I was impressed by their progress. It had only been a day, but all the students were now almost equal in addition and subtraction. I didn't care if they counted on their fingers, progress was progress.

"Well done, children," I beamed. "Well done, indeed. Let's see what else you can do. We are now going to move on to a reading assignment. Some of you may have to move to a new seat because we are going to have to share books. If you have to move, don't worry, we will move back to our regular seats after we finish."

I passed out the reading books. I would make notes as the children read to get a feel for the general level of each age group.

"Okay, we will start on the right side of the room, and we will go down the rows. Everyone will read a paragraph."

The first student, Weezer, looked up like he had just been called to give a testament before the Lord God himself. He was about eleven and was obviously well fed. His collared, orange-and-black striped pullover was easily two sizes too small for him. He was an unfortunate-looking child, and I could see someone had recently cut a large wad of something out of his hair.

He read slowly, wheezing through the gaps in his teeth. "The... dog... had fu... fu... found a boon."

"Bone," I corrected.

"... bone. He wa... wa..."

"Wanted."

"... wonted to keep it to him sleeve."

"Self."

Seven minutes later he was finished with the first paragraph, and I was pressing the tips of my fingers into my temples, wishing they were guns. I cut him off before he attempted butchery of the second paragraph. "Just one paragraph, let's give someone else a shot. Instead of going down the row, let's take a volunteer. Anyone?"

"I can keep going if you want me to," the chubby boy said.

I ignored him. "Anyone else want to read?" *Devil spawns?*

The twins sneered, and my eyes widened.

If you can hear me, I'm just kidding, I thought at them.

"Anyone? Older students? Yes, the oldest students will read so you can show the younger students there is nothing to worry about. Who would like to volunteer?"

No one raised their hand.

I looked at the back center of the class. "Peter?"

He waved me off. "Oh, no, but thanks."

I folded my arms. "Don't you want to set a good example for the younger students?"

He closed his eyes and made stabbing motions toward them. "I would, but I'm blind today. I was reading *Oedipus.*"

"You've read *Oedipus*?"

With his eyes still closed, Peter turned his face towards me. "Time, which sees all things, has found you out."

I lowered my chin and peered over my glasses. "An-y-one?"

Still, no volunteers. I scanned the class. Usually, the terrified kids would look away or down, but there would always be one kid who wanted to answer the question or read but was too afraid to start. Those students would make eye contact with you and wait for you to call on them, but no one did that either.

I moved my eyes to the large newcomer. "Montana."

He jumped. "What?"

"Don't look so scared. It's just reading. Will you read for us?"

"Um? I'm not sure..." he said.

Amy raised her hand.

"Yes, Amy? You want to read?"

"No, but..." Her head was turned down and she forced the words out, "I would love to hear Montana read... if he wouldn't mind?"

Montana shot out of his seat with such force I was surprised he didn't tear off the top of his desk. "I'll read."

I looked up at him. "Thank you, Montana, and thank you, Amy."

Montana looked over at her. They blushed at each other briefly, then she turned away. The other students *ooh'd* and *aah'd*.

"Okay, okay, class. Let the man read." I smiled and gestured for him to begin.

I wasn't expecting much after Weezer, but I appreciated the budding cuteness between him and Amy. However, when Montana began to read, I sat in my chair and admired his voice. Not only could he read, but his tone was strong and steady. He paused at the periods and even emphasized words; he was a natural. Once he was done, I stood and clapped. "That was great, Montana. It was very nice."

"Thank you, Mr. Christian," Montana said and smiled shyly.

"Did everyone enjoy that?" I smiled at the class, then raised my eyebrows at Amy.

She dropped her lower jaw and turned a bright red.

"I'll take that as a yes." I smiled. "Let's move on. Who would like to read next?"

I wished I could say that the rest of the class read with as much talent as Montana, but with a few exceptions, that didn't happen. I stayed hopeful until the last kid, but the reading level was so incredibly low that I would have to go all the way back to *Fun with Dick and Jane*. Well, it may not have been that bad, but I couldn't sit through another class like that. I couldn't help but find it a little sad. I had my work cut out for me, but I was determined to do my best.

Weezer raised his hand. I was hoping he didn't want to read again.

"Mr. Christian, I'm hungry!"

I put my hands to my forehead. "I'm sorry class, I forgot about lunch."

Weezer's face and eyes opened wide. "Geez, what did you eat for breakfast? A bear?"

"Actually, I didn't eat breakfast."

Scarlet raised her hand and grunted. "I ain't eat breakfast either!"

"Mr. Christian, what do you normally have for breakfast?" asked Carla.

"I love biscuits, gravy, and preserves," groaned Weezer.

I grinned. "I love all that, too, but I can't cook, so I just eat a lot of cereal. But this morning I was lucky and I had a biscuit."

Carla raised her index finger again and looked down at her desk. "If you were married then—"

Weezer laid over his desk. "I'm dying."

I held in my laughter. "Okay, okay, let's go to lunch."

31

By the end of the day, I had to stop myself from laying across my desk. The kids were worn out as well. "Okay class, that's it for the day. I know it was tough, but we made it through, all in one piece, together."

Scarlet wrinkled her face.

"What is it?" I asked.

Scarlet didn't respond and kept her face scrunched.

Allison raised her hand. "Mr. Christian, what about the question of the day?"

"Oh. Right. I forgot about that." That was, of course, a lie. I was unsettled about how personal these questions might get. Dread built as I pawed my shirt pocket to feel the outline of the pill against my chest. I became self-conscious and wondered if it looked like a third nipple.

I murmured, "Let's get it over with." Then louder, asked, "What's your question?"

The students' hands shot up like dandelions ready to be picked so I could grant wishes. A loud groan escaped me. It made some of the students giggle. At least someone was enjoying themselves. I tapped my chalk against my desk as I scanned the hands for my lucky executioner.

Some of the students grunted while they bobbed their hands up-and-down. Those students I immediately crossed off because they were far too anxious. Any question that called for such reaction was too much for me. A few of the students held up both of their hands, and I made Xs over their faces in my mind too.

Instead, I chose the sweet, innocent little girl, with her charming, innocent little headband and her sweet, cute, innocent smile. "All right, Carla, what is your question?"

The other students lowered their hands. Some of them protested, then collapsed onto the top of their desks like an old Kentucky house collapsing into itself.

I smiled at little Carla, and she asked, "Why aren't you married?"

Peter leaned his head back and laughed.

My smile melted away. *Carla, you little...,* I thought. I looked around, and the entire class was all eyeballs and ears.

"Well," I said, "I haven't met the right person yet."

Jason spoke, "My daddy said that you probably—"

I cut him off, "Jason, you didn't raise your hand, and no one asked."

One of the girls raised her hand. "Mr. Christian, my sister is single and said she wouldn't mind meeting you on a Saturday for ice cream."

"Don't do it Mr. Christian. Her sister is gross."

"Peter," I warned.

"She is not!"

"I was just kidding," he said. The girl turned around, and he looked at me and mouthed the words, "Don't do it."

The children continued to giggle. I could feel the heat in

my flushed cheeks. Carla raised her finger again. "When I grow up will you marry me, Mr. Christian?"

Scarlet cut in, "Hey! You can't do that—I was going to ask him."

I grinned and drew in a breath, I was touched and surprised, but I was also ready to change the subject. "Writing," I announced. "Tonight, I want you all to write me a paragraph. Now I know some of you are having more trouble than others, but I want you to do your best."

Allison raised her hand. "Mr. Christian? What are we supposed to write about?"

"Well, you can write about whatever you'd like. Maybe, something you like to do or something you collect."

"What do you collect, Mr. Christian?" Peter asked without permission.

I waved him off. "We've already had our question of the day, Peter."

Montana raised his hand. "I think it would help us if you gave us an example." Montana gave Peter a wink. Even the mighty were led astray by the evils of Mr. Janowski.

Peter leaned back in his seat and crossed his arms. "See? Tiny thinks you should answer, too."

"Don't call me that," Montana warned.

"No." I shook my index finger. "I know what you are doing."

"Now who's stalling, Mr. Christian?" smiled Amy.

"You too, Amy? Wow, are all of you in on this?"

Quiet giggles and snickers playfully teased.

"Okay. I'll play along. Fine. Um?" I drew a complete blank. "Well, this is harder than I thought. I don't collect anything. I mean when I moved here I only brought my clothes."

"I love clothes," beamed Allison.

I let out a half laugh. "Let's see. Clothes, a few kitchen things, but cereal is all I really eat cause I can't cook and my books. Books!"

"Books?" whined Scarlet, holding out the vowel sound and causing me to almost throw an eraser at her.

"All right, books. I like to read."

"I like books," said Weezer.

"See, Weezer likes books, too."

"Weezer likes his mom's—"

I pointed. "Quiet, Jason!"

"But to be fair, I like literature books," I said.

"What does that mean?" asked Allison.

"It means he likes books with stories in them," answered Carla.

"Yes, they all have stories," I replied.

"I think I'm going to write about war!" announced Jason.

"I don't want to write about war," cried Scarlet.

I took a breath and raised both of my hands. "Class. Everyone, listen. You can write about anything. Your favorite hobby or something you collect. I'm still new to this town. What is something you think I should know about?" These prompts got the children chatting with each other. I was glad this excited them, but they were getting too talkative. "All right don't tell each other, tell me..." They all raised their hands. "By writing it down tonight."

I couldn't help but smile. Sometimes kids are gullible, but they can be cute.

32

Once the kids were gone, I was astonished it was even the same room. Without all the little bodies and big noises, the schoolhouse was peaceful.

I walked over to the window and wrapped my arms around myself. The mine whistle blew over the hills. I didn't know what the whistles meant for sure, but it sounded like a good reason to go home.

I gathered up all my things—making sure I had my toothpaste and toothbrush—and walked outside, turning to face the door as I locked up.

"Mr. Christian."

I dropped my bag and everything inside it fell on and around the cinderblock steps. "Holy sh—! Peter? Christ!"

He was leaning on the school like he was waiting on me, one foot resting on the wall. "You sure are jumpy, Mr. Christian. I was just standing here."

Trying to control my anger, "No, you were hiding there with full intent to scare the shit out of me."

"Wow, the new teacher has a potty mouth. I would've never guessed," he said with a sly grin.

"I don't," I lied. "What do you want?"

"I want to know what you were doing outside after dark last night."

I straightened and glared at him. "That was you?" I rolled my eyes and threw up my hands, then moved to gather up everything I dropped. "I should have known it was a kid pulling a stunt. Is that how you get your kicks, scaring people?"

"What stunt? You saw me?" he asked with heightened curiosity, he dropped his foot from the side of the building and stood erect.

I scoffed, "What were you doing? Just waiting down the street watching me?"

"I wasn't watching you, I was down close to Main Street and wanted to know—"

"Then you circled around to my street? I'm going to call your mother. I'm going to call her first thing when I get home."

"I didn't follow you anywhere. I was down on Main Street—"

"Look, I don't have time for games. Go home," I said, digging out my keys from under the bench. "Wait. What were you doing outside last night?"

He wrinkled his nose. "Those rules don't really apply to me."

"Isn't that convenient," I said, snatching up some of my stuff.

He bent down and helped. "I don't want to have to tell Mr. Bankward about last night. Why were you outside?"

"Who is Mr. Bankward again?" I asked.

"Man, who are you and why don't you know anything?"

"What are you talking about? I can't learn a whole town in one night."

He stared at me, and, for whatever reason, I gave in. "I left my toothbrush and toothpaste in my bag, in my car, and I have a thing about brushing my teeth before bed."

He paused.

"You went outside after dark because of a toothbrush?"

"Yes. Don't you brush your teeth before you go to bed?"

"Yeah, but this is the backwoods, mister—"

"All right, I know. Why does everybody keep saying that? It's really irritating."

He looked at me like he was gob smacked. He finally shook his head. "Look, Mr. Christian, did anyone tell you the town rules?"

"Franklin told me the rules. I just needed to—Why am I explaining this to you?"

"Did you tell anyone you went outside last night?"

"No. Will you please—"

"Good. Don't. It's a serious thing around here."

Maybe he was actually trying to help me, maybe not. "To be honest, I didn't even think about it until I was halfway there. It's a stupid rule. I can't believe you saw me."

"This is Middwood, you're always being watched.

"That's disturbing. Now if you will excuse me, I need to go." I gestured to my things in his hands.

"I can carry it." He turned toward the trail, then glanced over his shoulder. "Come on, Mr. Christian. I'll walk you down."

"No," I said with a laugh not holding back my sarcasm.

He stopped. "We both have to walk down the mountain."

I paused. Peter had already proved to be a prankster, and I didn't want to deal with his intrusive questions. "No, actually, I forgot something inside, so I'll see you tomorrow."

He shot me an inquisitive stare. "What?"

I furrowed my brow. "What, what?"

"What did you forget?"

"My..." I shook my head. "My..."

"Come on," he said. "It will be fine." Then he walked away with half of my belongings.

I sighed, and, against my better judgment, I followed him.

We walked in silence for the first few minutes.

"Jeepers, Christian. Are you always such a stuffed shirt?"

"I'm not a stuffed shirt," I said hiding my offense. "I'm just your teacher."

"Well, we aren't in school now, so you are just another guy."

I taunted, "That's not how it works."

"Okay, fine. I tell you what. I'll be quiet, and you can talk. Here's Johnny!" he said motioning for me to take it away.

I grimaced at him, then set my sights back to the path. "I'm not a fan of talking."

"Well, I already know you don't want to hear me talk. Do you?" He glanced over at me. I was silent but gave him a plastic grin.

He huffed, "Oh boy, you're mean."

"I'm not the one who was spying on people."

He stopped and turned. "Christian, I told you, and I promise that wasn't me last night."

"Why is that?"

"Because there's no way you saw me.

I kept walking. "But you saw me."

"I did."

I stopped and spun. "Okay, then. How come the rules don't apply to you?"

He waved off the question. "That's easy. I'm Shawnee."

He sounded so sure of himself, like it was the most profound, indisputable truth.

"Because you're Shawnee?"

He nodded. "Well, half Shawnee. My mother is full-blooded."

"And that matters why?"

"She's a scary woman. Ghosts and monsters know better than to mess with us."

I continued my bitter stare.

He twirled his pointing finger toward my nose. "Don't do that or your face will freeze that way."

I swatted at his hand but missed.

He laughed, then he pulled a thin, black cord from around his neck and handed it to me. "See this? It's magic."

It was a simple leather strap with a crude flat silver charm about the size of a dime.

"Wonderful," I spoke again with sarcasm.

He laughed. "You're such a jerk. It's hysterical. But seriously, check it out."

Amusing him wasn't my intent, but I enjoyed the release being a jerk gave me. "Why is there a bug on it?"

He snatched it back, shocked. "It is not a bug. It's a hummingbird. They keep the ghosts away."

"Oh, forgive me. It looked like a bug. And here's the scoop, I don't have a problem with ghosts. Just possums, maybe raccoons, and prying eye teenagers." I glared at him.

He stared at me, and my glared faded into a sigh.

I looked forward shaking my head.

He jumped up and pointed at me. "See, you do like me. Good. I knew you couldn't be a sourpuss forever."

"I don't like you."

"Yes, you do. I'm your best friend."

I laughed. "No. You are not."

"I'm your best friend in Middwood."

"I don't have any friends in Middwood."

He laughed. "You do now."

33

At the base of the hill, we turned left toward the town, and walked to Keepers Bridge.

As we crossed over the bridge, Peter waved to Eddie as he was walking into the station. "What's new, Eddie?"

Eddie kept walking but waved a hand and shouted. "About to go take a shit. What about you?"

"Just walking with my new best friend."

"Don't tell people that," I scoffed with a nervous laugh.

"Glad to hear. Talk to you later." Eddie disappeared.

I glanced at Peter, "You aren't walking me home are you?"

"No, but I can drive you if you need a ride," he said gesturing with an open palm to the three trucks parked beside the station.

"No thanks."

He shrugged. "Suit yourself."

"Which one is yours?"

He pointed. "The rust bucket."

There were three old trucks, but his was indeed the most rusted.

"Like I said, which one is yours?"

"Haha, funny man." He strutted over and patted the back end of the middle truck. "Don't you love it?"

"It's pretty boss. Besides, if it's running, it's better than mine." I pointed across the creek.

"It runs great. Stopping is the issue. I usually cut it off before I get to the bridge and then coast in. He has a name, too—the Rustic."

"The Rustic?" I smiled. "Mine is the Falcon."

"No way? You named your car too?"

"Well, mine isn't as creative as yours. It's a Ford Falcon, so it came with the name."

"Still. Great minds." He gestured to my head, then to his.

"Oh, right. We're geniuses," I replied.

"We are, it's so cool." he turned and bowed as we parted. "Thanks for the talk, Christian. It's been swell."

I gave a fake grin, waved, and kept walking. A minor explosion made me duck in fright.

Spinning, I saw Peter waving, and I could barely make out what he was yelling. "She's a bit loud sometimes. Later, best friend."

I nodded. "You're a strange kid."

After parting ways with Peter, I made my way back to the house. I was aggravated when I found the frowning English bulldog, Franklin, sitting on my porch steps. At first, I was worried his scowl was because Grandma Rollin told him I had moved my bed. I didn't want to have to explain it again.

"Good work, Mr. Christian," Franklin said, his expression changing to a smile. "I listened to your lesson after lunch. How was the rest of the day?"

I cocked my head. "You listened?"

He nodded. "I was outside on the bench."

A great sense of relief washed over me. I couldn't

imagine Franklin hiding microphones around the school-house, but I wouldn't put it past him either. "You could have just come in, Franklin."

"I wanted to see how you did when you thought no one was watching."

"That seems to be the theme of the day."

"Welcome to a small town, Mr. Christian. Someone is always listening or watching. Speaking of which, you may want to start putting on more clothing before you step outside in the mornings. Our women aren't used to peep-show performances." He laughed. "Especially from a man without some meat on his bones."

I stood there not sure what to say, which made old man Franklin laugh harder to the point of coughing.

I cleared my throat. "Any luck on finding someone to work on my car?"

Catching his breath, he said, "I'd forgotten about that. Though I will admit we had a good laugh about you not being able to repair your own car." He chuckled. "He'll be by tomorrow, shortly after school. Old man Casteel. He does pretty good work. He owes me lots of favors. Time I started calling in some."

"That's amazing. Thank you." I grinned.

"But it does come at a price. You see, Casteel, he's a nice feller, but he is slow as molasses on cold shit."

My smile turned plastic. I turned my attention to the sky. "Well, the moon is up. I know how sundown is regarded and such. Thanks for looking into that for me, Frank. I need to get some work done."

"Good man. I'll check with you again soon."

∾

I opened the refrigerator, grabbed the remains of one of the dishes from Grandma Rollin, grabbed a fork, and headed to the porch. I stepped outside and sat on the top step. I kept my eyes on the mountain and sky above the rooftops of my neighbors while I ate the cold cubed steak and mashed potatoes.

I could feel my neighbor's eyes on me, but after a few minutes, they resumed whatever they were doing. I didn't want to be inside. That wasn't true. I didn't want it to get dark. However, the sun didn't care what I wanted, and there was a heaviness that set on me as the sun continued to sink. I held the empty, white-and-floral plate and stood. I watched the sky closely as I inched back onto the porch, and right before the last bit of the orange ball slipped behind the mountain, I shut the door.

34

Back inside, I went and opened the living room shutters. I looked down onto the calm, quiet village below and said, "Welcome, Mr. Baggins. You are a hobbit, hairy feet and all."

I sat on the sofa, took off my glasses, and set them next to me. I rubbed my eyes with my thumbs then blinked them open before leaning back against the pillows.

Movement in my peripheral vision caught my attention. It wasn't the moonlight.

I leaned forward on the sofa and my glasses fell to the floor. I reached down to grab them but stopped when something shot across the yard.

I stood and went to the window. My view wasn't clear and it was dark, but I could see the silhouette of the weeping tree beyond the wood railings of the porch. The view was no longer calming because with the warmth spreading over my face and chest, I knew I was being watched.

I scanned the yard and houses across the street. "Who's watching me now?" I wondered aloud.

When I looked away, another movement close to the street caused me to whip my head back.

I scanned the grass, my heartbeat increasing and the top of my shoulders tingling, turning into a dull ache. I rolled my shoulders back, then stepped closer to the glass. Who was it?

My eyes strained to focus in the darkness. However, I could tell there was... something.

In the lower corner of the yard, I saw something under the weeping tree. My curiosity pushed against my fear. My hands were shaking as I twisted the hairs on my chin, trying to zero in on whatever it was. It was hiding from me, moving when I moved, knowing at that distance it would be hidden. I looked for my glasses on the sofa, but they were gone. I searched the floor near the sofa, but I couldn't find them.

I bit at my fingertips, I wanted to go out there, but I remembered what Peter said, and remembered what I promised Philip and Grandma Rollin.

"Come on, Matt, don't cause any more trouble."

My stomach growled. "See, even your stomach agrees. Let it go."

I turned to get a bowl of cereal. I took two steps toward the kitchen when a light touch from cold, smooth fingers ran along my elbow. The sensation rushed up the back of my arm all the way up my neck and settled under my ear.

I spun, grabbing at my arm, but there was no one in the room. I cradled my elbow. It was chilled.

"Never turn your back on an open window," I recited. The hairs on the nape of my neck stood up. Cold washed over me, penetrating me.

I turned back to the window and leaned forward. Straining my weak eyes.

There. I could see it. It wasn't an animal. It was a person, a child? There was a porch post blocking my view so their face was hidden, but they were clothed in white. It looked like a dress with a puffy shoulder. A little girl, I assumed. She wasn't moving.

Goosebumps went down my neck and arms. I inched sideways, revealing more of the shoulder. The base of my throat was tight, bile threatened to come up. I slowly leaned farther to the right until I saw her.

The front of my body ached, like my skin was pulling away from the threat. Tears formed but didn't fall. Screams built but I washed them down my throat with the saliva flowing in my mouth. It was a little girl standing under the limbs of the tree looking at me. She was like a doll with her blonde hair and antique, white dress. She held perfectly still, with a blank, yet pouty expression on her face.

"It's just a child."

No, it couldn't have been. People here adhered to the rules. Never go out before the sun comes up or after the sun goes down. We both held the stare. I bent at the waist toward her, but then she moved.

I tripped backward over my ottoman and fell to the floor. I spotted my glasses under the sofa. My fingers clutched at them, and I popped up again, but she was gone. My chest rose and fell, anxious as I searched the yard. I shouldn't have been afraid of a little girl, but I was. All of my flesh still crawled. I was glad she was gone.

"I'm not turning my back," I said as I closed the shutters and backed away.

A creeping itch crawled under my skin to my right shoulder. It was like a bug.

I couldn't help but check the window and front door.

Backing up the stairs, I shook my head trying to get it on

straight. "Come on, come on, come on," I topped the stairs and went into the bathroom.

In front of the mirror, I placed my hands on the rim of the teal porcelain sink with my feet cooling on the smooth floor tiles. I looked at myself and said, "Come...on. You cool? When in doubt pop one out." I flung open the cabinet, pulled out my little bottle, opened it up, and took out two of the white pills for anxiety.

I closed the medicine cabinet door and put my mouth under the faucet. I caught myself in the mirror again and asked, "You cool? Yeah, I'm cool."

I took a deep breath in through my nose and just stood there looking down at the sink, biting my upper lip. There was no telling how long I stood there, but it must have been a while because my head started to swim. When my head made an involuntary dip to the right, I caught myself by reaching out to the wall.

35

Wednesday, November 4, 1964
Sunrise 7:00 AM. Sunset 5:33 PM

The sunlight split my eyeballs, cracked my head, and made my body ache. I shivered from the cold.

Something was wrong... Where was I?

I grimaced when I realized I was in the hall outside the bathroom.

I pulled myself up so I could lean against the hallway wall. I needed to stop taking so many pills, but I was sure that wasn't going to happen. I groaned.

∾

I was half asleep, writing sentences on the board, when someone entered. "Good morning, Christian."

I turned. It was Peter. "And the day just continues to get better and better."

Peter raised his eyebrows and cupped his ear. "What was that?"

I waved it off and turned back to the board.

"I'm sorry about scaring you yesterday."

"And what about Monday night?"

"I thought we'd already passed this. That wasn't me!"

"Come on, Peter. It's over now, just admit it."

"I'm being serious. I'd tell you if it was."

"School doesn't start for another thirty minutes."

He was quiet, which bothered me. He was behind me and my sense of being watched, or my paranoia of not seeing what was happening, kicked in.

I glanced back. "Did you need something?"

"Not really," He sat on top of the front center desk. "I just woke up early and thought I'd come in to see if you needed any help."

I wasn't buying it. "I see. That's nice of you, but I don't need any help."

"Sure, you do."

"Fine." I pointed to the broom. "You can help by sweeping the floor."

He wrinkled his nose. "Is sweeping my punishment or penance?"

I rolled my eyes. "You said you wanted to help, so help."

He shrugged in compliance. "Okay." He hopped off the desk and grabbed the broom. "Can I call you Matt?"

I pointed my chalk at him. "No."

"Why not?"

"I'm your teacher, and students should show respect to them while they are in school."

He swept. "What about after school and before school?"

"I'm Mr. Christian to you every hour of the day."

"Okay, okay, I just thought I'd ask." He paused. "Don't your friends call you Matt?"

"Of course, they do."

"Do you have a lot of friends?"

I tried to focus on writing my questions. "I used to. Why are you so curious?"

He opened the door and swept his pile into the yard. "Don't you ever get curious?"

"Of course, I do."

"Aren't you curious about why the town is so strange."

He was setting me up for something. "No. Franklin told me everything I needed to know."

"You sure?"

"Yes. Don't leave all that on the steps. Sweep it off or it will just get tracked back in here."

He moved outside the door, and I heard the bristles brush against the steps. He stepped back inside. "I don't really have any friends."

I shot him a glance. "I'm sure you do."

"Nope. People here don't really talk to me."

I grinned. "Is that why you run through the night scaring people?"

He lifted his chin and stomped his foot on every word. "I swear that wasn't me."

My eyes widened at his dramatics. "Wow, I hope I don't have to pay for that performance."

"It wasn't."

"Great." I turned and judged the floor. He had done a good job. "Want to pass out the science books?"

He didn't say anything, but he moved to the back table and began putting the books on the desks. An emptiness came over me. There was something more. "Is everything's okay, Peter?"

He shrugged. "Yes. I just wanted to talk to someone is all."

I looked at him in disbelief. "So you came to talk to me?"

"Yeah. Is that okay?"

Trying to hide my apprehension, I said, "I guess so, yes."

"Good." He walked over to my desk. "Here's a little something for your lunch. Since you said you don't cook. My mom made stew last night. I'll light the stove and if you put it on the coal stove, it'll be warmed up by lunchtime."

I regarded the bowl with a slightly hollow feeling in my chest. "Thank you. That was considerate. Tell your mother I said thank you."

"I'm the one that asked if I could bring it in."

"Thanks to the both of you, then." I grinned and took a breath. "To be honest, I didn't bring anything."

"No biscuits?" He laughed.

"None."

I joined in his laughter. I continued writing on the board, and he finished putting the science books on the desks.

≈

"Science is the devil," shouted Jason, ringing in the two o'clock hour.

"Well, then we won't worship it, we'll just study it," I said with a flippant smile.

That shut him up. We had forty-three minutes to go before we were free, but the students had been fighting me every step of the way. There weren't many kids I disliked, but Jason was one of those kids you wished you could feed to the wolves.

Of course, they thought science was the devil. I bet

whoever controlled the mines told them all that so that they wouldn't ask questions about why the grass and trees were all dead and why the water smelled and tasted like shit.

I rubbed my hands over my hair. Everything was starting to get to me. It wasn't just the kids and my lack of sleep. It was the whole "town rules" thing. I checked my shirt pocket, but, other than my nipple, there was nothing there. I had taken that pill hours ago. "Damn," I whispered.

On cue. "Mr. Christian?"

"All right, I know." I slapped my hand against my forehead. "Question of the day. Go."

Hands shot up, and I called on Weezer. "What do you miss most about Atlanta?" he asked.

Finally a decent question. I steepled my hands together and held them to my lips.

"What's he doing?" asked Jason.

Allison swooned. "I think he's praying."

"He's such a good Christian," beamed Carla.

"He's thinking, bozos," barked Peter.

"Language," I said instinctively.

Peter corrected himself. "He's thinking... dummies."

"Okay, hush. The thing..." I paused, still narrowing down my answer. "... I miss the most about Atlanta... is..."

... people who can read, the food, water you can drink, schools with other teachers and hot coffee, bedrooms with windows ...

"... The thing I miss most about Atlanta is the..." I straightened up and relaxed my shoulders as it came to me, "... are the trees."

There was a mixed reception toward my answer, but I nodded. "It's true. I really do miss the trees."

Jason crossed his arms. "We have trees here."

"You do, but I miss the pine trees and the evergreens."

"Which ones are they?" asked Scarlet.

"The ones that are always green," said Montana.

Amy chimed in, "And sticky."

Scarlet's nose was wrinkled, so I explained, "Pine trees are the trees that have needles instead of leaves. Not all pine trees are evergreens, but in Georgia, we have lots of pine trees and lots of evergreens. And here in Middwood, you...we have lots of oak and birch trees. I miss the green. In Georgia, there is deep green everywhere."

"What's so great about trees?" asked Jason.

"Well, they all add color to the sky. It's something to break up the blue. Gives you something to look at." I repeated a line I heard so many times, "'God made trees to hide the foolishness of man from his sight. They make the sinful world easier to look at.'" My heart kicked. "That's where my grandmother got her nickname, but her real name was Mary Rose."

"That's pretty." Allison smiled.

"She was so full of life, she was evergreen, so we called her Rose-Mary Grand." I put my hand on the back of my head. Then I let out a breath. Everything was tight inside of me, my neck, shoulders, and jaw.

Amy narrowed her eyes. "Mr. Christian, are you okay? Your face is red."

I cleared my throat. "Sorry. She passed away recently. It's still a bit new."

"I've never seen a man cry," said Jason, shocked.

"He's not crying, fool. He's just a little choked up," scolded Peter.

I took another deep breath and let it out in a choppy stream. "Luckily, it's time to go home. I want all of you to take a science book home and finish reading the first chapter. There are questions on page fourteen. I want you to write the questions and the answers as homework. You will turn your papers in tomorrow."

"We have to read fourteen pages?" moaned Jason.

"We have already read the first seven." I addressed the rest of the class, "If you have problems, you can get your parents to help you."

Weezer raised his hand. "Mr. Christian, my dad can't read."

I squeezed my eyes shut and released another sigh. I'd expected this would be the case with at least some of the students. I ran my hands through my hair and gently scratched an itch on my shin.

"That's okay. Some people can't read, but they are still skilled, smart people." I looked at Weezer. "Who knows? Maybe you can help teach him someday. Get your mom to help."

He replied with a smile.

Turning my attention back to the class, I added, "Just get it done."

The class looked at me with nervous frowns.

Carla raised a finger. "Mr. Christian?"

What? What can you possibly want? I thought. Venomous aggravation wished to spew from my mouth, but I thought about Darlene and held in my swelling anger behind clenched teeth. "Yes, Darlene—I'm sorry, yes, Carla?"

"Would you like me to take up last night's writing assignments?"

"Sure. Everyone, give Carla your homework before you leave, and have a good evening."

The class stirred like a storm with papers rising into the air, Carla taking each in her hands, protecting them from the chaos like they were baby birds. Once their assignments were out of their hands, the students raced to the door like lightning from the clouds.

She stacked and placed them on my desk.

"Thank you, Carla."

She curtsied and left.

The twins stopped in front of my desk and stared at me.

I looked at them with pained exhaustion. "What?"

They looked at the desks just inside the door. There sat two forgotten science books. I grunted as I pulled myself from my seat to grab the books and run to the door. "Weezer, you and Jason forgot your books!"

"Oh, no!" Weezer shouted. He threw his fists down to his sides as he yelled down the mountain, "Hey, Jason, come back and get your book!"

Weezer turned and trotted back to the school, but quickly downshifted into a fast walk. I knew it would take him a while. "I'll just put them down on the steps. Take your time."

I shook my head and walked back into the room. I leaned against the front of my desk and turned my attention back to the twins. "Thank you, girls."

They looked at me with their blank little faces.

In my mind I thought, *No, seriously, thank you, and I'm sorry for being a jerk earlier.*

Their faces lit up into smiles. They took each other's hand, swinging them as they exited the school.

They really could hear me…. *Of course they can, it's Middwood.* "This is the backwoods, mister…" I stopped myself. I was too tired to think about the oddities of the town.

Jason stuck his head in the door. "I got my book."

I tilted my head back in exasperation. "Where is Weezer?"

Jason checked over his shoulder then looked back to me. "He's almost here. You know he's fat."

I narrowed my eyes. "Will you take him his book?"

Jason snarled, grabbed the book, and rushed off, the sound of his running fading across the dirt.

"Thank you, Mr. Christian!" Weezer called from across the schoolyard.

Kids.

36

I wanted to lay down on top of my desk, but I staggered around it, plopped down in my chair, took off my glasses, and rubbed my eyes. I could feel the slight, gritty burn of chalk in them, but with my lack of sleep, there wasn't much of a difference. I sighed as I wiped my face and slapped my hands together to dust them off.

I awoke. I was falling over and I caught myself, but one of my hands struck my science book which somersaulted like an Olympic diver right onto my sore shin.

"Mary fucking shit!" Every muscle in my body tightened, and I shot up in my chair. I pressed down on the bruise and attempted to talk through the pain.

"What was all that?" asked Peter, sitting on his desk.

I jumped.

He laughed, "Oh man, Christian. You're a riot."

"Don't laugh at me," I grumbled and threw the eraser at him.

He dodged it. "I honestly can't help it, you are one jumpy cat."

"Well, you shouldn't sneak up on people. Especially tired people who live in shit-holes towns."

"Wow, you think Middwood is a shit-hole?"

"I didn't mean it like that."

"It's fine. It is a shit-hole."

"I shouldn't have said that. It just slipped out." I cleared my throat. "Why are you here?"

"I was going to scare you outside, but you never came out, so I came in. You were asleep, so I waited."

"You watched me sleep?"

"Yes." He nodded.

"That's odd."

"Definitely is," he replied.

"And you did all this because you wanted to scare me?"

"Yes." He kept nodding. "You're a gas."

"Shouldn't you be going home?"

He got up and straightened the desks. "I have work, but I still have a little bit of time."

I looked at my watch. "How is that possible, the town shuts down in a little over two hours."

"Remember, the town rules don't—"

"Apply to you, yeah."

"I work at Sears."

"The mines wouldn't take you?" I jeered.

"Gosh no, I couldn't work there."

"Too small?"

He lowered his chin and shot me a quick glare. "No, as a matter of fact, it's because of my—"

"Mouth?"

"—hands."

"Your hands?"

"Yes. I have magic hands."

"And you and your magic hands couldn't get a job at one of the mines."

"Well, they just work better at Sears. I'm a delivery boy. Isn't that great? Such a bright future."

I slid the writing assignments into my bag. "Well, I'm a glorified babysitter. Work is work." I crossed to the blackboard and wrote the next day's assignment on the board. The room was uncomfortably quiet. I wasn't sure what else to say, so I went with a standard teacher question. "What is it that you want to do?"

"I have no idea. Back to you, did you always want to be a babysitter?"

A laugh erupted from me before I knew it.

"What was that?" laughed Peter.

"Man, I don't know. It just jumped out of my mouth. But to answer your question, honestly? No. My Rose-Mary Grand was a teacher, so I became one, too." I shrugged. "I thought about being a lawyer once."

"A lawyer? I can't see you doing that. Oh," he snapped his fingers, "I could see you working in a library."

I wrinkled my face. "How boring?"

"Yes, but you like the quiet and you like books. You would probably love it. You'd fit in with all the old ladies in their shawls."

"Ha. Ha." I kept writing. "Am I that boring?"

"I was picking, Christian. You're not boring."

"It's fine. I do love the quiet." I glanced over my shoulder. "Anything to get away from you kids."

"Except me, of course," he said, pointing to himself with a sly grin.

"No, especially you."

"Haha. Right. I'm your favorite."

I laughed, and Peter's expression was so priceless,

amused and hurt at the same time, which made me laugh even harder.

My eyes teared from laughing so hard. "Oh man, that was a good one."

"I'm glad to see you can laugh. You always seem so darn serious."

"Well, life has a tendency of doing that."

"Tell me about it." He paused, then continued. "My dad left my mom and me. He was a jerk. It hurt, but we're fine. The river continues to flow." He shrugged.

Serious stuff, I thought. I cleared the webs out of my head. "I'm sorry to hear about your dad."

"It's fine. Can I ask you a personal question?"

"A personal question? Like the one Carla asked me?"

He gently tossed his head from side to side. "Maybe, but not so personal."

I mulled it over. "Sure, but then you go home."

"Deal." He paused. "Um, don't be mad for me asking, but... how did your grandmother die?"

His question clobbered me between the eyes. "Wow, that's a doozy." I pondered how to respond.

"I'm sorry. Never mind. It was stupid to ask. Sorry for being curious about ..." He picked up his book. "Don't be mad at me."

"Peter, I'm not mad at you for asking. It's just that." I sighed. "The answer is complicated."

He sat down. "How so?"

"She um..." I bit my lip, questioning whether or not I should answer. I shook my head. "She killed herself."

His mouth formed a perfect O, and his eyes went wide. His expression wasn't shocked, more like embarrassed.

"You don't have to say anything. I know it's terrible." I scratched my beard. "I shouldn't have told you."

"No." He raised one shoulder. "I'm glad you told me. I mean, thank you for telling me."

I let out a long steady breath. "Listen, you're the only one in Middwood who knows about this. Can we keep this between us?"

He grinned. "You mean, between friends?"

"Yeah, between friends."

He gave a proud nod. "Done!"

~

P eter waited while I locked up the school and we walked down the hill together.

It was strange. I wasn't a father, but I had been looked at as a father figure many times before. I had even had a few students call me "dad" by mistake. I could never, of course, be their parent, but as a teacher it was part of my job to teach them, and, from time to time, be whomever they needed me to be, even if I had no idea what a good father would act like.

37

After parting ways with Peter, I made the much-needed stop at the Sear's counter. If I was going to have to sleep in that room, I needed to have comfortable sheets. I think even if I took them out and beat them with a rock it wouldn't make a difference.

A bell attached to the top of the door rang as I entered, but no one came out to greet me.

"Hello?" I called. It was too quiet.

The bell dinged again behind me, and I jumped.

"Kinda jumpy there, aren't you?"

I turned and let out a quiet groan, "No, Clint. You just caught me by surprise."

Clint continued into the small store. "Lots of surprises around here, for sure. What are you ordering?"

I furrowed my brow but let it go. "Oh, some sheets."

He cackled. "What? The ones you have don't match your curtains?"

"You are a strange cat."

"Meow—"

The bell dinged again, and Pastor Gresham entered.

I couldn't help but think I would only be delivered because I'd gone to church on Sunday. If that were the case, I'd have to start going more regularly.

"Mr. Christian, how are you doing?"

He completely overlooked Clint.

"I'm doing well. Thank you, Mr. Gresham. Pastor! Gresham."

"Everyone treating you friendly like?"

The bell dinged again.

Gresham turned in time to see Clint leaving. "Get thee behind me, Satan."

"Sir, you are a Godsend."

"All you have to be is a willing vessel." He smiled. "But good timing comes in handy too. Was he bothering you?"

"No, sir. Just—"

"He's bad news and I'm a preacher, but God says we should love our neighbor."

"Luckily, he doesn't live next door to me."

Gresham laughed.

It was a big hearty bellow. I couldn't help but be amused by his good nature.

"I'm ordering my wife a necklace for her birthday. What about you?"

"Sheets, but what I need now is someone to help me with an order."

Gresham laughed and patted me on the back. "That's not how it works here. Peter is supposed to be here, but ..." he gestured to the empty store.

"Look here," he went behind the counter and pulled a receipt book out from below, "this is what you do."

He graciously walked me through the process.

"Thank you for helping me."

"I'm a preacher, I help the lost," he chuckled.

"Speaking of that, thanks for that introduction on Sunday."

He laughed. "Did you enjoy that? I was just funning with you. Since you're a teacher, I was sure you could handle it. Sarah always could."

"Sarah?"

"Sarah, Frank's daughter."

I froze. "Sarah, the former teacher, was Franklin's daughter? I didn't—"

A girl ran through the front door. "Sorry, pastor, but something has come up. Could you come to the church?"

"Is everything all right?" I asked.

"Oh yeah, it always is," Gresham replied. "Just town stuff. Good luck with your order, Matt."

"Thanks. I'll get the hang of it sooner or later."

"I'm sure you will," he said, and with a smile and a slap on my back, he turned and followed the girl out.

As I walked back home, I accepted I would have to change my way of thinking about how things were done here in the backwoods. It wasn't a big deal. It was only change.

I sleepwalked most of the way up Windy Hill, and as soon as I was inside, I made my way straight to my bathroom and dropped one aspirin and pulled out two Bufferin. One aspirin, even if it had been kissed, wouldn't help me. I had stronger pills for headaches, but I couldn't remember what bottle they were hiding in. I swallowed the Bufferin and the LSD along with it.

"Damnit!" I looked at myself in the mirror, realizing I'd just wasted a more intense trip. "Damn. Damn. Damn."

I walked into my Tomb, then walked straight back out. Exhausted or not, I couldn't stand to be in there. Instead, I went back downstairs to the living room, opened the shutter on one of the windows, and dropped myself down on the purple sofa to enjoy my trip.

I pulled the ottoman to me with my left foot. "Oh, brother that feels good." Unless a person spent extended time with twenty-one kids, they had no idea what real exhaustion was. It was calm and quiet in the house, complete and utter silence. Perfect, other than the low steady hum of the refrigerator, but even that was soothing.

The phone rang.

My first phone call, I thought as I stumbled into the kitchen. "Hello—"

"Matt, Casteel is heading down to tow your car," Franklin grumbled. "It's late as hell, but he wanted to grab it before it got dark."

"Thank you for the—"

He hung up.

"... call." I pursed my lips as I nodded. "Thanks, Frank." I hung up the phone.

"Shit." I closed my eyes.

I had about another fifteen minutes before the pills kicked in.

I rushed upstairs and leaned over the toilet. I stuck two fingers down my throat until I gagged. Nothing came up. I reached in farther but stopped. I had a limited number of pills and wasn't about to let one of them go to waste. I slid to the sink and put the stopper in the drain. I would fish it out and hope it was still laced enough to be good for later.

I pushed two fingers to the back of my throat and threw up in the sink. The remains of lunch and one Bufferin lay in the basin. I pulled up the stopper, rinsed the sink, and tried again.

Nothing.

After the third try, I still had not managed to produce the second Bufferin tablet, or, more importantly, the LSD.

My throat burned, and my eyes were ready to pop out. I gave up. Without looking in the mirror, I washed out the sink and splashed water on my face. I didn't want to face myself. It would be a hard fight, but I had to stay clear.

I could try throwing up again. I wasn't sure how long it would take for this Casteel to hook up my car, but I'd have to go down there to give him the key. "Fuck," I whined.

Fifteen minutes later I was leaning on the hood of the Falcon when an old orange truck pulled up beside me.

The driver raised his blue trucker's hat and rubbed his fingers over his red-and-gray buzz cut. "Are you that teacher?"

"Yes. I'm—"

He hit the gas pedal and peeled off.

"What is going on?"

About fifteen feet away, he slammed on the brakes, kicked the truck into reverse, and sped toward me. I jumped up on the hood as he stopped inches away from the front bumper.

"What the hell are you doing?"

"Hell, son, if your eyes got any wider they'da fallen out. I wasn't gonna crash into her," he hollered out of this window. "I figured you was smart enough to get outta the way. Guess not."

"Well, you drive like a madman." My heart raced as I

stepped down from the hood. I realized he hadn't stopped as close to me as I had thought.

"You're the madman, son." He kicked his driver door open. "I saw your flat tire on the mountain."

"It's you. The old bastard who drove past me after my blow out." I pointed. "I recognize the hat."

He gave me a quick once-over, and he didn't seem impressed. "City folk comin' to save us, poor hillbillies. I know who you are," he gritted through his teeth as he pulled at his right leg. "Go ahead and pop the hood," he ordered.

I reached under the hood and pulled it open. I tightened my jaw as he dropped out of the truck, grunting in pain.

"You okay?"

"Of course, I am," he snapped.

I noticed his shirt looked odd. I couldn't tell if it was real or the acid, but his right arm hung limp. Then I slapped my hand over my eyes; he didn't have one.

He cocked his head, and I looked up at his face. He glared at my stare. "You finished gawking?"

I giggled, "Sorry." Of all the times for my shit to kick in. "I'm really sorry."

He sighed, then pointed his chin at my car. "Keys in it?"

I nodded.

As he hobbled over to the driver's side he studied the Falcon. "Not the prettiest girl at the dance is she?"

My head swam. "Maybe not, but she's the only girl I dance with."

He snorted.

"I don't like anyone talking about my car."

He continued his examination, and to my surprise, kept his two-toothed mouth shut. He got in, leaving the door on the passenger-side open.

I pointed. "It doesn't start."

He sighed. "No shit, son. That's why I'm here."

"Right. Right." I said with a half grin.

"Are you okay?"

"I haven't slept much. No sleep since I got no windows."

After trying to crank it three times, he got out and walked back to his truck. I was about to ask if he was leaving but decided to see what he would do next.

"I'll have it back to ya in a few days. Ain't nothing major. Cracked fuel tank and a broken belt. Now, if you'd had one of those foreign cars you'd be up the creek. Good thing you bought a Ford."

I nodded like I knew anything about cars.

"I'll hook her up and haul her off."

"Need some help?"

He gave me an angry look. "Son, just because I only got one hand doesn't mean I'm helpless."

I shrugged. "I was just offering."

He went back to pulling the chain from the bed of his truck. "I know. You city types are always offering something, but no, I can manage just fine."

"Well, thank you for coming," I blurted out.

Still working with the chain, he nodded. "You can thank Franklin and the town. They're paying for it."

I gave up trying to be polite to him. "Okay. Have a good one." I saluted and turned to go back to town.

"Did you ever serve in the military?"

I turned. "No."

"Then you can take that salute and shove it up your ass," he barked, then spit.

Imagines of him in the war filled my mind. An explosion and him clutching his arm in agony. "I'm sorry. I didn't mean —It's the...Moons up!"

"Get on home, Big City."

I backed away from him, then turned toward home. I heard more grunts and strains over my shoulder as he continued connecting the two vehicles. I tasted my foot all the way up the hill. I decided I needed something to get the profound taste of stupidity out of my mouth.

38

After walking for what seemed an eternity, I finally found the house. I decided I would dine on the most exquisite cuisine in Kentucky, a cheese sandwich. Under the circumstance of the drugs, I knew fire wasn't a good idea. How I'd eaten all the food Grandma Rollin had brought I had no idea. I hadn't eaten in hours, and, since I'd emptied my stomach in the sink looking for a pill...

I moved to the living room and sat down with my dinner and the kids' writing assignments.

I needed to try and focus on their paragraphs, but afterwards, I would go straight to bed. If nothing else, I thought, the effects of the drugs would make the experience more bearable.

I opened the shutters. It was past six o'clock and the sun had lowered. I stared over the houses across the street, to the back of the bank building, all the way down to Keeper's Bridge.

I stared longer, and my mind started opening up.

A slight purple breeze caused the smaller limbs to sway

and the remaining leaves grabbed each other's hands and twirled. There was no sun, but all the shadows turned white and played "Do Wah Diddy Diddy" on the banisters and railings of my porch. "I love that song."

I glanced at the mountains and they pulsed in violent red. The music stopped. Witches flew around the summit of Black Bear Mountain.

I slapped my face. "Play the music and let's get to work."

There were about twenty assignments I would have the joy and horror of reading and correcting. Even if they were terrible, twenty didn't sound that bad. I divided the students' work into three categories: collections, hobbies, and facts of the town.

I read the collection papers first.

I like to read comic books, but my mom hates them. Sometimes I take them from the store. I know Jesus don't mind none because I'm reading.

I like frogs. I have tried to collect lots of them. I am sad though because I have never had more than six. I collect more than six but then some of them die. I like to collect them and make my sister mad.

I collect books. When I get older I want to read all the books so I can be as smart as Jackie Kennedy.—Carla

I like to hunt arrowheads. Arrowheads belonged to the Indians. Lotsa Indians were killed by the cowboys. But some live yonder on past mountain.

I have four hair brushes. I brush my hair each night 101 times. 101 is one more than 100. All the other girls brush

their hair 100 times. I want to be prettier than them.
Maybe if I get ten brushes, I will be the prettiest.-—Allison

I have a small ball of rubber bands. It is fun to play with. It
is fun to look at to. I want it to be the size of my head so it
can bounce to the moon. I'll be in all the papers.—Weezer.

I dont colect nothing. Mom hate me and wont let me she
colects men There is always a new man around all the
time She tells me not to tell or she will cream me Dont tell
her I told you she wonts to collect you two.—Scarlet

I laid my head against the sofa cushions and turned to
look out the large window onto my yard. My eyes were
moving slower than my head. I stared outside, but it took a
few seconds for thoughts to register.

The few leaves still clinging to the oak trees across the
street were twisting and turning in the wind. I relaxed into
the cushion, feeling myself slipping away.

I jerked awake. My head was groggy, but my eyes were
rejuvenated. How long was I asleep? Thirty minutes, an
hour? I went to the window and found the sky completely
dark.

Shining house lights from the next street over glowed.
As the wind stirred the branches, the lights danced through
the leaves. I closed one eye and held up the pencil in front of
the other. I pretended to erase one of the lights by covering
it with my eraser. When I moved the eraser, the light reap-

peared. It was silly, but wondrously entertaining. Swallowed or not the aspirin was definitely working.

I continued reading.

This town is a coal mining town. We make coal in the mountains. The coal keeps us all warm in the winter.
—Jason

My daddy was a coal man. He in heaven putting coal in the sun with jesus. I get to see him every day the sun is out.

Grandma Rollin is the best cook in town. She could put The Bucket out of business with one pan of biscuits. Once I get married I hope she will teach my wife to cook.
—Montana

This is a town in Kentucky. Kentucky sucks. I hate the smell of this place, I don't like the people, I don't like the politics, I don't want to work at Sears, but I gotta say I love that beard.—Magic Hands Peter

That one made me smile. I did have a proper beard. I pushed on with the few remaining papers:

This town is haunted. When kids die they turn into devils and hurt people. I don't want to die and hurt people like them.—Meg

Even with no windows I'm still scared at night. I don't like being afraid of the dark. I ask for a candle but my mom says I would choke with no air. I recently met someone though who makes me feel safe. Please don't tell momma I wrote this.—Amy

Since you are new you should know not to go outside after it gets dark. Joshua Johnson and the other ghost children killed the last teacher. I hope they don't kill you too.—Kate

"Who the fuck is Joshua Johnson?" But I finally had some insight into the town's crazy folklore. I read Kate's again. Middwood would make anyone go insane.

Kate's paragraph was cute. As absurd as it was, it was nice she was worried about me. All I had to do was figure out which twin was Kate and thank her.

I could make name cards and have the twins wear them while they were at school. They would read. "I'm Kate," and the other would read, "I'm Satan's daughter." I laughed so hard I coughed like old man Franklin.

I settled deeper into the sofa, warm and cozy. I moved the pencil's end to a different light and covered it. I moved the eraser, and the light was gone. "Magic," I whispered in delight.

My game was finished, I lowered my hand and opened both eyes, but was surprised to find the light was still gone.

My chest warmed and a dull pain tightened my shoulders.

"Dark magic," the words escaped my lips like someone else spoke them.

I leaned forward, and the light returned.

It hadn't gone out. Something was blocking it.

Something was out there. I was being watched.

39

I couldn't tell if I was I awake or not. Panic poured over me, drowning me in loss and confusion like my brain was melting.

"Matt, wake up. Wake up, Matt!" The serious tone of a voice I couldn't place shouted. Stinging slaps went across my face. I threw up my hands to block the blows but found no contact.

Shifting in my seat, I tried to get a full view of the lower half of my yard, but then something in the corner closest to the street moved. I craned my neck to see around the porch railing, but it was impossible from where I was.

"You're reliving last night, Matt. You aren't awake, boy." The words disturbed me, it was the tone of my father when he would give false warnings.

"Never go out after the sun sets..."

I advanced to the door. I couldn't stop myself, nor did I want to. I had to see. I opened the door and stepped over the threshold into the night. It was freezing, and the stirring wind carried the char of firewood.

"Go back inside."

"Voices in my head, visions of monsters, haunted dreams, damned rules. None of it's real."

I boldly stepped farther onto the porch and focused my sight on the tree.

There was nothing.

I scoffed. I spun to go back inside.

Look again. Look, my mind nagged.

I twisted and rotated around, and I realized I couldn't see the whole tree. There was still a porch post obstructing a small part of my view. My hands shook as blood pulsed in my veins. I was cold and my arms and legs felt weighted. My stomach churned, and I thought I might vomit. I tried to breathe, but there was no air. Every part of me was being pulled down. I fought against gravity. I struggled for control, but I was helpless.

I collapsed onto the porch banister.

I gasped for air. Blood flow resumed and gave me a dizzying high that made me feel like I was floating. I tried to steady myself, afraid I would faint.

"What was that?" It was the second time I had had that type of episode. The first time was on Windy Hill Lane when I went to get my toothbrush.

I pushed myself upright from the rail. My head swirled. "Easy does it."

At first, it appeared only as a blue haze, but after blinking again and again, my eyes cleared. The blur lifted.

There, less than ten yards away, stood a child.

I closed and reopened my eyes, but the child was still there. "Crap."

She wore a short, simple white dress, and from her height, she couldn't have been any older than five or six.

Her frowning chin stuck out as she watched me.

I glanced around to check if Peter was creeping in the

bushes, watching his theatre unfold—but no one else was out.

I closed my eyes and swatted away all the stupid moths and witches flying around in my head. She was probably scared to death. She must have been out playing when it got dark. Maybe she thought hiding under the tree was the safest place for her. Stupid town rules.

I walked barefoot across the grass toward her, "Hello?"

The little girl continued to stare at me. I moved closer. She didn't seem afraid but studied me with her big, innocent eyes.

I stopped several feet away when I thought there were two of her. I took a deep breath, fighting against the drugs. "Are you lost? I'm Mr. Christian. I'm a teacher."

From behind me, a voice snarled, "Turtle's not feeling well." I jumped forward with fright and fell beside the little girl. "Stay away from her!"

I looked up to see a taller, older girl, maybe nine or ten, standing over me. She was also wearing a dress, but her reddish-brown, shoulder-length hair and harsh scowl made her look like an old woman.

"You scared the life out of me!" I scrambled to my feet, dusting off my slacks. "I thought I was, my pills —Never mind."

The older girl stepped toward me. "Is he going to take us away?"

I didn't know how to answer that. "I can help you find your parents."

The girl's face hardened. She was a scary little thing. I was relieved when she took the little girl by the wrist. "You both will get the belt," she snarled at me.

The one she called Turtle stopped and turned, locking eyes with her sister. "Grace, I don't feel good."

"What's the matter?" her sister asked.

Turtle freed her wrist from Grace's and turned to me. "My tummy hurts."

Her expression was heartbreaking. Pouty lips and tears had never swayed me, but I could tell she didn't feel well. I couldn't help but want to help her.

"Of course, sweetheart. Where's your mama?"

Turtle became upset. "My tummy hurts."

"Try it again, honey!" shrieked Grace.

"Will you stop being a pest? I'm trying to help. Where is your mother?"

"This doesn't taste good" cried the youngest.

I knelt down. "Don't worry, sweetheart. I'll help you and your sister find your mother. Do you live around here?"

Grace crossed her arms. "This is our house."

I acknowledged Grace, softening my tone, "You're just lost because it's dark. I'm sure you live around here somewhere. Let's go knock on the neighbor's door."

I knew we wouldn't be received well, but I had to try. "Well, we'll just give it a try, okay?" I took Turtle's hand. "Oh my gosh, how long have you kids been out here? You're freezing."

"My tummy hurts."

We walked across the street to Amy's house, and I steadied myself against their door frame. I wasn't supposed to be outside, but there had to be exceptions to the rule.

The TV was on. I couldn't place the show, but the voices were familiar. Laughter rang out from the TV and the Tippett family.

I knocked.

Hurried steps rustled across the floor and the TV switched off. Except for the wind, it was now quiet.

I knocked again, and there were gasps from the other side, and a woman's voice said, "What do we do, Thad?"

"Mrs. Rebecca? Amy?" I called.

"What do we do?"

"Quiet!" Mr. Thad ordered.

Calling through the door again, "Hello? It's Matt. There are two lost children out here. I'm wondering if you could help me find out where they live."

"Mr. Christian?" His voice was closer to the door.

"Yes, the new teacher."

"Mr. Christian, get back to your house!"

"There are two lost children here."

"Get away from them. Run! Run!"

I jerked back to the space where Grace and Turtle had stood.

I scanned the yard and street for them, but the girls were nowhere to be seen.

A nervous chuckle escaped me, but when the lights inside Amy's house were cut off, my laugh dissipated into a despairing whimper. The girls and the light, vanished like it was all a cruel joke. Everyone was gone, leaving me all alone in the dark.

I bit my lip and closed my eyes. I was a crazy addict, and the whole town would know it by tomorrow. The truth of this made my mouth water as my stomach soured. I wanted to crumble to the ground, but I had to get back to my house.

"I'm sorry," I called inside. "I was mistaken. There is no one here."

I waited, but there was no response.

"Please don't tell anyone." I rested my head against their door. "Please don't."

The chilled air swirled around the valley. My arms hugged my body attempting to keep me warm. I slowly left their porch and labored over their lawn. The wind picked up in harsh gusts. I turned my head, trying to shield my face, but it was pointless.

Eyes.

Eyes were on me, numerous sets of eyes.

I imagined Amy's whole family watching me as I lumbered across the street. Mr. Thad had probably already called the sheriff. Someone was probably calling Franklin as well.

More and more eyes. The other neighbors must have heard the screams.

I stumbled and fell in the street. Tears rolled from my eyes.

With every stare, what I wanted so desperately, the job, the house, food, running water, were being dropped onto a table like coins in my pockets. Everything would be examined. I was a criminal. They would find out. Someone would make calls, and someone would find out who the new stranger was. They would find out I was an addict.

I wanted to run, leave Middwood like I had Atlanta, but I had no car. Without that, I was stuck here. I would have to deal with this. But not tonight, as exposed as I was in the open. The town rules finally worked in my favor. I'd be safe and left alone until morning. For the rest of the night, I could do what I so desperately needed, sleep.

I bounded up the porch, batted the door shut, and ran upstairs.

Crash!

The bloodwood door swung open.

The weighted impact sent me cowering into a protective ball.

I froze, staring out into the darkness.

Freezing gusts poured in. It was only the wind. That's

what I told myself, but my mind resisted. I had shut the door and bloodwood was one of the heaviest woods there was.

I thought back. I was emotional when I came in, and I wasn't thinking straight. I didn't shut the door all the way. I laughed. It was the drugs. Everything that happened was drug induced. I knew I'd gone outside tonight. I could tell by my cold toes and dirt on my feet, but nothing else was. There were never any girls.

I relaxed and rolled my hips to a sitting position at the top of the stairs. I shook my head at my foolishness. It was time I gave up the pills.

The porch boards creaked.

I looked up.

The girls were standing in the doorway.

40

M y brain reeled. I didn't know what to do, so I stood up.

The girls were silent. My eyes fluttered as my blood pressure spiked.

Part of me wanted to make a break for the Tomb, but I couldn't. For whatever reason, I couldn't.

"You two came back."

They were silent.

I had to be realistic. There was a high chance none of this was happening. I was an addict, and my mind was punishing me for what happened with Darlene. However, in the slim chance they were real, regardless of the town rules, it was my job to help children. Besides, they were in my house, and they needed to be somewhere else.

I cautiously moved down the stairs.

"Grace, I don't feel so good," pouted Turtle.

"I know. You told me that earlier. I don't feel so good either."

"What's the matter?"

I froze. They were repeating our previous conversation.

The youngest kept her eyes locked on me. "My tummy hurts."

I rubbed away the gooseflesh on my arms. "Who are you?"

"My tummy hurts." Turtle repeated.

I nodded. "I will help you."

The two small girls weren't staring, more like watching me. I didn't feel threatened.

My head was swimming, but two small children needed help.

"I'll tell you what, you two stay out here and wait while I call the sheriff. The phone is in the kitchen," my voice shook as I side-stepped through the opening. They followed me in.

I walked into the kitchen and, as I picked up the receiver, the front door slammed.

"Shit!" I turned to the door. The girls were standing next to the refrigerator. "Jesus!" I took a breath. "Sorry." We exchanged stares. "The door, it scared me. Sorry for swearing." In silence, we watched each other as I dialed the first few numbers with trembling hands. "He's big, but I think he's a nice guy."

The girls said nothing as they stood there, side-by-side, holding hands. There were so many thoughts going through my head, but I pushed through all of the chaos to focus on getting them out of my house. That's what I told myself over and over as my heart rate increased.

Holding her stomach, Turtle repeated, "Grace, I don't feel so good." She dry-heaved, and I dropped the phone and grabbed a towel.

"She doesn't like it," growled Grace.

Turtle cried, "I don't want anymore."

I knelt down to help Turtle.

Grace grabbed my arm. "She doesn't like it!"

Turtle started throwing up thick, white globs.

"What are you doing? Your sister is sick!"

Her grip grew in strength to double that of mine.

She stepped closer. "She doesn't like it." Grace's eyes, changed from brown to a dull, milky gray. Her face transformed from smooth tan to that of a bloated, milky corpse. "You both will get the belt, do you understand!"

She threw me, and I slid across the floor, stopping against the cabinets, hitting my head. I was dazed, but I saw her coming toward me with outstretched arms and pale blue fingers.

I pushed and kicked away from her, but I was trapped.

The cerulean veins in her neck and around her eyes pulsed. "Be the big sister and show her how to do it."

Her face slowly contorted into a dull show of pain. Her head tilted sharply to the right. A low rumble came from her belly. She stood straight up, throwing back her head. She shook her upper body back and forth like she was trying to control the pain. She grabbed her stomach, wrenching her clasped hands into her abdomen.

There was a brief silence.

I could only hear my teeth clenching.

There were gurgles of moving bile.

My own throat constricted.

She lurched toward me, her spine curled forward. She opened her mouth and she dumped her stomach's contents on me.

Both girls projected chunky, oatmealy bile.

I raised my hands to shield my face, but it covered me. Its heat and grainy stench assaulted my senses.

"Stop it!" I gagged.

The dangling phone filled the kitchen with a blaring busy signal.

They were gone.

I looked down, and the puke was gone.

I was shaking, in a fetal position in a corner on the kitchen floor. Slowly, my quaking and retching subsided into coughs. Although I could still smell the puke in my nose, there was nothing on me.

The buzzing from the phone continued.

I sat up.

My head was ringing. I ran my fingers through my hair to the back of my head. When I brought my hand forward it was covered with blood. Another unseen scar that my long hair would hide.

I leaned back against the cabinets. Something was building in me. It was growing from deep down in the pit of my gut. My body moved as it went up through my stomach and chest. I thought I was going to throw up, but instead, it was like a low sob. I bellowed like an animal.

I had finally lost it.

41

Thursday, November 5, 1964
Sunrise 7:01 AM. Sunset 5:32 PM.

I didn't sleep well. I couldn't. I was afraid if I did the two little ghoul girls would appear. When I closed my eyes I could see the pale, busted, veiny faces that housed their cold, milky gaze.

I staggered to turn on the light switch. I read my watch. It was already after nine. I pictured the entire town gathered with pitch axes and shovels outside in my yard. If I had a window I could have checked, I thought.

I crept down the stairs into the living room and peeked through the shutters. There was no one outside. I furrowed my brow. *How...?* I stopped myself. I decided to be grateful and not ask questions. Besides, there was a chance none of it happened.

Running out the door, I stopped myself and thought, *Screw it. I'll skip breakfast, but I'm not leaving without my coffee.* Caffeine was the only way I could get through the day. I was out of milk, but after the previous night's illusions, I didn't care if I was out of anything that resembled vomit.

"Matt!" Franklin shouted.

"Fuck the cow! Good grief, Frank! You scared the shit out of me."

"Well, you scared the shit out of me. Are you all right?"

I turned my chin. *What was he asking me about?* I thought. Dread built behind my eyes. *No,* I pleaded, *please don't be here about last night.*

"Last night, the children. Are you all right?"

So I had gone out last night. I figured that part was real, even though I tried to convince myself it wasn't. I wasn't sure what I should say. "Yes, I'm fine."

"Thad called Philip, and, of course, Philip called me—"

The feeling of being watched while crossing the street had been real, too. I didn't like where this was going. "It's a tight-knit town. You said that yourself."

"Matt, what happened?"

Oh God, I thought. What? What? What was real? What was the drugs? If I said the wrong thing, it would make matters worse. "To be honest, Franklin... I'm not sure what happened."

Franklin nodded with great concern. "Thad said you knocked on his door saying two children were lost."

"Yeah, I don't really remember."

"You don't remember?"

"Sorry, it's kinda foggy. I couldn't sleep so I took something. Whatever happened, I wasn't myself."

"A sleeping pill?"

I lied. "Yeah. I had one left that a doctor gave me when my father died. I forgot I had it, but I had a headache last night, so I got up to take a Bufferin... and I found it, and I took it."

"Matt, last night you had a run-in with the ghost children."

I paused, staring at him blankly. "The who?"

"The ghost children."

"The ghost children?" I repeated, giving myself time to think of what to say. Franklin was trying to trick me. I must have said something about ghost children to Thad, but I didn't remember that part. However, the neighbors saw me fall in the street. They knew I was wasted and they sent Franklin to get me to confess. All I had to do was tell the truth. "Like I said, Frank, I could have been attacked by a werewolf and I wouldn't have known. Besides, going out after dark is against the town's rules."

"Matt, other neighbors saw you, too."

"Did they see anyone else with me?"

"No."

I shrugged. "Hmm?"

"Matt, this is serious."

"I don't know, Frank. What do you want me to say? I'm sure everything is fine." I put my hands on his shoulders. "Look, regardless, I only had one pill, and thank goodness it's gone now."

He stared at me.

"Wow, that thing must have really sent me for a loop. I can tell, I'm not used to taking medication." I continued to nod.

All I needed was doubt.

Franklin looked at the ground. That was my cue. "The pill made it hard for me to wake up. I'm late for school. Do you need me to stay? I don't want to keep the kids waiting."

"Sure, sure."

I walked away.

"But we do need to talk. There have been lots of discussions."

I kept walking. "Sure thing, Frank. Thank you. Have a great day."

Jesus Christ, it actually worked. I didn't think I would be able to get away with that.

~

"**B**ut, Mr. Christian, Jason is looooking at meee!"
I held my hands over my ears, knocking the stick of chalk off my desk. I had a massive headache, and Franklin's visit had robbed me of going back inside to make my morning coffee. "Scarlet, if you don't stop whining I'm going to feed you to the cows."

Her nails-on-a-chalkboard voice cut through my brain, "We don't have cows around here."

"Then I'll throw you down a coal mine."

Amy gasped. "Mr. Christian!"

"Amy, I'm only kidding." I then gestured to Scarlet. "Relax. How will you work in the coal mine if you can't read?"

"Girls, can't work at a mine. It's bad luck," Scarlet pouted.

I rolled my eyes. "Luck, rules, bah!"

Carla sauntered up to my desk, picked up the piece of chalk for me, and then joyfully sat back down. I cringed. She looked to be about the same age as the older girl from my hallucinations. She and Grace were the same height, same little-girl build, and even the same hair color and length. Carla's face was innocent and hopeful, but Grace's expression had been hard, with a bitter distrust I had only seen in older people who had been dealt a lousy hand. My brain must have concocted the mental image of Grace from Carla. It was all about my mind working through what happened with Darlene, the girl I'd assaulted.

I shuddered, figments of the imagination didn't typically have names.

My heart beat faster. Last night was not real. Of course, it wasn't, I reaffirmed to myself. Regardless, my cheeks flushed. I lowered my head and rubbed my face under my glasses. I let out a deep, hot breath.

I glanced up. Grace was standing in front of my desk. Horrifically pale with that bluish hue, her skin was bloated and busted. She glared at me with dead eyes hidden behind thick fluid. She leaned in. "Are you okay, Mr. Christian?"

I yelped and so did someone else in the class.

"Are you okay, mister?"

I blinked. There was no one there. I jerked my head to Carla who was in her seat with a frightened, concerned look. I looked back to the nothing in front of me, then back at her.

I let out a short, absurd laugh. "Sorry, Carla. I know that was... I haven't been sleeping well. I think I dozed off."

"You okay, Christian?" Peter asked quietly as he moved to my desk.

Turning to the twins, I noticed their eyes. They were wide and shocked. Their hands clenched each other's arms like their lives depended on it. Their little chests were heaving.

"Did you see it, too?" I begged them both, but they remained quiet in their terror.

"Christian?"

"It's all right," I grumbled, waving Peter off. "I just had a bad dream."

"But, Mr. Christian," Carla said, squirming in her seat. "I didn't notice you falling asleep."

"Stop watching me so much."

Peter flipped out one of his tucked hands, then recrossed his arms. "We just care—"

"You don't care, if you did you'd actually have some friends."

He took a step back. "Damn man."

"Damn man," I mocked. "I'm not your father. Get over it."

What was I saying? I told myself to stop. My shoulders slumped. "Peter, I'm sorry. I didn't—"

"No," He waved me off. "You're right. You're not my dad." His face twisted, and his words sharpened. "My father wasn't a pill-popping jerk."

"Hey, I have an idea, why don't you get out. Go home and plan out your next 'fuck with Mr. Christian idea.'"

The class gasped.

"Jesus, Christian," Peter said, shaking his head.

I could feel the heat inside me trying to take over. "Peter, I'm sorry. I'm not sure what is happening to me."

"Well, good luck with figuring it out," he said and walked out the door.

"Peter, come back." I gritted my teeth. "Young man, get back here," I demanded and moved after him, but he ignored me.

I let out an exasperated moan as I ran my hands through my hair and hurried to the door. Standing on the threshold, I watched Peter run across the school yard.

42

I needed a pill more than ever. What the fuck was I going to do, take another pill and cause more hallucinations? Next, I'd be seeing spiders and unicorns. I'd be lucky to imagine anything normal. However, this one was harder to shake. It wasn't night time, and I was having a fit. I'd lashed out at my students. Worst of all, I'd attacked Peter. I hadn't physically assaulted him, but I knew what I'd said was just as hurtful.

Anger swelled inside me, but I blew off the absurdity, stretching my neck to the left and the right. I looked at my watch. It was 2:55. I shook my head and shambled to the blackboard. "I fucking hate this town," I said under my breath.

"Did you say something, Mr. Christian?" asked Allison.

"I said ..." I sighed. "Is it me, or is it hard to sleep in this town?"

It was a rhetorical question, but the kids all answered by nodding their heads. My churning anger faded. They understood. They had the same problem, and, as sorry as I felt for them at that moment, it also helped me. I let out a long satisfying sigh. "Okay, class. I'm sorry for being grouchy earlier. I'm sorry I was late, and I'm sorry we are already over our normal time. Let's relax, forget about this morning, forget about this afternoon, I'll find Peter and apologize to him later. Let's just finish up so we can all go home."

Their tired, little faces produced faint smiles. Finally, we were all getting back to the same page.

"Let's check our science homework and then get outta here. The question of the day, but this time it's for you guys, who did their science homework?" I said while performing an innocent hip-shaking dance.

The agreeable little faces diminished and were replaced by wrinkled frowns, surprised looks, and averted eyes. My hips stopped.

"I thought you just said we were going to forget about it," Weezer said.

"Oh, come on," I whined. "Are you serious?" I put my hands over my eyes and closed them tight. "Raise your paw if you did your homework." I prayed to the Lord God Almighty, Buddha, or whoever that there would be little hands up in the air.

I opened them.

I stood there licking my dry, lower lip as I marveled at all the empty space above my students' heads where their hands should be raised. *Empty spaces in their heads, too,* I thought.

There were only three hands raised, Carla and the twins.

"You three precious girls bring me your work."

They scampered up and tossed the papers on my desk then quickly darted back like their work was going to explode.

I looked down at their work. "Thank you, Kate, Meg, and

Carla. You three may leave. Thank you for doing your work. Have a nice day."

The twins looked at me like it was a trick, but then happily gathered up their belongings. Carla took more time, gloating in her pride. She grinned at the class and walked out of the schoolhouse with her nose raised.

Once the doers were gone, I turned my attention to the slackers. Scratching my head, "Unbelievable," I sighed. "Just unbelievable."

I sat in my chair and stretched out my legs. The class was quiet. I was trying not to have a meltdown. After a moment, I stood, then faced the blackboard. I reached into my pocket and pulled out one of my pills. "Screw it," I whispered and grabbed a second. I threw them in my mouth and swallowed them with spit—it was that kind of day.

I turned back to the class. "Okay. No homework?" I was speaking in fragments, which was never a good sign. "You have. To learn. To do. Your work. Or face the consequences. So, you will not be going home. You will stay here. Until you finish your homework."

"But Mr. Christian, it's already after three," Allison pleaded. "The moon will be up soon—"

"It's only 3:10, and I don't care!" I shouted, and the class jumped. "You are not going home! You will do as I say. Is that understood?"

The children cowered back into their seats like sinking shadows. There was a whispering wonder inside my mind, did I yell at Darlene like that before I hit her? I cast that worried angel out of my head. The kids needed to learn. I tilted my head from left to right. My neck was killing me. The punishment was justified. If only they had done their homework.

The mine whistle blew.

The arm holding my chin gave out. I must have dozed off. I looked at the class and then at my watch. It was an hour and fifteen minutes later, and the sun was sinking. "Are you guys finished?"

No one said anything.

"God," I groaned. I had wanted the younger kids to listen while I discussed the assignment with the older kids. Hopefully get them to ask some questions. It was a complete bust. "Eleven and younger can go."

"What about us," Amy asked?

"You guys have to stay."

There were mumbled words. "Yeah, mumble away the day. Just turn in your work and you can go."

"You know the valley gets dark thirty minutes before the sun goes down."

"Just finish your work!"

Thirty minutes later the jagged shadows of the dead trees were sprawling out along the floor of the schoolhouse. With every second and every inch of the shadow's invasion, the children became more and more tense. It was palatable.

The constant glances out the window annoyed me. No one had turned in their work. Their wide eyes darted from me to each other, then back to the windows.

"Focus on your work," I commanded for the hundredth time.

"Mr. Christian?" whined Scarlet.

"What, Scarlet?" I mocked.

She shrank down in her desk. "If we don't leave soon, we're going to have to stay here."

"Don't be ridiculous," I scoffed.

"My father told me if I ever get stuck somewhere before it gets dark to stay there, no matter where I am. Are we going to stay here tonight?" Weezer yelped.

"Class, it's not even dark yet. This is nonsense."

The children chattered. They were becoming more and more excited.

Jason stood. "Y'all, the sun sets at 5:32. The valley time will be five. My daddy is going to be pissed."

"Jason, sit down. I have no idea why the town has embedded these tales into your heads."

Jason pointed at me. "The ghost children are real, teacher."

The class erupted in emotional agreement. Their words and cries blending together in a child's hellish chorus.

I took off my glasses and rubbed my face. "There are no such things as ghosts!" I roared.

"Don't talk about them like that. They might hear you," warned Weezer.

"What if they are already outside...and they heard him?" gasped Scarlet.

"They might get mad!" exclaimed Weezer.

I threw my glasses back on and held out my hands to the class. "There are no ghost children. There is no—what's his name—Joshua Johnson!"

The class went silent, then stared at the window.

"Big City, you are going to get it," droned Jason.

The mine whistle blew, and the class froze.

I hesitated but then moved to the window. In the still

and quiet class my steps were loud. I peered out the window. "Why did they blow the whistle this late?"

The whistle blew again, and the class gasped.

"The double whistle," Amy stuttered.

The students became hysterical.

"What does it mean?" I asked raising my voice attempting to be heard.

"It means get home," Amy declared.

"You are gonna get it, teacher," Jason said shaking his head.

It was a losing battle. I was a fool to think they were going to complete any work under those circumstances.

A desk slid and crashed against the wall and the whole class jumped. Montana stood brooding. "Mr. Christian, we have less than fifteen minutes. It's time to go. I'm taking Amy home."

Literate or illiterate, I'd had enough. "Fine!" I erupted. I threw up my hands. "Run! Run for your little lives. Beware of ghosts!"

43

The children pushed each other to get out of the door first, pushing and shoving to the point of savagery, knowing freedom was only beyond the door.

One girl elbowed a smaller boy in the face. I expected he'd come crying to me, but he didn't. He just held his hand over the injured eye and continued the charge.

In less than a minute, the schoolhouse was completely empty. I looked around the room, shocked. Most of the children hadn't bothered taking their belongings. One student even left their shoes. I shook my head in amazement.

I went to the board and picked up a piece of chalk and wrote:

Town Foolishness:

1. Never turn your back on an open window.

2. Never go out before the sun comes up or after the sun goes down.

3. Unknown

Stepping back, I studied the words and read them aloud.

I looked out the window. It was indeed dusk. I continued to look outside. I was perplexed and angered, but still, the longer I stood there, the more I played over all the strange events that had occurred since I moved to Middwood: the animals, the dreams, the voices, the feeling of someone touching me when no one was there, and the girls last night. I hummed while I glanced around the room. I was cold, but more than that—I was uneasy.

The wind picked up.

I had been in a hurry that morning, so I hadn't brought a jacket even though I had intended to stay after school and catch up on grading. Except for Carla and the twins, I would fail them all on the assignment. I hoped a bad grade would encourage them to work harder next time. Make them think twice before not doing their homework. They had to learn.

I took off my glasses and rubbed my eyes. "What a mess."

Creak.

I looked behind me.

The blackboard was different. Even with my fuzzy vision, I could see additional words had been added under the town rules.

An overwhelming sense of a presence washed over me. I quickly put on my glasses, stood, and investigated the room. "Who's here?"

"Peter?"

I waited for a response, but there was nothing.

"Franklin?"

I walked closer to the board. The new writing was small and angled, written in an unsteady hand.

I stood shocked at the words.

"We want you to see us."

Goosebumps burned down my arms and back, the

words from the woman in my dream and the whispers on the street. A terrifying confusion overcame me. "How could —What is going on here?"

Again, the wind blew and rocked against the old outer walls. The room was cooler now, and my mouth and lips were dry.

Suddenly I couldn't help but think maybe if the whole town believed the rules perhaps I should at least be respectful of them. I gathered my things and fumbled as I stuffed them in my bag.

I stepped outside the school and pivoted to lock the door.

Sobs burst from below me.

I spun, dropping my keys. I didn't see anything.

The whimpers continued.

I stepped to the edge of the cinder blocks and peered under the school.

Scarlet jumped from her hiding place. "Let me back in."

"Scarlet!" I grabbed my chest, trying to regain some composure. "What are you still doing here?"

"I can't walk home alone. I just can't do it," she said crying.

I descended the stairs, knelt and retrieved my keys. "Scarlet, you will be fine." I locked the door.

"No, Mr. Christian! They'll kill me. I know they will. No one would walk home with me because they know the ghosts will kill me."

"Scarlet, why would anyone do that?"

"Not just anyone, the ghost children. And they would because I back talk my mom."

I was irritated by the absurdity of her fear, but I couldn't leave her. "Well, come on then. I guess I'll take you home."

She wiped at her tears. "You'll walk with me?"

"Of course, as long as you walk with me and keep me safe."

"Oh," she said more like a breath as she searched the growing shadows. "I wish I could, Mr. Christian, but, unfortunately, the rules do apply to me. We are on our own."

$$\sim$$

The great thing about walking home with Scarlet would be that she'd talk so much I wouldn't have any space between my ears to think. She might even give me more motivation to walk faster.

We made our way across the schoolyard.

"So, you've never been out after dark?"

She gasped. "No! Never!"

Okay, perhaps it was too serious of a question. "Um, what is your favorite subject in school?"

"What?"

"In school. What's the subject we've studied that you enjoy the most?"

She stuck her tongue out and nibbled on it.

Even though I wasn't surprised by her quirks any longer, I returned my eyes to the path.

"I enjoy the speaking portions the most," she said.

The child did have the singular talent of making the schoolroom's windows tremble with her constant chatter, but sometimes she could be funny.

"Yes, I agree with you," I said. "You are good at speaking."

She looked up at me. "What is your favorite subject?"

I grinned at her question. "Well, I have always enjoyed literature the best."

"Reading?" she groaned as she threw her shoulders and arms forward. "I hate reading!"

"Watch your step!" my hands fumbled as I grabbed her shoulder to keep her from toppling down the hill.

"I might have stumbled, but I didn't fall," she said in her slightly off-tune, melodic voice. She laughed and beamed up at me with her big eyes and a silly smile that sparkled even in the dimmed remains of the day. "It's the second time you saved me today."

"You're welcome."

"Do you think the other kids are jealous of me?"

"What do you mean?"

"You know," she said nodding her head, "because I'm your favorite student."

My jaw dropped as I searched for a response. She must have really gotten me with her question because my lungs sucked in all the smells of the tree bark, decaying leaves, and the burning stoves and chimneys of the town with my gaping mouth.

"Well, I shouldn't have favorites, but I won't tell if you won't."

"It will be our secret."

"Good." She craned her neck to look at the mountain. I thought she was being silly, but a deeper layer of shadow traveled up her little body, like a cloud was passing over or we walked under a tree with a massive canopy.

"Wow," I said with enthusiasm. "Scarlet, the light—"

"I know." She glanced down at my feet and then up to my face. "We are in the shadow of the mountain."

The path below was dark. I was so wrapped up in the conversation with Scarlet and distracted by her physical antics that I didn't notice the deep shadow that now lay before us. I watched as the darkness rose up my body like rising water. I'm sure it was only in my head, but as the darkness swallowed us so did the cold.

"Mr. Christian, you need to hurry. I can't protect you if you move that slow."

44

She took my hand, and her little legs more than doubled their speed. To keep from pulling her backward, I lengthened my stride. We speed-walked in silence until I couldn't take it. My head was rolling.

"This is the quietest you've ever been in your life isn't it?" I laughed.

"Keep your voice down."

"Oh because of the gh—"

She jerked my arm. "Don't say it."

I looked down at her as she pulled me along. "Okay, no more talking. You know, you're really smart."

We walked again in silence, but she beamed from my compliment. As I stumbled down the hill, I thought about how sickly-sweet it was, the student concerned for her teacher's well-being. She was protecting me, even if it was all stupid horse-shit.

She finally spoke. "My mom says I'm stupid."

Again, she caught me off guard. She was a special little girl, and she caused even my flat, tin heart to bend. "I'm sure she was only teasing."

She shook her head energetically. "Nope. She tells me I'm stupid all the time."

"My father used to tell me the same thing."

"Uh-uh?" She gasped in dumbfounded shock. "Doesn't he know you're a teacher?"

I nodded. "Yes, he did."

"What? Is he the principal or a mayor or somethin'?"

I laughed. "No. He isn't any of those things. What about you Scarlet, what does your mother do?"

"She works at the grocery store."

Holy shit. It all clicked. Wow. Magnolia was Scarlet's mom. Who would have figured? It made me mad to think about Magnolia calling her special child stupid.

I stopped. "Scarlet, listen to me, you are not stupid. You—"

"Why did you stop?" Her wide eyes darted all around us. Her voice was thin and panicked, "We broke the rule. We broke the rule. We broke the third rule."

"What's the third rule?"

"When out after dark, don't stop; never stop moving."

"Scarlet, it's been dark the whole time we've been walking."

Someone ran by us. They came out of nowhere.

I jerked my head after them. "See, there are other people out." My optimism faded as I said the words. The shadows swallowed the runner. "He came from the school?" The hairs on the back of my neck stood up.

I looked at Scarlet. She was frozen facing down the path where the man had disappeared. The only part of her moving was her chest, with shallow and rapid breaths.

"Scarlet, it's okay."

I put my hands on her little shoulders and peered into

her eyes. She wasn't looking at me. She was looking behind me. I whirled around.

It was the runner. He was blocking the path.

He stood before us, his shoulders bowed. He was shorter than me with a more narrow build. He looked like a teenager. His face was hidden beneath the hood of a gray sweatshirt. I stepped closer to him. "Peter?"

He crouched like he was going to attack.

"Take it easy," I said stepping back and pushing Scarlet behind me. "Who are you?"

He didn't answer, but his head jutted forward like he was sniffing the air.

I shifted my head hoping to catch any amount of light to see anything more than the void under his hood. It wasn't the fact I couldn't see his face that concerned me. It was his posture, primal and aggressive.

Reaching behind me with one arm, I moved Scarlet with me as I side-stepped. The boy's head followed me, keeping his face masked and his shoulders in line with mine. I didn't take my eyes off him.

"If you are here to mug me, I'm a teacher, so it's not your lucky day," I managed to keep a firm, steady tone, even though my heart was pounding.

I tried to penetrate the shadows of his hood. It was a strange sensation, but when I tried to focus on his face, it was like he was pulling me in. I shook my head, breaking off my scrutiny.

I pressed on. "What do you want, young man?"

Raspy, gritty gasps.

At first I thought it was a nearby stream mixed with the rustling leaves, but it was his breathing—long, thin, and hoarse.

"Say something!" I shouted. "You're frightening her. Is that what you want?"

No response. Nothing.

"I said you are frightening her. Please, leave."

He lowered his body like a coiling snake.

I stepped forward. "I said leave! Do you hear me?"

Scarlet whimpered.

He was locked onto us. I still couldn't see his face, but anger built in me. Clenching my fists, I took another step forward.

He charged me.

I threw up my fists and there was a sharp burst of blue light. I shielded my eyes.

When I opened them, he was gone. "What the hell?"

I spun to Scarlet. "Did you see that?" She didn't speak. I knelt and put my hands on hers shoulders. "Are you okay?"

Her sobs caused her petite frame to jolt. She was scared to death, but she was okay.

I looked up, and there he was. He was walking away from us, back toward the school. I almost called to him, but I held my tongue. I watched him walk into the darkness— one, two, three steps—then he was gone.

I strained to see into the night. He could easily circle us and attack from another direction. I broke my stare and scanned the left and right. I tried to listen, strained to hear his dreadful breathing. There was nothing, but that didn't mean he wasn't there. Scarlet and I stood quietly and still.

She whispered, "Is he gone?"

"I'm not sure, but I hope so."

He wasn't blocking us anymore, and that's all that mattered. I needed to get Scarlet home.

"Scarlet—"

"I told you he would come for me!" she whimpered.

"Scarlet—"

"I'll never back talk my mother again. I promise, God. I promise," she vowed.

My temples were pounding, and I was trying to regain my own composure. "It's all right. He's gone. He didn't harm either of us. Let's get moving."

She held on to me as we walked. "I knew he'd try to get me."

My eyes searched our surroundings, "Do you know that boy?"

"Of course, that's Joshu—I shouldn't say his name."

"Okay. It's okay. Are you okay?"

"I don't think so."

I looked down at her. "What's wrong?"

"I peed myself," she cried.

"Don't worry about that. To be honest, Scarlet, I almost did the same." The thing was, I was being honest, I wasn't just trying to console her.

"Don't tell any of the other kids. Promise you won't." She gazed up at me, pleading.

"I promise. It's none of their business. Besides, I'm a teacher, and as a teacher, I'm here to tell you it happens all the time."

"You think so?"

"Yes, you just don't hear about it because teachers are such good people they never tell the other students."

"Thanks, Mr. Christian."

"Now let's get you home. Your mother will be worried sick. She'll have me fired."

"Trust me, Mr. Christian, you don't want to owe her any favors."

45

Instead of going to the left toward the town, we took a right going away from it.

After we walked for five minutes, Scarlet pointed to a single dirt path on the left of the highway. There was a sign beside it that read, "Happy Valley Trailer Park." The bare trees hugged the road so close I was sure all the residents' cars were scratched to hell and back.

"How long have you lived here?" I asked, breaking the silence.

"A few months. We move a lot."

We didn't have to walk far. It was the second trailer on the right. The number once read "Lot 13" but someone had spray painted the number sixty-nine over it in glossy red.

Damn, that's mean.

I guessed that was part of the reason for the excessive moving.

I rapped on the door of the blue and white mobile home. I could see the light darken through the curtain behind the eye-level diamond-shaped window in the trailer door.

Looking down at Scarlet, "Do you think she will open the door?"

I turned back when the curtain moved. A cloud of smoke dissipated, revealing Magnolia's surprised face. She coughed as she took the cigarette from her mouth and opened the door. "Well, hello, handsome," she said unaware that her housecoat was open. I imagined she would wear black satin lingerie, but instead, she wore a gray and large, white flannel shirt. My mind instantly jumped to her mentioning her late husband the night we first met.

"Oh, hi. I didn't know if you'd open the door." I noticed the covering of the little window wasn't a curtain, but a hand towel that had been nailed into the door.

"I'd open for you anytime." She smirked, taking another drag on her cigarette.

"I wasn't sure with all the stuff—"

"Oh, honey, some things are worth the wrath of the dead," she gave a haggard laugh. She waved the smoke away between us. "Besides, those rules don't apply to me." Just then her eyes locked on Scarlet. She peeked back inside the house, then back out at Scarlet. Her forehead lowered, and she shouted through her bared teeth. "What the hell are you doing outside? Get in the house!"

Scarlet hid behind me. "Mom, don't be mad."

I stood between them. "I walked her home from school."

"From school? You haven't been home yet?" she hissed, grabbing at Scarlet until she caught her arm.

"You didn't even know I wasn't home?" Scarlet cried as her mother pulled her into the trailer.

"Why the hell would I know? There's no telling what you do all that time you're alone in your bedroom," she said pushing Scarlet behind her. Magnolia turned back and laughed and smiled at me. "That's none of my business."

From inside, Scarlet stomped through the living room and shouted, "I wish Joshua Johnson would have killed me!"

"He would have done me a big favor," Magnolia shouted over her shoulder.

I stood there, shocked, remembering all the terrible things my dad used to say to me.

Once Scarlet was out of sight, Magnolia stepped out onto the small landing. She was wearing short white socks. She crossed her bare legs at the ankle and let her back fall against the trailer. It wasn't precisely a graceful act, but I didn't think that was the point. She wanted to me check out her legs. It worked.

She lowered her smoky voice. "Thank you for walking her home. Very kind of you."

"It was no problem."

"No problem, huh?" She took a drag off her cigarette. "You like my legs?" She nodded. "Yeah, I got good legs. I'm only thirty-three you know?"

I was shocked that she was that young, but I didn't know what to say. "Yes, they're nice legs."

She tilted forward. "You want to touch them?"

My body was heavy. Even if I wanted to, it had been too crazy of a night. I took a deep breath to clear my resolve. "I need to get home."

She pushed off the trailer's hull and took a step a toward me. "Maybe you were already coming this way?"

I took a step back. "No, I'm on the other side of town. She... Scarlet was scared, so I walked her home."

Magnolia pushed her hair over her shoulder. "Oh, Scarlet, my little shame." She licked her lower lip and crossed her arms shivering. "Would you like to come in?"

"Oh." *Hello, Matt. Get the hell out of here.* "No. Thank you."

"Are you sure?"

"I have to get up early for school tomorrow."

"Well, it was just so nice of you to go through all that trouble. You should get something for it. Don't you think?"

"Mom," called Scarlet from inside the house.

"Damn kids, right?" she said.

I laughed awkwardly. "Yeah."

"Mom," Scarlet called again.

Magnolia continued, "You should think about—"

"She's calling you," I interrupted.

"I damn well hear her," she said and called over her shoulder with thick, fake sweetness. "I can't turn my damn back on the open door, sweetheart. I've already broken one rule, do you want me to die?"

"Don't die," I said.

"Aw. You're so sweet," Magnolia cooed.

What to do..."Rain check?" I squeaked.

"Oh! Absolutely. Absolutely. You take care, handsome."

"I will," I turned.

"Hey!"

I froze and looked back at her.

"Watch your back tomorrow. Folks in the town are crazy when it comes to their kids, and this is your second strike."

I furrowed my brow. I wanted to ask her what she meant, but maybe that was her intention. As hard as it was, I let it go. "Thanks."

I hurried away from the trailer and, of course, I could feel her watching me. I wanted to get away from her. I felt her eyes leave my ass, then heard her muffled shouts as she went inside and closed the door, "What the hell do you want, you little slut?"

Scarlet snapped back. "I'm not a slut!"

"You were running around with the teacher man. Did you play all scared so he would walk you home?"

Their voices diminished as I quickly moved farther and farther away. I hated hearing a child getting yelled at by anyone other than myself.

$$\sim$$

As I trudged to my front door, steps landed behind me. I whipped my head around, and the gray-hooded figure was standing directly in front of me. I jumped back, ramming my shoulders into the front door.

I held up my fists.

"Whoa, whoa, whoa," a voice from inside the hood said and held up his hands. "Christian, it's me." The menacing figure pulled back his hood to reveal Peter.

I shoved him. "Why do you keep doing this? What do you want from me?"

He held his shoulder where I pushed him. "I wanted to make sure you got home safe. I—"

"You're an asshole, and you scared the hell out of Scarlet."

"No, I was the one who drew him away from you!" he protested.

"Trying to help the pill-popping jerk huh?"

"Look, I shouldn't have said that, I didn't mean to."

I turned to the door. "How did you know?"

"I found your pills."

I spun around. "You broke into my house?"

"I'm good at things like that."

I shoved him again. "You went through my things?"

"I thought you were one of them."

I opened the door. "I thought you were better than that." I went inside and slammed the door in his face.

"I promise I'm not a bad kid."

I was having a fuck of a night, and I was a nervous wreck. My intention of moving to the country had been to relax, but after being in Middwood for less than a week, I knew that was never going to happen.

I went to the living room window. Peter was still on the porch with his back to the door. He pulled his hood over his head and then broke into a jog down the yard turning onto the street to the left. As he rounded onto the road, he turned, saw me, and waved. I backed away from the window and retreated to the bathroom.

With trembling hands, I reached into the medicine cabinet and pulled out my Rose-Mary's anxiety medication. I opened the bottle and turned out the contents into my hand, but the bottle was empty. The last of her was gone.

I chewed on the dead skin on my lip as I moved to the Tomb. I snatched my tote bag and pulled out my father's medication. Needing the bottle made my soul harden. I bitterly accepted that I needed something he had left me. The anger for him overcame my fear, which was good. I took two white pills.

Creak.

Someone was on the porch.

I returned to the living room window.

Peter was standing with his back to the window, his hood covering his hair and face.

I started to speak, but the hairs on the back of my neck prickled. I backed up.

He must have heard me because he slowly turned around and walked across the planks of the porch. His face stayed in shadow, hidden.

He crept closer to the shutters.

I crouched as some strange instinct took me over. I did not move.

"Go home," I whispered.
But the boy said nothing.

46

Friday, November 6, 1964
Sunrise 7:02 AM. Sunset 5:31 PM.

Again, I didn't get much sleep and what little rest I did get was filled with strange dreams. Luckily, I could only remember bits and pieces.

Knowing that I could have parents waiting for me at the school, one cup of coffee would not suffice. The dilemma was I didn't have a Thermos, and I was already thirty minutes late.

I tried to sip my coffee while I walked, but it was still too hot, and it burned my lips. I wanted to curse, but Amy's mother, Mrs. Rebecca, was out in the yard, so I bit through the pain.

Wiping the hot coffee off my mouth, I waved. "Good morning. Sorry. I just burned myself."

"Well, bad things happen to people who break the rules." She said with a sharp scowl.

I gave a little laugh.

"There's nothing funny about breaking the rules," she said, then walked behind her house.

I stopped. The words stung as they sank deep inside me. If kind Mrs. Rebecca was this upset with me, then there was no telling how the rest of the town would respond. I rolled my eyes at my own stupidity and continued to the school.

I took the street farther down the road that ran behind the Catholic Church. Clint was walking into the church, and we made eye contact. He shot me an evil grin and put his index fingers up to his head making horns as he shook his head in disapproval.

I narrowed my eyes at him. I wished that both of my hands weren't full so I could flip him off. I shifted my eyes away from him and continued on to work.

Walking up the hill, I soon realized the second cup of coffee hadn't been the best idea. I sloshed and burned myself, all the things any normal, well-rested person would have foreseen. I was a fool and decided to make the best of it the teacher way. I made it into a math problem.

Mr. Christian had two full cups of coffee. If he sloshed one-third of it on the ground after burning himself and spilled one-quarter on his shirt, then how much coffee did Mr. Christian have left in his cup to help him endure the day?

Less than halfway up the hill I could hear the children playing and yelling, which raised my anxiety, which made me push harder to hurry up the mountain, which made me spill more of my coffee. "Uhhrg!"

I hit the summit, and the kids perked up like kittens seeing their mom.

"Mr. Christian!" Scarlet said running to meet me.

"There he is."

"See, he's not dead," Amy said consoling, some of the younger kids.

Jason wrinkled his face. "Does he at least have a black eye?"

That last one caught me by surprise, but I ignored it. I was surprised no parents were waiting at the school door with shotguns and pitchforks. I'd received plenty of letters, calls, and personal appearances from parents. Thankfully, I'd never actually gotten pickaxes before. However, this is the backwoods, so I was ready.

"Sorry I'm late guys, but I'm even more sorry about yesterday."

Jason crossed his arms. "Did you get a whipping too for getting home so late?"

"No. You got a whipping?"

Jason nodded. "We all did. I was hoping you got one, too."

"Did you get whipped for not doing your homework?"

"Hell, no." Jason defiantly stated. "I only got the belt for getting home so late."

I continued staring at him even after he finished talking. I shook my head in shame. I had been so selfish yesterday. I hadn't thought about the kids getting in trouble. "I don't know what to say."

"Well, you should give it some thought because my daddy is pissed."

I gave him the *"I'm the adult, and you're the child"* look. "Jason, I know you're upset, but you need to clean up your language." I addressed the crowd. "Okay, guys, let me open the doors, and we can move inside."

Trying to save at least a bit of my coffee, I set one cup down on the bench, then went to open the school's doors, letting the kids go inside first. I scanned the group, looking for Peter, but he wasn't there.

"Anyone seen Peter?"

"No, sir," said Montana as he ducked into the schoolhouse. "Not since yesterday."

I followed and set my stuff and my other cup down on my desk. "Okay, okay," I turned to the chalkboard and erased the town rules I'd written the day before. I was writing a less personal version of my coffee math problem when I remembered my second cup out on the bench. I groaned and went outside to retrieve it.

When I got back inside, I put my second coffee on the coal stove to keep it hot, then I went to the board. The chalk wasn't there. I knew I'd put it down on the right side of the tray. "Where's the chalk?"

Children's laughter sang out and faded as they ran under the window and around the building. "Who went outside?"

Amy looked up. "I didn't see anyone."

I went to the door, sticking my head out. "Please get back in here and return ..." *There was no one there.* There was no one there, but I needed someone to be there.

I pressed my forehead into the door frame. "Not again. Oh, God, please, not again. There has to be someone there."

I turned my face back into the schoolroom. All the kids were staring at me with concern, confusion, and a few with amusement. I didn't care.

I slapped the inside wall with a flat palm. "I'll be right back."

I hurried around the side of the school. "Be real. Be real. Be real."

There were only leaves flipping lazily over a stack of cinder blocks.

"Shit!" I spat as I punched the sides of my thigh. I spun, scanning the outlying trees just beyond the dirt yard, shielding my eyes from the sun. No children were hiding behind the trunks, or none I could see.

"You want me to see you? Is that it? Then stop hiding! I'm not afraid of you. You're afraid of me."

I pivoted, then stepped out from the building, closer to the woods. "You're afraid of me," I hissed.

I held my arms out straight and gave the finger to the woods. "Fuck you!"

I huffed back inside, ignoring students' looks, though I could feel their eyes on me. I went to the board and found an unsteady, angled, smiley face. I stared at the board, then side-stepped directly in front of Carla's desk. "Who drew this?"

"Sir?" asked Carla.

I marched back to the board and pointed to it. "Who drew the smiley face on the board?"

"I thought you drew it," said Carla.

"No. No. I most certainly didn't draw that."

"Are you okay, Mr. Christian?" asked Montana.

"No, I'm not okay. I need to know where that came from."

"See, I told you he was crazy," ridiculed Jason.

I shot the little shit a death stare.

Amy stood. "I can erase it if you want me to."

"No, that's not the point," I groaned, leaning over.

Weezer raised his hand. "Maybe it was already there?"

I stood and wiped my face with my hands. "Yeah," I said with a long exhale. "That's it. Someone drew it this morning. You know how I am about saving the chalk," I lied, trying to save face instead of appearing batshit crazy.

"It's okay Mr. Christian."

"Well, I only have two more pieces left. I'm sorry for blowing up."

Scarlet stood. "We love you even if you are crazy."

I grinned at her. "Thank you, Scarlet." I forced myself to face the class. "Again, I'm sorry. Let's get back to class, shall we?"

Scarlet repeated, "Yes, shall we?" then sat down.

I picked up my coffee mug, and there, sticking out of it like a peppermint stick, was my chalk.

You little shits.

47

T he rest of the morning wasn't anything special. I mean that literally. I was kind of teaching, and the students were kind of learning. I could tell they were tired.

The children were moving so slow with their lessons I moved lunch and recess up an hour. It was a completely different version to my wild and crazy actions to the previous day. I needed to act like caring human being and be in the real world.

I scoffed. "Yeah, the real world here in Middwood. Ha."

Toward the end of our early lunch, the children were all outside and I was dozing off at my desk.

It was so quiet I could hear the birds chirping and the fluttering of squirrels through the brush. It was peaceful.

"The kids," I panicked.

I pushed my chair so hard I tipped over. I scrambled to my feet and bolted across the floor. I hit the entryway to the door.

They were all outside huddled together in a circle, quiet.

I rested my head against the frame. "They're okay."

There was no playing, no tag, no airplane, and no hide-and-seek. They were all in one group, talking.

Jason spotted me and slapped Weezer's arm, which set off a chain reaction until the entire class's wide eyes were on me.

"We weren't... We were just—"

I forced a smile and waved. "Take your time."

Rotating my shoulders, I dragged my feet back to my desk. "I'm a pill-popping jerk."

I lifted the hot mug of coffee from the stove and moved to my desk.

"Hello, Christian," a boy's voice greeted me from behind.

I jumped and dropped the coffee mug. It fell, hit my desk, then shattered on the floor.

Staring down at my drenched shirt, I exclaimed, "You! Of course, it's you!"

"It was an accident!" exclaimed Peter.

"Don't play dumb with me. You've had your fun," I said shaking the coffee off my arm. "That shit was hot! And you owe me a coffee mug."

"Okay. I'll get you one." He knelt and picked up the pieces. "I didn't mean to scare you—again."

"Of course not," I said sarcastically.

He stood with a grin. "So what are we learning?"

I leaned in and whispered, "What are you doing here?"

He whispered back, "I've come to be learned." He dropped the ceramic shards into the trash bin then sat on top of Carla's desk.

"You've come to be taught," I corrected.

"I know it's 'taught,' but saying it right isn't as funny."

"I don't want you here."

He leaned in and whispered again, "But that's before I saw you stand up to Joshua Johnson." He leaned back. "I

figured you were another boring square, but, boy, was
I wrong."

I crossed my arms. "I'm going to have a talk with your
mother about last night."

He threw up his hands. "That wasn't me. You can talk to
her if you'd like, but she knows it wasn't me either."

"Then how do you explain being out last night?"

"That's easy. When I heard the double whistle, I knew
you were in over your head... so I went to... help."

"Go home."

"It's the truth. My mom got a call from Carla's mom that
she hadn't come home yet. That's another part of the reason
I'm here. Listen—"

I crossed my arms and loomed toward him. "Why would
they call your mom? And I'm going to tell the sheriff you
broke into my house."

"I break into people's houses all the time. I didn't take
anything."

"Do you hear yourself? Doing it all the time doesn't
make it okay."

"I had to make sure you were clean, and you aren't, but
that's not the clean I'm talking about it." He shrugged. "My
dad was too, not pills, but a drunk."

I stopped.

A painful grin grew across his face.

I didn't say anything.

"No, wonder I like you so much, huh?"

I sighed, but I wouldn't let myself lose my temper. "Why
were you out after dark?"

He undid the first button on his shirt and flicked at the
charm on his handmade necklace and rolled his eyes. "I
already told you: the rules don't apply to me."

I held up a hand stopping him. "Magnolia said the same

thing last night, what does that mean 'the rules don't apply
to you'?"

His jaw dropped. "You were with Magnolia?"

I rolled my eyes. "No, not like that."

He doubled over laughing. "Oh my gosh, Christian. You
are full of surprises."

"Stop it."

"Fine. She's twisted. The rules most definitely apply
to her."

I sat back on top of my desk. "This is confusing."

He stood. "There's something you should know—"

Warm wet seeped into my pants, soaking my butt. I shot
up. "Oh shit," I groaned. "I sat in the coffee."

The student's whispered voices and dirt crunching shoes
approached. "Our talk will have to wait. They must have
finished with their little meeting." I strained to examine my
backside. "I would worry about my pants, but I don't think
they can think any less of me at this point."

"Christian, it's really important."

"I bet it is." I picked up the chalk and started writing on
the board. "I meant to have these questions on the board
before they came back in."

He paced behind me.

I glared at him. "Are you staying or leaving today?"

He widened his eyes. "You want me to leave?"

"Last night."

His face scrunched as his lips started forming words.

I held up my hand, "And don't give me any of that crap
that it wasn't you. It was. I don't know why you insist on
lying about it."

I turned back to the board. The rest of the class
continued to file in and took their seats, but Peter had
stopped.

My face went hot with anger. He was acting like a jerk. He couldn't deny last night. I heard him move toward the door. I saw him standing there. I pursed my lips in dismay.

"Teacher had a run in with Joshua Johnson last night, and he's not taking it seriously."

The students all gasped and exploded into chatter amongst themselves and at me in a chorus of chaos.

I raised my hands to the top of my head. "Peter, what are you doing?"

"I'm trying to save your life."

"It's true," cried Scarlet. "I was there. Joshu—the oldest one, he came for us last night!"

I groaned and pushed my palms into my eyes.

The class was arguing with each other. Jason yelled at Weezer, Montana was standing between Amy and Allison while they screamed at each other, Carla demanded the class be quiet, all while Scarlet sat alone sobbing.

My chest constricted. I pressed on my eyes harder, trying to hold in my seething anger. There wasn't any air in the room. I attempted a half breath, slammed my hands down on the desk, and I erupted, "Class!"

The room went silent.

"Thank you," I gritted my clenched teeth. "Now—"

Scarlet raised her hand. "Mr. Christian?"

"Not now, Scarlet!"

"But my paws up and..." whispered Scarlet.

Not holding back my irritation, I snarled, "What is it Scarlet?"

She pointed toward the door. "We have visitors."

48

I turned my eyes to see Franklin and the red-haired man from the church, standing inside the door. He was about half a foot taller than Franklin, and was wearing an impressive suit with a vest that hid his small round belly.

"Oh, fuck," said Peter.

Franklin was in full bulldog face. "Peter watch your mouth." Then he turned on me. "Mr. Christian, what in the hell is going on here?"

What little air remained in my lungs rattled out. I paused. "We were just..." My brain failed me. "Shit."

"Frank, I think I've seen enough," the other man said.

Franklin glared at me. "Mr. Christian, explain yourself before Mr. Bankward gets the wrong idea about you."

"I'm sorry, why are you here?" I asked the man.

The man gave me a stern stare.

Franklin shifted. "This is Randy Bankward, the trustee of the school." Franklin gave the word trustee extra emphasis.

"When we walked in the class was in hysterics. Surely, a

man of your age and experience can handle your students?" questioned Mr. Bankward.

"They were just excited." The words fell flat.

Franklin added, "As children get from time to time."

Oh shit, Franklin's trying to cover for me. This must be bad, I thought. I dug deep, trying to pull myself up. "Mr. Bankward, I apologize." I walked to him and shook his hand. "I'm Matt Christian."

He reached out and put my hand in a death clamp. "You'll need Jesus to deal with this."

"Really, they haven't been any trouble," I said as my face turned red.

Peter stood. "It was my fault." His tone prompted a certain level of respect, which confused me.

"Peter, I will handle this."

"Mr. Christian, please," he protested, shaking his head.

"Mr. Janowski? What are you doing here?" Bankward asked.

Peter stepped forward. "I've decided I want to finish school."

Mr. Bankward raised a finger to Peter. "Young man—"

Peter fired back, "Mr. Christian was attacked by Joshua Johnson last night."

Franklin turned sharply to me, his eyes full of confused fear. "Is this true?"

I stuttered as I regarded the three men bearing down on me. "I-I don't know who Joshua Johnson is. I wouldn't say we were attacked—Peter pulled a prank on me."

"It wasn't me!" Peter shouted holding his fingertips close to his eyes.

"Peter, it's not that big of a deal."

Peter screamed, his eyes at the two men, then pointed to me. "Do you see? He has no idea what's going on."

"So was it you or was it the Johnson boy."

Peter bounced on his feet in nervous anger. "He was walking Scarlet home, and Joshua attacked them."

Franklin turned to the class. "Where is Scarlet?"

She lowered her pouting face and raised her hand. "It's true."

Franklin and Bankward shot each other confused looks.

I raised my voice. "This is all ludicrous. He just ran past us and scared us. He didn't do anything." I flapped my arm at Peter. "Just say you're sorry and that will be the end of it."

Peter re-crossed his arms. "See, he has no clue what goes on in Middwood. That's why I'm up here screaming like a bozo. He deserves to know the truth before he gets himself or someone else killed."

The three of them continued to argue. The whole exchange was unexpected, but then again, the last six days had all been quite strange. I scanned the room; looked at my students' frightened faces. I snapped, raised my voice, and took control of the room. "Enough!"

Everyone went silent.

I caught a glimpse at the rage in Bankward's eyes, but I didn't care. "Gentlemen, you can finish your conversation somewhere else. You are scaring my students, and I won't have it."

"Son—" Bankward warned.

"Not in my school." I took a deep breath and pretended to calm, "We should get back to our lesson now. I'm sure you understand." I regarded Peter, "You. Sit."

Peter hesitated.

"Peter, sit!"

"Yes, sir." He quickly moved to his seat in the back of the class.

I waited for Bankward to make his next move. The silence was so loud I gulped.

Franklin slowly nodded his head like he was trying to convince himself to speak. "Mr. Christian is right."

Bankward sneered.

"Randy, we shouldn't do this in front of the children." Franklin leaned closer and whispered, but I could still hear him. "Now the entire valley will know."

Bankward moved his eyes to Peter and gave the slightest fake grin. I glanced at Peter, who waved at him grinning.

Mr. Bankward rotated and gave me a thin stare. "Matt, I'll wait for you after school, at my office."

"Where is your office?"

His eyes narrowed some more. I wondered if he could even see me. "The bank." Then he exited the schoolhouse.

Franklin shot me more of a look than a stare. His face was riddled with pain. "I'm sorry, Matt," he said with shame.

I was confused. "For what? Everything will be fine."

Franklin exited.

The children were all quiet, watching us with only their eyeballs, their little heads remaining stationary.

I took a deep breath. The room was still. I stood there, quiet and chastised. I was too tired to care.

Breaking the silence, Peter stood. "Well, that went great."

"Peter, sit down," I commanded.

The boy jumped and then sat.

I cradled my aching head, pained by the sound of my own voice. "No more out of you. You have done enough already. We will not discuss the previous topic any further. Is that clear, class?"

Scarlet raised her hand. "What about the question of the—"

I closed my eyes trying to save my head any further pain. "I said, is that clear, class?"

The students meekly answered, "Yes, Mr. Christian."

"Good. Now..." I was at a loss. I randomly picked a page and told them to start reading. Then I got up and walked outside.

I looked down into the deepest part of the valley. All the jagged rocks and space between me and the ground. I walked around the perimeter of the schoolyard. It was all the same, jagged rocks and air. I shook my head, thinking dark, damned thoughts. Maybe it was in my blood to suffer, to die, to drink, take pills, take my life.

"Mr. Christian," a little girl's voice said.

I closed my eyes and clenched my jaw. "I would turn around, but I know you aren't real."

"I'm not?" the high-pitched voice asked.

I turned. Carla was staring up at me.

"I'm real."

I nodded, then turned back to the valley.

"You are really messed up, huh?"

I rubbed the top of my head. "Carla, I think I am."

"It's okay. It happens a lot here."

"How do you mean?"

"Well, it's Middwood, the backwoods."

I rolled my eyes. "Not you, too," I whined, and she smiled.

"Everyone went home. I just thought I'd tell you."

I hadn't even noticed the kids leaving. They had either snuck past me, or I was that distracted by my own thoughts. "Thank you, Carla."

We walked side by side back across the schoolyard, and she waved to me as she too went down the hill.

"Have a good weekend."

"The weekend ..." How could I have forgotten about the weekend? But there wasn't the great thrill that used to come with the freedom. There was a worry, a fear. It would be a lot of time alone with my thoughts and my ghosts.

Before she was out of earshot I called, "Have a good weekend."

49

I trudged up the cinder blocks, which felt like I was climbing a full flight of stairs. I rubbed my face as I entered the school and crossed to my desk.

"That didn't go so well, did it?" Peter said.

I rolled my eyes. "Why are there kids everywhere I turn. Please, leave me alone."

"I can't do that."

Pointing as I walked toward him, I yelled, "Get out."

His eyes widened and he popped out of his seat. "You need to listen to me."

He slid one row over, but I pushed a desk out of my way so I could catch him.

He held up his hands. "Whoa, you're mad. I understand, but—"

"You have no idea. I'm tired and I don't have time for your shit."

He smiled as he backed away from me, which made me more annoyed. He jumped over another row of seats and ran out.

I grabbed all my crap and stuffed it into my bag. I stalked out of the school in a huff, moving away quickly.

Peter was waiting and followed after me. "I need to talk to you."

"Go home and... go scare some other people. God, why are you doing this?"

He caught up with me. "Do you know who that man was?"

"Bankward, who works at the bank," I grunted. "Don't make a pun joke."

"See? That's what I'm trying to explain to you. You have no idea who he is, what he does. Matt, stop!"

I stopped and turned to him, wanting nothing more than to drop to the ground. I'd never been so exhausted. My whole body ached, but I kept myself on my feet. "What I do know is that when you come around my life takes an even deeper downward spiral."

Peter lowered his eyes as he turned his face away. "He's the elder of the town."

"You mean like the mayor?"

"No, Christian, this is Middwood, the backwoods. He's an elder. He owns the bank. He owns the town."

I paused for a second, maybe more. I frowned. "So?"

"He came here to fire you."

My heart sank, and I could taste Peter's bitter truth in my mouth. "I deserve it. If I had my car, I would be out of here."

"If you had a car that's what I'd be telling you to do, but you don't, so you are in danger."

"In danger?" I said dismissively.

Peter looked at me with wide eyes. "He runs the town, and when there is a problem that Frank can't handle Bankward steps in. Bankward hates stepping in, and he's an asshole. However, you, you broke not one, but two of the town rules last night. Not only that, you also made every kid in Middwood break them, too."

"So, what does that mean? I have to say a few Hail Marys, walk backward in the moonlight? Why is everyone batshit crazy? I mean what are they going to do, kill me?"

Peter thrust his fingers from his temples toward me. "Yes, finally, you understand! When people break the rules, they end up dead."

"Oh." I faltered. "Wait. Are you serious?"

"Come on, man. I thought teachers were smart. When you go into Bankward's office you need to act like none of it was explained to you, get on your knees, offer your first born, suck his—"

"I get it."

"Do you?" Peter crossed his arms and did the one hand thing. "You seem to be taking it lightly."

"Well, I haven't slept since I got here and I'm a bit... out of it."

"Well stop by the Bucket, down a coffee, then go see Bankward. Just kiss his ass and don't be a jerk. Blame it all on me."

"Why?"

"Because I'm a troublemaker and I can handle the consequences."

"I'm not going to drag you into this."

"Don't worry about me."

"You broke the rules too, and I don't want you to get punished."

"Doesn't matter. I'll explain all of that later. Go."

I took a few deep breaths as I stepped away from the boy. If Bankward killed me, no one would come looking for me. I swatted that thought away. That was insane. If Bankward fired me I wouldn't have anywhere to sleep. Worst of all, I'd be outside with them, the ghosts.

"This isn't another trick, is it? To make me look stupid?"

Peter put his hands on my shoulders. "No. I promise."

"But—"

"I swear. I don't want you to get hurt."

For some reason, I believed him. If nothing else, I knew Middwood was a backwoods town and that I shouldn't put anything past the locals. Fear grew inside me as I decided to trust Peter.

"Okay. Okay." I walked away already planning the conversation with Bankward. I stopped and turned. "Hey, thanks for the ..." I motioned my index finger to him, then back to me.

"What are friends for?" he grinned.

Once I was out of Peter's line of sight, I broke into a steady jog down the hill. Not only did I need to pump some blood to my brain, but I also needed to get to the bank, and fast.

50

Once I got to the bottom of the hill, I crawled. At first I thought I was itchy from sweating despite it being full fall weather, but I wasn't cold. The top of my shoulders ached.

My brow scowled in furrowed contemplation. I stopped. *What was bothering me?*

I took a break from the puzzle as a dark car sped down the highway. It was going fast and weaving just enough to make me step farther onto the shoulder. As the car got closer, my heart rate picked up.

Move, move, my mind repeated over and over, racing with images of an event blurring so fast I couldn't make them out.

In complete juxtaposition to what was going on in my head, my feet sidestepped even farther away from the highway, closer to the railroad tracks. My eyes were fascinated by the blue car like it was the first I'd ever seen. My brain simply repeated the word like it was the only word I knew, *Car, car, car, car.*

I braced to feel the breeze of exhaust fumes, but instead of passing the car pulled into the shoulder, the rocks beating against its bottom like drunken curses. My feet continued to side-step as the vehicle corrected back into its lane, continuing its flight down the road. I caught a glimpse of the couple in the car, who appeared to be arguing while staring directly at me.

I followed the car with my eyes for at least half a mile as it continued down the road.

There was a pop inside my mind and what felt like a caffeine rush pulsed through me. I broke into a sprint. I had to get to my meeting with Bankward, but more than that, I needed to get off the highway.

51

At Keeper's Bridge, I slowed to a jog and looked over my shoulder at the empty highway. Still uneasy, I stopped. Closing my eyes, I listened for the sound of the angry car but heard only the rustle of a light breeze and the burbling of Looney Creek. I let out a sigh of relief and shed one layer of worry from my shoulders.

I dipped my head, wiped the sweat from my brow, and launched into another jog. Eddie watched me, but when I looked up to explain about the crazy driver, I was met with cold, stern eyes. Eddie held his hand up like a pistol and kept his aim on me as I crossed the bridge. I didn't stop moving, I couldn't. I didn't even allow myself to consider it. Instead, I focused my attention forward like a robot and continued to the bank. One fire at a time.

I turned left, and in the middle of Main Street on the left, I came to Middwood Bank. I paused outside. I didn't want to appear too out of breath when I met with Bankward.

The bank's architecture appeared to be like some of the

buildings I'd seen in books from the 1920s. The exterior was decorated with brick, wood, and mudstone. It had three large, plate-glass windows with pillars between each. The upper story had gabled dormers.

I walked through an offset entryway into the main lobby. My hard-soled shoes echoed through the cavernous space.

A young man came to greet me. "Yes, sir, how may I help you?" he asked, eying me with some suspicion.

"Matt Christian here to see Mr. Bankward, please."

"Oh. You. Wait here," he instructed, then went to a stairwell to the left of the teller line.

I tried to shake off his dismissive attitude. I swallowed hard and readied myself to go in. I had no problem kissing a bit of ass. Pride is for men who make more money than I do. I had to appear confident in front of the scary Mr. Bankward.

There were three teller windows with curved, brick adornments above each. I was admiring the copper plates on the walls when the young man cleared his throat behind me. "This way."

He led me up a stairwell that displayed more copper plates. *Fancy.*

At the top of the stairs, there was only one room. I was ushered in through the heavy, wooden doors and directed to take a seat.

Bankward's office was grand, the doors, the floor, and the furniture all made of rich wood. All together they gave the room a false warmth.

I sat alone in one of the two upholstered chairs facing his massive desk. I peered out the arched window to my left that looked down on Main Street. In front of the window stood an upright Zenith stereo with an open box of records beside it.

I wish I had that at the house, I thought.

To the right was a bookshelf that only housed two or three books. I strained to read the titles, but with my eyes and smudged glasses, it wasn't going to happen. Since I was already in the shit, I didn't want to look like I was snooping around.

Next to the stereo I spotted the crowning jewel of Bankward's office: a floating coal deposit on a two-foot-tall granite base. Of course, it wasn't floating, but the three thin metal rods boring into the rock from the base gave it that illusion. The inscription read, *"Coal, The Official State Mineral of Kentucky."*

My back was to the door of his office, and I didn't like that. I turned around in my chair to watch the door, playing nervously with my beard. The wait felt like an eternity, and my neck was starting to kink due to all my craning.

I returned my eyes to the Zenith. There was a light-green, forty-five-rpm vinyl leaning against the box of records. Since I had moved to Middwood, I hadn't heard any recorded music.

I got out of my chair and crouched in front of the record box. Zero Records was the biggest print on it, followed by Loretta Lynn.

The door behind me opened.

I straightened. "Mr. Bankward."

Eying me and pointing to the record, "Are you a fan of *Honky Tonk Girl*?" his tone was steady.

"I-I was just looking," I stuttered.

He walked past me, rounded his desk, and sat. "She was born and raised in Kentucky. She's a talent."

"Mr. Bankward," I sank into my chair giving my best humble tone. "I just wanted to apologize for earlier. If you had come any other day, you would've seen I manage my class quite well."

By the amused look he tried to mask with his developed poker face, I could tell he saw straight through my bullshit. "You don't say," he scratched the edge of his nose with his pinky finger.

"The students are already showing improvement in their writing and arithmetic. It's just we had a student, Peter Janowski. He showed up and—"

He was stern. "You can't let one student disrupt your class, Matt."

"No, sir, of course not, but he started in on some nonsense about ghosts and Joshua Johnson, and the class became hysterical."

"You don't say." Mr. Bankward searched my face for signs of something, but I did not know what. After a brief moment, he continued, "Well, stories of ghosts are popular in Middwood."

"I don't believe in ghosts."

"You don't?" he asked intrigued.

"No, sir."

"Well, Matt, real or unreal, the town has a certain way that it runs, and you are to abide by that. Whether or not you believe in ghosts, you are to follow the town rules." He paused and cocked an eyebrow at me. "Franklin did tell you about the town rules, right?"

I nodded.

He folded his arms on his desk. "What are the rules, Matt? Please, recite them for me."

I cleared my throat.

"No, stand up and do it. It will be like a lesson; I'll be the teacher, and you be the student."

Hot blood flushed my face as I rose out of my chair.

Maybe the bastard would like for me to get on my knees and lick his boots, too.

"Never turn your back on an open window. Never go out after dark or before the sun comes up. And ...run if you're out after dark."

He narrowed his eyes. "What's the third rule?"

"If it's dark and you're out, run home?"

"That's not the third rule." He narrowed his eyes. "Who told you that rule?"

"Scarlet."

"Scarlet?" he asked with raised eyebrows. "When did Scarlet teach you the rule."

"Last night."

"Last night? So, you lied to me? Franklin didn't teach you the rules?"

I'd rather take a pounding than listen to this man, but my conversation with Peter about me being in danger came forward in my mind, not to mention he had me by the balls when it came to my job. "I didn't lie. Mr. Mullis told me the first two. Scarlet told me the third."

"There. Franklin only told you the first two rules." He nodded. "Now I understand."

"Yes, sir."

"But still, you knew the first two, and you disobeyed them?"

"Yes, sir. I was trying to instill responsibility in the children. See, I assigned homework and the children—"

He waved a dismissive hand through the air. "I'll save you the breath, Mr. Christian. I don't care what you assigned or what they did or didn't do. Are we clear?"

"Yes, sir."

He pressed his palms on the top of his highly polished desk and stood. "You damn well better be. 'Cause if anything happens to my Allison or any of those kids because some big-city idea comes to your small-as-shit brain, then I will beat your ass into the dirt, and you better hope I don't come alone."

With small nods, I stayed silent as I took in his words.

"Good." Bankward straightened, then opened his arms and gave a smile like I'd just walked in to ask for a loan. "But listen, you can avoid all of that by just following the rules."

I sat quietly, and for whatever reason, I found my gaze on the floor between my shoes.

"But, Matt—Matt, look at me."

I met his gaze, trying to hide the anger in my eyes.

"Matt, I know it's hard to understand, but you just need to realize that what you did last night pissed off the entire town, because it affected their children."

I exhaled so hard I got dizzy. He was right. I screwed up. "I understand that now." I shook my head, pondering what to say next. I sighed. "I am sorry, Mr. Bankward. I couldn't live with myself if anything happened to one of the children because of my own prideful stupidity."

"You have those children one hour after sunrise to three o'clock. You are never to think or make decisions beyond your position. We won't have this conversation again. Are we clear?"

"Yes, sir," I affirmed.

He stared into me. "We'll start over and forget all about it. I'll have Franklin clean up his mess, and he'll take care of the town for you."

I mouthed the words, but it made me heavy as lead to do so, "Thank you, Mr. Bankward."

He grinned. "Great. I will be over in a few weeks to check in on you and your progress with the kiddies."

He got up and went to his stereo. He picked up one of his

records and then regarded me. "Have a good day. Class dismissed."

"Yes. Thank you."

I left Bankward's office with my ass chewed into pieces and stuffed into each pocket. Halfway down, Bankward turned on the Zenith, and heart-breaking country music poured down the stairs after me. Stepping into the lobby, the teller lines went silent. I tried to avoid the looks I got as I walked out. The clerk who had greeted me held his judgmental eyebrows high and his lips pursed.

I was a grown man, but I had gotten in trouble and had been sent to the principal's office, and everyone knew it. No wonder there were no parents at the school waiting to talk to me earlier. Middwood had its own punishment system, and it was effective.

Stop thinking, I told myself as I walked out and stared up at the steeple on the Methodist Church. The conversation with Bankward, the words of Mrs. Rebecca, Eddie, and the looks from the clerk looped in my head, churning with the events from the night before until I found myself working to hold in my screams.

I shook myself when I heard Eddie yell out curses that were nearly drowned out by the roar of an engine. I turned to see the blue car cutting across the little parking lot and heading straight for me. I quickly stepped back into the bank and watched through the glass door as the car rocked to a halt and a tall, slim man with barely any hair barreled his way to the bank's entrance.

Everything slowed down, and I became aware of seconds that seemed to hold on and stretch before they diminished into nothing, only to be replaced by another second. The man's feral growling, his skewed demeanor was unnerving. I focused on the object gripped in his curled arm: a rock. The stone resembled the shape and size of a human heart. The projectile left his hand and tumbled in the air. My chest pumped—upper chambers, lower chambers. Me, and everything around me, remained nearly frozen.

As the rock got closer to me, my focus moved to one side of it, where a painted white cross flashed.

52

The shattered glass of the door rang in my ears for several minutes after the rock connected with me, the impact sending me backward until I collided with the cold, smooth floor. My face burned.

Time resumed and gasps and screams from behind me echoed through the lobby. I touched my cheek to feel where I'd been hit. The left side of my face felt flat from the blow, but after a few touches, I found my cheek merely gashed. A mineral taste filled my mouth, and the top row of my teeth were in the most excruciating pain.

"Oh, shit," I groaned.

The broken glass door to the bank opened, and a pair of dark shoes approached me. I expected to look up and see the crazed man, but was instead met with the wide-mouthed shock of the pharmacist, Bill Self. The pain dug into my gums, and I had trouble pronouncing my words. I pointed to my face with pissed determination.

Self gawked at me. "Holy grits!"

"What happened?" I asked.

"You just had the shit knocked out of you, son. That's what happened. Are you okay?"

"I-I don't know."

"Come on, let's get you off the floor." He called to someone behind us. "Call the sheriff."

"Yes, sir," an effeminate man's voice answered. It must have been the snooty clerk.

"Tell him it was Gary Shindle."

"Who the fuck is Gary Shin—Jason Shindle? My student?"

"Yes, Jason's father."

"Good Jesus of grief!" I groaned.

Self looked up at the clerk. "I'll take him across the street and get him cleaned up."

"Where'd he go?" I asked looking up and down Main Street.

"He drove off. He won't be back."

"How can you be sure?"

"He smashed one of the bank's windows. He'll be so scared he might leave town," Self laughed.

I glanced at Self. Shithead would leave town, not for hitting a man with a rock, but for crashing the bank's window. I shook my head, but the pain stopped me.

Self helped me to my feet and guided me across the street while I recounted my dealings with the blue car on the highway.

Inside the pharmacy, he flipped the Open sign to Closed and directed me to a little closet of a bathroom. "Go in there and spit. It's good he hit you in the jaw and not higher up. Hell, then you might have a concussion, and there would be blood rollin' out everywhere. Bright side, right?"

"Right," I attempted to say, then stepped into the tiny bathroom. The phone rang somewhere in the store as I spit into the basin, expecting to see a tooth or two, but there was only spit mixed with blood. It didn't look that bad, but, damn, did it hurt like hell.

Bill called across the store. "Did you lose any teeth?"

I shook my head. "Nope, just some dignity."

"No, Frank, I think he's okay, just a bit bloody. Somebody is going to have to go have a talk with Gary." He paused. "Good, have Philip slug him in the face and see how he likes it, the bastard."

I spit again. "Well, hell, Frank, he threw a rock through the bank's window, so you know Randy is going to go jerk him bald." He paused. "Okay, okay. I'll holler."

A moment later Self pushed his way into the closet. "So you still got all your teeth?" He snorted. He handed me a small paper cup with a clear liquid in it. "Swish this around, but don't swallow it. It might burn a bit, but it will help clean your mouth out."

"What is it?"

"Moonshine."

I did as he said but swallowed it on purpose.

"Hell!" I gasped.

"You don't listen so good, do ya?"

He led me to a chair and gestured for me to sit. As I did, he pulled up another stool, looked at me, and smacked my face.

"What the fuck?" I stood, holding my cheek.

He looked at me apologetically. "Sorry, I was testing to see how bad the pain is."

I regarded him cautiously. "It's bad enough."

He sighed and patted the stool. "Sit down. I promise I won't slap you again."

I pulled the stool back and sat.

"You likely have a cracked tooth in there. You'll have to

go see the dentist, which is a fate worse than death around here. The actual dentist is fine, but his assistant—"

"Clint? Please, no."

"You know him?"

"He showed up outside my place the first night."

"Yeah, that sounds like him." Self shook his head in disdain. "I told that boy's aunt when he was young they needed to watch him. He was always experimenting or cutting on something. One time I think he boiled a cat just to see what it would look like."

"Seems like the type," I said.

He slapped his thighs then spun and headed toward the far aisle of the drug store. "The dentist comes through once a month. But you're in luck. He'll be here next Friday."

"I have to wait a whole week? Yeah, I'm real lucky."

Self laughed, "That's right, young man. Don't let Shindle break your spirit. The dentist sets up shop there in the big store. If you can't wait that long you can drive down to Lynch or Benham. They are two of the nearby coal towns, but then again, you don't have a car. Oh, well." He ducked down. "You will need an anti-inflammatory for your jaw and something for the pain." He popped up and pointed to me. "Are you allergic to anything?"

"Die don' dink sho," I said not even understanding the babbled words that came out of my bloody mouth.

Responding like he understood. "Uh huh. No matter." He moved toward the counter, placing aspirin next to the register.

He returned holding a bottle with a big "sorry you feel like shit grin on his face." "Use the aspirin, and I'll put some Anbesol in your bag as well, it will help some until you can get to the dentist." He looked at me empathetically. "It hurts pretty bad, huh?"

"Are you going to slap me again?"

He chuckled. "No. But I'm thinkin' that sucker is going to scream like a cat in heat later on." He flattened his huge lips. "Have you ever taken painkillers?"

My eyes flipped up to his. *Oh God, yes,* I pleaded. "Once or twice."

"And you did okay with them?"

"Oh, yeah, I did fine."

"Okay. Wait right here." He made his way back behind the pharmacy counter and searched one of the shelves.

He returned with a mischievous grin. "I'm giving you a few of these. You're going to love them. Go home and take one, then go straight to bed. These will knock you out. Tomorrow, if you don't get your car back and you don't have to go anywhere, you can take the second one, and the final one on Sunday." He grinned while he warned me with his index finger. "Don't tell Franklin. It will be our little secret."

A warm feeling ran through me. I have no idea what came out of my mouth, but it was meant to be a heartfelt thank you.

53

On the walk up Windy Hill, my face felt like a kickball, big, red, and fat. My jaw was loose and bouncy like there was a layer of water underneath the skin. The more I walked, the stronger the pain got. Self told me if he had a vehicle he would drive me home. Apparently, he lived in one of the houses close to me.

I wanted to be home so bad, but every step up the hill was like another rock to the face. This was the type of day where you needed a car, or maybe someone to go home to who would make you an ice-pack while you laid on their lap and complained. If I was getting weepy, then it was worse than I thought. I get weepy when I'm sick, but I wasn't sick. I'd been stoned for being a sinner by a Cro-Magnon Pharisee.

After the first two people glared at me on Windy Hill Lane, I stopped making eye contact with passersby. At that moment, I hated them as much as they hated me.

At the house, I went straight up to the bathroom and turned on the shower, then I took the bottle out of the bag Self gave me and shook out two pills and held them. "Up

yours, Randy Bankward." I spat. "That goes for the whole
back-ass town."

I dipped my wrist for the third pill to fall out. "Fuck
me, too."

The room filled with steam, so I got naked and got in. I
closed the curtain and plopped down in the shower, the
water flowing over me, burning hot. I leaned back against
the cold porcelain edge and screamed, jolting me and
sending pain to my cheek. I relaxed once my body warmed
the surface.

I tried to open my eyes, but they felt like they were glued
shut. It took three tries, but, finally, they opened. I stared
into the dark, sideways world of the hallway.

This is the backwoods mister. It's so backwoods its sideways.

I walked forward but realized I wasn't moving. I looked
down. My feet were walking, but they weren't touching the
ground.

I can fly.

I tried to soar to the end of the hall, but nothing
happened.

I can float at least. Who wants a stupid superpower like float-
ing? I thought.

I tried to reach the floor with my toes with a significant
lack of success. Then I decided to push off the wall my face
was up against. It took me a second, but I finally realized I
wasn't floating, I was on the hall floor.

I pushed myself up, and the vertigo was so severe I
gripped the sides of my head and squeezed my eyes shut.

I was in front of the Tomb, naked and soaking wet. I was
cold and starving.

Then I heard a voice. *"I will come for your ass, and you better hope I'm alone."*

A fearful frown bent my face. "Mr. Bankward?" I whispered.

"Do you understand what I'm saying?" the voice asked.

"Mr. Bankward, where are you?" I called out.

He cried with fake, pitiful, childlike agony, *"I'm in the closet. Let me out."*

I gasped. "The devil painting." I covered my mouth to keep from talking.

I lay there quietly and listened to the devil until my stomach's voice grew louder than his. Being hungry was enough of a reason for me to creep past the closet that held whispering devil painting. My courage rose, and I pointed an authoritative finger at the door. "You stay in there, Devil. You stay in that closet. Ha."

I was descending the stairs to the living room when they transformed into a flat, slippery rock. I slid with a whistle. I was on a mission. There was one thing that a man would do anything for. Unfortunately, I was downstairs, and I forgot what that was.

I rose and fell when a wave went through the room. I leaned against the stairwell like a drowning person would hold an ocean buoy. My face drifted toward the kitchen.

"The kitchen," I exclaimed. "That's right." I was hungry. I knew there was a reason.

I couldn't walk anymore, so I rolled myself along the wall toward my destination. I abruptly stopped. My stomach didn't like rolling. I was dancing with the room and the floor was stepping on my body. "Oh, boy, stop that." I squeezed my eyes together and took a deep breath. "Don't throw up. Do not throw up."

I was twirling around the room, despite walking in a

straight line. Or not so straight because walking into the kitchen, I found myself face-planted into the living room wall. "Why am I up? I need to go to bed before I hurt myself."

The kitchen answered in a roaring voice that seemed to come from God himself, "You want some food. You'll have to eat cereal again."

"I happen to like cereal, thank you very much," I answered matter-of-factly.

The voice was silent, and then in a softer tone replied, "Well, in that case, I'll get your bowl ready."

"Ah, thank you. You know, I'm not feeling so well, and I could use a friend."

"Matt, I know what it's like."

"I know you do and that is why I'm so thankful."

I smiled. Such a nice kitchen.

The living room carried me and dropped me off at the dining room, and there it was. My favorite bowl from my Rose-Mary Grand waited for me on top of the table. The off-brand cornflakes were already poured in the bowl with a spoon. The spoon was so shiny I shrieked in horror.

"I'm just as much afraid of you as you are of me, heifer," the spoon said.

I immediately picked it up and felt a few stray cereal flakes kissing my feet. I made peace with it and turned back to the spoon. "I thought you were too shiny, but now I completely understand."

I'm not sure how I got there, but I was in the dining room munching on dry cereal with my new best friend, Shiny Spoon. Spoon was talking a mile a minute about everything. He or she was giving me the scoop about everyone, which was funny because, while it was in my mouth, I couldn't understand what it was saying. I was being polite and listening, although I never cared much for gossip.

"Speaking of that, I'm surprised this crunching isn't hurting my tooth."

"I know, I know, it's good stuff."

The cold from the dining room window behind me was nice since the rest of me was so warm. Spoon was talking when my attention drifted to a warming sensation on my back. The living room shutters were open. It was nice to have something to look at even though it was dark outside. Something to distract me while I ate my snack and talked to Spoon. My head plopped to the left. I was dumbfounded because the shutters were open in the dining room, too. When had I opened the shutters?

I held my index finger up to my mouth. "Shhh," I told Spoon.

I was munching the cereal when a figure walked out from behind me. Spoon kept talking, but its volume rose as it spoke. My eyes followed the figure from my left shoulder as it moved around the corner of the table. It was human, but without detail, like a dark shadow. I tried to blink when it walked in front of me, but my blinks felt more like winks. "That's not right." My crunching slowed, but then I figured I was being rude.

"Oh, hello," I said, but it sounded like "herro" in my ears, and I laughed and spit, a few rogue flakes jumped from my mouth. "I'm sorry. I'm so high. Forgive me."

The figure moved into the kitchen. I shrugged it off, and I refocused on Spoon, who was complaining about the students. "Now, Spoon," I said, "You've to give the kids time to adjust. All that school stuff is hard."

I took another big bite to cut off whatever it was going to say next, but the taste was perfection. It was corny crunchy followed by fresh, creamy goodness.

"Hey, where'd this milk come from?" I looked to Refrigerator, but Refrigerator wasn't going to give me any clues. She had been quiet the whole time, like a good Christian woman who stuck to her morals. "Amen!" I held up my spoon in victory and shouted, "Thanks for the milk!"

The smell of a farm animal hit me, or at least the scent I associated with a cow. Maybe it was just the sound of my snoring or the ripples of milk washing up the flat side of my cheeks.

I raised my head.

I was face down in a milky pool at my dining table. There were two-toned corn flakes dried on the horizon. My eyes strained to focus on the living room window, but regardless, there was early morning sun shining in through the shutters.

I massaged my left cheek. The pain pulsed, but my skin was cold, clammy, and bloated from sleeping in the liquid puddle. "Great. I'm a ghost child." I said while I tried to hold my head steady with one hand and wipe the milk away with the other. I pushed the chair from the table and paused, making sure I wasn't going to puke. More milk and little tan shards lay on the floor between my feet. "What the hell were those pills?" I cocked my head to the side. "That shit was great."

54

S aturday, November 7, 1964
        Sunrise 7:03 AM. Sunset 5:30 PM.

I got cleaned up and dressed in my pajama bottoms, a white undershirt, a flannel shirt over that, and my cozy socks. I relaxed because nothing mattered, because today was a gift, a reward. It was Saturday, and Saturdays are a joy to teachers everywhere. Saturdays are a blessing from the Lord God Almighty, giving teachers a break from children, alive or undead. Teachers, we love our jobs and we love our students, but those two days away are the only reason we don't double our neckties or scarves around a water pipe and jump.

Sure, I could enjoy the sun for a full day, but I needed rest. Besides getting my car back and seeing a dentist, sleep was the only thing that could help me. I just wanted to open the shutters, relax on the sofa, and drink my coffee. Then, later on, revisit the kitchen for another bowl of the finest generic cereal Middwood money could buy, if I had any left. It would be heaven with no cares and no problems.

I made a pot of coffee and I settled onto the sofa. The dark, rich, caffeine aroma in my cup made my mouth water. I closed my eyes in sweet anticipation. I raised the rim to my lips and braced for the hot goodness.

Knock, Knock.

"Crap," I growled and whipped my head back onto the sofa's cushions, spilling some of my coffee onto my lap in the process. "Dammit."

I regained my composure but held a steady frown.

A dwarf of a figure appeared in my window.

"Shit," I hissed to myself.

"Matt, open the door," Franklin barked.

"Do I have to?" I whined.

"It's important."

Of course, it was important, important to him, but I'm sure I couldn't have cared less.

I cracked open the door. "I'm not wearing any pants."

Wrinkling his nose he said, "Let's not play this game again."

I sighed in defeat and stepped out of the way. I opened my eyes to shut the door. Franklin's Old Spice cologne overpowered the subtleness of my coffee.

"Have a seat," he instructed.

I waited on the sofa for what the elder of Middwood, Randy Bankward, had decided to do with me.

"Do you want some good news first?"

"They still make that?"

Franklin huffed out a laugh, "Casteel said he will drop off your car first thing after sun-rise."

I tried to be excited, but my tongue touched my tooth and I groaned.

"How's your tooth?"

My tooth throbbed so bad it was like it wanted to answer for me. "I'll be fine once I get to a dentist."

"I'm sure it hurts like hell. Bankward is furious at Gary, and since he shattered his door, he spent the night in jail."

"Because of the door? What about what he did to me?"

Frank held out a hand and started over. "Look, luckily Mr. Bankward is a sensible man."

"Is he?" I crossed my arms.

"Yes, that, and that Peter came forward about... the boy...the ghost."

I couldn't help but roll my eyes.

He searched my face, and he wasn't pleased by what he saw. "You making light of it isn't helping you."

"Not helping me? What do you mean?"

I wasn't sure if he was referring to my situation with Bankward or my lack of buy-in to Middwood's ghosts. To be honest, I didn't know what I believed at this point.

"Matt, I will admit I am not a fan of you acting like this. What you did yesterday, that is not the Matt that I hired a week ago."

I pointed to my face. "The Matt you hired last week wasn't getting stones thrown at his face by crazy ..." I trailed off because it wasn't true. Marbert had punched me in the face and the stomach.

I was a lousy teacher and probably, under it all, a terrible person.

I sank into the sofa. "I'll be honest with you. I'm trying, but this town is so... different."

He expression softened. "I'm sure it hasn't been easy for you."

"Easy? This town is anything but easy. I can't sleep. Kids keep playing nasty pranks on me... God, I hope they are real kids who are doing those things. Again"—I pointed—"rock to the face. Something is always happening."

He leaned forward. "Is Thursday the first time you were outside after dark?"

I didn't know how to answer that question. I didn't want to talk to Mr. Bankward again. "What happens if someone breaks the rules?" I asked.

"You're avoiding the question." Then he leaned back. "Well, it depends on the situation, but to be honest, when someone breaks one of the rules they often don't live to tell about it."

I indicated outside. "Is that because something happens to them out there, or is it because someone in the town does something to them?"

"There are reasons the rules are in place, and if you step outside of authority, then you're asking for trouble."

I narrowed my eyes and gave him an "eat shit" grin. "You're avoiding the question. Is that what your daughter did? She broke one of the rules?"

Hate pushed across his face and filled his voice. "I'm not here to talk about my daughter." He stood.

I waved my hands. "Okay, okay. Sorry. I'm sorry, that was a terrible thing to ask. Please, sit back down."

Franklin's glare subsided, and he sat back down.

I had crossed the line, but I was glad he decided to stay.

He took his time, then began speaking. "Mr. Bankward has made arrangements for you to make a public apology to the parents, children, and the rest of the town for your actions."

"Church?" I groaned. "Again? What if I don't go?"

"Matt, don't give me grief," he warned, impatiently. "Show up, say you're sorry, and then life will resume with no hiccups."

"That simple, huh?" I leaned forward on the sofa. "You know, Bankward threatened to beat me up."

"To be honest, Matt, I'm surprised no one took a swing at you. You can't mess with someone's kids and not expect to pay for it."

I knew all about people taking swings at me because of their kid. "Middwood is an eye for an eye kind of place. I got the message."

"I hope so. I don't want to see anything else happen to you."

His words made me feel better.

"Fine." I sat back on the sofa. "I'll be there Sunday."

"Good." He slapped his thighs and rocked himself forward to get momentum to stand. "And I suggest that you stay home for the rest of the day. The fewer people who see you until church, the better and safer for you. I'll have the sheriff pick you up in the morning."

"The sheriff? Are you serious? Isn't one rock enough?"

He ignored my joke. "He'll walk you in. Unless you want to chance another attack? Plus he volunteered. Luckily, you've made a few good impressions."

I raised my eyebrows. "I have?"

"Listen, Matt. This is serious. You haven't done anything else to break the rules have you?"

I had gone outside after dark numerous times. I wondered if I should tell him about the possum, that I moved my bed, or put the painting in the closet.

"No," I lied. "That's the only time."

He nodded. "Good. Make sure you don't get into any more trouble."

He slapped my shoulder, and every nerve in my jaw lit up. "Gaw, fuck!" I shrilled, holding my jaw.

"Good Lord, son, I barely touched you."

I cradled my face. "I know..." I sighed. "I just need to get to the dentist."

Franklin shook his head in concern. "We have a dentist, he's a good man, but that won't be until next week."

"I don't know if I can wait that long."

Franklin moved to the kitchen. "I'll do you a favor and get you taken care of, but you have to keep this to yourself." He stopped. "Can you do that? Keep a secret?"

"If it takes the pain away, yes, I promise."

Franklin nodded, then picked up the phone. "Tonya, do you have time today to help out Matt, the new teacher? He got the shit knocked out of him." He paused. "Gary creamed him in the face with a rock." He paused again. "Yes, that's what I'm asking." Pause. "I know." He paused and glanced at me. "I think so." Pause. "Yeah, can you send Peter to pick him up?" Pause. "That will be great." Pause. "One o'clock? He'll be here waiting. Thanks, Tonya."

Franklin hung up and grinned. "Peter will be by to pick you up in a few hours."

"Is Tonya a dentist?"

He searched for the right words. "Something like that. She'll get you taken care of." He pointed at me. "But remember, it's a secret."

55

A few hours later, Peter honked the horn, and I left to get my face fixed.

"Sorry I'm late, I had to work on the engine a bit to get her working."

"I would ask what was wrong with it, but I don't know anything about cars."

"Your face is fucked."

"Don't say that."

"Well, it is. So much for being new and shiny."

I grinned and shook my head. "After being a such an idiot, I deserve it."

"Get with the times. The word is bozo, but it's cool, I'm just pickin' on ya."

I shrugged. "I know, but...I'm sorry for all the things I said Friday."

"What about what you said on Thursday."

I huffed. "Jeez. I'm super sorry about that."

"Then it's cool."

I wanted it to be that simple, but I didn't know if it could be done. The "father" word fight had been terrible. My chest tightened because I needed him to know that I hadn't been myself that day.

I knew I shouldn't discuss this with him even though he knew about the pills. I was sure acting like Jekyll and Hyde was a pretty good indicator.

"I'm sorry." I didn't know what else to say, but I wanted to say something. He needed to hear it, and I needed to say it. "Thanks for looking out for me."

~

P eter's house was outside of town over the railroad tracks that ran parallel to Looney Creek. As Peter and I drove, I thought it was funny that his home was so far out that it was considered to be "in the sticks."

The drive down WPA Road was nothing but witch trees decorated with little white crosses. My toothache worsened every time we passed one. Finally, shanties and trailers appeared, but the composition of the homes was wild to my Georgian eyes. Some of the houses were level to the road, but the next could be ten feet higher on the mountain while the next looked like it was built in a hole. It was Kentucky's equivalent to a mid-rise apartment building.

"They'll stick homes wherever they'll fit, won't they?"

"We stick them where we need them, I guess."

I hadn't been to a student's house since the beginning of my teaching career, four years ago. It wasn't such a big deal then since I knew the family, and they even helped me get the job by making a few calls. Unsurprisingly, they disappeared after the incident with Darlene.

~

A fter about ten miles we turned onto what looked more like a wagon trail from the TV show *Bonanza*. Pebbles pelted the bottom of Peter's truck, and the ruts in the road from a previous rain caused us to shake feverishly. He slowed down until the truck only bumped along.

"We'll make it. Just hold on." He shook his head at me.

I hadn't realized I was gripping the seat with my left hand and holding my cheek with my right.

About a mile farther along, the road merged into a single lane. He pulled across the grass and parked next to a little, white Ford.

Peter lived in a simple, older, green house with yellow trim, but they had built on an addition with wood that didn't match.

Peter opened the door. "And here I go."

"What? Where?" I asked.

"Don't worry about it. I'll be in there in a bit." He pointed. "Just go up to the back door and wait." With that, he circled the back of his truck and walked toward a set of large, worn, wood outbuildings.

He left me sitting in the truck. I grumbled to myself anxiously and exited the vehicle, then walked toward the house. There were so many holes in the yard; little sunken pieces of ground. I, of course, almost stepped in one. I looked around the yard. They were everywhere.

Landmines, I joked to myself, but then the thought didn't seem so funny. *This is the backwoods, mister,* so I decided to proceed with caution.

After walking through about fifteen yards of peril, I made it to a set of rickety, old steps that led up to the porch. I was glad I wasn't a big man, I'm not sure the steps could

have taken the weight. The porch was in the same deterio-
rated state as the stairs.

Something buzzed past my head. I ducked and swatted.
It was big, whatever it was. It attacked again from the right
and then another from the left. I ran under the cover of the
porch. They were all around me, but I couldn't hone in on
what they were.

"Hummingbirds," a velvet voice said behind me.

I jumped and grabbed my jaw, then I let out a little
laugh.

Tonya grinned at them. "Beautiful, aren't they?"

"Yes. They are."

A hummingbird hovered at a little glass cup hanging
from a porch beam. Cups were hanging on every post, and
hummingbirds swarmed around each of them.

"You must be very intelligent." She smiled, relaxing into
the conversation. "Peter goes on and on about you. Every
day he comes home with a story about you. I'm so glad he's
in school. He thinks most people are boring."

A hummingbird darted past my ear with a strange
swishing, buzz that caused me to duck, which made my jaw
pulse. She laughed at my reaction. "They seem to be curious
about you."

"That, or they want to eat me."

"They're aggressive, territorial creatures," she said.

I eyed another tiny, winged creature scouting me. "I
see that."

"They don't attack humans. They probably think you're
another post on the porch or your beard is a nest." She
laughed, covering her mouth. I grinned back at her,
watching her trying to tame the laugh into a giggle. "I'm
sorry, Matt."

I finger combed my beard. "I'm not that skinny, am I?" playing along with her good humor.

"You'll be fine as long as you aren't evil."

How did she know? I raised my eyebrows. "Excuse me?"

Turning to the birds feeding from the small jars. "They're known for promoting happiness, beauty, and for warding off evil spirits." She spoke with a soft, confident passion and pulled out a pendant hidden between her breasts. "See?"

I regarded both the pendant and her breasts. "Yes, beautiful."

"Are you an evil spirit, Matt?"

"I'm not a spirit, and I don't think I'm evil, but sometimes I wonder."

"You mean you don't know?" she smiled with a laugh.

Oh, God. Is she flirting with me? Oh, brother, I haven't even made it inside the door. However, she was a beautiful woman, so I gave it my best try. "I guess you can give me a verdict at the end of the evening."

She laughed again. "Okay. I like that. You have a deal."

Peter ran into the front yard from the side of the house carrying a sloshing pitcher of water in one hand and a coffee mug in the other. Tonya slapped the side of her thigh. "Peter, there you are."

"No, there you are. I guess you guys have been getting to know each other?"

Tonya seemed embarrassed. "I was just telling Mr. Christian how much you're enjoying school."

Peter nudged her with the side of the pitcher. "Don't tell him that."

She shrilled, "Peter! That thing is freezing."

He raised his eyebrows and gave her a big grin. "I know, that's why I did it."

She swatted at his arm. "I'm going to beat you."

"Well, I didn't want him to know I liked school."

"Oh? I had no idea," I gloated.

"Well, it's mainly because you are so pathetic."

"Peter," Tonya gasped.

"I'm kidding, Mom." He shot me a look. "Trust me. I'm mostly kidding."

Everyone was quiet for a moment, then Peter broke the silence. "Oh, yeah, here you go." He poured the water into the cup. "May I offer you a drink sir?"

"Oh, thank you, but I'm fine."

Peter laughed. "No dummy, this is why you're here."

I glanced over at Tonya to inquire what he was talking about, but she gestured for me to take the mug.

"Oh. Okay," I said, taking it. It was strange because I had almost forgotten about my tooth, about that dull, burrowing pain. "I won't waste any more of your time. Franklin sent me over here for my tooth?"

Tonya and Peter nodded at each other.

"Have some water and tell me about it," she said.

"Well, I'm surprised you haven't already heard." I took a sip, but there was no nasty taste or odor. It was so cold I marveled at how it wasn't frozen.

"Holy shit that's—" I glanced at Tonya, grabbing the size of my face. "I'm sorry," I groaned.

"No, he's not. He has a filthy mouth."

I widened my eyes. "Don't tell her that."

"You two, stop." She swatted me on the arm. "Matt, drink."

"Yes, ma'am." I took another healthy swallow. It was so clean. I shook my head. "Oh my gosh, that's the best, frostiest water I've had," I said, then gulped down the rest. "Can I get another glass?"

Peter poured more water from the plastic pitcher. "Sure."

"So one of the dads was pissed at me and tagged me in the face with a rock. It hurt like hell."

"It looks like it," Tonya nodded.

"Can I do it, Mom?" Peter asked with eagerness.

"Let him finish his water."

"Do what?" I asked.

"Nothing," she said, waving me off.

I finished the glass.

"Here, Mr. Christian, I'll take that." He looked at his mom. "Now?"

She nodded. "Yes."

56

Peter slapped me in the jaw.

I held my cheek in surprise. "What the hell are you doing?"

"How does your jaw feel?" Peter asked with wide, excited eyes.

My mind raced with explosive expletives, but I guarded my tooth instead. I massaged my mouth, attempting to soothe the pain...but there was no pain.

"It doesn't hurt anymore, does it?" Peter asked with his face beaming.

There was a silence in my mind like a fuse had blown. "How?" I muttered, then turned to Tonya. "How did you do that?"

"Welcome to the backwoods!" Peter shouted and then laughed.

I looked at Tonya's grinning face. "Tell, Franklin he owes me one."

"Wait. You did this?"

"Not me; the land, the valley."

"The what?" I questioned.

She touched then squeezed my shoulder. "This is Shawnee land, and the land has power."

I cocked my head and nudged her with my elbow. "You mean like magic?"

She smiled and held up her hands to the sky. "The land, the water, all blessed by the spirits."

"The spirits of what?"

"Spirits of the valley."

I smiled in delightful confusion. "No really, what did you put in the water? BC Powders?"

She laughed. "Peter said you were funny. I do hope you will join us for lunch?"

I ran my fingers over where my cut was. "Well, I—"

"And, no offense, Mr. Christian, but you look like you could use a good meal. Peter said you only eat cereal."

"But my face?" I said pointing to it.

Peter chimed in, "I know. It's awful."

"Matt, stay for lunch and we can talk."

I was nervous because it would be my first meal with a beautiful, single woman in a long time, and on top of that, she may have just drugged me or healed me. Regardless, I was grateful.

Finally, I let go of my face. "Well, to be honest, I can also make a mean grilled cheese."

She and Peter both laughed.

Peter pulled on my arm. "Does that mean you'll stay?"

Oh, God. What was I supposed to do? Run. Throw up. Play dead. I looked at Peter's longing face, then Tonya's gentle grin. "I-I suppose so."

"That's great! She's a great cook, too, Christian."

"Here, Peter, take the glass back and bring Mr. Christian a mason jar of it."

"Okey-dokey," Peter said, then ran toward one of the side buildings.

A low growl came from inside the house, and I turned as a creature stalked behind Tonya. It looked like a shaved possum, a skeleton covered with gray fur. Even its eyes were gray. My breath went thin, a ghost possum.

I pointed. "Tonya, look out."

She turned. The creature barked. She grabbed her chest and began to laugh. "Oh, Matt, you startled me!"

"Is it real?" I asked blinking.

She knelt, picked it up, and kissed it. "This is Baby."

"What kind of animal is that?"

"Oh, Matt, you are too much. She's a Chihuahua."

"That's the largest Chihuahua I've ever seen." All I could think was how grateful I was to have already shaken her hand.

"She's a long-haired Chihuahua." She moved Baby's head toward her. "Aren't you, precious? She would have more hair, but she has the mange, but we can't seem to get rid of it."

"Even with your magic water?"

"Some things are beyond magic or"—she raised a finger —"they're illusions." She smiled.

"Which is it?"

"I'll never tell," she smiled coyly. "Poor, Baby," Tonya said. "She has cancer, too, and she's blind."

The dog was hideous and knocking on death's door. "Oh, God. I'm sorry to hear that."

"I know I should have her put down, but I just can't bring myself to do it. She doesn't seem to be in any pain." The two exchanged kisses. "Are you, sweetie? Momma loves her Baby."

Tonya was beautiful, but I was disgusted. Even though

I'd already shaken Tonya's hand, I realized she'd touched her dog before I arrived. I needed to wash them as soon as possible. "Poor... dog indeed," I said, not even wanting to wipe my hands on my pants.

The dog looked in my direction.

I closed my eyes. As if Baby knew what I was thinking, she growled at me.

"There, there, Baby. You know everyone is afraid of you at first. It's part of your charm, sweet girl."

Blind or not, Baby's dead, gray eyes swayed like she was trying to find me. I avoided her gaze by glancing over at the hummingbirds.

"Do you have any pets?" she asked.

"Um. No."

"A dog is a good thing to have in the valley—a living alarm."

Or a canine corpse with the mange, I thought.

Baby barked.

Tonya turned and walked into the house. "Come on. I hope you like meatloaf."

The door opened into a small room filled with mud-caked boots and coats, then opened into the kitchen. She led me into a small dining area. "Matt? Is that short for Matthew?"

"Yes, but please, call me Matt. Sometimes I'm called Mr. Christian so often I forget what my first name is." I moved through the kitchen to a simple table with two wooden benches and sat.

She placed Baby down on a mound of towels on the floor at the entrance of a hallway. "I'm sure that can be difficult with so many children. I don't see how you do it."

"Back in Atlanta I had more students, but that's completely different."

"Why did you leave Atlanta?"

"Um..." I stalled.

She put her hand on top of mine. "I'm sorry. I didn't mean to pry."

"I just needed a change. The hustle of the city was starting to get to me. My nerves."

She removed her hand and studied me. "But there's nothing to worry about?"

I continued, "I'm completely fine. I just decided the country life sounded better. I have enjoyed it..." I got stuck on my lies.

She forced a smile. "I understand. Everyone has something they'd rather not discuss."

The conversation had taken a wrong turn. I moved to adjust my glasses when the thought of Baby's skin on my fingers saved me. "May I use your restroom?"

"Of course," she pointed down the hall behind her. "It's the third door, down on the left."

I excused myself and circled wide to avoid the dog. Baby lifted her head as she searched for me with her foggy, granite eyes. She turned toward the hall entry, her nose pointed right at me, and let out a snarl.

"Baby, it's okay," assured Tonya.

The dog lowered her head onto her bed, but still showed her teeth in disapproval.

In the hallway, there was a musky scent, much like the one I'd noticed in the schoolhouse. The floor pitched downward. I assumed it was the recent addition to the house. The floor was more rigid beneath my feet, there was no pad under the carpet, and I could feel the change in the surface in my knees and back. The smell of moist earth got stronger.

All the doors in the hall were closed, so when I came to the third door on the right, I opened it. It wasn't the bathroom, but instead a small storage room with scents of fresh corn and fresh-cut wood, sweet and earthy. Leaning against the two adjacent walls were wooden frames that looked about ten by ten. Under the single window, there was also a table with sheets of burlap-like material.

Baby barked.

I pulled my head out of the room and turned to the other side of the hallway. It was the first time I had been in someone else's house since I had moved to Middwood. The older homes in the "country" were much different, but once I crossed the hall and stood in front of the toilet, I got a familiar fright.

"Hello, Satan," I said.

The devil painting in front of me was smaller than the one I had trapped in my closet. I pursed my lips. Perhaps the ghosts out in the backwoods were tiny, so smaller paintings were all they needed.

I wet my hands, but there wasn't any soap. I noticed a Lustre-Creme bottle, but the label had long been worn off. I opened it and took a sniff, and it was the same inviting scent of corn silk from across the hall. It would have to do. I couldn't help but take in the sweet smell as I lathered up my hands. "Get thee behind me, Satan, and get thee dog cooties down the sink."

I dried my hands and made my way back up the hall. Tonya was busy setting the table.

"Where did you get the soap in your bathroom?"

"I make all kinds of things," she put her hand to her chest and gave me a terrible imitation of a Southern Belle.

"I saw that. I mean, I didn't mean to, but I went into the wrong room by mistake. I saw your studio." I tried to cover my snooping and keep the conversation going. "I wish I was good with my hands, but that isn't my gift." I didn't know what she was thinking, but our conversation paused. "I have a hard enough time with my left and right."

She cocked her head. "And you're a teacher?"

I shrugged. I could almost feel her in my head. It was a strange sensation to have so much anxiety pop up so quickly.

She smiled again. "Well, I'm glad you like the soap. I'll have to send you home with some, but after that, you'll have to buy it. That is how I keep food on the table."

"Deal."

"Speaking of the table, have a seat." She crossed the living room and opened the back door. "Peter. Time to eat."

~

Once Peter came in, we all sat down to a good meal of meatloaf, carrots, and potatoes. Granted, it wasn't as good as Grandma Rollin's, but a darn close second place. I tried not to eat like a pig, but Tonya kept giving me more.

I finally held up my hands in surrender. "I'm not sure I can eat another bite."

"You don't like it? Or is it just you eat like a bird?" asked Peter.

I shot him a blank stare. "I ate everything on my plate." Then turned to Tonya. "I assure you, it's amazing."

"Good, 'cause there's more," Tonya said.

"Oh, my goodness," I smiled painfully.

"You can do it, Christian. I believe in you, but if not, then more for me."

Tonya stood and removed the pan holding the few remaining slices of meatloaf. "I'll wrap some up for you to take."

"Maybe you can put some meatloaf in a grilled cheese sandwich," Peter said with a spark of longing.

"That actually sounds good," I said smiling with my face and stomach.

"It does, doesn't it? We will have to try that, won't we, Mom?" he said, grinning with a full mouth of food.

Pointing to Peter, I asked, "But you? Where do you put it all?"

"Oh, I can eat. I'm a good eater," he said mocking his mom displaying both a mother's pride and a mother's pain.

We all laughed. His impression of her was spot on because she followed it with, "Yes, you are a good eater. Too good of an eater. Eating us out of house and home."

I immediately reached for my wallet. "Please allow me to pay you for the meal," but then I remembered I didn't have any money.

"No. Besides, that remark was for Peter."

Tonya sat back down next to me. "So, Matt, do you plan to stay in Middwood?"

A tension fell over the room. I stretched my neck slightly to each side to keep the tension from holding on to me. "I believe so. I like my students. I love the house I'm staying in, and the view, even though it's just of the yard and the street, it's a step up from where I was."

"So, you came to a haunted town to be calm?" Peter asked.

Tonya reached across the table and popped him on his arm. "Don't talk with your mouth full." She resettled her gaze on me. "But he is right. I'm not sure if the valley is the right place for calm."

I grinned. "I thought you said it was boring?"

"Boring yes, but calm, no. The dead have a problem resting here."

I paused, my eyes wide. I'm sure I looked like an idiot, but Tonya had just opened the door for a conversation about the town. I tried to chew my food quickly.

Trying to play it cool, I asked, "What is that all about, really? I'm not a superstitious person, and I can't wrap my head around all of it."

She looked at me. "Mr. Christian, the town is haunted. It's as simple as that."

I stopped mid-chew. Here was my chance to finally get some answers. "You can't be serious. The adults believe it, too? I thought it was just something to keep the children in line, like Santa Claus."

"I wish it wasn't, but it's all true," Tonya said.

"Mom?" Peter said in pain. "There's no Santa Claus?"

Tonya rolled her eyes and playfully swatted Peter. "Stop it."

Peter laughed, then pointed at me with his fork. "See, I told you. He doesn't believe it."

I shrugged. "Ghosts aren't real."

Peter shrugged, mocking me. "Yes, they are. Everyone in Middwood knows the story of the ghost children."

I looked at Tonya.

She shrugged. "Everyone knows the story."

"Except me," I said with a flat smile.

"Wanna hear it?" asked Peter.

"Oh man, yes."

"Can I tell him, Mom?"

"Since, apparently, no one else is going to," Tonya waved him on.

57

Peter turned in his seat and bent his arms at the elbow, throwing up his hands like he was catching a hiked football. "Thirteen years ago, at this same time of year, three weeks before Thanksgiving, the Johnson children, Grace, Isaac, little Turtle, and Joshua, went crazy. No one knows for sure why. Some people say it was something in the water. Others say it was the devils and witches, and some think it had to do with the old tales of the monsters from over the mountains, the changelings—"

"The what?"

"Old, old folklore. Hush and listen." He went back to his previous stance. "So, the Johnson children went crazy, and they took up an ax and hatchets. First, they went after their mother, Sarah, the previous school teacher, but her husband, Roger, saved her. Before they could escape, Joshua cut Roger's leg! Sarah and Roger made a run for it, and the kids chased their parents down the mountain, trapping them in old man Casteel's barn. Sarah and Roger barricaded the door, but the children chopped it down with the ax and hatchets. The parents had nowhere to run, and Roger was hurt, so the kids moved in..."

"And?" I asked.

"They killed their parents."

"Jesus, and they killed them with hatchets?"

Peter pointed. "Well, except for the oldest, Joshua, he had an ax."

"Good God. Well then how did they become ghosts, I mean, how did they die?" I asked.

"The next morning, they lit their house on fire and killed themselves, screaming out their confessions as they burned alive."

"Why did they kill their parents?"

"They went crazy," Peter said.

"There are rumors that the oldest boy, Joshua, talked his younger brother and sisters into it," Tonya said, shaking her head.

"But what caused them to kill their parents, and why did they kill themselves?"

"Regret, shame, penance, I don't know. Surrounding families rushed to try to put out the fire, but it was too late. They're the ones who heard the children confess."

"How is it possible they're ghosts?" I asked.

Tonya shook her head. "This is Middwood. Strange shit happens here all the time. Would you like some banana pudding?"

"Um ..." I regarded her offer, but my mind was still swimming with the story of the ghost children. "Maybe I'm not crazy after all."

"I sure hope not," she joked.

"Well, I want some banana pudding," Peter said, chewing with a smile. "But trust me, Mom, he's crazy."

Baby barked.

Tonya half-stood, craning her neck to see out the kitchen window. "Who is it, I wonder?"

There was a knock at the door.

"Peter, would you mind getting that?" she asked.

"It's not him, is it?" Peter groaned. On the second knock, Peter got up and walked heavily to the door.

Tonya slid closer to me and began to laugh, although I hadn't said anything.

"What's so funny?" I asked with pleasant, surprised confusion.

Baby yipped and yapped.

"Good afternoon, son," said the voice outside. "Is your mother home?"

"Yes, but we are having lunch. We have company. Can you come back later—"

Randy Bankward pushed past, Peter. "I'm sure your mother won't mind me coming in."

He was dressed in his Sunday finest on a Saturday afternoon. Baby growled at him. Looking down at her, he scolded, "I'll have none of that from you, old lady." He took his hat off as he crossed in and held his hat in front of his belly. He stopped smiling when he saw me.

"Oh, I didn't mean to intrude," he said with passive-aggressive sarcasm.

"Baby, hush," Tonya commanded. The dog sighed and reluctantly settled. "We were having lunch, Randy," Tonya said. "Matt was telling me the most amazing stories about Atlanta. We will have to go there sometime. Won't we Matt?"

All eyes were on me, and I had no idea what to say. I looked at Peter who was equally surprised, but then the boy's expression narrowed on his mother.

Completely confused, I played along, like some bad

improv game. "Yes. Atlanta is a great city. We should all go sometime."

"Peter, too, I suppose?" asked Mr. Bankward.

She laughed. "Peter wouldn't go with us on our trip, right Matt?"

"Of course, he could. Mr. Bankward could come as well."

"Oh, Matt, you are so fresh," giggled Tonya and rubbed my arm.

"I see." Bankward scrunched his chin. "Mr. Christian, what brings you here?" Bankward asked.

"Mr. Mullis sent me here," I replied.

Mr. Bankward stepped closer to me. "Well, did you get what you came for?"

I nodded.

"Good," he said. "Then why don't you get going? After Thursday's misstep, I'm sure you have plenty of work to do."

"Peter's my ride, and he's still eating. I don't want to be rude."

"I thought you said Peter was a troublemaker?" Bankward said crossing his arms.

Peter shot me a questioning frown.

"Well, there's no doubt about that." I smiled. "But that was before I got to know him better."

"Teachers and students should not—"

"Oh, Randy, stop. I invited him. I'm sure there is nothing wrong showing our new, young, handsome teacher a little hospitality," protested Tonya.

"That's very kind of you, Tonya," Mr. Bankward replied.

"Mom, just give him the rent money," murmured Peter.

Tonya walked to the kitchen and opened one of the canisters on the counter. "Here," she said as she handed him an envelope.

"Aren't you going to invite me to stay for lunch?"

She clenched her jaw. "Randy, would you like some lunch? I can wrap something up for you, and you can take it with you when you leave."

"Tonya, it's a nice offer, but wouldn't you like some company since the boys are leaving?" He put the envelope back on the table.

Peter shook his head. "Oh, I'm sorry Mr. Bankward, you must have misunderstood. We aren't leaving."

"Well, you're going to drive your teacher home."

"Mom?" Peter whined looking for backup.

She sighed and forced a smile at her son. "It's okay, honey. I do have business to discuss with him."

Peter shifted his eyes to Bankward. "Do you want me to stay?"

She crossed to Peter and ran her fingers through his dark hair. "Peter, you know your mother can take care of herself." She grinned. "Go on. We'll have dessert when you get back."

Peter stood, leaving everything in its place and stormed out the door.

The screen door sprung shut behind him.

I wiped my mouth and rose. "Thank you for lunch and... the afternoon." I faltered, "Are you okay to be with him alone?"

She gazed at me and anger flashed in her eyes. "I'll be fine."

I paused, staring at Bankward, then nodded to Tonya. "Thank you, again."

Peter honked the horn. The Rustic's sputtering and hisses masked the hint of a whispering choir blowing through the dead trees. I shuddered and moved quickly to the truck.

Tonya watched us from the screen door as I got in the truck. She looked sullen, then she backed into the house, the shadows swallowing her.

"He's a horrible man," Peter spat and pounded the steering wheel with the palm of his hand. He lowered his head but then composed himself.

I pushed my glasses up on my nose. "I can't say I like him much either."

"Rich old bastard."

"Rich old bastard with power. That's how it works. They're the ones in charge."

We drove in silence. I couldn't think of anything to say, and Peter was distracted with his own brooding. I had lots of questions, but asking a son about his mom's sexual partners usually wasn't the best idea. *I wish I kept up with sports,* I thought. It would have been the perfect time to bring up baseball. "Does Kentucky have a pro baseball team?"

"No. Why do you ask?"

"I like the sound of my own voice."

He looked at me, then gave the slightest smirk. "You like baseball?"

"I can feed you a line and say yes if it'd cheer you up."

He huffed. "Nah, I'm not really into baseball. I can't sit still that long."

"I would ask you about movies, but I see that Middwood doesn't have a drive-in movie."

He snorted. "Middwood doesn't have anything."

"It has magic water." I grinned.

He shrugged. "Old news."

"To you, maybe. But my jaw feels brand new. Besides, now you can tell the other students you decked me."

He let out a sound that resembled a laugh.

There was a lull, and we rode in silence again.

"Thanks, Christian."

"What for?" I asked.

"For trying to cheer me up. Thanks."

58

Even hours after Peter dropped me off, I was bothered. I tried to distract myself with reading and even a shower. I went to bed early, but my mind wouldn't settle. There was one thing that couldn't be silenced or pushed back: the ghosts were real?

If so, was it as simple as not breaking any of the rules to keep them at bay? Were the rules really that tried and true? How could a few ghost children watch all the windows in the town at one time? If they are ghosts, what keeps them from coming in at will? They were ghosts. They could walk through walls. They could be seen or unseen. They could be in this room right now, and I wouldn't know.

I shivered and peered around in the blackness and pulled the covers up a bit more. Maybe that is part of the reason there were no windows in bedrooms, in the pitch black, the living couldn't see the dead.

They had to be real. But I wasn't sure about the episode with the two little girls. That could have been the drugs. *Vomiting girl ghosts?* I scoffed.

I suddenly sat up in my bed. "I didn't take any pills

today." Just the words in my mouth made me want to run down the hall and stuff my face, to crunch on the chalky heaven.

However, I didn't. I couldn't.

"Ugh! What if I didn't even go to Peter's today?"

I slapped myself in the face. I waited for the pain, but there wasn't any.

I sighed and fell back on the bed. I recited the rules in my head. I wasn't breaking any of them at the moment, but it bugged me because I knew they could walk through walls, the little blonde one had touched the back of my arm the first night I saw her under the weeping tree. I rubbed my elbow to make sure it wasn't icy. I realized I had moved.

Hoping I didn't call attention to myself, I slowly moved my arms back to a resting place under the covers.

I had broken one of the rules that night. I had turned to go to the kitchen to make something to eat. I had turned my back on an open window.

"Jesus."

So what was the trick, the loophole? Was it that she saw me and I couldn't see her coming?

"Is anyone there?" I whispered into the darkness.

My heart rate increased, and my mouth went dry. I waited. There was no answer. I relaxed, rolled over onto my left side and closed my eyes.

I opened them.

What if I performed a test? It was a stupid idea. Let's piss off the ax murdering ghost children. *Really smart, dumbass.*

I couldn't help wondering, *What would happen ...?*

I threw back the covers, but I didn't move. I licked my dry lips and groaned at my stupidity.

I stood, checking my resolve.

I moved to the door and touched the knob to see if it was

cold. It wasn't. It was a good sign, I thought, but of course, it would only be cold if one of them was holding onto the other side. There was a chance Joshua was standing there, or perhaps the mean little girl was sitting and pouting across the hall.

Under the door, I thought.

I got down flat on the Tomb's floor. I closed one eye like I was aiming a gun. It was much easier to see through to the hall than I thought it would be. I could see a faint amount of light coming in, but no feet. There was nothing there but the sea of hardwood and a few collections of dust.

I got up and opened the door slowly. It could all just be a trick. After all, dead or alive, they were kids, and kids were sneaky. Perhaps being a teacher would give me a slight upper hand.

I exited the Tomb and crept down the hall. I was moving so slow I could feel the bottoms of my sweaty feet sticking to the floor.

The night was silent and still. At the landing, I peeked down but saw nothing. I inched down the remaining stairs, keeping myself hidden as much as possible. I peered into the living room, but unless they were hiding, there were no ghosts.

I relaxed and went to the living room shutters and peered out between them. The moon wasn't full, but there was enough light for me to see clear to the street.

Nothing.

Even though the shutters were closed, I made sure not to turn my back to them. I stepped backward until I was safely back to the stairs.

Just go to bed, I told myself.

I stalled. Again, I warned myself, *Go to bed. Don't do it.* I thought how beautiful it would be to have a good night's sleep. I pleaded with myself, but I couldn't make the nagging in my head go away.

I took a deep breath and marched back to the living room shutters. I reached out my hand to touch the little, brass hook that held them closed.

Such a small hook, I thought.

I flipped it up with my thumb, and in one motion I opened both shutters. I stood there looking out into the yard.

All was peaceful, calm, and still.

I stepped closer to the glass and looked across the street where the neighbors' houses were dark. The same was true for the homes to the left and the right. They were all closed up like clams. Nothing was stirring.

What was I doing? Why couldn't I just conform to the shitty rules and go to bed? I would never be happy in Middwood, but I could be content with what I had. Why risk everything for some simple curiosity?

My heart rate increased and my breath shook. "I have to," I said, even though the voice didn't sound like me.

I closed my eyes to gather my strength.

I slowly turned until my back was fully to the window. I bit my lip, and I took a step back. My bare skin touched the cold glass. My skin tightened from the touch of the surface; if nothing else I knew I was awake. I counted in my head, 1... 2... 3... Leaving the shutters opened, I stepped toward the stairs.

Instinct and fear told me to run, hide, but I just walked.

Two steps from the windows, my back flared with intense cold.

It was happening. Their eyes were on me. I'd called them.

I pictured a phantom soaring across the darkened lawns

and streets. Oddly, I only imagined one of them, but I couldn't tell which. My mouth spoke: "He's here."

The silence was deadly. Then footsteps crunched through the leaves on the yard. I kept moving, trying not to run. If I ran, they would run, and they would catch me. Hard-soled shoes marched onto the porch, unafraid of making their presence known. When I was halfway up the stairs, there were multiple raps and bumps against the window frame and glass.

Then it got quiet.

I didn't turn around. I couldn't. I knew they were there. At least one of them was in the house. Cold air emanated from behind me. The part of my back that had touched the glass was so cold it burned.

A dim glow from the opened living room window crept up the stairs. The light cast my shadow on the hall wall.

As I climbed, another shadow joined mine. We moved together toward the Tomb. I could hear their breathing. I could smell the damp air.

The bedroom was only three more steps away.

Hot urine poured from me, soaking my crotch until it ran down my leg.

I bolted forward, leaping into the Tomb and shutting the bloodwood.

Voices shrieked but were muffled when the bloodwood shut them out.

Why don't they come in? They entered the house some-how, so why not my room?

It hit me. They couldn't see in. Under the door, shadows frenzied about. If they got down on the floor, they could.

I lunged to my bed and whipped the sheet from the mattress. I turned, dove to the floor, and threw the sheet at the base of the door and stuffed it into the gap.

The ghosts wailed. Their shrill voices sent me backward against the farthest wall. They beat on the wood so hard I feared they would break it down.

I forced myself to my feet and moved to brace the door, the urine dripping from my pants around my feet. I pressed my hands flat against the freezing wood. The bitter cold was so much for my hands that I turned my back and pushed instead.

The added pressure made them even angrier.

"Stop!" I screamed.

The banging stopped. I listened, but my heart was beating so hard, and my ears were ringing so loud I couldn't tell what I was hearing.

I swallowed hard, and my ears popped.

My hearing returned to low moans swelling in and out of human octaves. It made tears swell up in my eyes.

The cries died out and hours passed, but I stayed firm, all night on my knees, holding the door.

59

S unday, November 8, 1964
     Sunrise 7:04 AM. Sunset 5:29 PM.

I woke up in the Tomb alive. Granted I was on the floor, and my back and neck were stiff from straining, but I was alive.

Last night wasn't a dream. I had turned my back on an open window and they came into the house. Their screams had filled the air, and I had felt the weight of their pushes and bangs on the bedroom door. All of it was real. The ghosts were real.

"Stop it," I shouted. My mind zoned out. I couldn't think. I was the blown bulb in the string of Christmas lights. Realizing and accepting the truth of ghosts changed everything. It would take me some time to understand how, but I decided sticking to the town rules was a good place to start.

I thought my students and the townspeople were simple backwoods hicks, but they had been living with the phenomena for thirteen years, some of them had been born into the madness. If they were ever to leave town, to venture out into the wider world, and speak of ghost children, town rules, or devil paintings, they would be put away in the nut house.

I had taken a glimpse behind a curtain I wished I didn't know existed.

"I should leave."

Then it hit me. "My car."

I rushed to the main floor, stopping at the bottom of the stairs. The living room window was still open.

I dismissed it and pushed opened the front door.

My heavy eyes focused on my beautiful, banged-up baby. The Falcon waited for me on the road right outside, flirting with me like a hot, willing woman. I bolted down to the street and hugged the warm hood. Let the world go to hell or fall away, I didn't care. I finally had my car back.

I got in the passenger side and slid into my seat. I gave myself a little bounce and settled into my spot as I gripped the steering wheel. I put my hand on the key and closed my eyes. Images of the Falcon eating white lines on the highway filled my rattled mind.

I turned the key.

She roared to life with a mighty greeting.

I glanced down at the gas gauge in shock. I had almost a half a tank of gas. No Christmas had ever been so sweet.

"I can leave," I whispered. I was sitting in my ticket out of Middwood. In a few hours, I would have to go before the town and apologize for my sins against their children. I would have to kiss the feet of Randy Bankward and stay in his good graces even though I knew he was a slime-ball, and, news flash, Daddy-o, the town was haunted.

"Yeah, let's get the fuck out of here."

I cut off the car and ran into the house. I frantically packed. I didn't sort anything, just started throwing my crap in any box or bag that was nearby. A voice in my head kept telling me to hurry. Hurry. Hurry.

Wiping the sweat from my brow, I threw my belongings in the back seat. I marveled that I'd gathered everything I owned in only one trip.

Back inside, I stood, looking around the living room. It was a beautiful house, but for each thing I loved about the home, there were bad dreams, two hellish little girls, and a hooded boy with an ax.

I left the key on the table behind the sofa and walked out. Some of the neighbors were looking out their windows.

Boy, they were nosy. "Good riddance."

The Falcon kicked to life, and I double checked the gas gauge—half full. "Thank you, Jesus!"

For the second time in just over a week, I raced to free myself from a bad situation with a gift of gasoline. I needed to break the surface for air, and that barrier was just beyond Keeper's Bridge and over the spine of Black Bear Mountain.

I threw the car into gear and sped off. It was too early for church, so I would be able to avoid unwanted attention, but I wouldn't have to tell anyone I was leaving because one of the many gossiping bitches would see me and the whole town would know before I hit the county line. I didn't have a full tank of gas, but I had enough to get somewhere else, anywhere else. Just not Middwood.

As I approached the gas station, Eddie was nowhere to be seen. It was like heaven was shining down its graces on me. "Let's go, let's go." My muscles tightened as I drove over Keeper's Bridge, but once I was over it, it was like my soul relaxed. Turning to the right, I floored it. My car was alive just like when I first got her. We were both free, and we would fly out of here, start over again.

The engine cut off.

Panic rose inside me as my heart and my jaw dropped.

"What? No. No!"

I stomped the gas. The engine didn't roar, didn't purr, nothing.

"I just got her back! Come on!"

I turned the wheel as hard as I could and coasted, pulling to the side of the road.

"It's fine. I'll just re-crank her, and we'll be on our way."

I turned the key... and nothing happened.

Nothing. No click. No tick. Not shit.

I punched the roof of the Falcon, and I put my head down against the steering wheel and screamed. "I just want to leave!"

I wanted to cry, but I lifted my head. Anger pooled and swelled in my jaw and face. "Shit!" I hit the steering wheel, took off my glasses, and threw them down. I was stalled out in the same fucking place as before, less than three hundred feet from Keeper's Bridge.

I got out, and I kicked the dirt, cursing Casteel and his entire family. I gritted my teeth until my jaw hurt.

I would be stuck in Middwood another night. People saw me load my stuff into my car and it would spread through the town. Fear hit my spine, and I stood at attention. What would they do to me if they thought I was fleeing? Would I be stoned in the church? I snorted at the thought, but then fear gripped me. "What will they do to me? What would Bankward do? Shit!" I put my hands to my lips and bit my curled index finger.

The evidence needed to be hidden. I pulled the two bags from the backseat, popped the trunk, and hid everything from view. If people heard I ripped out of town, they would come snooping around the car to see for themselves. I could call Peter to help me smuggle stuff from my car back to the house, if I was still alive.

I peered up at the mountains that surrounded me. If anyone was up there, they could be hidden from view, watching me. Maybe I was paranoid, but I still found myself squinting into the trees. It would take too long to scan such a large area.

I dug through my bags for something to wear to church. With my car between me and the town, I changed my clothes.

I would try and make it look like I was taking my car out for a drive. I would tell everyone, *Yeah, I was happy to have it back, but unfortunately, it died again.* I'd joke about me being a city boy and Casteel not being able to fix cars. Maybe everyone would laugh.

I heard a car coming, so I hurried and finished changing before they came into view. Of course, the car slowed as it veered into the other lane to avoid the Falcon's tail. I turned and did my best to grin and wave as all four heads in the car locked onto my face and twisted until they couldn't turn any farther. I looked away, but I imagined that their heads continued turning around entirely.

I couldn't leave the Falcon sticking out exposed like that. I put her in neutral and stood in the open door, pushing until the back was clear of the lane.

I sighed in relief, but my car continued rolling. "Whoa whoa whoa!" I shrieked grabbing at the frame, but she went down into the shallow ditch.

I grabbed two handfuls of my hair and pulled. "What the fuck is going on!" I roared as I stamped around in the dirt, having a conniption fit. "Fuck!" I slid down into the ditch and looked for damage. She was fine. "You are all I have, baby girl. I'll send help soon. I promise."

Another car was coming, and with that, I climbed out of the ditch, and stepped into the lane, stopping the vehicle. The couple rolled down the window. "Hi, I'm the school teacher. Would you mind driving me to church I don't want to be late."

"Of course, get in," the man said with Christianly concern.

"Thank you." I reached in and shook his hand. "Such a blessing. I just got my car back, and I wanted to go for a quick ride, but the devil had a different plan."

"That's where you are wrong, brother. God had a different plan."

"Amen. Thank you for that. That makes me feel so much better."

I got in the back seat and made sure to wear a grateful grin even though his words shook me. He said "God had a different plan." I wasn't sure it was God, but there had to be something at work against me. My car stopping in the exact same spot was too much of a coincidence for me to think otherwise. Could it be true? Were the unseen forces of the town keeping me here?

$\sim$

"So, we forgive Gary? Amen?" Pastor Gresham asked as I stood next to him on his right and Gary Shindle stood on his left. I couldn't believe what was happening.

The congregation repeated, "Amen."

He turned to me. "My people perish for lack of knowledge. This foolish young man, made a poor decision, putting your children in danger, but luckily, brothers and sisters, God had mercy on the children of Middwood. This time our children were spared. This time God's grace prevailed. This time we are able to learn and grow. Yes, we need to grow from this experience. Throw off spirits of hate, anger, murder, and walk in forgiveness. That is what God is saying to me this morning, forgive. Forgive not just Mr. Christian, but also our very own Franklin Mullis for keeping Matt in the dark about the true dangers of the town."

My eyes widened, and I turned to Gresham. I hadn't even considered Franklin getting blamed for any of this. He'd been sent to the principal's office, too. I couldn't help thinking I should defend the old man. I tried to hold my tongue, but I couldn't let someone get in trouble for me.

"Franklin told me about the rules, but I broke them. Franklin is a good man. He—"

Gresham put his heavy hand on my shoulder and gave my shoulder an uncomfortable squeeze. We exchanged a glance. I could only guess, but I felt like he knew what I was doing and even why I was doing it, but it didn't matter.

After a moment, I turned back to the congregation and regurgitated what I was told to say before the service. "Parents and children of Middwood, I want to apologize for my actions. I was in the wrong, and I thank Mr. Bankward for setting me on the right path. I can't begin to imagine how worried you were. Again, I ask for you and... God to forgive me. From now on, I will follow the town rules to ensure the safety of my students."

I couldn't believe I was able to get that out.

"Matt, that is honorable of you, and you are right, you are both good men. Brothers and sisters, we need a teacher up at that school and other than the mix-up on Thursday, the children have given only positive reports on this young man of God. That is why it is the decision of the elders of this church to forgive Matt Christian for his sin and we encourage the town to do the same. Can I get an amen?"

The amens were not all as quick as I would have liked, but the church was in agreement. For some reason the memories of getting baptized played over in my mind. Wearing a white choir robe as I walked down a path to a creek behind my Rose-Mary Grand's church. I'm sure the First Baptist Church of Middwood did baptisms, but I couldn't help but wonder if they also had a stake behind the church for burnings. I got their message plain and clear, and if I was going to survive long enough to get my car back and get out of town, then I'd have to lay low and play along.

Since I was stuck in Middwood, I'd have to eat. I walked to the grocery store and made my way to the bread aisle.

I was contemplating a loaf of Sunbeam Bread when a "hello" boomed, followed by a smoky laugh. "It's about time you came to see me," the words rang out from across the store.

"Oh, shit." I had completely forgotten about Magnolia. I was in the middle of the aisle, in the middle of the store, and there was no way to escape.

She was all smiles when she ran up to me with her arms open wide. The smell of alcohol and cheap cigarettes hit me before she did. She threw her arms around me. "I was beginning to think I wasn't going to get that rain check."

I glanced up over the low shelves to see a few onlookers. "Magnolia, please."

She laughed. "Yes, baby. Beg mamma for some lovin'."

"Stop. I don't think this is the time or place."

"Damn, baby, you look disheveled. Wild night? You cheating on me?" she slapped to my chest.

"No. My car broke down. I don't want to talk about it."

"I don't want to talk either. Once the church crowd leaves, we can go to the back room."

"No. You don't understand," I protested.

She grabbed my crotch. "That's pretty nice," she said with her smoky, boozy breath.

I pushed her hands off me.

She squinted her eyes. "What's your problem?" She waved it off. "Look, I've had a bad day you've had a bad week. We need this," she said, reaching for me again.

I stepped out of her reach. "I don't want you."

She put her hands on her hips. "I beg your pardon? That's not what you said the other night when you were at my place." The half dozen customers stopped their shopping to gawked at us.

I tilted my head back in exhausted aggravation. I sighed as I grabbed the loaf of bread and walked away from her.

"Don't you like women?" she snarled from behind me.

"That has nothing to do with it."

She caught up with me, walking as close as one of the ghost children. Her drunken breath made me nauseous. "Oh, I get your game. You like a woman who won't stop. What? You want me to beg?" she asked grabbing and pulling at the back of my belt.

She knelt on the floor. I glanced around the store, and the customers' faces were covered in shock.

"Get off the floor. People are staring at you."

"Baby, I'm Magnolia. I'm the only show worth watching in this shit-hole town."

"You're going to get in trouble," I warned.

"You want to hold me after class? I could probably fit into one of Scarlet's dresses if that is what you are into."

I backed away from her. "What is wrong with you?"

Her eyes darted around furiously as she became aware all the customers in the store were staring at her. She curled her lips in and spoke through her teeth, "Everyone out! The rules don't apply to me, you sheep. You pigs! This is my store! You hear me!"

"Magnolia, you are drunk. You need to go—"

She pointed toward the door and shouted, "I said get out, faggot!"

"Do you need me to get Mr. Self? Maybe he can—"

"Get out, or I'll kill you. I'll hit you with more than a rock. This is my store."

I didn't say anything else. I backed away from her and put the loaf of bread on the counter. Even Bobby, the clerk, left. I gave him a concerned look, and he shrugged. "She gets like this sometimes. No big deal."

I left the store. I couldn't get back to the house soon enough. The only thing on my mind was getting a shower. I needed to disinfect myself of her alcoholic, cigarette, cardboard touch. I could feel her witch hands caressing my back and the other one grabbing my crotch. I reached into my chest pocket and swallowed an anxiety pill.

60

"**G**et in," Peter called, reaching across the seat and opening the door.

I walked up to his truck. "I thought you were Gary Shindle with another rock."

"I wouldn't worry about that guy. He'll get what's going to him. Get in."

"Why?"

"I want to show you something."

"I can't. Franklin told me to stay at home."

"You're not at home now. C'mon, it's more fun when you break the rules," Peter said. "Christian?"

"I better not."

"Get in, or I'll lay on the horn and start screaming."

"Peter—"

Honk

"Okay, okay. Damn." I opened the door and got in. "Just take me home."

"I got something better." He turned to me with a hop. "Want to go see the ghost children's graves?"

My brain stopped, and my gaze froze on him.

A sly grin grew across his face. "Yeah, you do. Come on."

The words jumped out of my mouth. "Okay, let's go." *Did I say that?*

"All right." He turned the key and we roared off.

The road was a semi-graveled trail with a few strands of grass that still managed to grow in the center of it. Ahead, the path veered to the left. The birch and oaks lined the road leading us away from Peter's house and farther from the town.

A black mass walked out from the woods on the path. My eyes widened as I pointed and screamed, "Bear!"

A black bear stood on all fours in the middle of the road ahead of us. Peter swerved to the left, dodging it, but then stopped.

The bear stood on its hind legs and roared.

Peter rolled down the window. "Shut up and get out of the road!"

"What gives? Bears don't..." My words trailed off as the bear lowered itself and walked into the woods.

I twisted around in my seat, watching. "How did you ...?"

"He could've moved a little faster. I'm losing my touch."

"I'm not sure we should be going to the—"

"Are you whining, Scarlet?" Peter teased. "If anyone asks, I was driving to the graveyard to visit my dear, late grandfather and you were on your way to the graveyard because you have a thing for very old women."

"You have an active imagination," I said.

"And you don't?"

I gave a short laugh. "I used to not be such a stick in the mud."

"What happened?"

"I became a teacher," I said matter-of-factly.

He laughed. "You're such a bad liar. You love your job."

I sighed with a smile. "I do."

"Even after you got clobbered in the face with a rock."

"Stone for a stone. Eye for an eye."

"What does that mean?"

"I'm an odd duck, but there's more too it. The kids make the job or break the job. Plus, when you get older, you have to pay the bills."

"I thought teachers were supposed to be pretty, young women, not some skinny, hairy man."

"Just because you can't grow a beard yet doesn't mean that you can talk about mine."

We rounded the turn in the road and it emptied us out into a field with a view of the sky, and the sky was huge. The clouds were lit by the sun glowed in all the different shades of orange and light purple. Peter slowed and parked the truck.

"Why did you stop?" I asked.

He pointed to the corner of the field. "We're here."

There, on the sloping hillside next to a small pond, sat the graveyard.

"It's kinda late," I said, voicing my concern.

"Kinda late isn't late. We'll be fine, but hurry up," he said hopping out of the truck.

A red-brick wall that looked to be about the height of my waist surrounded the graveyard. The gate itself was enormous, at least ten feet of wrought iron extending up to the sky. If they were opened, they would look like bat wings. The mood and feel of the place were sinking as fast as the sun. "Why did they put it so far out?" I asked.

"So the dead would think twice about walking all the way into town."

"That's not funny."

"You'll be fine. We just need to watch each other's backs. Come on. Let's find out if anyone is here or not."

We walked the rest of the way in silence. *They're all dead,* I thought.

However, that wasn't always the case in Middwood.

My chest tightened as we got closer to the gate. I wasn't sure if it was fear or the cold wafting off the pond.

"Peter, let's see the graves and then get out of here. The moon is up."

Peter shot me a stare. "Look who's using the town lingo. We have at least an hour before sundown. We will be in and out of here in ten minutes."

"Maybe this wasn't such a good idea."

"Relax," said Peter, pushing open one side of the gate. The hinges screamed as they rotated like a train screeching to halt. "Oops. So much for being quiet. Now everyone knows we're here."

Waving him off I said, "Hurry up already. This place isn't sitting well with me." I pushed him to keep going. "Do you know where their graves are?"

He looked at me like I'd just asked the silliest question in Middwood. "Of course; everyone does. They are up on the hill there." He pointed. "See the big angel? They are directly behind her. Folks say they were put there, with the angel's back to them, because they killed their parents. God turned from them, and that's supposedly the reason they're still among us."

When we got to the top of the hill, I approached the statue. It was a marble piece of art, standing at least nine feet tall. Her wings were opened but slightly wrapped around her. Her face was calm and soft like she was resting, but she gazed over her right shoulder.

I rounded the statue and there lay four little tombstones. They were so small and already showed wear. It was apparent the town used whatever extra stone remains that were laying around to mark their graves.

"Laid, but not at rest." A chill hit me, and I couldn't help but look over my shoulder.

I moved closer, so I could read the inscriptions, but then stopped. I surveyed the earth that covered the graves. The ground was whole, smooth, with dead grass covering all the secrets these kids had. Whatever had come for me in the night hadn't crawled out of its coffin.

I inched toward the gravestones and adjusted my glasses. I read aloud, "'Joshua Johnson.'" Just saying his name made me uneasy and, again, I glanced around. I continued reading, "'1935—1951. A murderer. May the devil be kinder than you were to your own.' Wow."

I continued to Turtle's and Grace's markers. Again, under each of their names, it read, "A murderer. May the devil be kinder than you were to your own."

I thought Peter had been teasing me, but there was indeed another grave. It read, "Isaac Johnson. 1940—1951. A murderer. May the devil be kinder than you were to your own."

Peter walked up behind me.

"Isaac's the younger brother, right?"

I turned to see a small boy standing less than ten feet away.

61

He was soaking wet with his black hair matted to his head. He wore faded overalls and stood completely still. The only thing that moved was the water dripping off of him.

I closed my eyes.

I wished that when I looked again I would see he was just a little concrete statue, something I'd missed.

I opened my eyes.

The boy had closed the gap between us. He was just out of arms reach. He was so close I could feel the humidity emanating from him.

The boy moved toward me. "Is he going to take us away?"

I shot glances around searching. "Where's Peter?"

"There's a big gobbler at the treeline."

"I don't understand."

"I wonder how Joshua's doing?" He turned to walk away.

"Wait. I'm here to help." My words melted away as he stopped.

The boy's body tensed and he formed fists at his side.

"Why are you still standing there, boy?" his face soft and innocent. "Can you keep a secret?"

Finally, I was getting through to one of them.

His body twitched like someone changed the channel on a TV. Innocent eyes were replaced with an angry glare. Water flowed from his body, exposing bloated, pale blue, broken skin. He gargled, "They said they were going to leave us alone."

I stood frozen.

"Wait, why are you doing this?"

"Can you keep a secret?" he hissed.

"What?"

"Do you think you're strong enough to get them yourself? If you make this harder for me I'm going to make you suffer." He came at me, and I held up my hands.

He lifted me with ease and, with the force of two grown men, threw me like I was the child. I hit the ground, flipping over myself before tumbling to a stop. I looked up. Beside me was a looming tombstone. Six inches to the left and I might have been killed.

He curled his lip, exposing his bone-like teeth.

He stood directly over me, snarling in my face. Water dripped off of his body onto my face. I turned away. A chill came off his body, surrounding me with the cold mold from his clothes and rot from his flesh.

My eyes were closed. The pressure of his little hand grabbed my shirt. I trembled. I managed to form the words. "You wanted me to see you."

I looked again, and the boy was gone.

I scampered to my feet, grabbing my chest. I choked as I tried to breathe through the pain.

I glanced to my right.

Isaac stood there, dripping. "Do you think you're strong enough to get them yourself?"

I stumbled into a run. I ran as fast as I could. I glanced back to see if the ghost child was pursuing me, but, when I did, I collided with something.

We were both knocked to the ground. We instantly scrambled to get away from each other, but then realized neither of us was our pursuer. It was Peter.

"Who are you running from?" we asked at the same time.

I pointed behind me, "Isaac?"

"No," Peter shook his head. "Joshua Johnson."

A short distance away, Joshua rounded a row of graves. He was wearing the gray sweatshirt.

"What did you do?" I asked.

"I'm not sure, but he's pissed. Come on!" He pulled me up. I turned to get another look at Joshua. He picked up speed and broke into a sprint.

"How do you outrun a ghost?" I asked as we both ran.

Peter recited, "'When out after dark, don't stop, never stop moving!'"

The ground under my feet failed. I fell and kept falling. I couldn't tell if I had been hit again, but the impact felt the same. What made it different was the additional force of Peter's body falling on top of me.

I pushed Peter off, and we fought to get to our feet. We'd fallen in a pit of some kind. The walls were made of dirt, rotten roots, and worms. We were in a tight rectangular hole that was at least ten feet deep.

Peter's face grew in panic. "What is this? What is this?" He jumped and clawed at the cold dirt to climb up. "An open grave?"

I yanked him down.

Movement approached above us.

I pushed him into the darkest corner. Peter protested, but I covered his mouth.

We waited in complete silence. I removed my hand from his mouth. We glanced at each other then turned our eyes to the cloudy sky above. The only sounds were our heartbeats and our attempted quiet, shallow breaths.

Joshua's pace slowed, then stopped. I prayed he didn't know where we were. It was our only chance.

The steps got closer. I blocked Peter with my arm, keeping him behind me and pressed us into the pit's wall. Joshua was right on top of us, but from our angle, we couldn't yet see any part of him. He took another step, and I could see the tip of the hood of his sweatshirt. I hoped, if we couldn't see the opening of his hood, then he couldn't see us.

Peter and I held our breath.

Joshua whipped his head around and darted off. Peter and I let out sighs of relief. We stayed still for several minutes.

After a communication of charades, Peter and I decided I would slowly raise him up so he could make sure Joshua was gone. I leaned against the dirt wall. Peter climbed up my back and peered out.

He jumped back to the mud floor with a squish. "It's all clear," he whispered.

"Good, let's get out of this thing. Why is it so deep?"

"Christian, it's in a graveyard, it's a grave."

"Graves aren't ten feet deep."

"I don't know, I've never died before."

"Whose is it?"

"Probably no one's yet. This is Middwood. It's a tradition to have a least one grave always dug."

"Let's focus on getting out of here. Help me out first, and then I'll pull you up."

Peter looked at me.

"What?" I asked, "I'm not that heavy. Besides, you wouldn't be strong enough to pull me up."

Peter nodded and moved to the wall. He knelt and clamped his hands together. I grabbed a nearby root with both hands to help pull myself out.

He counted in the faintest whispered breaths, "One, two, three."

My head cleared the top of the opening, but I lost my grip and fell. Peter caught me.

"Maybe we should—"

"No," I answered, " it will work, we just have to get the timing right. I need to grab the ground once you boost me up."

He moved into the hoisting position. "This is fun, huh?" he said with sarcasm.

I grabbed his shoulder. "A complete blast." I wasn't about to start complaining. It wasn't his fault I was in an open grave in the middle of nowhere. It was mine. "Let's try this again."

"One, two, three."

I pulled harder, and Peter pushed. Once I cleared the opening, I grabbed at the dirt and thin grass. I kicked my legs against the inside wall. Peter continued pushing me up, giving me extra help. With one last kick, I'd be clear, but that one last kick made contact somewhere on Peter's body.

"Awh!"

I continued to pull myself up.

Boots stepped in front of my face.

Casteel stood looking down at me.

I let go of the grass and slid back down into the grave with a *plop*.

Peter looked at me. "Are they still up there?"

"No," I replied.

"Then why—?"

I pointed up. Casteel's face peered down on us.

"What the hell are you two doing?"

"Can you help us out?" Peter asked.

Looking at Peter, Casteel said, "And you, young man, your mother is going to tan your hide, but this one here—"

Peter pointed to him. "I'll give you ten bucks."

"I'll be right back," Casteel said, disappearing without a word.

Peter shrugged, "He's pretty easy to deal with."

A puttering engine approached.

Casteel reappeared. "Grab on to the rope. Can you pull yourself up? If not, I can pull you out."

Once we were out of the grave. "Hey, my car broke down again."

"Sorry to hear," Casteel held out his hand to Peter.

I watched Peter count out ten dollars, and I shook my head at the gall of the man.

"I'm sure daddy Frank will pay for your car there, sport."

Casteel got in his truck and left.

"Do you think he'll tell Frank?" I asked.

"Probably," said Peter as he moved toward his truck.

"So why did you pay him?"

He got in. "Well, probably telling Frank isn't the same as telling him."

I got in.

"Besides it wasn't even my money."

I sat up. "Where did you get?"

"Doesn't matter."

"Peter, you steal, too?"

He laughed. "Christian, relax. It's not like I killed someone."

I put my head on the dash. "Please, just stop talking."

Peter stopped at my car so I could get the rest of my stuff. After he dropped me off, I went inside and undressed. Not even fooling with the buttons, I pulled my shirt over my head.

As I worked on my belt buckle, a dog barked in the distance, answered by barks from across the street.

A rattle came from upstairs.

I froze awkwardly, with my spine curved and my pelvis thrust forward. With my face looking downward at my crotch, I could only shift my eyes to see the top of the stairs. I slowly straightened myself as I waited and listened. It could be a squirrel or another possum.

From that angle, I could only clearly see the ceiling of the bathroom, but there was nothing there. Light shone in from the window, but there was no telling what was lurking in the deep shadows around the bathroom door and hallway.

I tried to persuade myself that it was the pipes and returned to my belt.

The floor groaned as something stepped across the upstairs hardwoods.

Shivers shot down my back as the creaking footsteps continued. What the hell was it?

Clenching my jaw, I decided there could be no more lying. I ran my shaking hands through my hair. I knew what it was.

It's them.

Get out of the house, I thought. *Run.*

But I was a statue as I watched the staircase, waiting for one of them to appear, to present themselves, then roar down the stairs and attack me. The light outside faded quickly, as if a cloud had passed overhead.

All the windows were closed, or at least I thought they were. I glanced at the living room window and stretched my neck to look into the dining room. Yes, all the shutters were closed. "How did it get in?"

It became restless, and it began pacing, stomping up and down the hall.

I wasn't sure if my heart was beating or if it was just going so fast I couldn't discern the beating. I felt dizzy.

More dogs started barking. If I screamed for help, no one would hear me over all the noise.

My glasses fogged.

Get out! What are you doing? Get out!

I whirled and grabbed the doorknob, then it stopped.

Everything stopped. No sounds, no movement, but I knew it was still there.

I released the doorknob and took a deep breath.

Resting my head against the bloodwood, I whispered, "We want you to see us."

I turned and took a step toward the stairs. Still no sound. I waited for movement. I waited. "Where are you?"

A slew of sounds surrounded me.

I ran upstairs.

The noise sounded like it was coming from the bathroom, but when I got there, nothing. "Where are you?" I growled.

I stood in the bathroom doorway. The moon illuminated the porcelain sink and tub. There were small puddles of water on the floor. It was just a leak, my mind tried to tell me, but when I looked up to the ceiling, there were no water spots, no dripping. It wasn't the pipes.

I studied the puddles. There between my feet was another puddle. I turned to the right, to the shadows of the hallway and there was another small pool. I followed them toward the bedrooms.

I realized they weren't puddles at all, they were footprints.

I flipped the hall light switch.

Nothing happened.

I flipped it again, and the light popped, exploding.

My arms flew up to protect my eyes.

The Tomb was less than ten feet away, but to my eyes, the hall appeared to stretch in length. It started spinning. I staggered to the right wall. My face was hot and my eyes burned.

I backed into the bathroom and turned on the light. The

beam of light swatted at the darkness but fell short. Still, some light was better than none at all.

I crept along, following the footprints, through the threshold from light to darkness toward the Tomb.

Once there, I reached in to turn on the light inside my room but jerked my hand back when I touched someone wet. I examined my hand. I rubbed my fingers together and sniffed. "Water."

I peered into the room. The air was cold. I could see the faint highlight of the ruffles on the curtains against the wall.

Again, my eyes strained. My blood pressure was spiking.

There, in the darkest corner, a figure stood in the shadows, smaller than a man. If it weren't for his glistening hair, I wouldn't have seen him.

I couldn't make out his face. Then his shoulders rotated. His head spun toward me, shedding the shadows and revealing the face of a small boy. The faint light revealed the boy's broken, unnatural, grayish-blue skin.

"How did you get here?"

The boy was silent.

"You followed me home."

He shot out of the corner, gargling with broken shrieks.

He lifted me by the neck and soared, carrying me down the hall. I couldn't breathe. I grabbed at the wet hands clamped around my neck, but there was nothing but my own throat.

I was pushed into the bathroom, and I fell through the shower curtain into the tub. I grabbed at the cloth, pulling the fabric off the rings down on top of me.

My head struck the tile with a hard thud. My vision blurred. I could feel warmth pouring from the back of my head, but the rest of my body was cold.

I fought to stand, but he pushed me down.

The weight was released, and I finally took a breath.

My eyes darted around the room, but he was gone.

I reached up clumsily and grabbed the side of the tub. I winced. My stomach and ribs ached.

"Help me get this..." an unseen voice whispered.

"Wha?" I murmured. "What are you saying?"

"Help me get this—" it hissed.

I peered over the lip of the tub.

Nothing. The room was clear.

I laid back, my stomach aching.

Again, I grabbed the edge of the tub and slowly pulled myself up.

As I rose, pale, wet fingers reached up and touched mine. I gasped. A crown of wet, matted hair rose into view. A white, dead ear and then the milky silver eyes, sunken back in the head of a broken-faced little boy.

The corpse leaped from below.

His blue lips snarled.

Isaac's hand was on my chest, and it clenched my skin, twisting my chest hair as he climbed on me.

While one arm pinned me down, he used the other to turn on the faucet. Water spewed onto my face, impairing my vision, filling my mouth and nose.

I struggled with all my strength to pull myself up. As I choked, I tried to speak, tried to communicate, but the small hand immobilized me and forced me back down to the bottom of the tub.

I scrambled to escape the constant onslaught of water. Swinging my fists, I fought as hard as I could, but there was no connection, nothing to hit. My hands slammed into the tub and the shower tile, cutting open my skin with every useless swing.

I was jerked up by my neck. I gasped for breath, inhaling what air I could. Then I was slammed back down into the shallow water. Isaac grabbed my hands, restraining me.

The sound in my ears faded like someone had turned down the volume.

63

Monday, November 9, 1964
Sunrise 7:05 AM. Sunset 5:28 PM.

It was freezing. There was a stiff breeze. I must have left a window opened.

I shot to a standing position. That was a big mistake. I caught a blurred glimpse of brown, pre-dawn nature and looming heaviness before I sank to my knees. I held the sides of my head to keep the vertigo-like pain from splitting me open. As the sharp, cold November winds lashed my bare skin, I wrapped my arms around my chest. I was shirtless and in only my slacks. My nose, ears, fingers, and toes were all numb.

I tried to stay calm, but it wasn't working. "Why does this shit keep happening to me?" I pleaded to my hands as if they held the answer, but they were the only thing I could see clearly. I touched my hands to my eyes, but my glasses weren't there.

In hopes my glasses were close by, I dipped down, spreading my fingers wide, scrabbling through the grass, leaves, and dirt. Nothing.

I sat back on my ass and strained to study the foggy, grayish-blue terrain. There appeared to be a road cutting through a field in front of me, but behind me, trees and mountains. I wasn't sure if I was still in town. I turned to the left, and there was a dark-gray road leading up a purple mass that could have been any mountain of the Appalachians.

There was a gate of some kind about forty feet away with a billboard sign beside it. I couldn't read it at that distance because it blended in with the gray surroundings. I got to my bare feet and walked toward it across the brown grass, then stumbled along sharp gravel rocks until my feet found the comfort of turf once again.

The larger lettering made it easier to read: "Middwood Coal Mine." I wondered which mine I was at.

At least I was in town, but even Peter's house was considered to be in Middwood. I shivered, I could be ten miles away from Main Street. I didn't know how I would explain this to Franklin. Even worse was the fear of having to explain to Bankward, then apologize again to the church for running home half naked before sunrise.

The whistle!

I could hear the mine's whistle at the school, and I could faintly hear it at the house. If I was at the mine, then I was closer to work than home.

I spun and searched for some clue of the correct direction to start moving in. I hoped the heart of the town wasn't behind me over the mountain. I knew I could take the road to see where it would lead, but I was barefoot, and with all the broken bottles and trash along the roads I'd end up hurting myself.

My feet.

I plopped on the grass and pulled my feet up to my face. My toes were cold, but they weren't dirty. The bottoms of my foot and heel were clean, too. I was brought here. I tensed and scanned the horizon. Maybe the person or thing who kidnapped me was close by.

It was useless. I couldn't see. I ran my hands down my arms.

Instead of questioning why I had been taken from my house and dropped here, I pushed logic out of my head, and I closed my eyes. I'd always had a sense of when I was being watched. Whether I was high or just batshit crazy, it was all I had at the moment. I opened my mind, but there was nothing.

I ran my hands over my knees and decided to take my sense of nothing as a good sign. I slowly stood. To the right there were trees. To my left, the field appeared to open up about half a mile into the valley.

I went with my gut and went to the left. I walked gently back across the gravel to the grass. If I were caught out before the sun rose, I didn't know what the town would do to me. I tried not to think about Shirley Jackson's short story, "The Lottery"; getting hit with one rock was enough.

With any luck, I'd make it home before the people of Middwood woke up. I sighed, "Too bad, you don't believe in luck."

The school wasn't in sight, but I was sure following the valley would get me close to it. I would have to climb, but, if I ran, I could make it home before the sunrise. I didn't think about it another second. I ran.

The grass was soft beneath my bare feet. I watched the

ground as much as I could to avoid rocks, holes, or anything else that could hurt me.

I glanced up and my heart sank as I stumbled to a stop. There was an embankment blocking my path.

The incline ahead of me appeared to be mostly grass and dirt. It wasn't part of the mountain, but perhaps a road.

There wasn't time for second-guessing. I scanned the ridge for the lowest point. It was damn steep, at least twenty feet. The bank was the same height for as far as I could see, but there was a group of trees to my right that I could use to help me scramble up.

I ran to the trees and started the climb. I used a lot of energy, but, I was right, the trees made scaling the hill easier. I had to crawl to reach the top.

I stood and dusted myself off.

I had another choice: follow the road away from the mountain or go down the embankment and continue along the basin. The path curved, and trees obscured my view. I didn't like that I couldn't see enough to make a decision.

I squinted down into the ravine. It gave the appearance of rolling hills that led up to a group of higher ridges. I couldn't see the school of course, but it slanted downward.

"The bottom of the valley."

That was the way, I knew it.

Using the trees again, in the opposite manner, I ran down to the basin. My descent down the hill was my first breather for many of my muscles.

The sky was warming. I needed to move faster.

Once I reached the school, I'd still have to run to the bridge then cross over Looney Creek. I worried about Eddie. I wasn't sure if he'd be at the station with his shotgun. If I encountered Eddie I would more than likely see other people. Someone would see me, then everyone would know I had broken one of the rules.

There was something boxy in the distance. It was around the midpoint between me and the next ridge.

I didn't know what the little block-shaped thing was, but it felt right, so I continued running toward it. It was gray, like everything else in Middwood. It could be a tractor, an old wagon, but depending on the distance, it could also be a house. If anyone saw me, I could be shot on sight with the simple justification that they thought I was a bump in the night.

The more I ran, the more distinct the shape grew. It had to be a structure. It was smaller than I thought, and it was closer too.

The field started pitching up. I could see it now. Ahead, on a small swell, sat an old barn.

I stopped, attempting to catch my breath.

It was the barn, the one from Peter's story. If it was, then this was the most fucked up trick yet. Again, I knew better than to ask why. What was important, was that I knew where I was.

I knew I should keep running, but there was an unnatural attraction to the building, almost like its gravity pulled me in. The pure history of the location, the spot where the curse of Middwood began. There was an eerie darkness surrounding the barn. I felt it, rippling. It was calling me, communicating. Was it real? Was I awake, I wondered.

Early morning mist hugged the ground and hid my feet. With each step, cool mud spread through my toes. The waves from the building intensified, as if a hook in my chest pulled me forward. Its lure became stronger, almost seductive. More than anything, I wanted to get closer, see inside, touch the building.

As I drew nearer, the dank scent of rot and earth grew. Its wood was older than me, ancient like a treasure found in an antique shop that had been closed up for decades. I couldn't explain why I was still walking toward it.

I raised my hand to the door. There was a surge; the energy made my fingers go rigid. My hand hovered, taking in the ecstasy until my knees weakened.

My hand made contact.

An intense, splitting pain sliced through my shoulders, as my body cramped. It was like my bones were being pulled out of my body through my hand. There was a transfer between it and me, and, with every second, I feared it was taking, feeding off of what little soul I had left.

I opened my mouth to scream, but I couldn't hear my own utterance. There were two other distinct voices. A man and a woman cried in dreadful torment. There was something else stirring in the shed, too. It awakened. It saw me. It was coming.

I closed my mouth and the screams vibrated through my skull to the point that my teeth rattled.

A guttural call came from somewhere. It cascaded down the mountains, surrounding me.

The energy shift broke, and I dropped to the ground. I lay there shivering uncontrollably as my brain twitched.

A second howl stretched over the valley.

"It's coming," I whispered.

The grass and leaves stirred. The movement registered in my mind, but I could only stare forward.

"Home base. Home base," high voices chanted.

I stared into nothing.

"Home base. Home base," the voices repeated.

"Home. Base," I echoed.

The grass and leaves swirled again.

A palm slapped my forehead.

I jerked with a start.

"Where?" a man's voice asked in the distance.

I attempted to crane my neck, to scream for help, but the gust of wind ripped past me, pushing my head down to the ground.

My body ached, and my arms were so sore, especially my shoulders. They felt like they did before I saw the—

Something moved beside me. I looked behind me and stood up.

Little devil winds of swirling dead leaves blew around my feet. I relaxed. It had just been the wind, and my shoulders were likely sore from fighting with Isaac, waking up at the mine, or whatever touching the shed had done to me.

I closed my eyes to accept the breeze. I needed to breathe, gather my thoughts, then either ask the man on the mountain for help or run like hell. However, no breeze touched me. The air was still. My chest warmed. I wasn't alone. I opened my eyes. I didn't have my glasses, but I could tell something was off. I could see the ground, but it was as though there was something in front of it, a filter of some kind like a distorted pane of glass. I held out my hand, but there was nothing there.

I stepped closer.

Nothing.

I again, stepped closer.

Something started moving toward me. It was as if, the ground itself was rolling after me.

I spun and bolted.

The only thing I could do was try to keep running.

I checked over my shoulder. The blur was right behind me. I turned my head and saw another blur on my left side. I readjusted my course.

The blurs fell away, but I kept running at full speed.

I expected the voice from above to yell out a command to stop or even gun fire, but that didn't happen. Instead, a low howl bellowed then rose like a horn in military movie. Franklin warned me about the wild animals on my first night. Stupid me, I had just accepted the thought of ghost children, but there were more than spirits to fear and run from in Middwood.

Goosebumps rolled over my back as the call was echoed, the bass tones full of hunger. My pounding heart dropped, as a deeper horror washed over me. I understood; the pieces fell into place. I had fallen into a trap and I was both the prey and prize.

My legs were like bricks. My calf muscles cramped, but I kept running.

On the ground ahead of me, was the warm line of orange, the crest of the sun breaking over the mountain, but that no longer mattered. I ignored everything that wasn't life or death. First I'd focus on escaping whatever was chasing me. If I survived that then I'd worry about being caught outside before sunrise.

I shifted my weight forward, trying my best to flex and roll my feet as I ran in an attempt to stretch my calves. I huffed. My mouth was completely dry.

As I ran, howls echoed back from various positions of the valley floor. Whatever was behind me was a pack animal, and not the ghost children. I didn't want to stick around to find out any more. They had me surrounded, and they were coming fast.

I grit my teeth, the drive in my head and the pounding in my chest and ears pushed me on.

In front of me was more than three hundred feet of rock and earth. I had never attempted rock climbing, but I had no choice. I had to get to higher ground.

64

I hit the foothill, my bare feet ascending up the slope. The lower part of the ridge I was able to run up. Even when I got more than a hundred feet up, it was more of a hike than a climb.

Farther up, the dirt became rock. The cliff was cold, but I was glad most of the rocks had at least one flat surface. There was pain, but there were worse things at this point. I continued my climb, blocking out all thoughts and emotions except for a simple internal mantra. *Reach. Pull. Plant. Reach. Pull. Plant.* I was exhausted, but if I could keep going, I would reach the summit. It was there. I continued. *Reach. Pull. Plant.*

My arm reached up and over onto a more open area. I pulled myself up until I could roll onto my back.

I had made it to the top. My chest heaved in between shallow laughs. I opened my eyes. There was another twelve to fifteen feet of fucking rock.

"No. No!" I cursed.

I was on a narrow cliff that was tall and vertically flat.

A bellow boomed from the ravine. It sounded more like a man yelling out a single tone. Not being able to control myself, I twisted over to look below. The blurs shot out from the base of the ridge and raced along the valley floor toward the howls.

A clash of howls and yelps exploded as they fought over the prey.

Carefully, I stood and flattened my body against the mountain. Once I was balanced, I reached up with my right hand and then my left. I searched high and low for any surface I could clutch, but there was nothing to grab.

No! Keep trying, I argued, I couldn't see what I was doing and panic had already set in.

I bent my knees, searching with my hands for a foot hold of any sort.

Nothing.

"Come on!"

Down to my left was an indention. It was too shallow, but I was desperate. I planted my foot into the crevice and kicked myself up.

I fell.

I flipped over the ledge. Luckily, I only fell a few feet, and caught myself. I dangled from one of the many teeth-shaped rocks.

The growls were replaced with what sounded like happy yips. There was no telling what was below, but I couldn't risk my terror freezing me up. I'd already made that mistake once.

Using my feet, I swung and dropped onto the cliff without falling any farther. I dug my fingernails into the mountain, I clung to the rock.

Men's voices came from below. I couldn't tell what they were saying, but there were words. My brain wanted to explode. So many thoughts pulsed through my mind, were they animals or were they men? Had someone come to my rescue? I needed my fucking glasses.

I extended my reach to the next hold.

"Hurry!" a man's voice called.

My mind was playing tricks on me and my whole body hurt, and I couldn't feel my feet. I was exhausted, but I pushed on.

"Are you okay up there?" a man shouted from below.

I froze. Was it real?

"Are you stuck?" he asked.

I tried to swallow, to lubricate my throat to speak. "Hello?"

"Hello?" another man's voice mocked.

There was a murmuring of voices.

"Hey. Do you need help mister?"

I stopped climbing and trembled as I hugged the cliff. "I'm stuck up here."

"Climb down."

"I can't see. I don't have my glasses."

"We can help you."

"I don't have my glasses. My legs, I don't want to fall."

"Stop being a pussy and come down."

"Shut up, brother," the man cursed.

Another voice spoke. He was younger, calm, "I'll climb up and meet you half way."

I strained my eyes. He was nothing more than out-of-focus dot at the base of the ridge.

"None of us are good at climbing, but I'll try if you do."

He and I both held our spots for a few movements. My mind was fighting me; I didn't know what to do. He moved to the boulders and began to climb.

I pushed the flooding thoughts away and began my descent.

"He's coming down," the first male voice said.

There was a hushed exchange. I wanted to know what they said, but I was sure it was a joke at my expense. I reminded myself that pride was for men who weren't trapped. How the hell did I end up here?

"You're doing great, mister," the climber said. "Just a little bit more and I'll have you."

One of the men laughed.

I stopped. Something wasn't right.

"Come on, mister, you're almost there," the young voice encouraged.

I told my body to continue, but my body was ignoring my commands. I began to tremble.

"Sir, are you okay?"

"Come on down, man."

I wasn't even halfway down. "You'll have to come help me. I can't move."

"Move you scared little—"

The man grunted.

I opened my eyes and peered below. The men were scattering.

"I need you to come down to me now!" the younger man commanded.

"What's going on down there?"

"Nothing."

"Where did your people go?"

"Get down here!" he roared.

The boy stalked up the mountain. I froze, petrified at what I thought I was seeing. He moved so fast, covering tens of feet at a time with ease. A few feet below me, he reached for me.

I braced myself.

There was a reflection to his grasp like his hand bounced back. He jerked his arm back in a curse.

A streak of light blue shot up to us and the boy tumbled to the bottom of the gorge.

My eyes filled with tears. I wasn't sure if it was because I was afraid I'd just witnessed someone die, or because I was afraid to die, or because I truly didn't know what was really happening. I did the only thing I could, in frightful panic, I reached up and climbed. I fought through the pain, my shaking limbs, and the barriers in my mind, everything until I once again rolled onto the narrow slab, sobbing.

I tried to quiet myself, so I could listen. The voices below were silent. Another scheme, I surmised or proof that it was all trick my mind was playing on me.

"Mr. Christian?"

I gripped the ledge with my body.

"Mr. Christian!"

In a weak attempt to keep out of sight, I lowered my head.

"Oh, my gosh. Help! Help, someone. Montana, come quick!"

Help from above, I thought. I was saved from the men, saved from the animals, saved from the ghost children. Saved by my children.

"Wait!" I shouted. "It isn't safe. Go back!" I looked down to the valley floor and stared.

There were no men, no voices, no animals, no blurs. There was no movement, only distance, rock, and earth.

"Christian, what are you doing down there?"

"I-I." My mouth spoke still staring into space between myself and the ground.

"Someone, go get help!"

"No!" I shouted. I rolled over onto my stomach and rose to my feet. "I'm fine. I just need you guys to get me out."

"Where's your shirt?"

"I-I fell."

65

I only needed to climb ten more feet to get to the schoolyard, but with the condition I was in, it might as well have been the full four thousand feet of Black Bear Mountain. Regardless, I had been caught.

The kids meant well, and I was grateful they saved me. I would never forget that, but in doing so, they had sealed my fate. There was no way I could ask them to cover for me. I could, but one of them would tell, then I'd look guiltier.

The kids proved to be extremely resourceful. Montana lowered one of the double desks down, then he, Peter, and Amy pulled me up. I asked Peter to go get his truck. Luckily Montana gave me his coat. He didn't offer it to me, he just wrapped it around me.

They were all so kind.

Peter pulled onto the schoolyard and Montana helped me into the truck.

Once the door was closed. "What the fuck happened?"

I winced at Peter's volume.

"You didn't fall, did you?"

It hurt to talk. "I'll be honest, Peter. I have no clue what happened."

"You look like crap. You want me to take you to my mom?"

"No!" I took a breath. "I don't want to see anyone. I just need to go home, shower, and get back to school."

"Christian—"

"I have some of your mom's magic water under my sink. It'll be fine."

He turned back to the road. His concern was obvious.

He huffed and shook his head. He understood more than I thought he did. I made a deal with myself: I wouldn't worry about the circumstances until I got back to the school.

Peter offered to help me into the house, but I knew with the spying neighbors I would have to suck it up and make it inside by myself. Luckily, I was still wearing Montana's coat. The more normal I looked, the better.

I pumped myself up, thinking the worst angry thoughts I could, bit my lip, and powered up to the door.

I went to the kitchen and climbed onto the counter. I repositioned myself so that I could tend to my feet in the sink. I leaned against the cabinet letting the water run over my frozen, raw, bloodied toes.

Since I wasn't in flight mode any longer, the pain was excruciating. I clenched my teeth as the water washed over and into my wounds.

I pulled my feet from the water and sat there shaking. I knew I needed to call Franklin, but, instead I went for the mason jar Tonya had given me.

I gently lowered myself off the counter. Using my arms, I tried to control my position, but I ended up falling to the kitchen floor. After many curses, I pulled the jar from under the sink. I didn't even bother attempting to climb back up on the counter. I knew I couldn't do it.

Sitting on the floor, I carefully poured a thin stream of water onto my toes. There was immediate pain followed by warm relief. I sprinkled more of the water on my hands and ran my fingers along my lower legs and feet. As I rubbed, the broken skin fell away, leaving healthy, whole skin behind.

I ran my damp hands over my chest, then I drank the rest. I didn't know if it would help anything, but I was thirsty.

Once I could stand, I washed my face in the sink, but I still needed a shower. After nearly being drowned in the tub the night before, I thought there was no way in hell anyone could get me to go back in there, but I had to. I was covered in mud, I needed clean clothes, and I had to find my glasses.

After waking up at the mine and being chased across the valley and up the mountain, I couldn't help but wonder what would happen to me next. I wanted out of Middwood, but I started to believe the town wouldn't let me leave.

Part of me wanted to lock myself in the Tomb and hide, but I had to go to school. Everything needed to be seen as normal. I'd get myself together on the ride back. I'd call Casteel to have him tow and fix my car again, and then, the first chance I got, I would get the fuck out of town before they killed me.

66

I t had been a terrible morning, and even though the kids had saved me, they were all being absolute babies.

Everyone was tired and petty, and if they didn't stop complaining, I was going to... I couldn't have cared less if Joshua chopped up the entire class, as long as it was quiet afterward.

Amy and Montana were bickering at each other, and she and I locked eyes.

"What's wrong with you?" she asked with the most attitude she had ever displayed.

I fired back, "I live in Middwood."

Peter let out a grunting laugh.

I grinned at his approval and raised a finger. "And yes, class, that counts as the question of the day."

So much for keeping my head down.

"But, Mr. Christian," piped Scarlet. "I had a good one and—"

I held out my hand to her and gestured for her to zip it. If Scarlet spoke more than three words to me, I would probably kill her.

Hey everyone, Joshua Johnson did it. I smiled at my scenario.

The room grew dark as I imagined throwing Scarlet through the desks. She was so small the weight of her body wouldn't even push a desk askew, instead, she would flip and tumble over them. Of course, she would be crying, that crazy little face. What would really get me going was that obnoxious voice begging, "Why, why, why?"

She'd struggle to her feet, then I would backhand the whiny bitch back to the floor. I would break her spine with my knee as I threw all my weight down on her tiny, little frame. I would easily pin her down as I lunged down on her other shoulder. She would be so out of it she wouldn't even know I had killed her, but I would still do it. If my ax were out of reach, I'd use her bird face to balance myself as I grabbed it.

An ax would be overkill. You don't use a bomb to kill a blue jay. A young, fragile, but loud and annoying bird that deserves to die.

I snapped out of my trance.

What the fuck was that? I must have blacked out. Did I?

I shook. Images of Darlene filled my mind, her laughing, then crying on the floor. Had I done it again?

I searched the classroom in a panicked murmur, "Scarlet?" I couldn't find her. I scanned the concerned, questioning looks of the students, but I didn't see her. "Where's Scarlet?" I shouted. All the kids were there, but I couldn't find her. "Where the hell is she?" I demanded.

"Jeeeeez, I'm right here," she waved her raised hand. "What did I do now?"

I covered my mouth. She was right in front of me. Right next to Carla, where she always sat.

I went and knelt beside the little girl. I wrapped my arms around her. "I'm sorry, Scarlet."

"Mr. Christian's hugging me!" she laughed. "Why are you hugging me?"

"I don't know," I said as I continued hugging her, pushing all the vile images from my mind.

"Someone has already been by then?" a deep male voice asked.

I looked at the door. It was the preacher, Mr. Gresham.

His head was lowered, and his hands were clasped in front of his stomach. "Someone's already come by?" he repeated, then gestured toward Scarlet.

I lowered my arms. "I'm not sure I understand."

The preacher looked perplexed. "I just thought since you were consoling the child..."

"Oh, that, I don't know what came over me. I just thought she needed..." I stopped talking. There was nothing I could say that would make sense. I stood, my right knee—the one I used in the daydream to crush Scarlet's shoulder—was stiff. "What can I help you with?" I said with a slight sound of physical pain in my voice.

Mr. Gresham eyed me and looked down at my leg, but then he resumed in a low and steady tone, "There has been an... event."

The already quiet class went silent as a prayer. Even the background noise of the wind and birds was still. Gresham continued. "And I'm afraid it involves Scarlet's mother."

The children's faces went sullen. It was so quiet I could hear a high-pitched ringing in my ears and the faint sound of my heart.

"What is it?" I asked.

He looked at Scarlet and she met his gaze. Scarlet seemed to know what it meant, but she turned to look to her left and right in hopes of deflecting his eyes. She strained her neck and tightened her lips. She tried not to cry.

I shouted, "Will someone, please tell me what the hell is going on?"

No one spoke.

Peter raised his hand. "Christian?" he spoke quietly, "Mr. Gresham means to say that someone has passed."

I glanced at Scarlet, then back to Mr. Gresham. "Magnolia?" My voice was low and dry.

Gresham nodded. "Bobby called the sheriff to go wake her, same as always, but Philip had already gotten some calls from the trailer park about a commotion."

I knelt again, and Scarlet threw her small arms around me and began to sob.

"When?" the shock in my voice sounded familiar. I remembered asking that question when I was told about my Rose-Mary Grand and my father.

"The sheriff's not sure, but the neighbors said before sunrise valley time this morning.

"She didn't just pass; she was murdered," Gresham said with a hoarseness developing in his voice.

"What are you...? Why are you saying this in front of her?"

"They'll find out soon enough," he said in growing hopelessness.

"Who did it, preacher?" asked Amy.

"That, I shouldn't say. Something I didn't think I'd ever have to say again."

"What does that mean?" I asked.

"It was a ghost child wasn't it?" asked Jason.

"Was it?" asked Montana.

Other students chimed in. "Who did it, preacher?"

"It looks like one of the damned." Gresham's words sounded like they were boiling up from his lower gut.

Horror struck the class, as several whispered, "Joshua Johnson?"

Jason threw out his arm and pointed to me. "See what you've done, you son-of-a-bitch!"

Peter stood. "Hold on, kid."

I pointed at both of them. "Peter, Jason! Sit down."

Gresham's voice pulsed with panic. "She died from multiple ax wounds to the head and shoulders."

I shot to my feet. "I told you to shut up!"

Gresham's voice sounded like he was somewhere far away, "Whoever it was beat her up something awful. He broke her shoulder like it was chalk, and he chopped her up just like he did his parents."

"That's enough, Gresham," Sheriff Rollin said, stepping into the school.

Gresham's face tensed, which subsided when Franklin walked in.

Both the sheriff's and Frank's faces were long, tired, and covered with concern. The sheriff's eyes focused on me. "I need to speak to Scarlet."

Franklin reached out to the girl. "Come on, sweetheart. We're going to go see Grandma Rollin at the church."

Scarlet became aware that everyone was staring at her. She gathered up a maturity that amounted to more than her twelve years and sulked over to Franklin.

He ushered her out the door. "We're going to get you situated with a family," his words trailed off. I watched them through the window. She held Franklin's hand as they walked to the sheriff's truck.

Mr. Gresham tried to speak, but I cut him off. "Not another word!"

I turned and adjusted my clothes while I tried to calm myself. "Children, all of you, go home. Go straight home, and don't stop moving until you get there."

The children obeyed and exited.

I went to Philip. "Who will look after her?"

"The church will take good care of her. One of the families will take her in. She'll have her a bed, other kids, food. She'll be fine, Matt."

"Losing a parent like that? I'm not so sure."

I rubbed my hands over my hair and let out a deep breath. "Let me know if I can do anything."

"Of course." Philip put his hat on and stepped outside. "Come on, Gresham."

Gresham stared at me. "I want to know why you were consoling the child like you already knew what happened."

It was like a jab to the face. I knew I couldn't explain my daydream to him.

He narrowed his eyes. "What's wrong with your leg?"

"It's nothing."

"That's what I thought you'd say," he said.

"I'm not Joshua Johnson."

"That may be, teacher, but all of this stuff started after you came into town. Don't think people haven't noticed."

"Noticed what?"

He let out a cocky grunt. "You being out after dark on numerous occasions, knocking on people's doors, running home right before daybreak half-naked? Care to explain that?"

I didn't respond.

"Somehow you're in on it."

"That's ridiculous. I haven't done anything."

"You came to town."

"You think I'm a killer? You really are backwoods if you think that."

"Watch your words, mister," said Gresham as he drove his index finger into my chest.

I slapped his hand away.

He stepped closer, hovering over me. "I don't think you know what you've gotten yourself into, teacher. You might need to think about where you are—"

"Or where I need to be?"

"You said it not me. Maybe you can read minds?"

"Simple thoughts are easy to determine," I said.

He brought up his fist. I flinched.

Damn it, I flinched.

My embarrassment ran across my face.

He grinned, which was the worst insult. "You just watch that mouth, boy."

I'd gone from "sir," to "teacher," to "boy" in less than a minute. I tried to stand strong. "I have nothing to hide."

"We all do, boy." He shoved me, which was enough to make me stagger back.

"Let's go, Gresham," called the sheriff from outside.

"Don't turn your back on an open window," he said and walked out of the schoolhouse.

I slammed my palm down and leaned over the desk. I had shown my bluff. What's worse, I just made an enemy or created a bully out of the preacher. "What the hell?"

"Don't feel bad, Mr. Christian," a voice said.

"Why not?" I asked.

"He's bigger than you. Anyone would have been afraid of him."

I turned around.

There was no one there. The room was empty except for the slow rising dust floating in the yellow sunlight.

67

I needed to talk to Franklin, but I needed to go home first and get myself together. My head buzzed, and my eyes burned. No matter how many times, or how hard I blinked, they kept burning. Just one pill would get me together, then I would go to find him.

I opened the front door and slammed it. "Finally, quiet," I assured myself and then rested my head against the door.

"Have a bad day, Matt?"

I jumped and threw myself against the wall. Sitting in the armchair next to the fireplace was Frank.

"Frank, you scared the shit out of me."

He said nothing, just sat there with a stoic expression on his face.

"What are you doing in—"

He cut me off, "In my own house? I'm visiting my tenant. Sit down."

His tone was clear. This wasn't going to be good. I sat on the sofa, but then got up and started pacing. I took a deep breath and exhaled, rubbing the back of my neck.

His beady eyes studied me. "Matt, are you okay?"

"Yes, of course, it's just everything that's happening. Magnolia, I mean."

He held up a hand. "I didn't mean that. I meant are you okay?"

I paused. "I said yes."

He narrowed his eyes. "Are you fit to teach children?"

I stopped. "What the hell are you talking about?"

He shook his head. "I'll be honest with you, Matt, I've seen your bathroom and your bottles of pills. There are so many I had to call Bill. Some of them are serious medications prescribed only to mental patients."

"How dare you go through my stuff? You have no right—"

He deflected all the emotion I was throwing at him. "It's my house, I can do whatever I want. The pills, Matt. Or do I need to call the sheriff."

I stopped. "They're just for depression," I said in frustration.

"Not just depression—"

I spoke over him, "And anxiety. You don't have to tell me. I know the medications I take. They were given to me by a doctor!"

Franklin shook his head.

"I don't care what you think. You, Bankward, or the whole goddamned town."

"Speaking of Bankward, he made a phone call to your old school."

I recoiled and stared out the window.

"Turns out Middwood's newest resident has a few skeletons in his closet, and I'm beginning to wonder if he just added another one."

I turned. "Why didn't you tell me about the house?"

He held up his hand. "Don't change the subject."

I threatened, "No. No, you don't change the subject. Why didn't you tell me Sarah was your daughter?"

Frank fought to stay calm. "Matt, did you kill Magnolia?"

"No, I didn't." I pulled the ottoman close to him and sat. "Why didn't you tell me about the ghost children?"

"I asked you about them after you were outside in the middle of the night screaming your head off."

"But, Frank, you never *told* me about them!"

"We're not talking about children who died thirteen years ago."

I stood, throwing my hands up. "They're not in the ground! None of them are! It is so bizarre that a whole town will talk about them, but yet you work so hard to cover up—"

"What was the argument you had with Magnolia yesterday? You were screaming at each other. A lot of people said you got very heated."

"Frank, she had her hands all over me!"

"Scarlet told the sheriff that when you walked her home last Thursday night, you and Magnolia were discussing meeting up together—"

"Scarlet was scared, so I walked her home—"

"Were you sleeping with Magnolia?"

"God, no."

"What were you doing at old man Casteel's shed this morning?"

"How do you know about that?"

He crossed his arms. "So you admit it?"

"One of the bastards attacked me last night."

"One of the what?"

I pushed my palms into my eyes and leaned my head back. "The ghost children! Are you not fucking listening to me?"

"Matt, please—"

I paced the living room. "One did! The little one, dripping wet, attacked me upstairs and I woke up at the goddamn mine!" I shouted pointing out the window. "Now you explain that to me," I demanded.

"Maybe we can say that you were out of your mind and you didn't mean to kill her."

"Are you serious? I didn't—"

Franklin stood. "Why were you at the shed?"

I gritted through my teeth, "I didn't go there."

"Were you with Magnolia last night?"

"No!"

"Did you two get in a fight?"

"That was only at the store. She—"

"Is that why you were half-naked, trapped on the mountain? You were hiding?"

"I woke up that way—"

"I can't help you unless you let me."

"I'm telling you—"

"How many pills did you take today?"

"None!"

He stood face to face with me, raising his voice, "How many pills did you take yesterday?"

"I don't know!"

"Matt, the woman is dead. Killed in broad daylight and everyone is looking at you."

"She was killed with an ax. I'm not your grandson!"

Slap

The silence stung me more than his hand. My mind filled with so many options, actions, words, murderous urges, and fears following the strike.

I didn't look at him. "I didn't kill anyone."

"How many pills?"

"I don't know, I can't remember. I—"

Franklin's tone softened. "Matt, the children say you talk to yourself all the time. You see things, you hear things, and sometimes you just start crying. You were crying this morning when the kids found you."

"I was trapped on a fucking mountain cliff!"

"You were crying this afternoon when Pastor Gresham walked in. You were down on your knees telling Scarlet how sorry you were."

"That was just a daydream."

"A daydream? Matt, are you hearing yourself?"

I shut up. It was time to keep quiet.

In response to my silence, Franklin looked grim. "I see." He moved to the door.

"Franklin, I didn't kill Magnolia."

"I hope you didn't. I really hope you didn't, but until this is sorted out, I am closing the school. You are to remain inside until notified."

"What? Stay here? Am I under arrest?"

He stopped at the door. "Would you rather sleep in a jail cell?"

My heart beat hard, and my face burned red, but I didn't care. "If the devil chooses to take my soul because I broke this town's rules, then so be it. I'm guilty of that, but I did not kill Magnolia."

"I hope you're right." He turned to me, "because you don't want to know what we do to people who hurt one of our own. Do me a favor, remember what you just said about the devil." He opened the door and turned to me. "But, Mr. Christian, it won't be the devil who will be coming for you.

It will be his children."

I fumed as he left. I crossed to the door and slammed my fist against the wood.

I dashed up the stairs to the bathroom. The medicine cabinet was open, and my bottles were all out of order. I clenched my teeth as I swiped my hand across the shelves, sending bottles flying across the room and into the toilet.

"Dammit!" I shouted and dropped to my knees looking for Rose-Mary Grand's pills.

I stuck my hands into the toilet and pulled the bottle out of the basin. I twisted the cap, shook out two pills, and stood up.

I popped them in my mouth and turned on the water, but then I caught a glimpse of myself in the mirror. "Stop," I whispered.

I froze and looked at the bottle. Was there any truth in it? The dreams, the mine, the shed, the girls, and the pills?

I spit the pills out, and I put the bottle down.

I wandered into the Tomb and leaned my back against the door until it shut. If I could have locked myself in from the outside, I would have.

I was still. I was afraid. I left the light on. I'm not sure how long I stood there. I'm not even sure I was thinking. Every time I tried to think, my mind would snap back like a pulled rubber band to questions, lots and lots of questions, too hard, too locked away to mention.

I started crying. I wasn't crying out of fear, but because my mind wasn't able to comprehend what was going on. Why was I being haunted? Had I conjured the ghosts?

I started playing over my fantasy of killing Scarlet in my mind. It had been so real.

My legs started to tire, and I slid down the back of the door. "I'm going insane."

Like my father, and just like my Rose-Mary Grand, I was crazy.

But the real question clawed its way to the surface. My lips parted, moving on their own and I heard myself ask, "*Did* I kill Magnolia?"

68

Tuesday, November 10, 1964
Sunrise 7:06 AM. Sunset 5:27 PM.

Hours later, I cracked open the door to the Tomb. Amber light poured onto the hallway carpet from the bathroom. It was morning.

"I made it." I didn't wake up anywhere strange, I didn't have any crazy dreams, but that was because I'd fought all night to stay awake. I ran my fingers through my hair and let out a crazed laugh.

I went downstairs and opened the shutters. I glimpsed two of the neighbors closing their windows, and Amy's mother ran inside.

"What gives?" I shook my head. Why was she running? What? Were they afraid of me? I wondered.

I stood there and pondered that. They were. They were afraid of me. I chuckled. It was a new kind of feeling. Power. People were afraid of me.

"That's right, bitch! You better hide! I'll cut you up!" I snarled, then burst into laughter. I knew I was exhausted, which only made the laughter more amusing. I added some extra air behind it and out boomed an evil cackle.

I strutted into the kitchen and got myself some cereal. While I fixed my bowl, a mischievous grin grew across my face. I grabbed my bowl and went to the front door. I threw it open and walked out onto the porch and chomped and crunched as loud as I could.

The man across the street was heading off to the mine for his shift. I called out to him, "Good morning, neighbor."

He gave me a perplexed look. He didn't respond, but I waved at him until he waved back. I shouted, "I have to piss."

He turned his head and kept walking.

I looked back to the three houses across the street. I could feel their eyes on me. Of course, they were watching me. They didn't have anything else to do.

I put my bowl down on the porch rail, and I slowly pulled off my shirt. Then twirled it above my head.

I did have to pee.

A grin sprouted on my face, as I toyed with the idea of peeing off the porch. My dad used to do it all the time.

"Screw it." I stepped up to the banisters, and I lowered my zipper.

The phone rang.

I tilted my head back. "Dammit, people, the show was just about to start." I pointed to all the houses. "I saw you looking! I know you did."

Grabbing my bowl, I turned on my heels and walked inside, leaving the door opened.

I picked up the phone. I already knew who it was. "What, Frank?"

"Put some clothes on."

"Go fuck yourself." I hung up.

I laughed and took another bite of my cereal. I still had to pee, and I smiled as I walked back to the door. I crossed the threshold about the same time the sheriff's truck pulled up. I rolled my eyes and thought about doing a cartwheel.

He rolled down the window. "Matt?"

I leaned over the porch rails, smacking. "Yes, Philip Rollin? I mean, Sheriff."

He put his elbow on the door and leaned toward me. "How are you doing this morning?" he asked with a concerned smile.

"What, Sheriff?" I smiled. "I can't hear you. I would come down there, but Franklin put me under house arrest."

"Did he?" He continued his grin.

"Yep." I gave a deep nod.

He snapped his fingers and pointed his index finger at me like you would when you caught someone in a white lie. "You heard me that time."

I copied his gesture. "Yes, sir, I did."

Rollin eyed me.

"But don't worry, Sheriff Philip Rollin, I'm staying right here. I'm just eating some cereal. Would you like some?"

He gave a laugh. "Would I like some cereal?" he asked, and he got out of his truck.

"Oh shit," I said, and I couldn't help but let out a nervous laugh. *Well damn, there goes my badass to dumbass.*

As he got closer, I remembered how hard a simple back slap from him was. "Are you going to take me to jail?"

Slowing shaking his head, he walked toward the porch. "No."

I scratched my beard. "Are you going to beat me up?"

"No." His foot hit the first step.

By the time he got to the top of the stairs, I was reminded that Philip was a good foot taller than me. I bit my lip and stayed quiet.

He raised his chin. "It's a bit cold out to be shirtless."

I said nothing.

"Matt?" he asked raising his eyebrows.

"Um," I tried to think. "It's too warm inside."

"Maybe you're just sick."

"That's what they tell me." I laughed, but I was talking like a crazy person, like I was drunk. Like Magnolia.

"Are you? Sick?" He put his hand on my forehead. His fingers reached more than halfway around my head.

"Don't kill me."

"What?" He laughed. "If I killed you, I couldn't get my cereal."

"Oh. You really want some cereal?"

"Well, you did offer, and I am hungry."

"Oh." I began to move but jerked to a stop. I didn't know if he was toying with me or if he was being serious. I stepped to the door. "Um, sure. Come on in." My breath came in shallow gasps. I stopped. "On second thought, why don't you wait here and I'll bring it out to you?"

"No. Thanks. I don't like the cold. Let's go inside."

He followed me into the kitchen. While I poured him a bowl, he took off his hat. We ate our cereal standing up, him leaning against the refrigerator and me standing in front of the sink.

I felt exposed. "I'll be right back."

"Where are you going?"

"I left my shirt outside."

I moved toward the door, but he sidestepped, blocking my path. "I thought you were hot?"

"No, I'm good now."

"You wanted it off so leave it off."

I returned to my bowl and went back to eating. I forced down the remaining three spoonfuls. It was like eating sandpaper.

He finished and held the bowl out to me. "That was great. Thanks."

I took it from him and went to put it in the sink. I didn't want to turn my back to him, but I didn't want to make him angry. I turned.

He rushed up behind me, grabbed me by my shoulders, spun me around to face him, and lifted me off the ground.

My eyes widened and I stared at my feet as they dangled. He had me in his vice-grip hold. Even if I was dumb enough to try and fight him, he had my arms immobilized. I wasn't about to start kicking him.

I didn't do anything.

"Look at me," he said calmly.

I did.

"You know I could hurt you if I wanted to, don't you?"

I stared into his eyes and my chin melted into a nod.

"Good. But, Matt, I don't want to do that. So will you do me a favor?"

I nodded.

"Will you do that for me, Matt? A favor? I don't mind coming over here again. I don't mind at all. I enjoy the company, but Bankward is a man you don't want to dick around with. And Franklin is trying to help you. Are we clear?"

"Yes, sir."

"Good."

He dropped me, and I stumbled back into the counter.

"Thanks for the cereal." He put on his hat and his heavy

boots stomped through the living room, out the front door, and down the wooden steps.

When I heard his truck drive away, I ran to the door and locked it. I then crept to the shutters and closed them without exposing myself. I reached for my shirt, but it was gone. I looked all around the kitchen and in the living room, but it wasn't there. I peered out the shutters. It was laying on the front steps. I shrank away from the window. I didn't dare go back outside.

The phone rang. I picked it up but said nothing. I hated Franklin Mullis at that moment. I'm not sure I ever really liked him in the first place.

"Matt, I'm sorry for having to do that."

"I'm sure." There was a biting restraint in my voice like a collared dog.

"Don't be sour. Be an adult about this. I'll get it sorted out as soon as possible."

I didn't say anything, but he didn't hang up. Finally, I said, "Do you think I killed Magnolia, Frank?" There was a clicking sound in my throat.

"I'll be honest with you, there is always something strange going on in Middwood. I don't know if you did it or not. If you did, I'll find out. If you didn't, I'll find out. So if you are innocent, you can relax. That I can promise you."

"How will you know the truth when you find it?"

"I have my ways, and I've never been wrong before."

"What about your daughter?"

He was quiet. "Try and get some rest."

I hung up and waited a few minutes to see if he would call back. He didn't. Even though he had sent the sheriff over to put me in my place, I knew I was the one being a dick.

I squeezed my burning eyes as I leaned against the

refrigerator. I exhaled, and my throat gave another click. It only did that when I was exhausted.

I decided I'd had enough fun for the day, and I was ready to do something I didn't get to do much. I made my way upstairs. For once, I wanted the darkness.

69

I woke when several knocks rapped on my front door. My temples ached while the rest of my head pounded. *How long had I slept?*

I covered my ears and laid back down.

The chipper pecks continued on my door.

"What?" I croaked.

More damn knocking.

"Go away, ghost children," I moaned to myself. My mouth as bitter tasting as the venom in my words.

I yawned through the cotton dryness on my tongue, as I smacked my lips, pouted, and crawled toward the noise.

I made my way to the door and opened it. A small brown package floated in front of my face. I was instantly annoyed.

"Did someone at this address order a Sears package?" a voice asked in a bad New Jersey accent as from some old detective movie I would have hated.

The box was lowered to reveal what was behind it: the smiling face of Peter.

"Hey," I said blankly. "What are you doing here?" I asked leaning against the door. "I'm sleeping."

"I'm delivering your order, sir," Peter informed as he danced the box about.

I covered my eyes with my palms. "Don't move so much so quickly, I might throw up."

"Oh, brother. Are you drunk?" Peter asked, enjoying himself way too much.

"No," I said the word in two syllables.

"Someone is being a grouch."

"Sorry. I'll be back to myself tomorrow."

"Sign the paper, and then you can have it. I don't know how you guys do it down in Atlanta, but this here is the back—"

I lowered my hands. "Please don't say that."

He held out a worn, brown mini-clipboard.

"Oh, you were being serious? You work for Sears?"

"I make a few deliveries in the afternoon."

"I thought you were just being... Peter."

"Since Magnolia died there is no school, so here I am."

I signed the slip and took the box. He looked at me with his stupid smile. He was waiting for something. I stared at him blankly.

"You're welcome," he said.

"Oh, okay, good. I thought you were waiting for a tip," I said, then I chuckled. I began to shut the door, but he didn't move.

My laughter subsided. I shifted my weight and let the box rest on my hip. "Okay. I got it. Thank you."

"What's in the box?" he asked with youthful curiosity.

"Peter, I'm really beat."

"Mail-order bride?"

I sighed. "Bedsheets."

"Why do you need bedsheets if you never sleep?"

"Peter—"

He stepped into the doorway. "Aren't you going to invite me in?"

"It's getting late."

"Well, I want to hear what happened."

My shoulders drooped lower. "Have a good night, Mr. Janowski."

"I like the way that sounds. Will you start calling me that?"

"Goodbye," I said, pushing him out of the threshold.

"Okay, have a good night," he said and spun to go.

I turned my head and started to shut the door, but before it closed Peter rushed passed me and bounced up the stairs.

"Peter, not now. Please." I shouted after him.

He went into the bathroom, then came back out. He leaned against the banister, pointing his thumb back like a cocky hitchhiker. "Why did you take the painting down?"

I frowned. "I thought it was silly."

"You took the painting down because it scared you, didn't you? Did you burn it?"

"No, I put it in the hall closet."

"Takes balls. Big, hairy balls," he said with prideful, dramatic nods.

"Well, that's lovely," I said with unease. "Have a good night." I moved back toward the opened door and held it for him.

He looked down at me. I thought he was going to smile or say goodbye, but he didn't.

"It's almost one of the town rules."

"But it's not," I said.

"But it almost is, and you're breaking it. God knows you're already in deep shit," he assured me.

"I'll put it back."

"You don't have to. I'm your friend, so I'm not going to tell on you. I just haven't seen anyone without a painting in the john."

"Peter, go home before you get us both in more trouble."

"I have to use the bathroom."

"You were just in there."

"But I got distracted by the lack of the painting."

"Why didn't you just say you needed to use the bathroom when you got here?"

"I n-e-e-d t-o p-i-s-s."

"I'll give you a quarter if you go pee on Mrs. Rebecca's flowers."

"Come on!"

"Do you really have to go that bad?"

He didn't answer.

"God." I sighed and pointed to the bathroom.

He hopped in and shut the door.

I guessed he did have to go. Moments later he flushed and reappeared.

"Good, now go home."

"I can't go home," he said with a serious face.

"Why not?"

He did a little twirl. "It's too dark. Joshua Johnson will get me," he joked, then disappeared down the hall. "Let's see. What other kinda crazy stuff have you been doing?"

"Do not go down there. Stay out of my room—Peter!"

"No, no, Mr. Janowski, please," he corrected from out of sight.

"Please, come back downstairs!" I muttered, "God, I hate children."

From upstairs exploring, he called, "Oh, a locked door. What's in here?"

"I have no idea."

"What do you mean? It's a locked door in the house you are staying in."

"Franklin said it was to remain locked—"

"Want me to pick it? You know I can."

"No. Stop." I shook my head. "Where does a kid in Middwood learn to pick a lock anyway."

"Boy's Life."

My face went blank.

"Come on. Don't you want to know what's in there?"

With a firm tone, "I said no!"

"God, you are uptight." He moved into the Tomb, and I could hear his voice and footsteps through the floor. "You know, Christian, it's almost a criminal act."

"I know, and that's exactly why I want you to leave."

"You wear funny underwear."

"Peter!" I demanded.

"I'm just kidding. There isn't any up here."

I held my temples and walked through the kitchen and sat at the dining room table. If I ignored him, maybe he would finally come downstairs. I took the box he'd brought. The photograph displayed the perfect bed with correct sized, perfect, turned-down sheets topped with two big, fluffy pillows. It read, "You'll sleep like a dream." I sighed longingly.

"I wish Joshua Johnson would come. I'd give you to him," I said to myself with a smirk.

Peter shouted, "Hey! Why did you lock the door?"

I yelled up to him, "I'm downstairs, you bozo!"

Snap.

A branch of a bush broke outside the window. I shot to my feet, spinning to window behind me. My spine still tingling and radiated with heat. *Run, run, run,* the voice in my head clear and sharp.

I grunted at myself as I rubbed the nape of my neck. "This town has made me one jumpy cat."

Peter called again, but his voice sounded farther away. "Okay, okay. Open the door."

"Just a second, I'll- "

The bushes rustled, and I slowly lowered my arm.

My heart rate quickened, as I examined the closed shutters. There was nothing to be afraid of, I told myself. The shutters were closed, but eyes touched me like unwanted hands. I glanced through the dining room door to the window in the living area. It was shut.

I held my eyes on the window in front of me.

My chest expanded. I must have been holding my breath. I was being silly, I told myself. Even though I slept all day, I was exhausted, hearing things.

"Matt?" Peter called.

My words failed me. My throat was like lead.

I hesitated, but I slowly reached out of my fingers towards the little gold hook that held the shutters closed.

"Stop being a child," I told myself.

With both hands, I grasped the two little knobs and spread open the shutters.

I froze face to face with Joshua Johnson.

The eldest ghost child peered at me his eyes somewhere hidden under his hooded sweatshirt with only a thin sheet of glass between us.

The boy stood still.

I clenched my fists to my sides. "Leave me alone. I don't want to see you. Do you hear me?"

He stepped closer to the glass.

"No. I won't turn my back on the window."

Joshua Johnson lifted his arm and revealed an ax in his

right hand. I regarded it, but then glared back into the darkened hood.

"Go away," I shouted.

Joshua raised the steel point of the ax and placed it against the window. He raked it across the glass. The screech was loud enough to drown out the double bass of my heart.

I reached out and flung the shutters closed.

"Go away! Do you hear me? Go away!"

"What's going on down there?" Peter shouted, beating on the door.

I fixated my widened eyes on the window as I retreated toward the kitchen. "I'm not turning around. I'm not turning around."

The glass shattered and the shutters burst open. My arms covered my face, as shards of glass and splintered wood sprayed across the room.

70

Joshua Johnson stepped through the window.

He was here to kill me, but . . . *Oh no, Peter.*

As I kept my eyes locked on the darkness of the hooded face in front of me, I tried calling out to Peter to stay upstairs, but my voice was hardened lead.

Joshua took the blade from the window, drew it back, and shattered the glass with one swing. My arms covered my face, as shards of glass and splintered wood sprayed across the room. When I looked up, his ax was coming straight for my head.

I ducked and dove to the right.

Joshua's blade cut into the frame of the dining room door jamb.

His blade was embedded so deep he had to use both hands to retrieve it. With that much force, he would have easily taken my head off.

I scurried away under the dining room table as he recovered his weapon and looked down at me on the floor. He raised the weapon above his head.

I dashed for new cover, as the ax blade ate through the table top protruding only an inch from my scalp.

Peter pulled and banged on the door. "What's going on down there?"

I wasn't going to make it, but I hoped Peter stayed in the Tomb.

Joshua kicked the table, and it flipped over, uncovering me. I scrambled through the doorway to the living room, but he grabbed me by the back of my shirt. He threw me head first across the room into the staircase wall. My face cracked the plaster.

He immediately grabbed me again by my arm and my hair, lifted me up, and flipped me down into the table behind the sofa. The table and I crashed to the floor.

I was dazed and had lost my glasses in the attack, but, from the floor, I could see part of his face. I could make out a huge devilish smile.

I couldn't look away.

He raised his ax.

"What the fuck?" Peter shouted somewhere toward the top of the stairs.

"Stay back," I struggled to say.

Peter stuttered a chant, fumbling over his foreign words.

Joshua turned his attention to Peter. I pushed myself to my feet and jumped onto the stair's banister. Peter, still trying his chant, cursed at himself, then grabbed my arm and helped pull me over. My foot struck something as I hurdled over the railing.

I couldn't see what was happening behind me, but somehow we managed to get up the stairs.

"Come on!"

We made it down the hall to the Tomb, but the door was locked.

I shoved my weight against the bloodwood, but it didn't budge.

"Hurry, Christian!"

I panicked as I slammed myself against the door. "It's locked."

Peter pushed. "I swear I didn't lock it."

We were trapped. The door was too thick and heavy to kick in. The thing that was supposed to keep us safe was keeping us out.

"Matt, he's coming!"

I spun, and Joshua Johnson came into view as he reached the top of the stairs. He moved in a graceful rocking motion with steady, calm steps. Joshua swung his arm out, and the metal point of his ax penetrated the wall's plaster. He held the handle firmly, and the blade dug an unsteady trench down the length of the hall.

As the chipping paint flaked and fell, I remembered swinging punches at Isaac as he held me under the tub's faucet. It was pointless to try and fight a ghost.

Peter held his leather chord in his hands, saying a silent prayer.

Pointless or not, I would do my best to protect Peter, or at least give him a chance to escape.

I stepped forward, putting myself between Peter and Joshua. I gritted my teeth. "Come on you bastard."

Joshua pulled back his ax and swung.

I raised my arm to take the blow, but I was pulled into a room.

My ass hit the floor as Peter slammed the door between Joshua and us.

It took me a second to orient myself. "What?" was all I could say, while I stared at Peter. "What just happened?"

His eyes and mouth were wide as he shook his lower jaw. "I don't know! I tried it again, and it opened."

"How did you open—"

I noticed the light-purple walls, oak furniture, and a single bed covered in a solid purple quilt.

We were in the locked room, the secret room on the left. "How did you—"

My eyes fell on a picture frame that set on a light oak dresser. I moved to it and picked it up. The frame held a photograph of a beautiful young woman with shoulder-length hair. "The woman from my dream." I whispered. "Sarah, this is Sarah's bedroom."

It had to have been her. Before Turtle revealed her true ghost form she was just a sweet little girl. The resemblance between Sarah and Turtle was remarkable.

A heavy chop boomed into the door, breaking my reverie and causing me to jump.

The second slash came with such force it splintered through the upper left corner.

I marveled in terror at the supernatural strength Joshua Johnson had to break through the dense wood. Then he started hacking into the middle of the door near the frame.

Horrified, I realized what he was doing. "He's cutting away the wood around the hinges." He would be inside the room in minutes.

I rushed to the dresser. "Peter, help me brace the door."

Peter's shoulders and neck strained as we pushed the barrier into place. "I wish we had that devil painting."

"Why?"

"Because if something bad happens, you are supposed to hide in the bathroom!"

"What?"

"It's another unofficial rule—" Peter gasped. "What is that? There's a window!"

"What win—"

The door disintegrated into flying chunks of splintering wood, revealing Joshua Johnson.

I held my breath.

Somehow, my heart pounded even faster. It was deafening. I wanted to scream because there was nothing else I could do but wait.

The dark stirred.

The killer stepped into the light, like death breaking through a grave.

71

J oshua kicked the dresser. It crashed into me.

Everything seemed to slow down as I flew backward and collided with Peter, sending his smaller frame soaring. He grunted as he landed on the bed and bounced off, then hit the floor. I fell on my backside as the frame shattered, rose into the air, and peppered me. I watched as the frame spiraled across the room until it bounced off the window.

I couldn't see what Peter was doing, but I heard him gasp. I wanted to ask if he was all right, but my concern came out as a whimper. I couldn't look away as Joshua entered the room with his ax.

I lay on the ground, but I needed to move.

Joshua chopped downward. I pushed away, and the blade landed between my legs.

Joshua seized my foot with one hand and yanked me to him. I grabbed at the floor, but his strength was unnatural. He jerked me off the ground like the nothing I was to him.

He held me with his left arm, and he lifted the ax with

his right. He gave me a sharp shake. It was like the wanted to make sure I was awake, so I could see what was coming.

I was paralyzed with fear as he held his shining ax less than an inch away from my cheek. He slid his blade into my skin. Blood dripped onto my exposed neck. I trembled in terror that was far worse than the pain.

"There are two more!" Peter shouted. "There are two more ghost children outside!"

Joshua's hood looked to the window. I crumpled to the floor as Grace and Turtle phased through the unbroken glass with a shriek.

I didn't wait to see what was next. I had barely survived a single encounter with one of the brothers or the two sisters, but three of them together was an entirely different situation. Pushing all thought out of my head, I twisted around and grabbed Peter by the back of his collar and lugged him over the bed. I could hear him choking, but he could forgive me later. Peter kicked his legs to scoot closer to me. He pulled at his collar, so I grabbed his hand, lifted him up, and we bolted down the hallway, but Peter stopped.

I pulled at him. "Come on!"

"The painting." He flung open the hall closet, reached inside, and held the painting to his chest.

Screams clawed out of the bedroom at the end of the hall, stabbing at my spine like ice picks.

Joshua was thrown from Sarah's room and slammed into the door of the Tomb. The screams escaped the bedroom in blue light as the girls launched themselves at Joshua. They snatched him in a blur and returned to the room. The sound of breaking glass followed the frenzy of the commotion.

"They're fighting over us like a pack of hungry animals."

"Fuck, I don't know what to do," I spat.

We could go downstairs, but there was nowhere to hide.

"What are we waiting for!"

"Peter, wait!"

The front door rocked.

"He's run around," Peter said.

Grace and Turtle stepped out of the second bedroom.

I shouted, "You've got to be kidding!"

Even with the girls stalking toward us and another ghost at the door, I couldn't help but stare at the painting.

Peter moved in front of me. He knelt and placed the devil painting on the hardwood floor between the ghost sisters and us. "Eat this, bitches!"

The ghosts continued.

Nothing happened, and my heart sank.

I began to move, but Peter held out his arms for me to stay put.

It shifted.

I swallowed.

The image of the devil spun and slid toward the girls.

Grace and Turtle regarded the painting but kept moving toward us.

The reds swirled into the black as the painting melted, becoming a black puddle in the hall. The dark pool boiled and a wail rose from a deep place far below the first floor.

The banging on the door stopped.

The girls stopped.

Peter ran back to me.

"What's happening?" I asked.

The shriek, from whatever depths it flew from, was sharp and moved fast.

A dark, slimy, claw pierced the breach of the bubbling paint, and I jumped back. "Oh, my God!"

Sulfur and char filled my nose. I covered my ears as the

echoing scream rushed outward. A black, dripping arm, rippling with lean muscle, cut through the filmy fluid. Long, thin fingers stretched and stabbed into the hardwood and flexed as it pulled itself out of the tar-like liquid. The head of the creature emerged. My eyes couldn't comprehend the demon. It looked like a bat, a wolf—hell itself. It had glowing orange eyes and long, black, razor-sharp teeth.

Fear.

My thoughts were broken. There was no logic.

Fear.

"Oh, Jesus. Please." Tears formed in my eyes.

The ghost girls cried out. I couldn't tell if they were challenging it or afraid of it.

"Go. Go!" I shouted at them.

"What are you—?" Peter questioned.

The creature flipped its orange eyes on us.

"Oh, fuck." I backed into the corner of the wall.

Peter threw out his arms in front of me.

The girls rushed the demon. It whipped around to face them with a roar.

Grace and Turtle bolted down the hall, and the devil creature pursued them, cutting into the house with its spiked talons, every swift motion moving it forward.

"What was that thing?" I murmured frantically.

Boom.

The front door shook.

"We've gotta get into that other bedroom."

"On it." Peter ran down the hall, checking the other bedroom first. He gave me a thumbs up that the room was clear. He knelt down and got to work.

Bangs erupted against the door.

I glanced into the bathroom. *A weapon, any weapon,* I

thought. There was nothing but pill bottles and my cereal bowl. I grabbed the bowl. It was the only thing with weight.

The door cracked.

"Hurry, Peter!"

"I'm working! It's different under pressure."

I clutched the bowl to my chest. Pain built in me. It was a new kind of pain, a sort of surrender, an acceptance. Tears formed in my eyes. I didn't feel weak. I couldn't pass that judgment on myself. Humans weren't meant to face these forces.

The front door crashed inward. I jumped back from the surge.

Joshua Johnson walked in. His face hidden, but he was bowed, heaving with anger.

I looked down the hall to Peter, bravely working on the door. He was a strong kid. I was glad I got to meet him.

The ghost's worn boots sprinted up the stairs.

Gripping the green bowl, I thought of my Rose-Mary Grand. The thought of her smile warmed me. I knew I would be with her soon.

72

J oshua continued his rush. I pulled the bowl back and threw as hard as I could.

The jadeite bowl disappeared under the monster's hood, and Joshua's head snapped back. I froze.

He staggered and fell down the stairs.

I ran down the hall to the Tomb. "Hurry up. I don't know how much time we have."

Peter focused on the lock. "What did you do?"

"I threw a bowl at him."

"Hmm," he grunted and kept working.

Heavy-soled boots bounded up the stairs.

"One more second."

Joshua Johnson rounded top of the stairs and raced down the hallway.

"Peter!"

"Got it!"

The door opened, and I pushed Peter in.

"Close it!" Peter shouted running to the farthest corner.

My fingers weren't cooperating.

"Christian, shut the door!" he pleaded.

Green light shot past me, and the bloodwood slammed. I jumped to lock it.

"Holy shit! It worked." Peter shouted.

"Peter, help me block this thing!"

Peter nodded and grabbed the bed, and we shoved it across the door, barricading us in.

We stepped back. As I held my breath in the bottom of my chest, waiting, I noticed the room pushed in on us. It felt smaller than before, tighter. The single lightbulb burning with its tungsten yellow confirmed how artificial the room felt.

There was nothing but tension and silence.

"Why isn't he breaking down the door?"

"Shh!"

I crept to the wall that ran along the hall and placed my ear to it.

After several minutes, "I don't hear anything."

"The golem chase them off?"

"Golem?"

"The thing that came out of the painting."

I gestured for him to stop. "Are you all right? Are you hurt?"

He kept his eyes locked on the door, listening. "I'm fine."

Neither of us were fine. Neither of us were safe, but we were alive.

A rustle behind us from outside the house made us both whirl around. It was like a restless wind, but it grew from being merely eerie to the crushing and breaking of brush, branches twisting and popping.

Peter moved to the center of the room.

I followed him. "Is that the ghosts?"

We both stood still and watched the walls where the

windows once were, long before the town went insane, before four children killed their parents.

I glanced at the bloodwood door. I wanted to run. I didn't care where. "Maybe they are all out front, and we could—"

"Christian? What are you thinking?"

"We could run to your truck and haul ass."

"Christian, are you crazy? Where?"

"Your magic house. Look, I know what the rules say, but—"

"We can't open the door. They're outside. They're just trying to trick us. This is the safest—"

"We're not safe," I scoffed. "Something is wrong. Something is different."

"This is where you're supposed to go."

"Exactly, this is where you're *supposed* to go. Now we're in here and it gets quiet."

"Mr. Christian going out at night is one thing, but driving at night? Cars have lights, and they're loud. There are more things to worry about in Middwood than just the ghosts—"

I held up my hand stopping him. "Don't. Just don't. I can't take any more fucked up things in the backwoods." I readied myself and grabbed the doorknob. "I'm going to peek into the hall—"

Peter pushed me away. "Get your mitts off that. He has an ax. We are not leaving this room. There's no way in hell I'm going—"

BOOM!

The foundation shifted and rocked beneath our feet.

Everything slowed as fear spread in Peter's eyes. His arms shot out as the floor beneath him broke away. His mouth formed words, and from the strain in his face and neck, I was sure they were shouts. But I only heard a distant cry. I lunged for him, catching one of his hands as the inner concrete walls of the room crashed in around us.

I had him and I would not let him go. The boy's faith in my determination showed on his face. His mouth was speaking unheard words, but I knew he trusted me, and his belief in me made me stronger.

"Hold on," I pleaded, the words sounding as if I were underwater, as I thrust my other arm toward him. My fingers clutched at his. I had him. I just needed another inch to get a firm grip.

A second explosion tore through the house.

His hand slid out of mine. My insides turned to liquid as our fingers slipped past each other.

"Peter!" I cried out in raw anger.

I laid flat, searching for him, trying to pierce through the black billowing smoke.

I caught movement out of the corner of my eye. I turned in time to see the bloodwood slab of a door fall from its frame and crash into me.

The Tomb's floor collapsed, and I fell.

73

My ears and head rang dizzyingly.

I tried to think, clear my head, but the air was filled with smoke. If the flames didn't get me the fumes would. I tried to reposition myself, to push whatever was on me off, but it was no use. I struggled to find enough air to cough.

I feared death even though it had always surrounded me. My family was cursed to hold its blessed hand, but it was I who watched those around me get ripped away, which was its own form of torture. I prayed that God would let me pass quickly. I always wanted to go fast, not enter hell through the smoke.

Someone stepped through the fire.

"Over here!" I shouted.

Isaac, the ghost child, approached me.

"The fire will cover it all," he said.

Exhausted and broken, I didn't have the will to fight. "If you've come for me, then take me. Just get it over with."

Tears filled my eyes from deep sadness. "Are you here because I am about to die?"

Isaac knelt and extended his hand. "We don't have much time."

I hesitated but reached up and took his swollen dead hand.

～

I woke up. I was on an old, worn area rug laying across an unfamiliar, worn wood-plank floor. There was no consuming fire or lack of air. I was safe, but I didn't know where I was.

A vehicle roared, closing in from a distance.

A child's voice said, "Someone is pulling up."

There was a gentle crinkle of light fabric. I raised my head and saw Isaac peering out a large window.

"It's probably just Grandpa Frank," said Turtle. She sat on the rug playing with blocks. The little ghost child I'd first met, beautiful blonde hair and rosy cheeks, was no less than three feet away from me.

"Nope. It's not him." Isaac said, facing the room. "It's all right. It's just Mr. Bankward."

"The banks are closed today. Why would the bank come out here on a Sunday?" asked Grace, stepping into the living room from the kitchen. I was so close I pulled back my hands to keep her from stepping on them. She moved next to Turtle, placing her hand on her little sister's shoulder. "Joshua!" Grace called. "Is he going to take us away?"

A shadowy figure moved toward the living room from the hallway directly across from where I lay. My heart rate picked up.

As Joshua entered the light, he lifted his arms and his sweatshirt above his head. He slid the sweatshirt over his head, concealing his face. Only his lower stomach was exposed. He walked past me and pulled at the bottom of his sweater.

He tussled his little brother's hair. "No one is taking us anywhere. This is our house. Even with mama and daddy gone, it's still ours, that's what Grandpa Frank said." Isaac smiled up at him. "Now everyone keep quiet, and I'll talk to him."

Isaac smiled. "Like diddy?"

"Yes, like dad," Joshua replied and made eye contact with each of the other children. And for the first time I saw him —Joshua Johnson. He wasn't the hard-faced killer I imagined, but rather a handsome boy. He had dark, wavy hair and dark brown eyes that did their best to hide his concern.

I hesitated, then held my hand up to Joshua. His eyes looked through me like I wasn't there. I spun my head to Grace, waving my arms in front of her. "Can you see me?"

No response.

I stood, but none of the children noticed me. I followed Joshua when he went outside onto their porch.

Joshua stood. His stance was wide and his arms were crossed. He glared at Bankward through the windshield of his car. "What can I do you for?"

Bankward sat in the car for a moment longer. When he exited the vehicle, I moved behind a porch post. I wanted something between the vile man and me.

Bankward approached with a slight bow but kept his eyes on the boy. "Good afternoon, Joshua."

"What can I do you for?" Joshua repeated.

"There is no need for that tone, young man—"

"I say there is. Grandpa Frank—"

Bankward cut him off. "Son, you lost your mother and father. I just came to check on you, is all."

A second car pulled into their driveway.

"Why is there another car?"

"Son, the church always reaches out to families in times of need."

Two men got out and walked over to stand behind Bankward.

My eyes narrowed. It was the pharmacist, Bill Self, and the pastor, Gresham.

"How are you kids holding up?" Pastor Gresham asked.

"See, Joshua? It's pastor Gresham. We've come to bless you."

Gresham cleared his throat. "You guys got enough food to eat?"

Joshua relaxed. "We got a bit."

"I didn't think so. But you're in luck! On our drive up we spotted a big ole gobbler at the tree line. What do you say you and me go down there and check it out?"

"Preacher, I need to stay here with my brother and sisters."

Mr. Gresham started toward the porch. "Joshua, you're the man of the house now, and it's up to you to provide for your brother and sisters. Do you know how to hunt?"

Joshua straightened. "Sure, I do."

Pastor Gresham smiled at him. "Have you ever shot a gun before?"

"Yes, sir, of course. Diddy and I used to go hunting all the time."

Mr. Gresham laughed. "Then why are you still standing there, boy? Let's go get that turkey." Mr. Gresham continued laughing as he started walking toward the woods. He turned. "You comin' or not?"

Joshua ran inside and grabbed his father's gun, then ran back out the door.

Grace shouted, "What do you need that thing for?"

He answered over his shoulder as he ran, "I'm going to go shoot us some dinner. Pastor Gresham says there's a big gobbler at the tree line."

Isaac and Grace moved to the window to watch as their brother ran to catch up with Gresham. Once Joshua caught up with him, the preacher put his arm around his shoulder.

I turned to the sound of lighter steps as Isaac walked out onto the porch. "Some turkey sounds real good to me."

Mr. Bankward laughed. "Good turkey is good eating, my friend. Let's go inside and get out of this chill. They shouldn't take too long. That turkey was so fat I bet it couldn't run off even if it wanted to."

Isaac giggled as the men moved into the living room and everyone sat down together. Isaac kept shifting his eyes to the window.

Mr. Self finally spoke. "You girls have breakfast yet?"

Grace shook her head. "We had some butter cookies at the church this morning."

"You were at church?"

"Yes, sir. Pastor Gresham is a truly anointed man."

Self eyed the girl with fearful curiosity. "You thought so?" He flattened his lips. "I didn't see you there."

"Oh, yes, sir, we were all there. Grandpa said it would be best for us to sneak in up to the loft so we wouldn't distract the service."

Self's face went white. "Oh?" he asked as he narrowed his eyes on Randy Bankward.

Backward ignored Self's stare. "Well, I love butter cookies, but I'm sure you kids are starving. We brought you some groceries. I hope you like oatmeal."

Isaac laughed, "Grace doesn't like oatmeal."

Bankward smiled. "Don't worry, we brought a bag of

brown sugar and raisins, too. Come on into the kitchen and Mr. Self will cook up a pot for you and your little sister."

Turtle spoke up with a worried face, "What about the turkey?"

Bankward smiled. "Even if they get a turkey, it will take them an awful long time to clean it and cook it. You girls will be skin and bones by then."

Grace nodded. "They're right, Turtle. It takes a long time to pluck all the feathers off a chicken, and a turkey is much bigger."

"That's right," said Self. "Let's go make us some oatmeal. We'll tell Joshua you made it all by yourself." He looked at Isaac. "That is if Isaac won't tell your big brother."

Mr. Bankward leaned to Isaac and asked, "Can you keep a secret?"

74

Isaac sat up straight. "Yes, sir."

Mr. Bankward smiled and patted him on the shoulder, "I bet you can." He looked to Mr. Self. "Bill, go on and help the girls get started."

"Okay, girls, you heard him. Let's go make some breakfast."

I followed as Mr. Self led the girls into the kitchen. Looking around, Mr. Self asked, "Where are the pots?"

Grace ran to one of the lower cabinets. "I'll get it." She raised a pot to him. "Here you go."

"Thank you. Well, it's real simple to make oatmeal. You put three cups of water and then a cup and a half of oats. Oh, and don't forget the salt."

Turtle crinkled her nose. "Salt?"

"Yes, but just a pinch. It makes it taste better. Isn't that right, Mr. Bankward?" Self called through the doorway to the living room.

Mr. Bankward walked into the kitchen. "Oh, yes, yes indeed. You girls come here for a second. I've got a surprise for you two and your brother."

"What is it?" asked Turtle.

Mr. Bankward leaned over to them. "Is everyone listening?"

I too fell for Mr. Bankward's distraction, but I was facing Mr. Self. With the children and Bankward between us. Mr. Self's eyes hardened, at first I thought he was looking at me, but he took a small bottle out of one of the bags. He opened it and poured it into the pot.

I lifted my hands to my head. "No. No, no, no."

Mr. Bankward continued, "I've got some oranges for you kids in the back of my car, but you have to eat all your oatmeal first."

The children's faces lit up with joy.

Turtle held her doll close and squeezed it with excitement. "Oranges are my most favorite."

"No, don't listen to them," I growled.

"Mine, too," beamed Isaac.

Bankward grinned. "I thought they might be."

"Stop hogging those kids. I don't want their oatmeal to get cold."

He stood. "You got breakfast done already in there, Mr. Self?"

"Yes, it is," Self moved to the kitchen doorway. "Let's get this over with. Who wants brown sugar and raisins?"

"Me! Me!" Grace and Turtle said raising their hands as they rushed into the kitchen. The two girls sat down at the table where three bowls were already sitting out for them.

I rushed to Isaac who remained. "Grab your sisters and get to your brother."

Grace called out, "Come on, Isaac! It's oatmeal time."

I knelt in front of him. Tears built in my eyes. "Isaac, get out. Please!"

Isaac sauntered back to the living room. "I wonder how Joshua is doing?"

My eyes widened. "Yes! Good."

"I'm sure he's doing just fine," said Mr. Bankward. "He probably has that turkey by now."

Isaac frowned. "Not yet, Mr. Bankward. We would have heard the gunshot."

I nodded. "That's right. Don't listen to him. Call for your brother."

Bankward and Self exchanged glances. He cleared his throat and gently prompted. "Go on and eat your breakfast, Isaac."

"No. I'm not hungry."

Bankward lowered his chin in a stern, but playful scowl. "Little man, you need to do as you're told."

"Thank you, but I'd rather have the oranges, Mr. Bankward."

Wiping his forehead, Bankward said, "Okay. If that's what you want." He looked to Mr. Self. "You go ahead without us, Bill. I'm going to spend some time with Isaac here."

"What are you going to do, Randy?" asked Self, his voice shaking.

"Don't worry yourself. We are just going to go get those oranges out of the car." He turned his thin gaze down at Isaac. "Do you think you are strong enough to get them yourself, little man?"

I covered my mouth with my hand. "You've said this before. Oh, no. Don't go outside. I was wrong. Don't go outside."

"I can sure try," smiled Isaac.

He led Isaac out. "I'll be right back, Bill."

At the table, Turtle made a yucky face. "This doesn't taste good."

"Oh, no," I ran to the girls, my feet heavy as a last breath.

"Turtle! That ain't polite."

"No. It's fine. I don't like oatmeal either without a lot of brown sugar." Mr. Self mixed another large spoonful into her bowl. "Try it again, honey."

Turtle took another bite.

"Is that better?" Grace asked. Turtle didn't respond. "I don't think she's going to eat it, Mr. Self."

"Well, Grace, be the big sister and show her how to do it."

I stared at Self. "You bastard. You horrible, horrible ..."

She picked up a big spoonful. "Watch me, Turtle. This is how you do it." Grace put the spoon in her mouth. A disgusted look showed, but she chewed it up and swallowed it.

"See. Your mother would be so proud," Mr. Self said. "Let's put some raisins in that. If you eat it fast, it will be better."

The girls both took another bite. It was hard for me to watch.

Turtle put down her spoon. "Grace, I don't feel good."

"What's the matter?" her sister asked.

"My tummy hurts."

My knees gave out, and I crumpled to the floor.

"I don't think we should eat any more of this, Mr. Self," Grace said.

Self planted his palms on the table and spoke low and firm. "You are both going to keep eating or you both will get the belt, do you understand?"

Turtle whimpered.

I spat. "I'll kill you for this."

"Just eat one more bite, Turtle. It will be okay," Grace said in a comforting tone.

Turtle spat up some of the oatmeal onto the table.

"Turtle!" Grace grabbed a towel and wiped her little sister's face."

"That's okay," assured Mr. Self. "Just a little more brown sugar will help it go down."

"They don't need any more brown sugar!" I swung at the box, and it flew off the table.

Self jumped and looked around the kitchen.

Turtle put her head down on the table.

Grace's head swayed as she regarded her sister. "I'm sorry, Mr. Self, but I think she fell asleep. Excuse me, I need to go to the—" Grace's words fell off, and she fell out of her chair and threw up.

I stood there looking at the two girls as they lay curled up on the floor in pain. They might not have been dead yet, but they soon would be.

I stepped up to Self. "What have you done?"

"What I have done?" he whispered to himself.

I ran outside to Isaac, his voice calling from behind the cars. "I don't see any oranges, Mr. Bankward."

As I rounded the side of the house, Bankward grabbed the boy by the back of his hair.

Isaac pulled at the man's hands. "What are you do—!" Isaac's scream was cut short as Bankward threw the boy's head down onto the tailgate of his truck.

The dazed boy attempted to hold his injured head, but Bankward slapped him across the face, and Isaac hit the ground.

The grown man reached down and picked him up by his overall straps. The boy struggled, but he was only eleven. He was no match for the monster, but he did manage to do one thing.

"Joshua!" he screamed.

Bankward struck Isaac in the throat, and the little boy fell, jerking and gagging. Bankward bent and tried to catch hold of Isaac, but he kicked his way under the truck.

I stepped to Bankward. "I swear, I'll make sure you suffer for this."

"I swear boy, if you make this harder for me I'm going to make you suffer." Bankward dropped to the ground in his expensive suit. "Do you hear me?" he said grabbing at the boy's legs.

Isaac squeezed himself into a ball just out of Bankward's reach.

"You piece of shit," he spat. "Fine!" He stood and walked around his truck as he beat the dirt from his suit. "You stay under there, and I'll crush you like a possum." Bankward threw open the driver door.

I threw a punch into Bankward's face, but my fist went through him.

I threw another swing.

I screamed and threw another.

Bankward smashed into the ground so hard he rolled.

Joshua stepped through me.

"Get away from my brother!" he roared readying the piece of firewood for another blow.

Bankward pushed himself off the ground.

Joshua gripped the wood and threw it down against Bankward's back. Joshua held his glare on Bankward. His face was pure rage to the point of seething tears. "Are you okay, Isaac?"

Isaac let out a cry.

Joshua growled and raised the wood again. "I swear, I'll kill every last one of you."

A distant gunshot.

Joshua's left eye exploded, spraying Bankward's face with blood.

Joshua dropped to his knees and fell on his stomach.

I rushed to catch him, but he fell through my arms.

"About damn time," said Bankward as he staggered to his feet.

"Are we finished?" Self called from inside the house.

"Yes," Bankward replied as he pulled a cloth from his suit and wiped the blood from his face. "Where is Gresham?" Bankward scanned the tree line and saw Gresham running back to the house.

Self walked outside. "What the hell happened to you?"

"That bitch of a boy hit me with a piece of firewood." He raised his voice as Gresham neared. "How did you let Joshua get away from you?"

Mr. Gresham huffed and was bleeding himself. "He knew something was up. Then he pegged me straight in the nose with the stock of the gun when his little brother screamed for him."

Under the truck, Isaac choked and sobbed. Bankward turned his attention back to him. "Damn boy. Just die."

"Shoot him and get this over with. He's suffering," said Self.

Gresham dropped to the ground to peer under the truck as Bankward went around the other side.

"One shot isn't a big deal. Two shots get people's attention," Mr. Gresham said.

"Well, he's not going to be eating any oatmeal with a crushed neck," Bankward said catching the boy's foot and dragging him out from under the truck.

Gresham got to his feet. "What are we going to do with him?"

"This whole thing has pissed me off," said Bankward as he flung Isaac, rolled him over on his back, and grabbed him by his shirt. "If you would have eaten the oatmeal, it would have been painless. But you had to be a little shit, didn't you?"

Isaac choked. "Don't—"

"Don't what?" asked Bankward and he punched him in the face.

Self turned away. "Good God, Randy."

Bankward glared at Self, exposing his wild, crazy eyes. "Don't judge me, you prick. You just poisoned two little girls." To Isaac, "Did you hear? That man poisoned your two little sisters. How do you feel about that?"

"Get it over with, Randy," said Gresham firmly.

"What's the rush? We can do anything we want with him. There isn't anyone here."

"We are here to do a job, not anything else," Gresham warned, walking up to Bankward.

"Fine!" he spat through his teeth. Bankward looked around and spotted a filled washtub. He dragged Isaac and pushed his head down into the water, which overflowed.

I went to Isaac and dropped to my knees, trying to pull the boy from the water.

Isaac's hands flailed, but Randy's strength held him down.

"What do we do now?" Self asked.

Randy stood. "We burn the house. The fire will cover it all."

I screamed as loud as I could, but no one heard me.

A small hand took mine, and I opened my eyes to see Isaac's milky, dead eyes and blue face. "That's how we died. We wanted you to know. We wanted you to see us."

75

I woke to searing heat burning into my face.

The fire had grown hotter.

The ghosts were gone, but I was trapped under the weight of debris.

I tried to find a pocket of breathable air while I pushed with all my diminishing strength against whatever had me pinned.

My eyes were boiling, like hundreds of fire ants were eating them. My breaths were short, thorny inhalations. I tried to focus and not panic. There was no time for extra complications. Peter was trapped somewhere, too. I needed to find him. I just hoped I wasn't too late. That fear made me fight harder, but I was losing my struggle.

I knew the truth. I knew what had happened to the Johnson children, and I had to get out of there so I could tell the town.

I pushed against the weight on top of me, but I couldn't catch my breath. My lungs were dry and brittle. I was suffocating.

Something banged. I readied myself for more of the house to fall in.

Fear filled me.

I pushed against the door with my back, arms, and stomach. Adrenaline rushed through me as I fought to get out. Using my hands, arms, and elbows, I pushed.

The living room fumed with smoke. Fire blazed from the kitchen. The heat burned the left side of my face. Memories of falling off my bike on the summer Georgia asphalt raced through my mind. I clamped my eyes shut. It was like we were swimming in a lake of smoke, and I needed to break the surface.

The ceiling in the kitchen caved in, and burning boards fell. The white roof of the living room was black and danced in red and yellow flames.

Freed from the smoke, I took half a breath, but everything went black.

~

Smoke stung my lungs as I hacked for air.

"He's waking up," a man's voice said somewhere beyond my tear-blurred vision.

"I told you we should've checked," a higher pitched male voice said.

My gasps for air clashed in between shallow choking coughs. My muscles were fatigued from straining to free myself from the weight of the rubble, but I was able to roll onto my stomach.

A muffled conversation swarmed around me.

"I was hoping he wouldn't make it."

"The smoke might still kill him."

"Are you deaf and blind? He's alive."

"He still might not make it."

I was fighting to take in little amounts of air, as I fought to push out the fumes that filled my lungs. I needed to try and stay calm. Cough out the smoke, let the air find its way in.

"Anyone want to make a bet?"

The first wisp of breath that filled a small portion of my chest was cool. It sent me into a stronger fit of coughs, but through that grasp at life, I was able to focus on my other senses. I wasn't surrounded by heat. The threat of the fire was gone.

I pushed my palms against the ground. I was on dirt. I could have been on any road or dead field in Middwood. I wasn't sure. Wherever I was, I wasn't pinned any longer, but I knew I was still in danger.

"Hurry up and take care of him," said a horribly familiar voice.

Anger flared inside me. A hate strong enough to push down the fear that should of have had me scurrying to get away. My earlier thought was correct, I was in danger. I was in the presence of a murderer, the child killer, Randy Bankward.

Bankward scoffed, "Do it and get it over with."

"No, none of that. We aren't going to kill an innocent man."

"Bill, there's no way he's innocent."

In front of me, a weathered brick wall ran at length. It was an open area with a few trees close by. I dropped my chin to the left and saw a stagnant, film-covered pond.

I was at the graveyard.

I rolled onto my back.

"Damn, he isn't going to die." Bankward huffed, "Try it your way."

Pastor Jimmy Gresham knelt beside me. "You are one lucky man."

"What? Your fire didn't kill me?" my voice croaked.

"Kill you? Matt, we saved your life," said Bill Self, stepping up behind Gresham. Without my glasses, I couldn't see Self's face clearly, but it appeared bloodied and his eyes were darkened.

"Save me? Did you? You killed—" more coughs erupted from my burning chest.

"Yes, we pulled you out of the house," said the pastor. "Just in the nick of time."

I fought out my words through hoarse coughs, "Where's Peter?"

Gresham shook his head. "No more tricks, Matt. It's time—"

Weakly, I grabbed at Gresham. "Where is he!"

Gresham's tone firmed with concern as he shrugged me off, "There wasn't anyone else with you." He rose and turned to Self. "Was there?"

"Peter was in the house," Self said.

"What?" growled Gresham.

Self stuttered, "Yes, but—"

Gresham grabbed Self. "You idiot! Why didn't you tell us!"

"Quiet!" ordered Bankward. "We can deal with that later."

Gresham pushed Self away from him. "But what about Tonya?"

I rolled onto my side. "Are you going to kill her, too?"

"We didn't kill anyone," Self said in a defensive plea.

I tried to stand. "I swear—"

I took a boot to the face, and my neck jerked back. My head fell to the dirt with a dull *thud*.

"What the hell?" panicked Self.

"We're here to do a job. I'm not going to play around like last time. You have really screwed this up, Bill."

"Me? The boy was there and the ghost children. I didn't know what to do. Randy, you're the one that wanted to move on this so fast."

"Don't you question me. Gresham is the one that came to me about Magnolia."

They continued to argue amongst themselves. I noticed Self's gray sweatshirt. I strained my eyes. His eyes appeared dark because he had a black-eye. "That was you? You were dressed up like Joshua Johnson?"

Self hurried to me and clamped his palm over my mouth. I pushed against his grip, but I couldn't move him. In my weakened state, all he would need to do was hold my nose to easily kill me.

His eyes searched mine with a crazed intensity. "Matt, I need you to listen. Shut up and listen."

I stared at him.

"Blink your fucking eyes, if you understand."

I blinked, and he removed his hand from my mouth.

He pressed his hand down onto my chest. "I'm trying to save your life. You need to leave town. None of this happened, you see?" His pitch rose as he leaned harder into my chest. "None of it. I'm sorry about Peter. I didn't mean to kill him."

Gresham pulled Self back. "Get yourself together. We'll deal with Tonya."

"How? She'll kill us all. You know she will."

"Bill, if you won't get yourself together, I'll have to kill, you too."

Gresham shot Bankward an angry look. "Don't worry,

she won't ever know because Mattie Junkie boy is going to work with us."

Randy Bankward marched to me and gripped his fingers into my hair and yanked me up to my knees. "This is our scapegoat, here. This is all your fault, Matt. Before you came to Middwood everything was fine. But with you here, within a few days the ghost children get stirred up like hornets, someone breaks one of my windows, and people start dying. You have a real gift of causing all hell to break loose."

"Don't kill him, Randy. Don't," blubbered Self.

Bankward jerked my hair harder and spoke through his teeth, "Now is the time to use that teacher brain of yours and listen. Your car is fixed. The tank is full. There's some money in the glove box. Get in, drive away, keep your mouth shut, and never come back. It's as simple as that."

"How much money?" I asked.

Bankward let go of me and I dropped to the ground.

He smiled. "See, boys. I told you he would take it. Junkies are simple folk."

"How much money you pig? How much money is Peter's life worth to you?"

Bankward's smile faded and he spat on me. "Leave or die, junkie."

Gresham spoke up. "Middwood isn't the right fit for you. Take his offer. We won't offer it again."

"Do we have a deal or are we going to have to throw you in an open grave? You're afraid of your own shadow so I know you'll make the right choice. I'll even get Bill to throw in some of those happy pills you like so much."

The fire from the house couldn't match the blaze inside of me. "You think it's that easy? Give me some pills and wish me on my way?"

"For an excuse of a man like you? Yes."

"I can't do that."

"Why not?" Self pleaded.

Gresham shook his head. "Think about what you are doing—"

I shouted, "I don't need to think about it."

"Then we kill you," Bankward said.

"Coward," I growled.

Randy Bankward's face twisted into an angry grin. "Why are you calling me a coward?"

"Because I know what you are. All of you!"

"You're a dead man," spat Bankward.

"Death would be a mercy."

"What in God's name?" asked Gresham.

Bankward stepped back. "It's the devil in him. He's made a pack with the devil."

I glared at Gresham. "Were you behind putting Bankward in charge of the town?"

"The town made that decision," sneered Gresham.

"Then when did the bank start making so much money?"

"You don't know what you're talking about," Bankward insisted in a near-calm voice.

"I know you killed those kids," I spat blood in Gresham's face. He threw me to the ground.

I coughed. "You killed them! You murdered them and then you all burned down the house."

"How does he know this?" Self wailed.

"What did you do with the money?"

Gresham leaned over me. "There was no money from the land, you idiot. No one would touch that land for years."

"Careful, Gresham," warned Bankward. "Don't let it in your head. The town voted to turn that land over for mining."

"The new mine is on the land Sarah and Roger owned. That's why they put me there."

"Who put you where?"

"The ghost children. They put me at the mine."

I made my way to my feet. "Did you kill Sarah and Roger, too."

"No, we wouldn't kill innocent people," Self insisted.

"You killed those kids."

"How does he know that?" Gresham growled.

"They showed me. I saw it."

Gresham stepped forward. "That's not possible."

"The devil's work," insisted Bankward.

"There is no devil at work here. Matt, please take the deal and leave," Self said, dropping to his knees beside me.

There it was, a simple, pretty package of freedom, everything I wanted. For a moment, it felt the world was pushing in on my hollow chest. The void sucked all the life from this dead place into the hole inside me and continued down into my nothing.

"I have nothing," I uttered.

"See boys. He's not dumb. He knows a deal with he sees it."

I looked to Self, to Gresham, and to Bankward. "No."

Bankward scowled, "My offer only stands—"

"Your hands are too dirty to take anything from."

"Fine. He's made his decision and I've made mine," Bankward rushed me, but Self stood between us.

Self struggled to hold Bankward back. "Randy, I'll get him to change his mind."

"I won't change my mind. Those four poor kids."

"Then you die," Bankward spat.

"Do it, coward."

Bankward grinned at me in disgust and stepped away from Self. "Kill him, Bill."

Self backed away said, "I'm not killing anyone."

"It's not like it's your first time," Bankward said reproachfully. "He's not some little girl. This time you're going to have to get your hands dirty."

"Randy?" Self cried.

"He knows! He has to die now. The devils we cast out of the Johnson children live in him. He's been sent by the devil to destroy us!" Bankward warned.

"Tell me your name, demon? Did you kill, Magnolia?" demanded Gresham.

"No." I scanned the faces of three men. "What has this bastard made you do?"

"What is he talking about?" Self panicked, turning back and forth between the two men.

Bankward stepped forward. "I'll take care of this."

I held up my fists and threw a punch.

He jerked back with annoyance. "You can't even throw a punch."

I let out a grunt, but it grew into a roaring laugh.

Bankward punched me in the eye. "What's so funny?"

Huffing out a breath, I pointed with my chin, "Behind you."

"I'm not a fool who falls for simple tricks," he spat.

"No, you're a murderer, and they've come for you."

76

Bankward threw me to the ground as the two other men spun around.

Bankward's eyes were full of crazy rage, but his movements were calm as he took off his watch and wedding ring and placed them in his blazer pocket. "We killed you once, and we can do it again." He folded his coat and dropped it on the ground. "Ghosts or not, you're just dead kids. You'll just run away like you always do."

I stood dumbfounded at his cocky arrogance. The man was about to attempt to fight the ghost children.

Flanking Bankward, Gresham flung off his jacket, gritting his teeth. "We're hunters," he roared in righteous anger. "We killed you once. And we can do it again!" The preacher crouched, preparing for engagement.

Something fell and dangled around his neck. It was a black cord with a dull metallic medallion.

"Peter's necklace." I scrambled to my feet and tackled Gresham. Even with all my weight, he didn't budge. He batted me away like a fly. I hit the ground, but I recovered. "Where's Peter!"

The preacher lumbered toward me. "It's your time as well."

A blue light flashed and Gresham flew away from me, slamming into a tree.

Another blue flash. About twenty yards away, Isaac materialized in front of Bankward, with water dripping from his hair. Isaac blankly stared at Randy Bankward. "I'm going to spend some time with Isaac here."

Bankward curled his lips. "Listen to me, you little shit."

Isaac's boyish face peeled away to a bloated and brutal corpse. The boy let out a shriek, attacking Bankward.

A man screamed behind me.

I whirled around.

Grace and Turtle stood between Bill Self and me. "Stop hoggin' those kids," Grace hissed.

Self readied his stance but faltered. He kept shifting his weight and his face was unsure. Self broke into a sprint and ran for the trees. Grace and Turtle slowly stalked behind him.

Gresham's large frame jumped in front of me. He shoved me to the ground. I jerked away from him as I kicked as hard as I could.

He grabbed at my leg, and I stopped. "Made you look."

I grabbed a fist full of sand and threw it into the preacher's face. I got up and heaved the hardest punch I could.

Gresham went down, and I fell over. But it wasn't from the punch, it was from a loss of balance. My fist never made contact.

The preacher yelled out curses as Joshua disappeared with Gresham.

"They can do that?"

"Joshua!" Isaac screamed behind me.

"Remember this, you little fuck?" shouted Bankward as

he dragged Isaac by his shirt down to the pond. The boy struggled, but he was no match for the grown man.

The preacher was dropped on the other side of the pond. Joshua manifested. Gresham jumped to his feet and began throwing punches.

Joshua dodged each of them, swirling in and out of physical form. "You're the man of the house now, and it's up to you."

"I'm. Not. Afraid. Of. You!" roared Gresham, punching after each thunderous word.

Shots rang out, and I ducked to the ground.

"Get away from me!" yelled Self firing off another four rounds. The bullets rippled like little blue circles as they passed through the girls.

Turtle phased in front of Self taking a bullet through the head with no reaction. "I don't feel good."

Bill turned to run, but Grace blocked his path. "Do you like brown sugar and raisins?" The girls stalked closer.

Self fell to his knees and sobbed.

Turtle walked up and touched his leg. "Just a little brown sugar will help it go down."

"You girls have breakfast yet?" asked Grace.

Self grabbed her. Somehow able to hold the ghost in his hands. He screamed and shook Grace violently. Her neck snapped, and her head fell back as her body went limp. He dropped the girl's body and stood, trembling.

The top few buttons of Self's shirt had come undone. I stared at his pale chest. Against his skin, hung a black cord with a small silver amulet.

They all have one. How is that possible? I thought.

Grace's head moved, and she sat up. "You both will get the belt." She thrust her little hands into his knees, and they bent with gruesome snaps.

Self screamed in pain. He wormed away. As he crawled, Turtle dropped and stared at him, eye to eye. She grabbed her stomach, lurched over, and threw up on him. Self raised his hands. The white, sizzling liquid splattered over his fingers and chest.

He swung his arms, groaning in agony. The liquid ate into his skin.

"I didn't know!" He screamed, "I didn't know!"

"I don't feel good," the two girls said in unison.

Both girls vomited the flesh-eating oatmeal onto Self's face. He threw himself onto the dirt, trying to roll away from the liquid. The white foam ate into his eyes. He gargled as his throat was eaten away.

I couldn't watch any longer.

Bankward jerked Isaac into the shallow water and held him under. As he leaned over and held the boy, a silver amulet fell from his neck and dangled from a black chord. Isaac gripped at Bankward's arms, but the little hands sank slowly down in the black water. Randy proclaimed, "They can be killed."

I had to help. I ran toward Bankward, but a flash of blue light took me to the other side of the graveyard.

"No!" I shouted and ran back toward the fight.

"What are you afraid of, demon? Fight me," challenged the preacher.

Joshua threw another jab that missed Gresham. Then he stepped forward and took a direct punch in the face, causing a flash of blue light.

"Feel the wrath of God."

Joshua spun around. The eldest ghost child threw one punch, connecting with Gresham's jaw. Gresham stumbled toward me and we made eye contact. "God have mercy on you," he said.

I shook my head in sorrow for the man.

Joshua grabbed the back of Gresham's head. "Then why are you still standing there? Let's go get that turkey." Joshua pulled back his fist and punched a hole through the back of the preacher's head. Joshua grabbed his killer's eye from the inside and yanked it out. Gresham's body twitched, then crumpled.

Joshua vanished.

Bankward stood shocked as he watched Gresham fall and looked at the remains of Self. He locked his rage on me and charged out of the water. "This is all your fault!"

Vengeance boiled inside of me. "You're the killer here."

I charged forward. I let loose a punch, but he blocked it. I kneed him in the stomach. As he hunched over, I jumped up and brought my fists down on his back. He went to his knees.

"You killed them, and now they've come for you, Randy!"

Rising to his feet, he backhanded me.

I landed on my back and floundered to get to my knees.

Bankward picked up a nearby brick from the cemetery's wall. Through gasping breaths, he said, "I'll make sure to take one more person with me to hell."

A shot rang out.

Bankward cried out in pain, but followed through, slamming the rock down into my skull.

Warm blood poured over my eyes.

"No!" a shout screamed.

It was Peter's voice. He was okay. As I fell to the ground with a grim satisfaction so did the reality around me. The dreamlike space between this world and the next buzzed with desire. Whispers crept from the darkness. The wheel of fate clattered like demonic chants.

None of it mattered. I was ready to die.

The voices hidden in shadow hissed as an invisible veil fell across my being.

My head hurt like a motherfucker, but other than the pain, I was fine. I was breathing. I was thinking. Why wasn't I dead?

I lifted my face out of the mud.

Bankward had his back to me, and the sheriff had his pistol aimed at him, ready to take a second shot.

"You better hope you kill me, Philip, because if you—"

"Randy, what are you doing? Please, stop this."

I stood. "Don't shoot him."

Randy Bankward turned to me with shock. Holding his bleeding right shoulder, he spat, "Why the hell aren't you dead?"

"I wonder if it has anything to do with this?" I opened my fist and let the silver amulet fall from the black leather cord that hung from my index finger.

He snarled.

"You belong to them now, and I'm glad I'm here to watch."

Bankward charged me, but Isaac materialized and blocked his path.

"Out of the way." He swung his fists, but his punches flew through the boy.

Bankward turned his eyes to me, then ran to his left, toward the pond. Grace and Turtle flanked him from both sides, bearing their eroded teeth, snapping at him. He evaded them and darted into the shallow water.

Joshua appeared and punched him with an uppercut. Bankward flew farther into the pond with a splash. His arms sloshed as he struggled to stand.

"You can't kill me!" he shouted with determination.

Joshua waded into the water as the girls closed behind him on the pond's bank, chomping like animals at the air.

Bankward jumped as though something under the water grabbed him. The surface of the pond rippled, and he leaped away.

The water began to bubble as Isaac rose from underneath. His body continued to rise until he stood on the pond's surface. The boy held out his arms, and Bankward's body washed toward him.

His chin fell to rest in the little boy's hand.

Bankward grabbed at Isaac's arms, but his efforts only passed through the ghost's form.

Isaac looked into his killer's eyes, intent with questioning purpose. "Help me get those oranges."

"No! No!" screamed Bankward, as Isaac grabbed him by his hair, then plunged them both under the surface.

Bankward fought in desperate and violent attacks.

Randy Bankward erupted from the water once more, panicked eyes finding mine for just a moment. They reminded me of a cruel man who once thought he was the predator. A man whose eyes bulged in shock at the flash of the eternity of death as his own son's hands choked the life out of him. He reminded me of my father.

Joshua held up the man's struggling body above his head. "I swear I'll kill you for this," Joshua said.

Bankward screamed out, but his screams were cut short, as Joshua thrust Bankward underwater, baptizing him for death.

Bankward gasped and gagged as Joshua held him by the neck and shoulder, then pulled, ripping the two apart.

The violent churning diminished until all was still and silent.

77

The ghost children glided slowly to the edge of the pond.

They halted and stood together in a straight line. It was the first time I'd seen them all together.

They stared at me.

"I don't know what will happen next but thank you for saving me."

"Children," Franklin's husky voice called from behind me.

I turned to see him, shaking his head. He tried to speak again, but no words came out. Tears welled in his eyes. Straining, he tried once more. "Children..."

The children saw their grandfather, and they soared toward him. I feared for Franklin, but a blue light enveloped each of the ghosts. The surge of energy caused me to shield my eyes.

I lowered my arm, afraid what I might find, but instead of the horrid ghosts, Joshua, Isaac, Grace, and Turtle ran to their grandfather. They weren't ghost any longer, but children, whole, innocent, with eyes and smiles beaming.

They shouted, "Grandpa Frank! Grandpa!"

Franklin struggled but dropped to his old knees to embrace little Turtle who, even though she was the youngest, raced to him the fastest. One by one, the children wrapped their arms around him.

Franklin cried out in surrendered joy, "Oh, my. My, my, my beautiful grandbabies."

Tears of joy fell from my face as I watched the reunion.

"Where have you been, Grandpa?" asked Turtle, but it came out as "Ganpa."

"We've been looking for you this whole time," said Grace.

"We thought you had left us," said Isaac.

"We kept trying to find you, but we couldn't see in any of the windows, and the house was gone, and we didn't know where to go," said Joshua.

Franklin began to sob. "I'm sorry, children. I didn't know. I didn't know. I'm so sorry."

"Why are you sorry, Grandpa?" asked Grace.

Holding her tighter, he said, "I made a mistake. I thought something I shouldn't have thought. Can you ever forgive me?"

They all hugged.

"I want you to know I love you all, every one of you," said Franklin.

"We love you too, Grandpa," the children echoed in chiming voices.

Joshua stopped and turned to the mountain. "Hey! Did you hear that? I think it's time to go." The boy's eyes filled with delighted joy. "I hear father calling us."

"Diddy!" squealed Grace.

"And Sarah?" asked Franklin.

Joshua nodded wiping tears from his face.

"Oh, it's Mommy," beamed Isaac.

Franklin reached out to Joshua and pleaded. "Please. Can't you take me with you, too?"

Joshua touched his face. "Oh, Grandpa," he hugged the old man. "You still have work to do here."

"Please. Sarah. Sarah! Please!" He cried out.

His grandchildren surrounded him with hugs and kisses.

"We love you. All of us. Always," Isaac said.

"I'll never forget about any of you," Franklin promised.

Franklin and his grandchildren hugged one last time.

The children began to walk away, but Turtle turned and ran back. She whispered something into his ear, then kissed him on the cheek. She joined her brothers and sister, and they ran into the mist through a blue light, leaving only the rustling of dead leaves.

Franklin collapsed, sobbing.

I continued to cry, too.

"What was that?" Peter said wiping his face, standing beside me.

"Peter!" I shouted and pulled him into my arms.

Peter laughed. "Yeah, I'm fine. I'm glad you're still alive, too."

"So, you run into a fire to save me and still come back for more?"

"What are friends for, right?" he asked.

"Right. What are friends for?" I put my arm around him and smiled. "So, what happened to you after you pulled me out of the house?"

"I'll tell you all about it, just not right now."

Philip walked down to Franklin, but I stopped him. "Let him have some time. It's a lot to take in."

Franklin had been carrying his family's burden for thirteen years. He needed time to let it out.

Philip nodded. "It's a lot for all of us. More than I think you'll ever know. His family's name is cleared."

I turned to walk away.

"Are you just going to leave him there?" asked Peter.

"Yeah, I figure he needs some time. Are you okay?"

"Yeah, no big deal," Peter scoffed waving it off. "Just another night in a boring town."

I laughed. "Yeah, mountain life sucks."

"Tell me about it," he grinned.

78

Wednesday, November 11, 1964
Sunrise 7:07 AM. Sunset 5:26 PM.

The next morning, the Falcon was finally repaired and holding all my worldly possessions. I was leaving Kentucky. There were still plenty of states to dream in, but I couldn't stay here.

It seemed necessary to say goodbye to at least one person. If it was going to be anyone, it was going to be my closest friend, Peter. As I pulled into his yard, I swear I could feel it, the lighter side of life, the lesser burden, the magic. Whatever it was that caused the hummingbirds to stay, even in the late fall. It allowed Tonya to have a dog that was at least thirty years old. Not to mention she made paintings that demons crawled out of.

Baby howled, then wandered outside sniffing the air as her glazed eyes searched for me. Tonya appeared to identify the cause of her howls. She walked out with her posture echoing the question on her face, but once she peered through the windshield, she relaxed into a state of disappointment.

As I slid out of the passenger door, she spoke before I did. "You're a light packer."

"Yeah, I'm leaving with less than I arrived with." I gave a brief grin, but she didn't react.

"I don't blame you for leaving." She shook her head holding her shoulder with crossed arms. "God knows I would if I could."

"It was... an experience."

She shook her head with a dismissiveness. "It's just life in Middwood."

I didn't reply, and she didn't speak. I wasn't sure what else to say. I couldn't give her my condolences for the loss of her friends. Friends whose deaths I had played a part in.

She was so quiet and distant, and I knew she blamed me at least for part of what happened.

Finally, after an uncomfortable silence, I said, "Is Peter here? I want to tell him goodbye."

"I'd like to tell him that myself." She looked down. "He's gone."

"What do you mean?"

She shook her head. "I was hoping when you pulled up he would be with you, that you had talked some sense into him." She ran the tip of her shoes along the grass. "You weren't the only one who was of thinking of leaving."

"I'm so sorry."

"Was it you who gave him the idea?"

"What? No. No." Looking her in the eye. "He never talked to me about it."

She pursed her lips and looked away.

"He was really fond of you, you know?"

I nodded, as a hard swallow moved down my throat. "He's a great kid."

"No. He looked at you more than that, Matt. I think he left because he knew you were going to leave. All his father figures leave."

I looked away.

I came to say goodbye to Peter, but the fact he decided to leave without saying goodbye to me stung more than I'd expected. I was worried about how he would react to me going, but he turned the tables on me.

"He'll be back, Tonya, and when he does come back, please tell him I said goodbye and that I hope he finds his way. Tell him I said thanks."

I walked back to my car and slid in through the passenger door. Once I got in, the humming of the Falcon's engine gave me a sense of relief, but also an urgency to get out of Middwood as quickly as possible.

Tonya leaned over to the window. "Matt. Do yourself a favor, never come back here."

I looked in the rearview mirror as I drove off. I knew Middwood would forever haunt me wherever I went, but I hoped I'd find my place and that the Falcon would get me there.

I pulled out onto Highway 421, but then I pulled off to the side of the road. I left the engine running. I wasn't going to tempt fate by cutting it off. I reached into the back seat and pulled one of my bags to me.

I hopped over to the passenger door and pushed it open. I unzipped the bag and dumped the remains of my coated pills onto the dirt.

I bit my lip as I thought about saving one or two, but I closed my eyes and let them fall.

I threw the empty bag in the back seat, slid back behind the wheel, and drove on.

I didn't stop until I was out of Kentucky.

The End

EPILOGUE

Wednesday, November 11, 1964
Tonya

I stood watching Matt's car as it turned out of the yard. Once it disappeared behind the trees and the sound of the engine faded in the distance, I cleared my throat and said, "He's gone. I know you're hiding out there."

Franklin nodded with a grin and walked out from the trees. "Are you worried about Peter?" he asked as he walked into the yard.

"I wish he would have let me know where he was going, but as long as he's gone, he'll be fine."

He studied my face, but I didn't look at him. "Are you sure you're up for this?"

"The mourning moon has already come and gone. The winter will be rough, but it will all be behind us soon."

"Well, there turns out to be more to this story than we thought."

I finally broke my stare from the empty road where the car disappeared. "What is it?"

Franklin paused and thought about the words before he spoke.

I was concerned. "What?"

"It turns out Self, Gresham, and Bankward weren't the ones who killed Sarah and Roger."

"What?" I gasped. "Who told you that?"

"Turtle did," he said with a tinge of pain in his voice.

I stared at Franklin, looking for answers. I took a deep breath. "Then who did?"

He shook his frowning face. "That, I don't know."

I narrowed my eyes at Franklin. I wasn't sure if he was telling me the truth or not.

"We'll figure it out," I said, my voice dry.

He lowered his eyes and put his hands in his cardigan pockets. "Yes, we will."

We both turned our eyes to the Black Bear Mountain.

<<<<>>>>

TO THE READER

I appreciate you taking the time to read Ghosts of Black Bear Mountain. I hope you enjoyed reading it as much as I enjoyed writing it. Please consider leaving a review on Amazon at www.amazon.com/Marc-Monroe

If you would like to learn more about me or my upcoming work, including the second book in the Middwood series, The Hunter and the Hunted, please visit my website www.marcmonroebooks.com and sign up for my Reader's List.

Thank you again for being a crucial part in this new exciting journey. - Marc Monroe

ACKNOWLEDGMENTS

First of all, I'd like to thank the Acting Class of 2016. I told you guys about the dream that spawned the idea and that I was thinking about turning it into a book. You guys were so excited, enthusiastic, and supportive. You gave me the encouragement I needed to start this journey, and I'll always be grateful for that. Thank you to Hallie Goodwin, Ethan Pettepher, Grace Ward, Kallen Urfi, Uzomah Onovoh, Jaysen Jolicoeur, and Marcel Mendoza.

Big Thank You to my former student and friend Cameron Darby for being the alpha reader on most of this project. Love you.

I want to give a special thank to my beta readers for their support and insight: Betty Mackey, Caitlyn Davis, Melanie Bartram, Teresa Baxter, Shane Mangham, Mike Miller, Anne Ledford, and Jason Courson.

Thank you to my beautiful, supportive family: Mama, Diddy, Wendy, and the best three nephews in the world: Taylor, Cody, and Mason.

Finally, thank you, to my members of my launch team: Abi Lehmen, Ali Palen, Alisa Le, Alison Asberry, Allison

Faulk, Amy Fountain, Amy Magnus, Andrea Alburn, Andrea Wie, Anna Connor, Anna Kiristin, Anne Ledford, Betty Mackey, Caitlyn Davis, Catherine Baxter, Catey Funaiock, Charles Swint, Cheri John, Cheryl Coleman, Chris Bass, Chris Smothers, Christina Sickbert, Cliff Donlan, Cody Guilfoyle, Cody Mangham, Crystal Hales, Dawn Hendel, DJ McMullin, Eric Kuhn, Ethan Murphy, Grace Ward, Hallie Goodwin, Dr. Hannah Oldham, Heather Harbour, Hedi Schardine, Iman Hinton, Jacob Rollen, Janna Schaeffer, Jason Litterick, Jason Meeks, Jason Mourray, Jaysen Jolicoeur, Jillian Lambert, John Tribble, Josh Holloway, Josh Valdez, Julia Hogue, Kallen Urfi, Kate Jason, Kelly Cody-Grimm, Ken Ramsey, Keryn Key, Kham Chai, Kristen Dunn, Kristin Storla, Laura Melissa, Lisa Stricklin, Madeline Norton, Mallory Nonnemaker, Maria Melissovas, Mariah Kemp, Mary Simmons, Max Cobb, Melanie Lee Bartram, Memre Savant, Olivia Gowan, Paige Hutchinson, Palmer Farrar, Paula Axford, Raquel Dominguez, Veronica Jaques, Santana Whitham, Savannah Bradley, Sean Magee, Shane Simmons, Shannon Jenkins, Stacey Mason Mullis, Susan Blanton, Susan Holmstrom, Sydney Wynn, Taby Solorio, Tania May, Teresa Baxters, Terri Robbins, Tessa Brooks, Tina Kalvelage, TJ Wonders, Todd Hefflinger, Tracey Kemp, Trevor May, Van Nguyen, Wes Robertson, Wesley Boutillier, Wille Keck, Zach Simmons, and Zacki Malik.

Made in the USA
Columbia, SC
20 November 2018